Living in
Harmony

Living in Harmony

MARY ELLIS

HARVEST HOUSE PUBLISHERS
EUGENE, OREGON

Cover by Garborg Design Works, Savage, Minnesota

Cover photos © Chris Garborg

This is a work of fiction. Names, characters, places, and incidents are products of the author's imagination or are used fictitiously. Any resemblance to actual persons, living or dead, or to events or locales, is entirely coincidental.

LIVING IN HARMONY
Copyright © 2012 by Mary Ellis
Published by Harvest House Publishers
Eugene, Oregon 97402
www.harvesthousepublishers.com

Library of Congress Cataloging-in-Publication Data
Ellis, Mary,
 Living in Harmony / Mary Ellis.
  p. cm. — (New beginnings series ; bk. 1)
 ISBN 978-0-7369-3866-2 (pbk.)
 ISBN 978-0-7369-4286-7 (eBook)
 1. Couples—Fiction. 2. Amish—Fiction. 3. Maine—Fiction. I. Title.
PS3626.E36L58 2012
 813'.6—dc23

                                                          2012001363

Printed in the United States of America

       12 13 14 15 16 17 18 19 20 / LB-CD / 10 9 8 7 6 5 4 3 2 1

"If the Lord would tarry another hundred years,
what kind of world will we leave to our children?"

Old Order Amish father of ten,
Waldo County, Maine

৵

"The Amish are a tremendous asset to our community.
They are restoring the agricultural vitality
to the land I grew up on."

Jim Kenney,
lifelong area resident and son of a farmer

ACKNOWLEDGMENTS

Thanks to local resident Jim Kenney, and Ted and Rhonda Barnes and their daughter, Sarah Poulin, of Farmer's Corner Restaurant, of Troy, Maine.

Thanks to Diana Avella of the Copper Heron Bed & Breakfast for opening her lovely home to me and answering all my questions.

Thanks to Rosanna Coblentz of the Old Order Amish for the delicious recipes.

Thanks to Peggy Svoboda for traveling with me during what seemed like the hottest summer in recorded history, and thanks to Rosanna Huffman, dear friend and fellow writer, who helped find the perfect Scripture.

Thanks to my agent, Mary Sue Seymour, who had faith in me from the beginning, and to my lovely proofreader, Joycelyn Sullivan.

Thanks to my editor, Kim Moore, and the wonderful staff at Harvest House Publishers.

Finally, a special thank-you to Lewis, Kenneth, Ervin, and other members of the Old Order Amish community of Waldo County, Maine, for providing general background information and agricultural detail for my novel. Though Waldo County is real, Harmony is a fictional town.

ONE

Rock of Ages, cleft for me

Mount Joy, Pennsylvania

The rain's finally stopped. We're late. I'd better get you home before your father comes looking for us carrying his squirrel rifle—thunderstorm or no."

"Hmm," replied Amy. John's attempt at humor fell short of its mark.

"With my next paycheck, I should have enough money for a load of insulation to be delivered next week," he said with great animation. "I'll check the total weight. If it's not too heavy for my flatbed wagon, I'll pick it up at the lumberyard with your *daed*'s Belgians. That will save us the delivery charge."

"Mh-hmm," replied Amy, trying to shake off the odd sensation snaking up her spine. It was probably the two lemon bars she ate after the sloppy joes. Sweet and spicy didn't always set well in her stomach.

"And I'll pick up one of those fancy whirlpool tubs with at least a dozen water jets and also a tanning bed so your *mamm* won't get so pale during the winter months."

"That's nice. Whatever you think would be best for the *dawdi haus* addition." Amy laced her fingers together and pressed both palms down on her roiling belly.

John Detweiler pulled on the reins and steered the open buggy to the side of the road. "What has you distracted, Amy? You haven't heard a word I've said since we left the cookout and singing at the Lapp farm." His expression revealed concern rather than irritation.

Amy straightened against the bench seat, grinning as his previous words took root in her mind. "*Mir leid,*" she apologized. "I don't feel quite right. I should watch the combination of foods I eat at get-togethers instead of nibbling on a dozen different treats." She offered an apologetic smile. "I do believe *mamm* and *daed* would frown on the Jacuzzi and tanning bed ideas, so just stick to insulation."

They laughed companionably as John checked for traffic and then guided their buggy back onto the roadway. "At least I got your attention." He patted her knee. Even though her legs were covered by a pine-green dress and black apron, it was still an inappropriate gesture.

But Amy didn't scold him for his affection, because everyone in the district knew they would announce their engagement this autumn and marry in November—the traditional wedding season in Lancaster County. She opened her mouth to ask him to explain his house addition plans when the acrid smell of wood smoke assailed her senses.

"Fire!" she gasped. Alarm turned her voice into a childish squeak. Her mild sensation of unease quickly escalated into full-blown dread.

"Easy, now. We just left a bonfire and s'mores roast. Who's to say some *Englischer* isn't doing the same thing over the next hill?" Nevertheless, he clucked his tongue to the horse to step up the pace.

As they rounded the bend in the road, Amy saw a streaky

orange glow reflected against low-hanging clouds. "Oh, dear Lord," she gasped, half standing in the buggy. "Bonfires don't light up the entire sky, and that's the direction of our farm!"

John gently pulled her down to the seat. "There are plenty of houses in that direction, Amy. Let's not get worked up until we know for sure." He spoke words of assurance, yet his tone wasn't very convincing.

She squeezed her eyes shut and began to pray. Over and over silently in her head, she pleaded for the blaze to be a brush fire, or perhaps an abandoned ramshackle barn torched by the volunteer fire department for training purposes. Every few years the fire marshal scheduled an exercise and invited all surrounding fire departments to participate. Amish and *Englischers* arrived with lawn chairs to watch the volunteers battle the flames.

"Git up there," John shouted, slapping the reins with urgency. The Standardbred complied, breaking into a fast trot.

The horse's effort only hastened the inevitable conclusion for Amy King. As they reached the top of the next hill in Lancaster's famous rolling countryside, she stared across hay and wheat fields at a daughter's worst nightmare.

Her fervent prayers weren't to be answered.

Her parents' farm—her home for all twenty-two years of her life—was fully engulfed in flames. Sparks from the inferno shot thirty feet into the air as the entire yard glowed with eerie yellow light. Paralysis seized every muscle in her body. She tried to scream, to holler for more people to come help, but no sounds issued forth. Hot, stinging tears filled her eyes and ran down her cheeks as the breeze carried smoke and soot in their direction. The horse neighed loudly and fought against the harness, expressing a strong opinion about getting closer to the fire. John slipped an arm around her shoulders as he turned the buggy into the next driveway.

She barely felt his touch as she again tried to speak. "Why is no one ringing the farm bell?" she managed to say between choking coughs.

John jumped out to secure the horse to the hitching post of the house next door—the home of Amy's aunt, uncle, and grandparents. Then he reached up for her hand. "I'm sure they rang the bell plenty. Everybody who could come is already here." He also coughed from the bitter smoke that drifted across the yard like a heavy fog.

Avoiding his outstretched hand, Amy jumped from the buggy and sprinted through the meadow separating the two farms. She scrambled over the split rail fences with childlike agility.

John followed close on her heels, trying without success to catch hold of her. "Slow down, Amy! You'll twist an ankle or break a leg."

She ignored his warning and focused solely on the total destruction of the hundred-year-old wood-and-stone structure. When the wind shifted, her vision cleared briefly. The back and side yards were swarming with people. Two neighbors aimed green garden hoses ineffectually on the fire. The fire department's larger hoses rained a steady stream on the back of the house, the side still intact. Firemen in full gear pumped water from the King pond using diesel generators. Some Amish men still clutched full buckets of water, passed to them by lines of women and children from the pond, but the intense heat prevented them from getting close enough to dump their buckets on the blaze. With soot-darkened faces they moved back, acknowledging the inevitable.

Amy stood rooted to the driveway, watching as the roof collapsed in a shower of sparks. Her home was lost. For a minute she stood transfixed, unable to look away. One by one, firemen repositioned the hoses on the barn to keep the blaze from spreading to other outbuildings. She heard the mournful bellowing of cows in the pasture, terrified by sights and sounds and smells they didn't understand. John again tried to offer comfort with an arm around her back, but his touch merely galvanized her to action. She ran pell-mell through the crowd, amid smoke and sparks and confusion. Hoses and equipment lay everywhere, ready to send the unobservant sprawling.

"Where are my *mamm* and *daed*?" she screamed. Yet her strangled wail was barely audible. "Rachel, Beth, Nora—where are my *schwestern*?"

Several Amish women of their district hurried toward her, but Amy shrugged off their restraining embraces. Headlong toward the inferno she ran, and she might have slipped between firefighters and into the house if John hadn't caught up to her.

He grabbed her around the waist and dragged her none too gently back from the heat. "Get hold of yourself!" he demanded, pinning her against the trunk of a maple. Even the bark felt warm through the cotton of her dress. "Two of your sisters were with us at the singing. Don't you remember? Nora and Rachel said they would wait out the thunderstorm and walk home if no one offered them a lift. They chose not to ride with us to give us a chance to talk." John's face wavered in front of her, speaking words that took time for her to comprehend. "They are fine, Amy."

She sucked great gulps of air into parched lungs. "And Beth?" Her voice sounded raw and hoarse from the smoke. "Where is she?"

"You told me your youngest sister was spending the night at Aunt Irene's. She was disappointed because she's still too young to attend social events." John released her shoulders but didn't step back. He remained vigilant for another sprint toward the fire.

"They're safe?" Amy repeated the idea before asking a new question. "And my parents? Where are they?"

"I have no idea," he moaned, his expression a mask of shock and horror.

Slowly, Amy stepped away from the rough tree trunk without her earlier panic. On tiptoes she scanned the throng for several moments before spotting Aunt Irene and Uncle Joseph. *Mamm*'s sister and brother-in-law had lived next door for as long as she could remember. Uncle Joseph seemed to be supporting someone to keep her from falling to the ash-covered ground. In her stupor, Amy didn't recognize the elderly woman in the dark-brown dress, soot-speckled *kapp* and sturdy lace-up shoes. But the tall white-haired man at the woman's side was very familiar indeed. "*Grossdawdi*," she murmured. Her grandfather. With growing horror, Amy recognized the bent, sobbing woman as her grandmother. She could think of only one reason for *grossmammi* to carry on so. On unsteady legs, she staggered toward her family as John remained at her side, supporting her arm. Onlookers and would-be helpers parted before them like the Red Sea.

"*Grossmammi*, Aunt Irene," she said as she approached.

Both her aunt and grandmother looked up with red-rimmed, watery eyes, confirming Amy's suspicion.

"Amy, I'm glad you're home," said her aunt as *grossmammi* wrapped her arms around her. They both patted and hugged and attempted to console what was inconsolable. Amy allowed herself to be enfolded in their embrace, feeling exhausted and numb, as though she'd run all the way from downtown Lancaster.

"Where's Beth?" she mewed, sounding more like a kitten than a grown woman.

"Your cousins are keeping Beth away from the fire. She's safe at our house." Aunt Irene sounded distant and muffled, as though she were speaking underwater.

"And my *mamm* and *daed*?" she asked with her face buried in the soft cotton of her grandmother's dress.

"No one can locate them in the crowd."

Aunt Irene's words were little more than a whisper, but Amy heard the pronouncement clear as a clanging farm bell. She squeezed her eyes tightly shut.

"Amy! John!" A shout pierced Amy's semiconsciousness.

Amy peered up at two of her sisters running toward her. Stiffening her spine with resolve, she pulled away from her grandmother. As the eldest daughter of Samuel and Edna King, she must be strong. "I'm here, Rachel, Nora." She opened her arms to them.

Sweating and panting, with dirt-streaked faces, they hurried forward. *How long had they been running?* The glow from a house fire could be seen for miles in a night sky. The two girls fell into Amy's arms, crying and hiccuping like young children.

"We're so glad to see you," said Rachel. "Is Beth okay?"

"She's fine." Amy delivered a flat, emotionless statement, knowing what question would come next.

"And *mamm* and *daed*? Where are they?" asked Nora, extracting herself from the embrace.

Amy locked gazes with Nora, younger than her by only two years. "No one has seen them since the fire started."

Nora crossed her arms over her ash-speckled apron. "That doesn't mean they are still in the house!" she protested, outraged at such an idea. "They could have gone for a buggy ride or a walk in the moonlight, or maybe they both went to check on the livestock."

The third oldest sister, Rachel, also crossed her arms, looking hopeful rather than cross. "Maybe we should check the barn."

Amy forced her mouth into a smile. "That's true. It's entirely possible," she said, even though she'd never witnessed her parents doing any of those things in the middle of the night. "Why don't we bow our heads and pray they will soon be home?"

Nora and Rachel wrapped their arms around Amy's waist, and they all took a few steps toward the fire. The girls watched the flames consume the final side of the house with savage fury. Then they bowed their heads in silent prayer. Relatives and friends huddled close to pray, but they didn't intrude on the sisters' private anguish.

Amy kept her head down and eyes closed to the stinging smoke as the sound of their home crashing into a pile of embers rang in her ears. But she couldn't keep her mind focused on her pleas to God. She wondered instead about how she would manage as the new head of the King household. *What will I do when others turn to me for direction, support, and comfort?*

❦

The following days passed in a blur. Blessedly, no one looked to Amy for anything. She and her sisters had spent the waning hours until dawn next door in her aunt's kitchen. They did not return to the smoldering remains of their home. Uncle Joseph and her cousins cared for the livestock and began moving them to their own herds. The county fire marshal arrived before noon to confirm that he had found the bodies of Edna and Samuel King in the debris. Investigators would conduct a full inquiry, but it appeared the fire started in the attic, most likely from a lightning strike during the thunderstorm. The marshal asked Amy about working smoke detectors. She explained her father wouldn't allow them, preferring to place their safety and fate in God's hands. With the marshal's terrible news, destroying their hopes of possible alternatives, the younger girls broke into sobs. Amy wouldn't let herself give in to sorrow.

Her solemn grandmother organized a closed-casket viewing in Aunt Irene's front room and the funeral two days later. It seemed that half of Lancaster County stopped by to bring casseroles or desserts or to offer words of condolence. After the burial, the Kings served at least two hundred people at the luncheon, yet so much food remained they had to pack it up to send home with neighbors. Amy moved through the interminable days nodding her head to sympathetic mourners and murmuring the words, "They'll sleep peacefully, waiting on the Lord's return," over and over. But she didn't cry or shake an angry fist at the sky. The thoughts jumbling through her brain like puzzle pieces were of her future.

Should we plan to rebuild the house and try to keep the farm going?

We should just sell the place while the prices are high and move else-where, her *daed* had said several times.

It's getting too crowded in Lancaster—too much traffic. It's dangerous to even cross the street for the mail, her *mamm* had muttered too often to count.

With so many Englischers *settling in the area, it's getting hard to keep the Plain ways.*

Amy remembered her parents' complaints and those from other district members with bitter nostalgia. Now Edna and Samuel King no longer had to worry about the number of buggy accidents or increased land taxes or aggressive tourists trying to take their pictures in town. They wouldn't fret about anything ever again.

Now, two weeks later, Amy was no closer to figuring out what to do. Impulsively, she stalked away from those clustered on her aunt's porch following a preaching service. She headed across the meadow toward a stand of tall pines. Talk, talk, talk—that's all her Amish family ever did, just like *Englischers*. Maybe it's all human beings ever did. But she needed to think, alone, in only God's presence.

Ever since the night of the fire, the bishop, ministers, and elders had been dropping by to speak with her *grossdawdi*, Uncle Joseph, and John. Even though she loved her fiancé with all her heart, they weren't married yet, so why did the elders speak to him more so than her? They hadn't yet announced their engagement, although everyone knew they were courting. They had both taken classes and joined the Amish church. John had moved to a room in their barn loft so he could spend his free time helping with the remodeling to the King home. The long-range plan had been for *mamm* and *daed* to eventually move into the new *dawdi haus* addition, leaving the main house to Amy and John. That unfinished addition had gone up in smoke along with everything else.

Amy swallowed down her selfishness. Because her mind just now was a confused stew of emotions, she should feel grateful that others were concerned with her well-being. Settling herself on a sunbaked boulder, she turned her face skyward to plead once more for guidance.

But the answering voice came from a tall, muscular man rather than from a merciful Lord.

"I thought I saw you slip off," said John, striding toward her. "Too many folks around your uncle's house, no? It's hard for a person to find a quiet moment." He sat down in the tall grass by her feet, tipping his hat back to catch the warm sun on his face.

"That's the truth. And four girls to one bedroom is three too many," she joked—her first attempt at humor in weeks.

He reached for her hand, cradling it gently inside his. "I imagine so. When one gal runs out of things to say, someone else pipes up." He focused his sea-blue eyes—truly his best feature—on her. "You've been given much to think about the last few days. I know your uncle and the bishop spoke to you about selling your parents' farm."

"*Jah*, they have." She wished this discussion could be postponed indefinitely.

"Plenty of people are interested in the land, English and Amish, besides your uncle and his sons." John paused, waiting for a reply. When she sat mutely watching a bumblebee's move between clover heads, he continued. "And I hope you've seriously considered my idea. I have nothing left here in Pennsylvania except for you, Amy. The addition I was building onto your parents' house is gone. I can't continue to live in a barn loft on property about to be sold. Both of my brothers reside in Maine. I can't afford to buy your *daed*'s acres here in Lancaster, not since the proceeds must be split among your sisters, but my older *bruder* says I could buy decent farmland up north with what I've already saved…and your share of the inheritance." John's assurance slipped a notch when she failed to respond. "That is, if you're still willing to marry me in the fall." He seemed to be holding his breath, waiting.

She turned to face him and ran her index finger down his smooth-shaven cheek. "Of course I'll still wed you, John. My parents' passing didn't change my feelings for you."

He smiled, blushing like a schoolboy. "Whew, that's *gut* to hear." He leaned up to brush a quick kiss across her lips.

He tasted of peppermint candy and sheer devotion. John was the only thing Amy felt certain of. She'd fallen in love the night they met and had never doubted his commitment to her for a single moment.

"Thomas said his district grows larger each year. The *Englischers* have welcomed Plain folks to the community, but there's little chance the area will become a tourist hot spot like here—at least, not in our lifetime. What say you, Amy? Land in Maine costs a fraction of what it does in Lancaster. I want to farm, but I can't afford to do so here. I don't like working construction, but I'll continue if you don't want to leave your family." His ruddy complexion glowed with health and hopeful expectation.

Amy pulled back her hand and rose to her feet. Clearing her throat, she composed her thoughts—the ones that had been churning in her head for days. She'd discussed John's ideas with her sisters and grandparents. She'd prayed nightly for direction, and finally it had been delivered. Now she needed to stop behaving like a child and speak up. "I have talked things out with my family, and I've decided to accompany you to Maine. We can marry before we leave, or, if you prefer, your brother can marry us upon arrival. But there is one catch." She paused in her narration to meet his gaze.

He opened his palms wide. "Name it. I only wish to see my future *fraa* happy."

"Nora wants to move north with us. None of the young men in this district interest her in terms of courting. She yearns for a fresh start where everyone isn't as familiar as old shoes."

John's brilliant smile slipped a notch. "Thomas and Sally have a large home, according to his letter. I'm sure they will take in Nora until we marry and buy our own place."

"*Danki.* Having one sister near will lessen the pain of leaving home. Rachel and Beth refuse to leave our grandparents. They are planning on moving into the attic of the *dawdi haus* and adjusting as well as can be expected."

"We're not moving to the moon, Amy. You'll still see them occasionally."

"I've looked up Maine on a map. Visits will be few and far between." Amy inhaled a deep, calming breath. "As the eldest King sister, I've made another decision too. I refuse to sell my parents' farm to an English developer. I don't want dozens of houses springing up next to my grandparents. The traffic on this road is bad enough already."

John's smile vanished altogether. "But no farmer can afford to pay what this land is worth."

"You mean worth by English standards. This land has been in my family for generations, constantly divided up into ever smaller plots for sons who marry. My uncle wishes to buy our acres and combine them with his. My cousins want to farm. They will secure bank loans to add to Uncle Joseph's down payment. The amount won't come close to what a land developer would pay, but it will be enough for the four King girls to make new beginnings." She lifted her chin. "As you already pointed out, land in other places is far cheaper than here."

He opened his mouth to argue, to protest the foolish idea of turning down a million dollars, but stopped. Maybe it was her ramrod posture, or the set of her jaw, or the hard glint in her cornflower eyes, but he closed his mouth before it started catching mosquitoes. "Your sisters agree with you?" he asked after a pause.

She nodded. "*Jah*, they do. Perhaps for the first time the four of us see eye to eye."

John pushed off the rock to rise to his feet. "Then it's settled. I'll tell the bishop and Uncle Joseph of your decision. Shall we head back to the house? I could use a cup of strong coffee." He held out his elbow toward her in a gentlemanly fashion.

Amy stood and hooked her arm through his, and then they strolled across the meadow back to the house. A long-absent sense of relief settled deep inside her. Finally she felt she could breathe again.

෩

John Detweiler stared across starlit fields under a full moon, trying not to cough. The foul smell of smoke still hung in the air of his austere quarters. The night of the fire, he'd left his windows open to catch the evening breeze before taking Amy to the social gathering. Instead of cool air, the windows had allowed in thick, cloying smoke. District women and the four sisters had washed his walls and floor and laundered his bedding, yet the stench still remained throughout the barn, including his loft bedroom. Amy's aunt and uncle invited him to bunk with their sons next door, but he'd declined. He could tolerate the loft for a while longer. Because the woman of his dreams had agreed to become his wife, he was a happy man. They would soon leave the fast-paced, crowded world of Lancaster County, Pennsylvania, for the tranquil countryside of Waldo County, Maine.

Maybe the winters would be long and harsh.

Maybe the soil might be less fertile than that of the Garden Spot of America.

Maybe he would have to build a house from the ground up for his new bride without the plentiful able hands in his current district. Amish homes without electrical wiring wouldn't be readily available in a four-year-old community. Four years in existence—as opposed to nearly three hundred years in Lancaster.

But those years had wrought much change to the lives of the

descendants of the original Swiss refugees. And in his opinion, those changes hadn't been for the better. Scouting parties of Amish had been quietly looking at land in other parts of the country for years. For the price of a farm in this part of Pennsylvania, a father could buy several homes for his sons in other states. What drove the Amish from Lancaster wasn't tourism but its consequences. Once *Englischers* visited, many wanted to stay and build houses, driving up prices and clogging the narrow roads with increased traffic. They demanded things like city water, professional police forces, and modern schools, raising taxes for everyone.

Many Amish families earned great sums selling quilts, crafts, furniture, and baked goods to the constant stream of tourists…and had become corrupted by the almighty dollar in return. He'd heard of Amish with gas-powered air-conditioning, modern propane-powered light fixtures, and women no longer content with traditional clothing fabrics, not when permanent press made ironing an unpleasant memory. Many had forgotten that subsistence existence, demanded in the *Ordnung,* had served the Amish for generations.

Almost every young woman he knew worked for a while in the English world, facing the temptations of a fancy lifestyle. He didn't want that for his sweet Amy. So far she'd remained home, helping her *mamm* with housework and occasionally babysitting for the English woman down the road. But once he overheard Nora and Amy talking about looking for jobs in a tourist shop to help their parents pay bills. John cringed, thinking about Amy with women who wore short skirts, low-cut blouses, and heavy makeup. Already he'd noticed subtle changes in her demeanor he didn't like. He hadn't appreciated the way she'd turned his words against him regarding land prices up north. She became evasive with his questions and forthright with her opinions, even on matters she knew little about. It's not that he thought women shouldn't have a say, but why should she burden herself with difficult choices when she had a man who loved and cherished her?

John walked to his cot and withdrew a tattered, dog-eared road atlas from beneath the mattress. An *Englischer* had either lost it or thrown it out a car window when it no longer served a purpose. He had found the atlas in the ditch and taken it home to study when sleep wouldn't come. By kerosene lamplight he located Indiana, Kentucky, Missouri, Tennessee, and Wisconsin—states that many Old Order Amish had settled in when Pennsylvania and Ohio had grown overcrowded. His fingers quickly found his favorite map— Maine—home to his older brother, Thomas, and Thomas's wife, Sally, and his younger brother, Elam.

John slipped on the reading glasses he'd purchased at the dollar store. He stared at the small dot that would become the new home of the John Detweiler family. Even the town's name portended a good life for those wishing nothing more than to farm and serve God—Harmony. Now that the prettiest woman in the world would be at his side, perhaps harmony would replace the doubt and disappointment filling his heart of late.

TWO

From Thy wounded side which flowed

Amy King had never felt so tired in all her life. When John said they would travel to Maine by train, she imagined herself sitting comfortably in a train car watching pretty scenery pass by. She had no idea how long it took to get to the Amtrak station in Philadelphia, first by hired driver to Lancaster and then by bus. The train itself rattled down the tracks so fast, she felt as though her stomach had taken permanent residence in her throat. But the countryside fascinated her and Nora—what they could see from the moving bullet.

John buried his nose in a paperback from the bus terminal bookstore, purchased before they boarded: *The Agriculture of New England.* He couldn't wait to take up the reins of a draft team or feel rich, soft earth between his fingers. Amy couldn't wait to sleep in a real bed instead of in a seat with her head bouncing against the window. She had no clue regarding what their accommodations would be like in Harmony because John had not yet visited his brother in his new home. He had never met his nephews or his sister-in-law, Sally. The eldest Detweiler had left Lancaster a long time ago, moving originally to Missouri before settling down in the Maine community—the first of New England—with his bride of one year.

After the train deposited them in the seaport town of Portland, they caught a bus to Augusta and then climbed into transportation arranged by his brother. She begged John to see the ocean for the first time, but he promised they would travel there for their honeymoon. Fortunately, Thomas had received John's letter in time and had arranged a van. Otherwise, they would have been looking for hotel rooms in the middle of the night on foot. It seemed strange to carry all her clothes and personal items in one large cloth duffel bag that held Nora's things as well. House fires never announced their arrival, allowing people to safely remove their possessions beforehand. With a stab of sorrow, Amy remembered whom she and her sisters lost that horrible night. Odd how she could mull over the destroyed fabric for her wedding dress, her hairbrush and pins, and her brand-new tennis shoes, but she couldn't think about the parents she wouldn't see again this side of heaven.

"This is it, folks," announced the driver in an unfamiliar accent. "This is the Thomas Detweiler farm."

Amy shook her head as though waking from a dream. In the darkness she saw nothing but the gaping mouth of a dirt lane.

The driver lowered his voice to speak to John, who sat next to him in the front seat. "Would you mind much if I left you off here, young man? We've had a lot of rain recently. I could get the vehicle stuck if the driveway has turned muddy."

"Not at all." John sounded cheery, as though he were chatting at a potluck instead of having just traveled a thousand miles by six different conveyances. "We have little luggage, so the walk won't be any trouble to us."

"Wake up, Nora." Amy shook her sister's arm. "We're here."

"Where?" Nora straightened, peering around with a frown. "I don't see a thing."

"Harmony, Maine." Amy accepted John's hand as she climbed from the van's backseat.

"It's about time," muttered Nora, not hiding her crankiness.

John paid the driver and hefted both bags by the shoulder straps. The van disappeared down the road in a great hurry. "I can't wait to see my brother's face. It's been years. He's gotten married, become a minster, and fathered two boys during that time." He slipped an arm around Amy's waist.

Amy clung to him and breathed deeply, glad to be out of the stuffy vehicle with odors of onions and garlic. "That driver must eat his lunch and dinner in there on a regular basis."

"*Englischers* love to eat on the run." John filled his lungs too. "Smell that fresh clean air. Do I detect a hint of pine and not the exhaust fumes from tour buses?"

Amy grinned at him despite her overwhelming fatigue. Beyond them lay only inky darkness. "No buses filled with shutterbugs will be nice for a change."

"How will we find the house?" wailed Nora. "It's pitch-black out here."

"You can see the dirt and gravel at your feet, can't you?" John mustered an easygoing tone. "We'll put one foot after the other until a house appears in front of our noses. Grab on to your sister and hang on tight."

His tender patience with Nora warmed Amy's heart. He'd had to call upon it many times since they left their other two sisters and grandparents in Lancaster. Even though Nora begged to accompany them north, she'd done an uncharacteristic amount of complaining on the trip. Amy snaked an arm around Nora's waist. "Lean on me. I'll catch you if you fall. It's been a long day."

Nora turned her face up. Moonlight filtered through the

canopy and glinted off her cat-green eyes. "What if they don't like us?" she whispered close to Amy's ear.

"What's not to like? Two sweet, always cheerful, hardworking women like us?" Amy patted her back as John laughed under his breath.

"That's what I'm worried about." Nora's whisper floated on thick humid air.

"We have a clean slate with an opportunity to make good first impressions," stated John. Then he added, "All three of us, I mean. I've never met Sally before."

As they walked up the lane, Amy clung to John while Nora clung to her. *Please Lord, don't let John's kin be in talkative moods tonight,* she prayed. *I just want to sleep.*

A serenade of nocturnal animals and insects closed in around her, but it did not offer the familiar comfort as it did back home. These critters might be dangerous for all she knew. According to John's book, moose, black bear, fox, and coyote filled the Maine woods. What would prevent a lost wolf from wandering down from Canada? They owned no maps to confine themselves to acceptable national forests.

But before a predator could strike, a rambling white house with a green metal roof and long front porch loomed before them. Flowers bloomed on both sides of the steps, while vines encircled the posts and entwined the handrails. Somehow she'd envisioned Maine's landscape inhospitable to climbing roses, clematis, daylilies, and black-eyed Susans.

Without warning, the front door swung open as they reached the porch. "Welcome, welcome!" a deep voice boomed. Soft yellow light from a kerosene lamp framed a tall man in the open doorway. Amy spotted a second lamp burning on the table behind him.

"Thomas," greeted John, hurrying up the steps. "You're a sight for sore eyes." The two men hugged clumsily with much backslapping. "This is my intended, Amy King." John pulled her up the steps. "And this is her younger sister, Nora. She was eager to try out your new community."

Nora stepped into the light and nodded demurely. "*Danki* for letting me come to visit."

Thomas appeared momentarily befuddled. "Oh…of course. We'll all be joined as family when John and Amy tie the knot. Come in. Meet my *fraa*, Sally." He stepped aside, and they entered his austere but pleasant front room.

Amy's gaze fell on a tiny woman holding a sleeping infant. She looked no more than twenty—*younger* than she was. Another child peeked out from behind Sally, clutching her dark-brown skirt in his tiny fist. Amy held out her hand to the woman. "I'm Amy King. *Danki*, Sally, for opening your home. I hope you haven't kept your *kinner* up waiting for us."

Sally stared at her hand as though handshaking weren't a common practice. She squeezed Amy's fingers rather than shaking them. Amy filed away the information for future use.

"Oh, no. This one woke up with a wet diaper. Then his howls woke up his brother. This is Jeremiah." Sally hoisted the *boppli* up on her hip. "And this is Aden." She dragged the toddler out from the folds of her skirt. "His shyness will only last a day or two. Then he'll talk your leg off."

Amy bent down to the boy's perfect oval face. Thick lashes framed his huge dark eyes. "Good evening, Aden," she greeted in *Deutsch*. The boy blinked several times, frightened by so many new people.

"Are you hungry or thirsty?" asked Thomas, looking from Amy to John and back again. "Sally can heat leftovers from supper in no time at all." He took one bag from John and closed the heavy wooden door against the night. Even in thin lamplight, Amy could see the deep lines that etched his eyes and mouth. Flecks of silver peppered his dark hair, and his beard reached his chest.

John shook his head from side to side. "No, we ate several times during the last twenty-four hours. We're eager to lay our heads down, if you don't mind. I can sleep in the barn if you have a spare blanket."

"No need for that. There's room in the house. We have four bedrooms—one for us, one for our sons, one for Amy and Nora, and you can have Elam's old room."

"Where is our little *bruder*?" asked John, looking around as though Elam was also hiding behind someone's skirts.

Amy watched the smile fade from Thomas's face.

"He's not here, John. You'll have the room to yourself. He's away, working on a logging crew up north. And even when he's home, he's taken to sleeping in the basement."

"On an English crew?" asked John. "I thought the Amish in Maine didn't work for outsiders the way they do in Lancaster. That's one of the reasons I wanted to move here."

Thomas walked to his wife's side. "Usually that's true, but you know our brother. A bull moose separated from his heifer isn't as stubborn as the youngest Detweiler." He punctuated his sentence with an unconvincing laugh. "But we have plenty of time to catch up on family news. The women need their rest." Thomas guided Sally toward the foot of the stairs. "Amy and Nora can follow us up. You'll find your new room down that hallway. It's the last door on your right. Take along that lamp to find your way."

John nodded in Amy's direction. "*Gut nacht*. Sleep well. Before you know it, we'll be wed and looking for our own place."

Stopping in his tracks, Thomas turned back to his brother. "We'll also talk on that matter tomorrow. You indicated in your letter that you wished to marry as soon as possible."

"We've both taken the kneeling vow and have been baptized," said John. "We were about to start the marriage classes with the bishop when—" He faltered, reluctant to mention the fire. "When we decided to relocate."

"*Jah, gut*, but things are different here in this district. The bishop will want to meet you both. Then he'll want you to adjust to our ways before taking the next step." Thomas spoke almost melodically.

John opened his mouth to speak but closed it again quickly. "We'll talk tomorrow, then." He lifted the kerosene lamp from the table and headed down the hall, not quite as cheery as when they arrived.

Sally leaned over to brush Amy's cheek with a kiss. "Welcome," she whispered. Then she trailed her husband up the steps as he held the lamp high.

Nora staggered up behind Sally, dragging their one bag as though it weighed a ton. For a moment Amy paused to admire the plain, homey furnishings of the kitchen and front room, and then she followed last with a springier step. She slumbered that night in her new bed in her new room in an unknown land as though a choir of angels stood nearby, singing sweet lullabies.

❧

Sally didn't sleep anywhere near as well, even though the house's nighttime creaks and groans rang familiarly in her ears. Although she welcomed more females into the household to help with housework and offer feminine perspective, she shuddered at the thought of these two making such a disastrous move. Even though both sects were classified as Old Order, a world of difference separated their Maine community from the Lancaster Amish. Close proximity with the English had changed the Pennsylvania brethren's ways, making them more worldly and tolerant of independent, willful behavior, especially among young people.

Here in Harmony, there was no *rumschpringe*—no testing of the waters before joining the church and committing your life to Christ. The elder sister, Amy, might adjust fine because she had already been baptized and found her life mate. But the younger King girl? Sally had gazed into those moss-green eyes and seen herself as she was many years ago, before her redemption by the patient love of a good man.

"Is the room too warm for you to sleep? I'll open the window across the hall for cross ventilation." Thomas's low-pitched words floated in the darkness.

Sally felt the mattress move as he shifted his weight to an elbow. "*Nein*," she whispered. "I'm just worried about the new arrivals."

"My *bruder* and his future *fraa*? They'll be fine after a good night's sleep and some of your delicious vittles under their belts."

She laughed at his teasing—her cooking wasn't her best skill. But she soon sobered. "Don't underestimate their transition."

He sighed so softly she almost missed it. "True enough. The bishop prefers people to visit first and try out our ways before making the move. Many change their minds once they experience the long Maine winter."

"And discover we are but a dozen families."

"But we're growing larger all the time."

Sally reached for his hand atop the quilt. "You're the best supporter Harmony could have."

"I am content. The Lord has blessed us richly. There's no reason why John and Amy can't make a happy home here too."

"It's not about them I worry, but the younger one."

This time Thomas's sigh sounded like a mule's grunt. "John made no mention of an uncommitted youth tagging along. If he had, I would have discouraged the idea, but I couldn't turn someone away in the dead of night. She looked as though she were about to fall asleep standing up." He chuckled.

Sally clucked her tongue. "I doubt she will stay. And the expense of her travel will be wasted money."

"If you are worried, send up the matter in prayer." Thomas spoke now as one of the district's ministers rather than her *ehemann*.

"I was praying when you decided to chat about the heat upstairs." She pinched his arm lightly.

"Once you have prayed on the matter, then there is no cause to worry." He leaned close to brush her forehead with a kiss. "Go to sleep, *fraa*. God in His infinite wisdom will sort out this dilemma."

ϨϾ

The next morning Sally awoke to the steady beat of rain on the metal roof in an otherwise silent house. Even her infant slumbered after his last feeding several hours ago. Dressing quickly, she went downstairs and brewed coffee before setting out fresh bread, strawberry preserves, and a bag of cracked wheat. Creamed wheat sweetened with maple syrup would make a hearty breakfast for Thomas when he returned from early chores. With the pot of hot cereal simmering, Sally settled down with a second cup of coffee. A patter of feet on the steps soon broke her solitude.

"Good morning," greeted Nora King in English. "Amy's snoring woke me up, so I thought I'd see if you needed a hand with breakfast." The girl lifted the lid and gave the contents a stir. "What's this, might I ask?" She scraped the sides of the pot with the wooden spoon.

"Our version of Cream of Wheat. The wheat comes from your home state but is ground locally in town."

Nora tried a sample with a teaspoon and wrinkled her nose. "It tastes fine, but I'm not much for cooked cereals. *Mamm* usually keeps dry cereal on hand for me when we're not having eggs—" her face suddenly paled. "She *kept* it, I mean."

Sally's heart ached, witnessing the fresh pain of loss. "Do you mean an English boxed cereal?" she asked.

"*Jah. Mamm* bought them from the closeouts at the salvage store or sometimes from the dollar store. She would never pay grocery store prices, no matter how finicky I was."

Sally noticed that the girl was practically skin and bones, which probably justified her *mamm*'s indulgence. "I'm sorry, Nora, but

we have no outlets or dollar stores in Harmony. We have one grocery store, but the Amish usually shop at the community co-op.
That's where I bought the ground wheat and strawberry preserves.
My berry patch didn't do well this spring. Thomas said it takes several years for a patch to become fully established and productive."

Nora poured herself a cup of coffee. "Your breakfast will be fine,
Sally. I don't mean to sound troublesome. Shall I toast the bread?"
Her pretty face bloomed into a smile, making her look heartbreak-
ingly young.

"*Jah*, there's the cutting board and knife." Sally pointed at the
counter and hurried from the room at the sound of a baby's cry.
"I'll be back soon."

By the time she returned with her two sons, washed and dressed
for the day, Kings and Detweilers filled her kitchen. Amy scurried
around filling mugs with coffee and ladling creamed wheat into
bowls. Just as Sally settled Aden into his high chair, Thomas and
John rose to their feet.

"I'm taking my brother for a tour of the farm." Thomas lifted his
hat from the peg by the door, while John drained his mug. "Later
I'll hitch up the buggy and take our guests on a grand tour of the
town." He winked at Sally. "I'll show them what Harmony has to
offer."

"I can't wait." John's enthusiasm flowed like a mountain stream
in spring. "Can we stop at the bishop's house? I'm eager for him to
meet Amy and me. Once he sees our commitment to each other
and to the Lord, I'm sure he'll have no qualms about marrying us.
Must we wait until November like back home?"

"No, we have no wedding season the way they do in Lancaster
County. Folks can marry any month, time permitting, but our
bishop doesn't live here. He lives in our sister district up north,
close to the Canadian border."

"Further north than here?" asked Amy in a tone that doubted
the possibility of such a thing.

"How can you share a bishop?" asked John, simultaneously.

Thomas answered Amy first. "*Jah*, about a hundred and fifty miles. He hires a car to get him here and back." Then he turned to John. "He comes every other week to hold church services. On the opposite weeks, the other minister and I conduct Sunday school and Bible study, all in English."

Three pairs of eyes stared at him. Nora was first to speak. "You have preaching *every* Sunday? No off week?"

Thomas pulled on his suspenders. "Every week. There's so much to learn in Scripture that I feel we can't miss a weekly opportunity to be in God's Word together."

"Why in English, this Sunday school?" John sounded almost accusatory, as though the Maine congregation was misbehaving in some way.

"We welcome outsiders to our services, even *Englischers*. All are invited to hear about the Lord and His Son. It's the same up north, only on reversed Sundays."

John reached for his hat, momentarily speechless.

"I told you things were different here," said Thomas, opening the door.

"I'm sure we can adjust to minor changes." John stepped onto the porch, tugging down his hat brim against the rain.

"We haven't even scratched the surface yet." Thomas followed him outside, shutting the door behind him.

Sally was left with two women looking like deer facing a woodland hunter with a drawn crossbow. But after a moment Amy and Nora began clearing the table and were nothing but helpful for the rest of the morning. They cleaned her kitchen, washed the dishes, and started the laundry. While she hung wet clothes on the line under the covered porch, Nora ironed the basket of shirts in the living room from yesterday's load. Amy fixed sandwiches to take for lunch during their tour. Then she breathed a sigh of relief when the King sisters climbed into the buggy, leaving her alone with her boys. She wasn't used to so many people underfoot. And she wasn't used to other women scrutinizing her housekeeping. Wouldn't you know that when the rain stopped the bright sunshine illuminated windowpanes desperately in need of washing and a huge, lacy cobweb in the corner of the room? How does one whack down a web without being obvious?

Amy and Nora pretended not to notice the spider's handiwork, the dying pot of herbs on the windowsill Sally had forgotten to water, or the fact she hadn't knitted a single sofa throw to add some warmth to her bland living room. These were well-mannered Christian girls well raised by their *mamm*—a *mamm* who probably never overcooked noodles or burned a batch of cookies in her life. Sally shook off her self-pity as she remembered that their mother had gone home to the Lord and would never have an opportunity to overcook or burn anything again.

While Aden played with the small wooden horses carved by his *daed*, Sally decided to cook a memorable dinner for their first supper in Maine. But good intentions will never fill the silo, as her *grossdawdi* used to say. She underestimated how much a big, strapping man like John could eat. Her two roasted pullets proved inadequate for five adults and one toddler. Once she sliced up the meat on the platter, she flushed with embarrassment. In addition, her stringy green beans apparently should have been picked sooner. And she should have mashed the parsley potatoes, because that's how they looked in the serving bowl anyway. When Aden had doused himself with juice, his midday bath had distracted her from the boiling pot of spuds.

"Everything is delicious," said Amy after swallowing a dainty forkful of potatoes.

"I'm glad you like it," said Sally, sipping a glass of water. She hoped the Lord would forgive Amy's well-intentioned fib. The younger sister, Nora, looked pale and distraught, as though she'd witnessed something unimaginable on the trip to town. "How was the tour?" Sally hoped livelier conversation would divert attention from the empty chicken platter.

Amy glanced up with unreadable cool blue eyes, but John was quick to answer. "*Gut, gut.* The town's smaller than we expected, but everything a person needs is here. Farmland everywhere and not a single housing development in sight. Your cooperative market is a good place to buy what we need and sell whatever we grow, if we ever have more than what our family needs." His handsome face couldn't look more enthusiastic. "And they sell fresh donuts there on Wednesdays."

"Do you really hold preaching services in a new building like the Mennonites?" asked Nora.

Thomas smiled patiently at her. "We do. It's our meetinghouse, school, and church. We don't worship in one another's houses."

"So you just hang around there, visiting after lunch?"

Thomas paused a moment. "We eat a simple meal after services, but after that we usually have hymn singing for the whole congregation and then go home."

Nora nodded while pushing green beans around her plate. "Where's the closest Walmart?"

"I have no idea," he said as Sally burst out laughing. "Probably in Bangor, but that's too far for us to go by buggy." Thomas set down his fork. "You'll find things much slower and quieter here than what you're accustomed to."

"That suits me fine." John dabbed his mouth with his napkin. "Say, do I smell something burning?"

Sally leaped to her feet. Eager to hear about the tour, she forgot about two apple pies still baking.

Thomas jumped up too. "Careful now, *fraa*. Don't burn yourself on those hot pans." He grabbed oven mitts from a drawer and carefully removed the smoking pies from the oven. Sally opened the window and set two trivets on the sill. Thomas placed them so smoke would drift outside and then leaned over to inspect them.

"Only the crust is burnt," he announced. "I trust the insides can be scraped out with a spoon just fine."

Sally smiled at him gratefully, but she couldn't wait for supper to be over with, especially after she'd noticed her brother-in-law's expression of utter disapproval.

❧

"Walk with me, *bruder*," said Thomas.

John jumped to his feet. Dessert had been a disaster—the apples were as mushy as the parsley potatoes earlier in the meal and just as lumpy. "*Jah*, sure. I could use some exercise. I'd love to look at your workshop again."

"A man needs a way to keep his hands busy during the long winter." Thomas held open the kitchen door and they stepped into a warm summer night.

"With weather as hot as this, cold temperatures are hard to imagine." John gazed at a sky already beginning to darken as the sun slipped behind the hills.

"Our hot weather lasts barely a month, not three like in Pennsylvania. And the growing season is shorter here. We can't plant until late May and must harvest silage corn in September, not November. At best we'll get three hay cuttings, not four, and sometimes snowstorms come in October."

"You don't say? I bought a book to read about New England agriculture for the bus ride. I worked on a construction crew back home to save money toward a farm. Because I already know carpentry, maybe I could learn woodworking and help out in your shop this winter." John paused to admire the three-story barn with a gambrel roof. "Almost every barn I saw today was brand-new like yours."

Thomas batted away a mosquito. "Most barns in Waldo County

have to be knocked down. Farming dried up here forty years ago, but it's slowly coming back. Young *Englischers* have started organic produce farms and welcome us with open arms. Everyone wants this section of Maine to return to its former productivity."

"Did you buy an English home?" asked John, selecting a hay bale for a perch.

"*Jah*, the house came with the land. The bishop gave me a year to pull out the electrical wiring, but it needed lots of other work. Nobody had lived here for years other than mice. But at least we had a roof over our heads during the reconstruction." Thomas peered up at the rough-sawn rafters overhead. "The old barn was falling down, so we had it demolished by a materials recycler. He paid me enough money to buy lumber for the new one. *Englischers* and Amish alike turned out to put the barn up, but it took several days, not one like back home. There are probably more folks in Lancaster County than Maine has in the entire state."

"That's what I like to hear," said John, splaying his hands across his knees.

Thomas nodded. "We'll have time to discuss crops and farming down the line when you start looking at land or a farm to buy. Right now we have more important things to talk about."

"Should we light up a pipe of tobacco like *daed* did when he needed to talk man-to-man with his sons? We'd better be careful none of the womenfolk smell it on us." John snickered companionably.

His older brother didn't laugh. In fact, he looked as sour as sugarless lemonade. "*Nein*, there's no tobacco use in our district. None. And no alcohol use, either. No one here allows the last batch of cider to ferment into apple jack for a midwinter nip during a blizzard." His expression didn't soften.

John shrugged his shoulders. "Fine by me. You know I don't smoke, and I've never even drank a beer, let alone anything stronger. Very few districts in Lancaster allow members to imbibe."

"I'm relieved to hear it, but there's something else. You didn't tell me Amy's younger sister would be coming with you."

John felt a muscle tighten in his neck. "I didn't know about her plans until shortly before we left, Thomas. There wasn't time to write to tell you." The overcooked dinner and burnt apples churned in his belly.

"If you had I would have told her to wait a bit."

"She's not welcome in your home?" John stared at him. Had his brother lost the charitable side of his nature since becoming a minister? That didn't make sense. Surely he knew what the Good Book said about taking in strangers.

"No, no. She's welcome here. Forgive me. I'm not expressing myself well. It's just that Nora hasn't committed yet to the faith. She hasn't taken the vow to the Amish church." Thomas met and held John's gaze. "There's no *rumschpringe* here—no testing of the waters and deciding if a person wants to remain Amish. We have no big volleyball parties or cookouts or bonfires or any other social events for the youth. For one thing, we're only twelve families. There are not enough young people for a decent volleyball game." His forced laugh rang hollow in the cavernous barn. "If you had written, I would have advised Nora to remain in Pennsylvania until her running-around days were behind her. She will probably find our conservative district too confining for the uncommitted."

John blinked several times. "I don't know what to say."

Thomas placed a hand on his shoulder. "There is nothing to be said. She is here now, and here she'll stay with Sally and me. But don't be surprised if Nora doesn't buy a one-way ticket back to Pennsylvania. I wanted you to know the lay of the land, and I don't just mean with agriculture." He patted John's back and walked out through the open doorway

John was left alone with his thoughts—and he had much to think about. He'd never heard of no *rumschpringe* for youth, although the practice had always been optional. He remembered his own running-around days fondly—playing a battery-powered CD player in his buggy, going on a canoe trip down the river one hot summer afternoon, and taking a bus trip to see a minor league ballgame with his pals. All in all, he could have skipped both events and still died a contented man. But Nora? How would she react to no socials to meet eligible young men? She would probably go back to Lancaster to live with her grandparents. And that might be a good idea, as far as he was concerned.

His Amy would make a smoother, easier transition to their new district if her willful, free-spirited *schwester* wasn't a constant companion.

THREE

Be of sin the double cure

Amy awoke to sunlight streaming through her curtainless window. She left her bed to push up the pane and inhale fresh and decidedly cooler air. Yesterday's showers had washed away much of the heat and humidity, leaving the world a more comfortable place.

Nora burrowed her head deeper under the covers. "Haven't they heard of shades in Maine?" she muttered from beneath the quilt.

"Upstairs windows don't need shades. And if the sun's up, that means you should be too." Amy slapped the rounded hump playfully.

"Ugggh, please leave me be a while longer. I have a headache. Make my excuses to Sally and Thomas." The lump didn't budge.

"All right, but you'll go hungry until lunch. No one caters to spoiled women here." She poured a glass of water from the pitcher on her dresser and dug out the bottle of aspirin from her suitcase. "Except for me. Sit up and take these." Amy shook two tablets into her palm.

Nora complied, looking haggard with red-rimmed, watery eyes. *"Danki.* What would I do without you?" She swallowed them with a long drink before retreating into her cave.

Having showered the evening before, Amy washed her face and hands at the basin, slipped on her favorite navy dress, and headed downstairs.

In the kitchen, Sally hummed a hymn while spreading grated cheese on what looked like an omelet. John and Thomas were already at the table. John appeared to be studying the local newspaper, while Thomas played a game of peekaboo with his infant son. The father laughed as heartily as the *boppli.*

"I was ready to rap on the ceiling with the broom handle," teased John with a wink. "We don't want the day to get away from us."

"*Mir leid* if I'm late," she apologized. "I'll have to set my alarm clock."

"You're fine," said Sally over her shoulder. "They just returned from chores, and you're in time to lift the bacon from the grease." She handed Amy a pair of tongs.

Once all the strips were draining on paper towels, Amy poured herself a much-needed cup of coffee. "What do you have in mind for us today?" She aimed her smile in John's direction.

"You, Nora, and I can take Thomas's buggy into town for some more exploring. And I have a surprise for you." John set down his newspaper as Sally carried the omelet to the table.

Amy brought over the platter of bacon and then slipped into a chair across from her fiancé. Everyone bowed their head in silent prayer. After Thomas said "Amen" and Sally began serving the eggs, Amy cleared her throat. "I believe the field trip will be just the two of us. Nora has a headache and will stay in bed a while longer." She looked at Thomas and then Sally. "She's prone to migraines."

Thomas hesitated while scooping up eggs, his spoon aloft. "Normally unmarried couples do not take buggy rides together unchaperoned."

John glanced at Amy and then his brother. "But we were published in Pennsylvania—our intentions to marry have been made clear."

"I understand that." Thomas put a small portion of breakfast in Aden's bowl. "But as I explained, we're more conservative here. Because you're new, and many will assume only visiting, I give you my permission." He dug into his food with gusto.

Amy picked up her fork and ate too, hungry because she'd eaten only a chicken wing and some potatoes last night at dinner. Although curious about the district's rules, she realized this wasn't a good time to ask. Once Thomas left for morning chores and John to hitch up the horse, Amy rose to scrape plates into the compost bucket. "*Danki* for loaning us your buggy."

Sally fed her son eggs while finishing her own meal. "I'm glad Thomas will let you go today. I was worried about that." She wiped the boy's chin with his bib.

Let us go? Amy didn't know what to make of that. At twenty-two, it had been a long time since she'd had to ask anyone for permission for anything.

"Be sure to wear your full black bonnet as though going to church." Sally gazed up at her. "Women don't go to town in just white prayer *kapps*. They're okay for working in the garden or hanging laundry, but not out in public." Then she added in a barely audible voice, "We might have to widen your brim. I'll have to check it."

Amy glanced at Sally over her shoulder to make sure she wasn't joking. She'd heard of districts that required brims so wide on either side that you had to turn your body to see left or right. The head coverings sounded like blinders for an easily distracted horse.

But she looked perfectly serious.

Once Amy finished the dishes and put them away, she went upstairs to hunt for her full bonnet in her suitcase. She'd worn it while traveling and then tucked it away. It was a good thing Aunt

Irene had insisted she take an extra one because she had no time for sewing. Nora still slept soundly, a soft snore emanating from her cocoon. With bonnet in hand, Amy ran down the steps and out the front door without asking Sally to check it.

John pulled up in the buggy just as she reached the driveway. Soon the issue of full blinders seemed trivial as they trotted down the road toward Harmony. Once beyond sight of the farmhouse, John brushed her cheek with a chaste kiss. "You smell nice," he said.

"Raspberry shampoo—that stuff smells good enough to drink." Amy leaned out the side window to catch some sun on her face. "What a gorgeous day for an outing."

"We have several hours before I must help Thomas cut firewood. Sounds like folks here spend half their summer getting ready for winter."

When they reached the center of town—a crossroads where the bank, post office, historical society, the English church, and an insurance office stood—he turned right instead of left.

"We're not heading toward the grocery store and pizza shop?" she asked, remembering yesterday's tour.

"No, but don't worry. Thomas gave me good directions. We won't get lost."

"Our second day in Maine and we disappear, never to be seen again."

"Only if we want to." After a mile he turned left down a road into a public park.

"We brought no picnic lunch today. What a shame. The benches in the shade look cool and inviting."

"No need for packed sandwiches." John remained secretive, however, as the lane continued past picnic tables and swing sets. Dense woods encroached on both sides as the roadway narrowed. Two vehicles could barely fit side by side. They drove past a well-kept cemetery, but no houses, cabins, or even driveways into the dense forest.

After several miles she asked, "Are you sure about this? You didn't misunderstand your *bruder*?" No sooner had she voiced her concerns than the road curved and a parking area opened up before them. Cars, trucks, and boat trailers filled at least half the spaces.

"Goodness, John. Who would know this was back here?" Amy gaped at a large body of water not fifty feet away. Dappled sunlight sparkled off the smooth surface for as far as the eye could see. Boats crisscrossed the waves, their white sails fluttering in the gentle breeze.

"Only the locals, and now that description includes us. Welcome to Harmony Pond." He stopped the buggy in a parking space and set the brake.

"*Pond*?" she squawked. "I've seen lakes smaller than this." She jumped down and ran toward the beach. Several families had spread blankets across the sand to enjoy a day in the sun. Children filled colorful buckets with plastic shovels, giggling merrily. No one gave her more than a passing glance as she approached the water's edge. Apparently the Amish here, though few in numbers, generated fewer stares than in well-populated Lancaster County. Amy walked onto a fishing dock that dipped and swayed under her weight. "It floats," she called back with hands cupped around her mouth.

John climbed down too, but he remained with the horse as there was no hitching post. He grinned from ear to ear. "*Gut* idea. The dock can rise and fall with the water level," he hollered back.

Shielding her eyes from the glare, she gazed across the water. Tiny cottages dotted the far shore, but to her left she could see no end to the so-called pond. She loved watching the boats, the children splashing in the shallows, and seagulls diving for fish that ventured close to the surface. "What a hidden treasure," she called on her way back to him. "I wish Nora were here to see this." Impetuously, she threw her arms around him and hugged.

"According to the book I read last night, glaciers formed this lake. It has only one water source—no separate intake and outlet." He helped her back into the buggy. "I wonder what happens during heavy spring rains."

"You'll have to keep reading that new book of yours." Amy only vaguely understood the concept of glaciers, but it didn't matter. "*Danki* for bringing me to see this, John. I love it here. Do you think someday we could come back when Nora can join us?"

"Maybe after we're wed, providing you wear the proper head covering." He winked for the second time that day. "We should start back so we have enough time for lunch. I spotted a deli on our way here."

"I thought you might have a plan up your sleeve." She settled back to enjoy the scenery, relaxed now because she knew they weren't lost. At the main road, she noticed there was no sign pointing the way to the lake. Harmony *Pond* truly was for locals and not tourists.

⁂

John parked the buggy in a grassy area near the railroad tracks within an easy walk of the local diner. Inside, Amy found more than delicious food. She spotted a "Help Wanted—Part-Time Baker" sign in the window. She inquired about the job while the woman fixed their sandwiches.

"Three days a week ought to do it," said the manager. "Mondays, Wednesdays, and Fridays. You could bake enough on those days to last for two. We're closed on Sundays. Everything in town is closed around here."

"May I talk to my fiancé and come back to fill out an application?"

"Sure. I've had that sign up for two weeks with no takers."

Amy hurried back to the buggy with their lunch and her news. She began explaining the details before even climbing inside. "I could work for a year or so until *bopplin* came along to help pay for our new farm. What do you think?" she asked, breathless with excitement.

John unwrapped his chicken salad sandwich, laughing. "If working for a while would make you happy, why not? On your days off you can teach my sister-in-law to bake. Did you ever taste such awful pie as last night's? I thought apple was just about foolproof."

Amy pinched his arm. "Be kind to Sally. Any woman can lose track of time. I've burned a few things myself."

"Never when you were cooking for company, I would venture to say." He easily guided the buggy onto the road. Harmony had little traffic no matter what time of day.

"John Detweiler, show some compassion. Anyway, we're family now, not company." She nibbled her ham-and-cheese.

"You're right. Sally is my brother's wife, but Thomas would benefit if his *fraa* took a job as a baker." He tried to slide away from her, but she pinched his arm once more in the small buggy.

As it turned out, neither Amy nor Sally were destined for such a vocation. At supper that night, Amy told Thomas and Sally about the Help Wanted sign in the restaurant's window.

Thomas's jaw dropped down to his chest. "Impossible," he said without hesitation. His gaze shifted from her to John, where it stayed. "She cannot take a job. That's simply not done here. Women do not work outside the home, even if they are still single."

John's features registered surprise. "We didn't know that, but it's no problem. We can swing buying an existing house and de-electrifying or building on bare farmland without Amy working. It was just an idea." He resumed eating his supper of stew and pickled beets without another word on the subject.

But Amy's head swam with ideas—all of which she kept to herself. She ground down on her back teeth, annoyed that Thomas addressed the matter with John and not with her. Thomas hadn't

glanced in her direction again—not after his original shocked
scowl. But for now she held her tongue. What choice did she have?
Her home in Pennsylvania was nothing but a pile of ash and debris.
She'd sold the land and ventured north into a new world, never
imagining just how different that world would be.

℘

John didn't know if his indigestion stemmed from supper or
from the recent turn of events. Sally's beef stew had been so bland
and flavorless it couldn't have caused stomach acid. The meat was
tough, while everything else had been cooked so long it looked like
rainbow mush in his bowl. Her biscuits were dry and the pickled
beets too sour. Only her peanut butter cookies tasted good. He'd
contemplated stuffing his pockets with the rest but stopped himself with great self-control.

He tried to remember that Sally's cooking was not his problem.
His brother cleaned his plate and smacked his lips no matter what
his wife prepared. And the more he thought about it, John was
happy local *Ordnung* wouldn't permit Amy to work. He suspected
Nora triggered his latest bellyache. Did the girl think she was on
vacation? When he and Amy returned from town, Nora had been
sitting on the porch swing, reading a paperback novel. Had she
even asked Sally if she needed help with supper? Sally's garden
overflowed with produce ready to pick. Tomatoes were so overripe
that their skins had split. Green beans dangled from heavily laden
bushes, while carrots and green onions pushed themselves up from
the soil. If someone didn't start harvesting and canning soon, those
plants would go to seed, spoiling the vegetables. Couldn't Nora
see weeds sprouting between garden rows or shiny apples hanging from tree branches on her frequent strolls around the farm? At
supper she had rambled on about fictional characters in the novel

she read. Didn't she know nonsensical conversation was inappropriate at a minister's table?

John scrubbed every feed or water bucket, mucked out the stalls for Thomas's twin Belgians and his buggy Standardbred, and then swept the barn floor with the push broom. Hard labor worked wonders for a man's soul…and for a woman's too, if Nora King cared to give it a try. After washing at the barn's hand pump, John strolled back to the house, tired but in a better mood. His temperament further improved when he spotted Amy sewing on the porch.

"Good evening," he greeted as he climbed the steps. When she scooted over, he sat beside her. "What are you making?"

She lifted one eyebrow. "I'm altering my bonnet because the brim isn't wide enough for district rules. Sally found some matching fabric, so this shouldn't be too difficult."

"Must not let anyone see how pretty you are. I won't stand a chance." He snaked his arm around the back of the swing.

"Seeing at all will be the challenge." She focused her lovely blue gaze on him instead of the bonnet. Her eyes matched the deep color of Harmony Pond. "All's well with the livestock tonight? Thomas said you volunteered for evening chores to give him time to work on his sermon."

"*Jah*, but his goats are an ornery lot. One of them tried to butt me when I retrieved his water bucket for cleaning. I can't figure out why Thomas keeps such troublesome creatures." He dropped his voice to a whisper.

"You're joking, *jah*?" Her dimples deepened. "The females produce milk, which Sally turns into delicious cheese, and she also uses their milk when the Holstein heifer dries up. Thomas raises the males for meat. They pasture better on rocky, hilly land than cows. That was boar goat meat in the stew tonight. *Gut*, no?"

"Ah, I'd wondered what that was. Now I know." He moved the swing with a boot heel. "But I don't want to debate goats and cows with you."

"I take it you're a beef man." Amy knotted the thread and then broke it off with her teeth.

"I am, but we need to talk about Nora."

"She went to bed early with a couple more aspirin. I hope she feels better tomorrow. Those migraines can last for days." She held up the bonnet to inspect in the fading light.

"Your sister needs to pitch in while we're living here. And Sally could certainly use help with two little ones. Nora is no *Englischer* on vacation."

Amy suppressed a grin as though he'd said something funny. "She doesn't think she is. She wasn't feeling well today, that's all."

"You have a tendency to baby her."

She pondered that for a moment. "Perhaps I did back in Pennsylvania, but I promise I won't here." She patted his arm. "If the migraine is gone tomorrow, I'll stand over her with a stick to make her work."

"*Gut*," he said, louder than necessary.

"Should we go inside? Mosquitos are starting to feast on us." Amy rose gracefully to her feet, repaired bonnet in hand.

"Another minute, please. I've more to say." He patted the swing. "Amy, her dresses are inappropriate—dark pink, pale green, light blue. Women in Maine don't wear those colors."

"She's still in *rumschpringe*, John." Amy sat back down.

"*Nein*. Not here she's not. Young people in Harmony don't have that option. They join the church and commit their lives as young as sixteen, but certainly by seventeen or eighteen. Nora is twenty— it's time for her to make a decision. And until she does, she must wear more appropriate clothing."

Amy blinked, staring at him. "We'll go to the co-op store tomorrow if we can borrow the buggy again. We'll buy black, brown, and navy fabric and start making new outfits and bonnets."

"*Danki*. I don't mean to sound cross with you, but your sister needs to understand Harmony's ways."

"We've only been here two days, but I'll speak to her during the drive. Now, if you don't mind, I'm going inside before these bugs eat me alive. I'll take a cup of valerian tea up to her to ensure she's as good as new tomorrow." Amy jumped up and left without another word.

John would have liked to spend time with her without discussing goats, cows, or cures for migraine headaches. He enjoyed their ride to the lake earlier, secretly glad Nora hadn't tagged along. Amy pampered that girl. So had her *mamm*, by buying and cooking special food just for Nora. Finicky eaters became less so once hunger took over. "*Ach*," he muttered as one uncharitable idea after another flitted across his mind. It might be better if Nora returned to Lancaster sooner rather than later. With her willful independence, she would never conform to district *Ordnung*. And the longer she remained, the more influence she exerted on Amy. If the bishop met the undecided Nora, he might not approve their marriage.

John clenched his eyes tightly shut, ashamed of his thoughts. He should encourage the younger sister to find the one true path instead of wishing her shuffled back to Pennsylvania.

Forgive me, Lord. I should concentrate on my own sins instead of pointing fingers at someone else.

෨

The next morning Amy almost didn't see John standing beside the horse and buggy due to her newly widened brim.

"*Guder mariye*, Amy," he greeted. "I hope you're feeling better, Nora." He perused Nora from her green dress up to her black head covering, a perfect copy of Amy's.

"I am, *danki*," Nora replied, staring down at her shoes.

"Sally loaned Nora her bonnet, and that dress is the darkest one she owns. We're not the same size." Amy tried to keep pique from her tone but failed.

"It'll be fine for one day." John offered a hand to step up. "Would you like me to drive you to the store? Thomas said he can spare me for another morning because I accomplished so much last night."

Amy tugged the reins from his fingers and tucked her skirt around her legs. "How can we have a woman-to-woman chat with you along?" She clucked to the horse. He pulled hard against the harness.

John grabbed the bridle and held on tightly. "But you're not familiar with Thomas's horse or the way to town."

Amy exhaled through flared nostrils. "I will drive two miles down this road, turn left, and drive two more miles. I don't think anyone could get lost going to Harmony. And I know how to handle a Standardbred. I owned one in Lancaster until I sold him to my cousin." She held his gaze.

"As you wish," he said, releasing the bridle.

"See you at lunchtime." Amy nodded to him as the buggy rolled down the driveway.

Nora turned to look out the back window. "I'm surprised he's not running after us. He has changed."

Her three emotionless words duplicated Amy's suspicion of the previous night. She'd replayed the porch scene several times when sleep refused to come. "No, he hasn't," she said after a pause. "But we live in his brother's house. Therefore, we must abide with their district's rules."

"Thomas seems nice to Sally, but he barely tolerates us."

"That is how it should be, no? And not the reverse?"

"Why can't he be nice to everybody?" Nora leaned her head back and closed her eyes.

"Don't be quick to judge. Maybe he has more on his mind than us. Now, put on your sunglasses to prevent another headache."

"I doubt they are permissible with the new *Ordnung*." Nora crossed her arms.

Amy glared at her, but Nora kept her eyes closed. "They are for medical reasons, not to look fancy. Please don't get cranky with me."

Nora dug in her purse for the sunglasses, donning them before she replied. "I'm sorry, Amy. Thinking about no *rumschpringe* in Harmony has made me cranky. How do young people meet and start courting? You said at breakfast there were few social events to speak of."

Suddenly, she pivoted on the bench. "Surely you don't mean they arrange marriages—fixed-up deals between parents and the bishop?" Nora pulled her glasses down her nose and peered over the top. "If that's the case, you can point this buggy toward the bus station and mail my meager belongings whenever you get a chance."

Amy burst into laughter, as did her sister. Near hysterics lifted the somber mood that had prevailed since John relayed Thomas's expectations. "No, nothing like that, but courting is far more… conservative. I asked Sally to spell out the particulars while you were in the shower." She glanced at Nora.

"Go on."

"They do hold singings, but everyone attends them, including parents and children. Remember, there are only twelve families here until more folks move to town. The other two Maine districts are far away. "

"I never realized there would be so few people."

"After a singing or a preaching service, a boy could ask to walk a girl home, but her parents will walk a few paces behind them. They aren't left unchaperoned."

"Except when he takes her for a ride in his courting buggy, *jah*?" Nora's question was filled with hope.

"*Nein*. No courting buggies here." Amy shook the reins to hasten their pace.

Nora stared, wide-eyed and frightened. "How exactly do people fall in love? Surely a man doesn't walk up to a woman and say,

'You look like a pleasant enough person to spend my life with…
how about we get hitched a week from Thursday?'"

Amy laughed but without much humor. "I asked Sally about
that. After a few walks, if the boy is still interested, he talks to his
parents. If they think it would be a good match, then the boy
speaks to her parents."

"Wait a minute, *schwester*—"

Amy held up her palm. "Let me finish. If her parents agree to
the relationship, then they will talk to their daughter. If she says
'Not interested,' the matter is dropped and never discussed again.
You must admit this saves the boy time and energy if a gal has her
heart set on someone else."

Nora rolled her eyes. "Seems to me time is all they have in
Maine. There's not much else to do. Okay, what happens if the
girl says *jah*?"

Amy stifled her grin. "The plot thickens, no? The boy will spend
Sunday afternoons at the girl's home. They get to know each other
better. They can sit on the porch and talk, or they can take a walk
as long as one of her siblings tags along. At any point either can
decide this isn't the right one for them. But there are no romantic buggy rides or holding hands or stolen kisses under the stars."
Amy studied Nora's expression to make sure the point hit its mark.

"I get the picture." She sounded uncharacteristically meek.

"I love you and would like you to stay in Harmony, but no one
will think badly if you choose to return to Lancaster County. This
isn't exactly what you were expecting." She slapped the reins on
the gelding's back.

"Is it what you were expecting?"

The question caught Amy off guard. "No. I had planned to
work before I had children. But I have John. My future has already
been determined."

Nora squared her shoulders. "You're not married yet."

"What's that supposed to mean?"

She shrugged. "Nothing, I suppose. All these strict rules are hard for me to take in."

"Would you like to go home? You could live with *grossmammi*, same as Rachel and Beth."

Nora remained silent for so long that Amy assumed she had no answer. But as the buggy turned into the Amish co-op parking lot, she replied quietly, "No, I don't want to go back there. Despite hundreds of young men, no one interested me. I'll stay to see what prospects Harmony has to offer." She hopped down when the buggy rolled to a stop. "Besides, I need to prevent my sister from making any stupid mistakes." Nora ran toward the store before Amy could demand an explanation.

Once she followed Nora inside, she soon forgot what had irritated her. "Oh, my," she enthused, starting down the first aisle. "Who knew a general store would have all this?" During Thomas's initial tour of Harmony, they hadn't had time to see more than the outside of the building.

"Just about anything a person needs or wants." Nora ran a finger down a display of beeswax candles, scented lamp oils, and hand-wrought iron candelabras. Row after row of shelves held hardware, housewares, shoes, boots, and bulk foods. Handcrafted furniture, birdhouses, and birdfeeders were displayed on the covered front porch and against the back wall. The farmer's market offered every sort of garden produce beside cookies, pies, bread, and baked goods. Woodstoves and other equipment designed to be diesel, propane, solar, or wood powered were sold in a room in the back. A sign on the wall advertised colors and prices for metal roofs, outbuildings, and custom-made siding. The two women wandered the aisles, wide-eyed as any tourist.

"Something for everyone, both English and Amish," said Amy.

"Look at this!" squealed Nora, turning a corner. Dozens of bins of bulk candy, sold by the ounce or pound, tempted those with a sweet tooth. She began scooping sugary confections into little bags.

"I've found my favorite section." Amy grabbed a couple of plastic sacks for herself. "Save some of those Jordan almonds for me."

When they approached the front counter with their candy selections, a clerk stepped forward shyly. Then an older woman hurried up behind him. "Be sure to visit the building next door," she said, leaning around the young man. "You'll find fabric and thread, as well as handmade throws and quilts both new and used. Lots of unique patterns you don't see anymore. Oh, and welcome to Harmony," she added after a small hesitation.

"*Danki*. Dress material is what we're here for." Amy addressed the woman while the young man rang up their purchases. They both placed money on the counter for the candy, but he couldn't take his eyes off of Nora. He blushed all the way to his earlobes. Nora seemed more curious about the taste of purple gumdrops than her admirer. After Amy accepted her change, she stuffed the sweets into her purse and headed for the side door.

"How did that woman know we're new?" asked Nora, stealing glances at the young clerk over her shoulder. It seemed she had noticed the man's attention after all.

"Don't be a goose. Because she doesn't know us, we must be new." Amy pulled open the door and nudged her sister outside.

They immediately noticed a log cabin-style building with a straightforward sign: "Quilts and More." When they entered they saw that new quilts hung from the ceiling on all four walls, their craftsmanship a testimony to Maine's long winters, along with price tags that reflected the amount of time involved. Amy spotted bolts of cloth standing on end on tables against the wall. "You start picking out fabric and thread," she said, pointing toward the back. "Buy enough for three dresses in navy, brown, or dark-green. I want to check out this table of secondhand quilts."

Nora dutifully shuffled toward the sewing supplies while Amy rummaged through the used items. As the storekeeper had predicted, she found many unique quilt patterns. The colors and materials had softened from daily use and repeated launderings. One particular quilt caught her eye.

"How about this beauty?" Amy held up the end for her sister to see. "These are the prettiest shades of blue and lavender."

Nora peered up from measuring a length of olive-colored serge. "You love anything blue."

"Doesn't this look like waves in the sea, rising from the darkest depths to meet the sky and clouds? You can practically feel the undulating waves." Amy set the quilt into motion.

Nora scrunched up her face. "How would you know what the ocean looks like? That just looks like crooked strips of blue and purple to me." She turned her attention back to the drab green.

Suddenly, Amy's gaze landed on a small bug stitched onto the quilt's binding. "Come look, *schwester*. I believe the quilter marked her work with a signature." She pulled the fabric up to her nose to study.

Nora abandoned her selections to join Amy at the table. "*Mamm* would call that vanity," she said, peeking over her shoulder.

Amy's breath caught in her throat. "She *did* call it vanity— every time her sister added a red-and-yellow ladybug to one of her creations."

The two sisters stared at the embroidered insect and then each other. "It can't be," said Nora.

"But it is. Look at those tiny black antennae. Who else would go to such trouble?"

"Aunt Prudence." They uttered the name of their mother's sister simultaneously. "The aunt who was shunned and left Lancaster County in disgrace. We never knew where she resettled." Amy refolded the quilt with near reverence.

Nora's eyes rounded like an owl's. "I guess we do now."

"Finish your shopping. I'll wait for you at the front register. I'm buying this quilt."

Nora gasped at the price tag. "You could make a brand-new

one this winter. You'll certainly have plenty of time. And you can add your own ladybug—"

"No. I just know this once belonged to our aunt. I want it." Without another word she pulled out her checkbook and marched to the checkout.

FOUR

Save from wrath and make me pure

Thomas arched his back, working out the kinks in his lower vertebrae. Because John insisted on finishing the barn chores and the last of the alfalfa was cut, he had time to find his *fraa*. She proved easy enough to locate.

"Hullo, Sally," he called, approaching the kitchen garden. "Aren't your helpers back from shopping yet?"

Sally straightened to greet him, clutching a ripe tomato in both hands. "No. I told them to take their time and stop for lunch. Once they start working on Nora's new dresses, they won't see the light of day until Sunday school this weekend." She offered him a smile before returning to her vegetables.

Thomas hopped over the low rabbit fence. "Then I'll give you a hand. You have more tomatoes than a catsup factory."

"And what if someone sees you doing woman's work?" she asked, not taking her focus off the plants.

"You let me worry about my reputation. My lesson on the parable of the lost sheep from Luke fifteen will give our church

members so much to think about that they won't have time to pon-
der what constitutes men's work." He picked up an empty bushel
basket and began picking two rows over. "What are your plans
with these? They'll need to be processed as soon as possible." Juice
and seeds ran down his wrists from split skins on several tomatoes.

"Tomorrow I'll wash, blanch, and cut them up. Then I'll start
canning chopped tomatoes to use in chili, sloppy joes, and stew.
I'll also cook the mushy ones down to make spaghetti sauce and
tomato soup. I might also give homemade V8 juice a try. I have
carrots, celery, parsley, chives, green onions, and Swiss chard to
add to my pot of tomatoes." Sally swatted away a deerfly without
breaking stride in her plucking movements.

Thomas extended his fingers one at a time as he counted silently.
"That's only seven vegetables."

"Seven veggies will be enough to simmer and strain into juice. I
don't want folks at the Campbell Soup Company getting nervous
about the competition."

Thomas laughed easily despite his misgivings. He knew that if
Sally took on too much, she would fail at all tasks. "I hope Nora
and Amy will put off sewing for another day and help you tomorrow. This many tomatoes will require more than one pair of hands."

"*Ach*, if Nora has something suitable to wear on Sunday, then
I'll suggest it. Otherwise, she must sew at least one dress and bonnet by then. We can't have the preacher's future kin wearing spring
green, can we?"

He didn't know the light, soft shade of green even had a name.
"*Jah*, true." He tossed a few rotted tomatoes close to the gate to add
to the compost pile later. "Have you planned lunch for the district
after Sunday school? Folks will need something to eat before our
hymn service. We can't have growling bellies drowning out voices
lifted in praise."

Sally's head bobbed up from behind a huge plant. She'd
dropped to her knees to reach low-hanging fruits. "I haven't given

it a thought! With this garden demanding so much attention I forgot about Sunday's lunch. I never asked anyone what they could bring." Her sweet face filled with alarm.

The meal occurred on a weekly basis, which should make it difficult to forget. Nevertheless, Thomas smiled with the patience of Job. "Just keep it simple, *liewi*. Folks don't need a banquet. That only encourages gluttony. How about bread, spreadable cheese, lunch meat, and some chips? Then the only thing you need to prepare ahead is dessert—nothing fancy, though. This isn't the time to try out new pie recipes. Maybe just a simple cobbler with some of our peaches."

Sally perched a red-hued fist on her hip. "What's that you say? I had my heart set on Baked Alaska."

"I don't even know what that is, *fraa*."

"It's like a giant hot apple dumpling with vanilla ice cream hidden inside." She moved her hand over her belly in a circular pattern. "Sounds delicious, no? I read about it in a magazine at the doctor's office."

"How do you bake a dumpling without the ice cream melting and draining out?"

"I don't know. The nurse called me in for my exam." She reached for another empty basket behind her.

"Forget about Alaska. If you keep lunch simple, you'll be able to relax during my fascinating lesson. And you won't have to run around like a rooster without its head afterward."

Sally stopped picking and jumped to her feet. "Is that how I appear to you, Thomas? Like a headless chicken?" Her flushed cheeks matched the tomatoes.

Thomas bit his tongue with the thoughtless remark. "I misspoke. Forgive me." He stepped between plants to reach her row. "I meant you wouldn't be so rushed if the meal were simpler."

Her pink cheeks lost none of their heightened color. "Maybe you picked the wrong woman to turn into a preacher's wife." Her posture slumped. "I'm supposed to lead the other women into service, but I'm usually late and dashing in at the last minute. Either Aden falls into a mud puddle or Jeremiah spits up down my back before we leave for church. Do you remember your first day here as minister? I wore black running shoes instead of high-buttoned leather oxfords like a proper preacher's wife. I thought the older women would have a heart attack, while the younger ones looked downright fearful for my sake."

Thomas reached out to touch her face. "Yet everyone survived the day, to the best of my recollection. God brought *you* to be my beloved *fraa* and then delivered us here." He waved his hand at their garden, the hayfield where just-cut hay lay drying under warm sunshine, and the low Dixmont hills on the horizon. "And our family will bloom where we've been planted."

A smile lifted one corner of her mouth. "I suppose I shouldn't question His judgment."

He laughed wryly. "He makes no mistakes, Sally. Trust in Him and in yourself, and you will grow into your role."

"We'd better take these to the house and get out of the sun." She hefted one basket to her hip. "You're starting to talk in garden analogies. Besides, I need to cook something for supper."

He grinned with affection. "You go inside. I'll finish picking the rest before they rot. There are not too many rows left. Then you and the King sisters can start canning."

She started to protest until Jeremiah released a loud wail, indicating he was either hungry or wet or both. "*Danki*, Thomas. I'd better see to that *boppli* before he wakes the neighborhood." She giggled at her favorite joke, set down the basket, and headed toward the playpen.

No one was sleeping at this hour.

And no one lived close enough to hear a baby cry anyway.

Sally lifted Jeremiah into her arms and planted a string of kisses across his forehead, quieting him instantly. Aden raised his arms above his head to indicate he too wished to be carried. Sally complied, settling one son on each hip.

As Thomas watched, his breath caught in his throat, while his heart swelled with emotion. "Don't forget to ask the girls to help when they get home," he hollered.

She nodded her head to indicate she'd heard as she struggled up the porch steps.

While Thomas picked more tomatoes than any human needed, he brooded on the new potential threat. Sally had gained little approval among the older matrons. She certainly didn't need Amy's and Nora's liberal ways to reflect on her. Especially Nora. Thomas doubted that the girl would remain in Harmony. A small community offered little compared to Lancaster County. But Harmony was exactly what his family needed—a place for Sally to forget about her willful past and walk the straighter, narrower path. Nora wouldn't be good for Sally, nor Sally for her. He hoped both would come to this knowledge before any real damage was done.

୧୦

Amy stopped the buggy midway between the house and the barn, and stared at the ten bushels of tomatoes across the porch. "Goodness, Thomas," she called as he set another in the long line. "Did you pick all those today?"

"Along with Sally I did." He brushed off his palms as he approached. "Are your errands done?" he asked, peering up from beneath his hat brim.

"*Jah*. We found everything we needed to make Nora three dresses—one for Sundays and two for weekdays. There's a nice shop next to the co-op market. Inside it—"

"*Gut, gut*, but my wife can use your help with dinner. Tales from your travels can wait until later."

Tales from my travels? Amy blinked as Nora jumped down from the buggy. "Of course," she said. "Let me take the horse to the barn and we'll be happy to—"

"I'll take the horse." He interrupted her again. "John can rub him down while I wash up."

"*Danki* for the use of your buggy." Amy handed him the reins as she stepped past him.

"Amy?" he called.

She halted on the stone walkway and turned around.

"Could you hold off with the sewing for another day? Sally needs help with these vegetables and might be too shy to ask."

"Of course. I assumed as much when I saw the bounty. The Lord has been generous with the harvest, no?"

"That He has." Thomas perused Nora with a silent head-to-toe assessment before leading the horse away.

But once Amy and Nora opened the kitchen door, they had little time to puzzle over Thomas. The room was in complete disarray, yet Sally greeted them cheerfully. "Back so soon?" she asked. She tucked a lock of hair beneath her *kapp*. "Where did you eat lunch?"

Amy hung her purse on a hook and slipped a clean apron over her head. "At the deli by the railroad tracks. We split a chicken salad sandwich."

"I always wanted to try that place. Maybe someday I will." Sally dropped a raw piece of fish into a bowl of flour.

"I see you've been busy with the garden. What can I help you with?" Amy walked to the sink to wash her hands, trying not to stare at the variety of vegetable trimmings littering the floor around the trash can. Sally's aim was terrible.

"I'll put these bags in the front room and come right back," Nora whispered in Amy's ear.

"I'm breading some haddock I found in the back of the freezer. Once a month a seafood vendor comes to market day and sells his fresh catch. Thomas loves fried fish." Sally dipped a floured piece into an egg mixture and then dropped it in a bowl of breadcrumbs.

A wisp of smoke rose from the frying pan as Amy smelled oil beginning to scorch. With a pot holder she moved the pan off the burner before the grease burst into flames. "Why don't I fry the fish while you make the rest of supper?" she asked, discreetly lowering the heat. With the crisis averted, Amy walked to where Sally was coating fillets with flour, egg, and breadcrumbs.

"Good idea. We'll have yellow beans with boiled new potatoes. I just dug up these spuds. Because they are small they won't need much slicing."

Amy grinned into the bowl of plum-sized potatoes. "They are adorable. A perfect size."

When Nora returned, she set to work cleaning the kitchen. Within an hour the extended family sat down to a delicious meal in a tidy room. Sally had fed both *kinner* ahead of time, allowing her a chance to enjoy an adult supper.

John, who had been quiet since chores, finally spoke after sampling the fried haddock. "I thought you would return for lunch." He pulled a small bone from between his teeth.

Amy smiled across the table. "We would have practically had to turn around the moment we arrived. And you know how women love to browse in stores."

"Our co-op is a gem, no?" Sally popped a bean into her mouth. "It has a good selection of bulk foods, both grown locally and trucked in from out-of-state."

"It has everything a person needs," agreed Amy. "And I loved the quilt-and-fabric shop next door. I imagine it's crowded with tourists on Fridays and Saturdays."

Sally laughed uproariously. "You're not in Pennsylvania anymore, Amy. Tourists don't come to Harmony."

"None at all?" asked Nora. She took a second fillet from the platter. Fish hadn't been commonplace back home.

"Let's see." Sally tapped her jaw with one finger. "There were those elderly ladies looking for a giant flea market. They were definitely lost. I hope they found their way home safely."

"As far as I'm concerned, no tourists means no traffic." John scraped two more pieces of fish onto his plate.

"Some would be nice," said Thomas. "The Amish in our community make woodcrafts and furniture to sell over the winter that we must ship elsewhere right now."

"*Elsewhere* will probably bring you better profits anyway." John sounded like an English businessman instead of a farmer waiting to buy his own land.

Amy sipped her iced tea. She'd taught Sally how to make sun tea with cool well water, a few tea bags, and a sunny window. "Nora and I found something interesting in the quilt shop next to the market." She dabbed her mouth with a napkin, waiting for everyone's attention.

"What was that, three different shades of black thread?" John directed his quip at his brother, who chuckled good-naturedly.

"Even better. We found a quilt for sale we believe our aunt made. She left Mount Joy about ten years ago, shunned. We girls never learned where she moved to when she left town." Amy glanced at Nora for confirmation.

Nora looked up with her green eyes shining. "We might not know where she went originally, but she must have lived here at some point."

Two people at the table stopped eating. "Why do you think this aunt made the quilt?" asked Thomas.

Amy leaned forward in her chair. "Because she always marked her work with a little ladybug embroidered on the seam binding. It was like her signature."

"*Mamm* called it vanity, but she always laughed about Aunt Prudence's little bugs," added Nora with a giggle.

No one else seemed amused.

"Oh, my, Prudence Hilty is your aunt?" asked Sally, setting down her fork. "She did live in Harmony for a while." Sally cast a glance in Thomas's direction. "But word of the Lancaster shunning eventually followed her here and she left."

Amy turned toward Thomas, who looked as though a fish bone had lodged in his throat. "What happened?"

"Divorce goes against God's law," he stated simply. "It is an abomination."

Amy lowered her gaze to her plate. "That's what my father and my *grossdawdi* said. *Mamm* wouldn't tell me why she left Uncle Leon, but she must have had her reasons." Amy breathed deeply to calm her nerves. She sensed that becoming emotional wouldn't serve the situation.

"She was always nice to her nieces and nephews." Nora's voice sounded weak and frightened in the quiet room. "God never blessed her with *bopplin* of her own, so she loved to spend time with us."

"Prudence *did* have her reasons," murmured Sally.

Amy and Nora stared at the tiny dark-haired woman. "What did you hear?" they asked simultaneously.

Thomas cleared his throat, but Sally forged ahead. "Her husband was fond of strong drink."

"You should not gossip or state with conviction what you haven't witnessed," Thomas said, frowning at his wife.

Sally turned to face him. "I'm not spreading gossip, *ehemann*. Prudence herself told me this. And you don't have to catch someone holding an empty whiskey bottle to know when someone is drunk."

"Did Leon follow her to Maine?" asked John. Even he'd stopped devouring the delicious fish, intrigued by the bizarre story.

"*Nein*," Thomas said softly. "He was never here. The bishop questioned Prudence, and she explained everything to him."

"And you ran her out of town?" Amy's voice rose with indignation.

"No, we didn't. We asked her to kneel and confess her sins." Thomas focused on Amy and her alone. "We told her Scripture was clear. She may live apart from an abusive spouse, but she should not have sought a legal divorce in English courts. She and your uncle are still married in the eyes of God."

Nora pushed away her plate. "Do you mean Aunt Prudence hired a lawyer and divorced Uncle Leon?"

Thomas nodded. "This isn't conjecture. She told me so. We advised her to repent of her sin and live in peace here, away from the man. We would have helped her." He lowered his voice to a whisper and didn't meet anyone's gaze.

Sally groaned low in her throat and shook her head sadly.

"But soon after Prudence left our community." When Thomas raised his head and glanced around the table, his face seemed to have aged during the meal.

Amy was stunned. She could sense Nora's and John's eyes on her, but she focused on a stain on the oilcloth table cover. *Was it beet juice? Had Aden smashed a raspberry?* Dwelling on the possible nature of the stain provided distraction from her confusing emotions. "I hope she's happy wherever she went." She spoke only to break the uncomfortable silence.

"Apart from God there can be no joy." Thomas rose to his feet to get the coffeepot.

Sally scrambled up for her baked dessert. "Anybody for peach cobbler made with our own peaches? Georgia has nothing on peaches over the state of Maine." She set the pan on the table and began to slice.

"Cut me a small piece." Amy had seen the peaches for sale at the co-op compared to the Georgia peaches purchased back home at the IGA, but the cobber turned out to be equally delicious.

After the dishes had been washed and put away, Amy followed John out to the rockers on the front porch. As she sat down next to him, she spotted Thomas taking the living room chair within view of them. "Don't try to steal a kiss," she whispered. "Your *bruder* can see us."

John smiled. "Don't be too hard on him. It's no easy task ministering to a congregation." He spoke softly so as not to be overheard. "Most district members express words of condolence when a man draws the lot to become preacher. It's a heavy burden."

She nodded in agreement. Around them she heard comforting night sounds: the wind through tall pines, the drone of insects, and a train whistle at a faraway crossing. Amy closed her eyes and began to rock. After a few minutes of companionable silence, she spoke. "I will write to *grossmammi* and Aunt Irene before bed. I want to tell them their daughter and sister lived here for a while."

John stopped rocking and reached for her hand. "Do you think that's wise? Prudence knew her actions would lead to shunning, yet she acted anyway with total disregard for Amish *Ordnung*."

"Sometimes both of your choices are bad."

"True," agreed John. "But we must pick the choice in keeping with Scripture."

"It's not that simple."

"*Jah*, it is." He shook her hand as though trying to wake a child from a bad dream.

Amy faced him in the darkness. "Are you judging her?"

"*Nein*. I'm only cautioning you to let this sleeping dog lie."

"My aunt is a human being, John, not a dog." She pulled her hand back. "I want to let my family know she's still alive and well. I see no harm…or sin…in a letter like that." She rose to her feet and strode toward the door. "*Gut nacht*." The screen door slammed behind her as though punctuation for her parting comments.

❧

John was only too glad to climb into Thomas's buggy and leave the farm for the day. His meager breakfast had consisted of toast, coffee, and sliced peaches. By the time the men left the room, the women had turned the kitchen and porch into a tomato processing plant. Every pot, kettle, and cauldron had been appropriated for cooking down the garden bounty.

"This will be a good day to be gone," said Thomas, as though reading John's thoughts. "What do you suppose supper will be? BLTs with tomato soup?"

John laughed heartily until he noticed that the little flag had been raised on the Detweiler mailbox. Amy had written to her family after all and set the letter out for pickup. He ground down on his molars to rein in his temper. "We'll be hungry enough for anything by the time we get home," he said from between gritted teeth. "I want to buy a buggy, harness, and my own horse today. I can't keep borrowing yours, Thomas. Besides, Amy likes to run errands whenever the notion strikes her." He grasped the window opening as they rolled over a pothole. "How far away is this carriage maker?"

"A good fifteen miles on the road to Waterville. The man sells quality buggies at a fair price. And he usually has horseflesh available for sale too. His brother is a breeder and trainer, so if you see something you like, the beast will already be trained to the harness."

Another pothole jarred John's kidneys. "I'm not picky with horses. I'm obliged to you for taking me there."

Thomas squinted from sun glare. "My alfalfa could use more time to dry before we rake and bail. Anyway, I was ready to get away from rocks and clay for the day."

"Clay soil?" asked John. "I thought land this close to the sea would be sandy."

"We're thirty miles from the nearest inlet to the ocean. The land you'll buy will probably be hard clay that will need plenty of building up. Better to buy fallow farmland so most rocks and boulders will have already been removed."

"Did you buy fertilizer to enrich the soil when you started out?"

Thomas shook his head. "No, I compost horse, cow, and goat manure and then till it under in the fall. Most *Englischers* around here grow organic produce. Their harvests fetch good prices. Folks in Boston will pay dearly for no pesticides or chemical fertilizer residue on their vegetables. You should look into organic farming for yourself."

John scratched his clean jawline. "Right now I just want to grow enough to feed my family. I'm not interested in a cash crop."

"For the three of you?" Something seemed to lurk beneath the surface of Thomas's question.

"*Jah*, the three of us until Nora makes up her mind. I'm hoping by then that we'll have a little one on the way to give Amy plenty to do."

His brother made an odd clucking sound that didn't seem intended for the horse. "You're getting ahead of yourself, no?"

"I hope to wed and be living in our own place by first snow." John braced as the buggy took a tight curve in the road faster than he'd expected. "On the way back from Waterville, let's stop at any farms for sale."

Thomas tugged his hat brim lower. "I can think of one or two places that might warrant a look-see. Depends on how long you take to negotiate a price on your new buggy and horse."

"I'll pay whatever's fair. I'm not much of a haggler. Tell me what the English organic farmers grow up here."

"You name it—potatoes, squash, onions, peppers, broccoli, cabbage, spinach, and several kinds of lettuce. And tomatoes, of course. Cukes too, but beetles infested ours this year. I had to till the plants under."

"Have any Amish farmers obtained organic certification?"

"*Jah*, two so far. Lots of paperwork to fill out, but our bishop stands behind the idea. Too many chemicals are dumped on the land and end up in our water supply these days."

"What about wheat? I haven't seen any yet."

"Wheat doesn't grow here, nor rye or spelt. No sorghum or soybeans, either."

"No grains of any kind?" John cocked his head with surprise. "Then where do you get your straw?"

"We don't use it. Only wood shavings for animal bedding. Barns stay cleaner and smell better with pine shavings."

"Lots for me to learn," John murmured.

"Plenty of time to learn it." Thomas slapped him on the back.

"What about dairy herds? Any Amish selling milk to cheese producers?"

"Most district cows or steers are for family use. *Englischers* supply the milk in the area to bottlers and cheese houses. So if you have a hankering for a dairy farm, you won't have much competition. I recommend goats, though. They are less troublesome with our hills and long winters. Goats will put up with just about anything."

John remembered the nasty varmint that tried to make him his supper and shook his head. "No, goats and I don't see eye to eye."

"That's because you're *never* supposed to stare one down." Thomas chuckled. "Just sit quietly and tell him your life story over a bucket of wormy apples. You'll both gain new perspective."

John's mind swam with new information and ideas. Later that afternoon he bought a fine Morgan-Standardbred gelding and a well-made two-seater buggy with plenty of room behind the backseat. Thomas and the carriage maker chitchatted so long that they had no time for house-hunting on the way back, but John didn't mind. He enjoyed getting to know another member of his new district. And the more he admired the undeveloped acres of land waiting to be farmed, the more certain he became. God had brought him to the right place. He and Amy had found a home.

FIVE

*Not the labors of my hands
Can fulfill Thy law's commands*

Nora took one look at her hands and sighed. Every one of her nails had broken during the past few days of canning, while her skin had taken on a pinkish hue that would probably last for weeks. She had never seen so many tomatoes in her life. *Grossmammi* and *mamm* always put up many quarts of each variation, but Sally's harvest exceeded that. What would her small family do with so many jars of stewed tomatoes? At least with Amy, John, and herself living here, they might be able to reduce the inventory.

Two days of nonstop canning had forced her to rush through cutting out and stitching up her new Sunday black dress. But at least the garment was finished, giving her a much-needed Saturday afternoon of relaxation. Nora tucked her wide-brimmed bonnet into an apron pocket in case she decided to walk on the road and set off through the mowed portion of the backyard. A craggy tree stood sentinel at the pasture gate, one that demanded a closer look. As she neared the droopy-leafed tree with cigar-shaped seed-pods, the sound of a squalling baby grabbed her attention. Nora ran in the direction of the cries and frantically searched the thick weeds and wild sumac. Had one of Sally's sons wandered off and become entangled in barbed wire? Sally might not be the world's best housekeeper or baker, but her children were never out of view or earshot. The woman fed, changed, bathed, and coddled the boys all day long.

Pushing back the brambles of overgrown wild roses, Nora found the source of distress—a baby goat caught in the fence. The kid's bawling sounded almost human. A nanny goat stood a few paces off, watching Nora suspiciously. "Easy there, Nelly. Let me see if I can help your little one." But when she bent down to lift the animal free, the nanny charged with an evil glint in her eye.

For a moment Nora contemplated continuing on her stroll through Thomas's farm—the first leisure time since her arrival—and not get dirty, cut by barbed wire, or bit by a protective goat. But the kid's plaintive cries melted her heart. She reached between the barbs to pat the furry head and the nanny lunged again. "Stay right there," she ordered, withdrawing her fingers just in time. "I'll come back with help."

Seeing no one in the fields, she hurried to the barn. Inside the cavernous interior, which smelled of fresh-sawn wood, sweet timothy hay, and not-so-sweet horse droppings, Nora found only animal occupants. "John?" she called. She cocked her head to listen, yet heard nothing but the usual huffs and snorts of live-stock confined to stalls. She hurried down the main aisle to the attached workshop, where Thomas built birdfeeders and carved wooden weather vanes during the winter months. "Thomas?" she called, despite a seemingly empty shop. Again she waited, listen-ing. Through the doorway to the corral, Nora heard the distinctive whinny of a horse. With no other options, she entered the outdoor paddock, calling the name of her future brother-in-law once more. "John, are you out here?"

Nora peered around. With a start she spotted someone bent over a black horse. The man appeared to be digging something out of the animal's hoof. She marched to the outdoor stall, careful as to where she was stepping. "Why didn't you answer me?" she demanded, making no effort to hide her annoyance.

"Because my name isn't John." The man gazed up with mild interest, but he didn't release his grip on the horse's hoof. His eyes, dark and intense, seemed to bore holes through her as they traveled from her feet to her *kapp*.

"Who are you?" she asked, suddenly nervous and self-conscious.

"Elam Detweiler." After digging another piece of gravel from beneath the horseshoe, he lowered the animal's hoof to the ground. "Your turn. Who are you?"

She wiped her palms down her skirt. "Nora."

His expression didn't alter with the slightest sign of recognition. "Is that right." His reply was a statement, not a question

Finally, her common sense returned. "I'm Nora King, sister of Amy King, who is engaged to be married to John Detweiler, who is your brother."

His smile started out small but soon filled his face. "That last part I already knew, but at least now we're getting somewhere." He walked around the horse and pulled up the other hind leg. It was actually more of a smirk than a smile.

"I'm pleased to make your acquaintance."

"Likewise, I'm sure. They didn't get hitched yet?"

"No, not yet. Thomas wants them to get to know the district first, and for your bishop to know them."

He grunted and rolled his eyes. "*Jah*, that's sounds like my brother."

"Anyway, I'm sure you would have been invited to the wedding, had there already been one."

Elam laughed as though he'd heard a good joke, but he didn't glance up from his hoof trimming. "I wouldn't be so sure of that, Nora King from Lancaster County, if I were you."

Suddenly, she remembered the reason for her barn visit. "Could you stop for a minute? I need your help. A baby goat is tangled in a fence, and I couldn't free him by myself."

"Thomas and his goats. If it's not one thing, it's another." He sounded angry but backed away from the horse and tossed his tool into a bucket by the stall wall. "Show me the way, Nora King." Elam dusted off his palms, grabbed a garden rake and a pair of snippers from the bucket, and followed her around the barn.

Nora walked as fast as her not-very-long legs would carry her. "They are over this way." She pointed toward the fence.

"I'd venture a guess they are in the goat pasture, no?"

She bit down on her lip, deciding to wait until they had freed the poor creature to give the man a dressing-down. Surely house-guests warranted more gracious treatment.

His stride was so long she had to jog to keep up. If there were two things Nora didn't like, sweating and running topped the list. "Here, behind this bush," she gasped breathlessly as they reached the barbed wire. Nora pulled back the branches to reveal the trapped kid. He peered up with moist black eyes and released a plaintive wail.

"Hold those branches away with your backside and be ready with this." Elam handed her the rake.

"What am I to do with a garden tool? Clean out last fall's dead leaves?" Nora positioned herself in between the bush and the fence, trying not to think about his embarrassing reference to her backside.

Elam snickered, revealing straight teeth and two dimples. "Use it to keep that nanny from biting or head-butting me while I free her baby."

Nora had barely raised the rake in place when he reached into the tangled wires, grabbed hold of the goat's face, and snipped the wires snared in his fur. *Snip, snip, snip*—three cuts and the kid was loose. Elam lifted up the little goat to inspect him for injury.

"Could you hurry?" Nora shook the rake menacingly as the fifty-pound mother advanced toward her offspring. "Shoo! Get back! Stop!" Her commands did little good as the nanny grabbed the rake handle with her teeth and pulled it from Nora's grasp.

"He looks fine to me. Just a few minor scratches," announced Elam. When he set the kid down in the grass, he quickly scampered to rejoin his mother.

The nanny dropped the garden tool, nuzzled her young, and then the two headed up the slope without a backward glance at their rescuers.

"Stay back from the fence, you pair of dummies!" Elam hollered before bending to repair the cut fence as best as he could. "That should hold until I can restring this section." He straightened his back, squared his shoulders, and gazed down his nose at Nora. "*Danki*. You were quite helpful until she took your rake away. How will you finish cleaning up the yard now?"

She tried unsuccessfully not to laugh. "A rake in a goat's hands can be dangerous. We're just lucky she dropped it." Suddenly, Nora spotted blood running down his fingers and dripping into the grass. "You're bleeding. Let's go to the house."

"No, I'll wash at the pump instead. It'll clot soon enough on its own."

"Don't be a mule. I'll meet you at the pump with paper towels, antiseptic cream, and bandages." She headed for the house without further argument.

Five minutes later, she found Elam with both hands under a stream of cold water. Blood dotted his pants and shirt and tinted the drain water. "Didn't clot as well as expected," he mumbled as though angry about all the blood.

"I didn't think it would. But it was noble of you to sacrifice your skin for Thomas's goats." She dried his hands with a clean towel and applied some salve.

"Don't be impressed. It was a rare, weak moment. I'm usually callous and insensitive." He focused only on his hand being bandaged.

"How come I haven't met you yet, Elam Detweiler of Harmony, Maine? Have you been hiding?" *Two could play his game.*

One dimple deepened. "I work on a logging crew, so I'm not home much. Thomas prefers it that way, if you catch my drift."

As soon as she applied the last strip of bandage, he picked up his tools and headed toward the barn. He was already ten paces away when he called, "Thanks, Nora." His words floated over his shoulder, appearing to be more of an afterthought than anything else.

♔

Amy loved this time of day when she could sit and rock, sip tea, and think about her life—past, present, and future. The supper dishes had been washed and put away. Sally was tending her children, while Nora worked on her second dress of navy blue. John sat in the living room, hunched over the classified ads of the local paper, searching for farms or land for sale. The heat of the past several days had broken, leaving far more hospitable temperatures for sleeping in upstairs bedrooms.

"Mind if I join you for a spell?"

Amy jumped, spilling tea down her skirt. Dabbing at the stain with her handkerchief, she looked into the piercing blue eyes of not John Detweiler, but his older brother. "Of course," she said, lifting her Bible off of the other rocker. It had been her mother's and she treasured it, despite its smoky odor. The Bible had been plucked from the debris and returned to her by the county fire chief.

"I wanted to talk to you about your Aunt Prudence." Thomas lowered himself stiffly onto the chair. "I didn't tell you everything the other day, and I'm not sure why, but I want you to know all that I know." He paused, letting an uncomfortable silence grow between them.

Amy felt oddly frightened by his admission. She didn't know if she should prod him to continue or run upstairs to her room and hide.

"We welcomed Prudence into our district. She confessed her sins on her knees to God in front of the entire district. Our Lord forgives sins, and after that day no one ever brought the matter up again. But it wasn't long after that Prudence visited the bishop again." Thomas rocked slowly in the chair, stroking his beard like an elderly sage sitting atop a mountain rather than a thirty-year-old farmer and preacher from rural Maine.

"What did she talk to him about?" Amy felt beads of sweat form on her brow, as though *she* were the one who had approached the preacher with some grave misdeed.

"Prudence had connected in a special way with someone new to our district, an Amish man from Michigan. He was a widower with grown children, and he knew about her divorce." Thomas leaned his head back and closed his eyes, while Amy sat very still. "Prudence told the bishop they were *en lieb* and wished to marry. In love—as though that emotion changed something." He stopped rocking and faced her. "It changed nothing, Amy. They could not marry. Prudence was still wed to Leon in the eyes of the Lord. The Good Book has no fine print that says if you're married to a mean-spirited drunk, biblical laws are suspended."

Amy was shocked by both his sarcasm and her aunt's behavior.

"There are clear instructions in First Corinthians, chapter seven, verses ten and eleven." He began to recite Scripture from memory. "'For those who are married, I have a command that comes not from me, but from the Lord. A wife must not leave her husband. But if she does leave him, let her remain single or else be reconciled to him. And the husband must not leave his wife.' And in verse thirty-nine:

'A wife is bound to her husband as long as he lives. If her husband dies, she is free to marry anyone she wishes, but only if he loves the Lord.'" Thomas shook his head. "As long as the husband lives, a wife may not remarry. Our hands were tied. God's Word is law. Soon afterward, Prudence packed up and left...with him."

"Did they move to Michigan to live close to his kin?" Hope filled Amy's heart that her long-lost aunt, a woman she hadn't seen since she was a girl, had found compassion and acceptance with this Amish man's family.

"*Nein*," said Thomas, dashing her idea. "His Michigan district would have viewed the situation the same way. They are banned, Amy. Their sins are grievous."

"Maybe they never went through with it. Maybe they came to their senses and simply parted ways."

"I hope so, for the sake of their eternal souls." The zeal had gone out of his voice. He sounded sad and weary.

For several minutes they rocked in the growing darkness, each lost in their own thoughts. *Prudence going against the* Ordnung *in so many ways? Who was this man from Michigan who turned her away from the Amish community after she'd regained a home?*

While Amy tried to understand another woman's motivations, Thomas simply rocked, seeming troubled and anxious. He didn't return to his evening Bible study or check on his wife and sons. Then he spoke in a soft, troubled voice. "I have her address. The bishop supplied it, in case you wish to write to her."

"*Jah*, of course I do." Amy sprang from the chair.

But Thomas stopped her with an upraised palm. "She is banned and will remain so as long as she lives in sin. But in God all things are possible, including Prudence's salvation. Write to say you have come to live in Harmony." He met and held her gaze. "Tell her about the unfortunate passing of her sister and brother-in-law. She probably knows nothing about the fire. Perhaps she will be made to consider the brevity of life. We are here for a fleeting moment, but eternity is forever. Let Prudence know she still has family and friends who care for her and pray for her." He stretched out his hand with the slip of paper. "Here's the address. Tell her God won't turn His back on a penitent heart."

"*Danki*, Thomas. I will write tonight."

He struggled to his feet, as though stiffer than when he sat down. "*Gut nacht*, Amy."

After Thomas walked into the house, she was left with only questions. What would make Aunt Prudence turn from her faith and the Lord? Had her husband been so horrible that only an English divorce could provide the peace she sought? Amy clutched the piece of paper tightly in her hand. A woman married to find a sense of security and protection. Could a husband be the source of fear and suffering? It was a blessing Prudence and Leon had no children. God, in His infinite wisdom, had protected the unborn from a life of turmoil. But according to Thomas, God would close the gates of heaven if she married again. What was this new *ehemann* like that Prudence would risk the fires of hell for him?

For a moment Amy wondered if she would chance such a destiny for John's love, but it didn't take long contemplation to figure that one out. She would not. There was too much ado made about love. Some things were more important, such as a person's soul. And feeling safe and secure. Strong people knew how to feel secure inside. It seemed to come easier for men, but Aunt Prudence must have found some sense of it, or she never would have struck out with this new man. Ever since the fire, Amy had felt like a leaf on the wind, helpless to determine where she would land. But one thing was certain. Her *mamm* had loved Prudence and had never given up on her sister, shunned or not.

Amy opened the screen door and crept to the kitchen table, careful not to wake the rest of the family. She drew paper and pen from one of Sally's drawers and began her letter to the long-forgotten aunt. She had barely explained her present circumstances in Maine when John strolled into the room. He carried an empty coffee cup with the newspaper tucked under his arm.

"Ah, Amy," he said. "I'd hoped to see you yet tonight." His eyes twinkled with excitement.

She smiled fondly at him. "I'm writing another letter before bed."

"*Gut, gut.* I just read an interesting story in the Harmony paper." He paused, waiting for a murmur of acknowledgment before continuing. "A while back, a reporter from a Boston newspaper wrote an article about how the Amish have been welcomed by the *Englischers* of Harmony." He settled into the chair next to hers and then picked up the paper to read aloud a sentence. "Folks are eager to restore the proud agricultural heritage of the area, and the Amish will be a tremendous asset in that regard."

She glanced up from her writing. "That's nice."

"Well, some rich person in Boston liked the article and the town so much he sent a check for twenty thousand dollars to the fire chief for a new truck." He laid the paper down, beaming.

"Why?" she asked.

"Because the community needed a new fire engine." His nose twitched as though it tickled. "The department is all-volunteer and operates on a small budget, as you can imagine." He folded back the paper to a different page.

Amy shrugged. "Couldn't Boston use some new equipment?"

John furrowed his brow. "I have no idea. That's not the point. The generous man wanted to help Harmony, not where he lived."

"I see, but I wonder if he told his wife about the donation."

He lowered his brows and stared at her. "Why don't we change the subject?" He tapped the classifieds with a finger. "I found listings of land for sale in the area. Shall I read you the descriptions?"

She shook her head. "Why don't you read them at breakfast? I'm sorry, John, but I really want to finish this letter and post it tomorrow."

His face turned dismal as he set the listing aside. "Who are you writing to? Rachel and Beth?"

"No, to Aunt Prudence. Thomas gave me her address. She still lives in Maine." Amy unfolded the slip of paper.

"Do you think that's wise? She is banned, Amy."

She patted his clenched fist. "I know that, dear heart, but she hasn't heard about the fire. Even your brother feels she should know that her sister is no longer among the living." Amy's voice cracked as a lump formed in her throat. It still hurt to say the words about her parents' deaths.

"That is true. She needs to know about the fire." He pushed back his chair and stood. "I'll tell you about the farms for sale in the morning."

As he reached the doorway, Amy asked, "John, did you know Elam was home? Nora spoke with him this afternoon."

"I didn't. I'll seek him out to say hello."

"I can't believe he prefers to sleep in the cellar with the spiders." She shuddered at the thought.

John rubbed his eyes. "It's his choice to separate himself from the family. He hasn't joined the church yet and refuses to abide by district rules. The cellar has an outside entrance for his comings and goings, and his old bedroom doesn't."

"I look forward to meeting him."

"Don't expect too much, and you won't be disappointed."

"Isn't that how life is in all regards?"

"More so for some than others." He turned on his heel and marched down the hall.

Amy picked up the pen for the third time, puzzling over his cryptic remark only briefly. She had plenty to say to her banned and mysterious aunt without worrying about John and Elam's strained relationship.

❧

When Wednesday finally arrived, Sally breathed a sigh of relief for a pair of reasons. First, Elam had left at dawn to return to his job up north. Because an unseasonable rainy spell gave the workers a couple of days off, Elam had come home. Although he'd tried to stay out of Thomas's way, she had listened to several conversations with raised voices. He hadn't gone to the meetinghouse for Sunday school with them. He hadn't sat down to a single family meal, preferring to forage like a raccoon after everyone left the kitchen. In fact, she could think of plenty of critters to compare him to. Although he worked around the farm, he avoided people like a coyote. Elam was wild and impetuous, while Thomas was tenderhearted and predictable. It was hard to imagine that those men shared the same parents.

The overdue reunion between Elam and John had not been warm and cuddly, either. From what she'd overheard, Elam seemed determined to talk John out of buying property in Harmony, while John appeared determined to keep Elam away from Amy and Nora. When Amy finally met her future brother-in-law, she shook his hand and then jumped back as though he might bite. She hid behind John's back for the rest of the get-acquainted conversation. That gal needed some backbone. Elam wouldn't hurt a fly, despite his rather unkempt appearance.

However, Nora marched right up to him asking question after question: *Where do you sleep? Why don't you eat meals with us? How do you get back and forth to the logging crew? Why is your hair cut like that?*

After a while Elam stopped answering her questions and just stood there laughing. But John found no amusement in the situation. He finally sent Amy and Nora inside so he could have a private chat with his younger brother. Unfortunately, Sally couldn't listen to their conversation because they had wandered into the woodshop. But when John returned to the house, he wasn't smiling.

When an *Englischer* arrived to pick Elam up, he filled his jacket pockets with muffins and biscuits and took the leftover fried chicken and pie. Sally didn't mind. The young man needed to eat. Besides, she'd baked several more pies for tonight's special supper—her *other* reason to rejoice—an evening in town for the women. They would attend a fund-raiser at the community center for a local family who lost their furniture and personal possessions in a trailer fire. Every Amish family in the district would be there, as well as most of Harmony's English population.

Who would think a metal enclosure could possibly burn? mused Sally, setting her three peach pies into a hamper.

"Those look delicious," said Amy from over her shoulder. "Dinner will be worth the price just for a slice of your pie."

"*Danki.*" Sally felt her cheeks warm from the compliment. "Everyone is bringing food for the potluck. The organizers are hoping that twenty dollars a plate will raise enough cash to pay the family's rent for the next six months. People will also bring whatever they can spare to help furnish their new home. I'm donating two quilts and two sets of sheets. A furniture store in Waterville promised new beds, and an appliance outlet here in Harmony donated a washer and dryer."

"Very generous," said Amy. "Because Nora and I brought little other than our clothes with us, we're each chipping in a hundred dollars. I placed the cash in an envelope."

Sally gasped. "Talk about generous!"

"I transferred my portion of the farm sale to your bank here, so I have enough to share with the less fortunate. Nora left her inheritance in Lancaster, so I've covered her portion too. How did the fire start?" she asked softly.

"A malfunctioning hot water heater allowed propane gas to leak. A single spark set off the blaze. By God's grace, no one was hurt."

The kitchen door swung open, and Nora stuck in her head. "Come along, you two. The men are already in the buggy." She tugged on her full-brimmed bonnet with a scowl—horse blinders, as she called it—and marched back out.

"I hope the ladies like my pies. I don't bake much for potlucks. My baking doesn't stand up to local standards."

"Everyone will enjoy them, I'm sure." Amy lifted one handle of the hamper. "And it's a standard crust recipe. What could possibly go wrong?"

Sally took the other handle and followed her, pulling the door shut behind her. She appreciated Amy's flattery because she always cringed whenever her cooking or handiwork was subject to Amish scrutiny. Two elderly widows acted like self-appointed county fair judges, despite the fact that Plain folks didn't enter competitions. With any luck, *Englischers* would select her pies from the buffet.

But luck—or divine providence—wasn't kind to Sally that night.

The Detweilers and Kings paid for their suppers at the door and then greeted the organizers and the needy family. Amy and Nora slipped their contribution into the envelope box and, as newcomers, were soon surrounded by district women. Sally placed her pies on the dessert table and wandered over to the housewares collection area. Fine-looking cookware, dishes, towels, and bedding had been donated, as well as a large amount of children's clothes. With Jeremiah perched on one hip and Aden clinging to her skirt, she took up a position by a post to watch the English couple welcome each new guest. Truly, they didn't seem to have expected such an outpouring of goodwill.

"No need to brace up the pillar, *fraa*. The building will stand without your assistance." Thomas materialized by her side and draped an arm around her shoulders.

"I'm just making sure. These people don't need any more nasty surprises." Sally smiled up into his handsome face. "Almost everyone brought something practical for them and put money in the box besides paying for supper. Why do *Englischers* always seem shocked by Christian charity? The husband and wife look ready to faint."

"That they do," he agreed. "This family will never forget tonight and will probably be the first to help others in need for the rest of their lives." He took her arm as the organizers signaled it was time to eat. "Let's get our dinner. I'm starving."

Sally and Thomas loaded their plates and found seats near Amy, John, and Nora. The assortment of food was exceptional, encouraging everyone to indulge more than usual. Thomas foraged the dessert table, returning with several things to share with his tablemates. "I would have sampled your peach pie, *fraa*," he said, "but there was none left. The lady in front of me took the last piece."

"Was she an *Englischer*?" Sally asked, feeling a twinge of unease.

"No, a district woman, even though all of you probably use the same recipe." He swung his long legs over the bench and looked at his brother. "There is no figuring out women."

"I'm starting to discover that myself," agreed John, taking a brownie from the plate.

Sally slouched lower in her seat and tried to finish her potato salad and ham. Within another minute, a woman's voice rang out from the table behind them.

"Goodness, Sally Detweiler, there's a housefly in my dessert! Aren't these the peach pies you brought?"

Sally turned around to watch in horror as Clara Yoder flung the offending bug off her fork to the floor. Murmurs rose from the table of Amish diners.

"Everybody's heard of shoofly pie, but you shouldn't take the name seriously," Clara said, not trying to be subtle.

People in the nearby vicinity broke into peals of laughter. All except for Sally. She prayed that the town hall floor would open up and swallow her alive.

SIX

Could my zeal no respite know

On the final stretch of open road, John slapped the reins on the new gelding's back, encouraging him to go faster. He was eager to get back to his brother's farm and even more eager to talk with Amy. The information he'd learned today was too good to keep until dinnertime. If he was fortunate, everyone would still be at the table eating lunch.

John felt certain that Thomas and Sally would appreciate some good news to wash away the memory of Friday's potluck and yesterday's preaching service. How could Sally have been so careless as to not notice a fly in her sliced peaches? The district ladies had giggled and guffawed merrily, but the *Englischers* within earshot hadn't looked quite so entertained. John noticed more than one poking around their desserts for unwanted ingredients.

But Thomas, always the indulgent husband, had made light of the situation. "Oh, that little fly wouldn't even hurt...a fly." All the district men laughed, diffusing the uncomfortable situation. The pie went into the trash and the elderly woman selected a different dessert. Sally had been mortified—and rightly so. She'd sat pale and silent for the rest of the meal, as though waiting for someone to arrest her for pie sabotage or attempted assault.

John liked his sister-in-law. She was a fine mother, but her careless housekeeping and bad time management made her a poor example for Amy and Nora. But after what he'd found out today, they would soon be moving to a farm of their own.

He turned the horse into the driveway, pulling hard on the reins so his new buggy wouldn't topple over on its side. Inside the barn he rubbed down the Morgan and filled the water trough and grain stanchion with a bucket of oats. When he entered a nearly empty kitchen twenty minutes later, Amy stood washing dishes at the sink, elbow-deep in sudsy water. "Am I late?" he asked. "Did I miss lunch?" He hung his hat on a peg.

She glanced back at him. "I'm afraid so. If you give me a minute, I'll fix you a sandwich."

"*Danki*. I need to wash anyway." When he returned two sandwiches, a pile of potato chips, and a glass of lemonade waited at his usual spot at the table.

Amy sat down across from him with a drink of her own. "How did it go in town? Did you find the information you were looking for?"

"Indeed, I did. I visited the office of the Maine Organic Farmers and Gardener's Association."

"That's quite a mouthful." She took a swallow of lemonade.

"They use letters to abbreviate the name. Anyway, they explained the whole process of how to get part or all of my acres certified organic. A woman even gave me the necessary forms to fill out."

"This special certification is important to you?"

"*Jah*, I want my...our...future *kinner* to eat fruits and vegetables without toxic chemicals stuck to the skin." He bit into sliced roast beef hungrily.

Her left dimple deepened. "You could refrain from spraying or adding dangerous substances without bothering with English paperwork. Plain people have used good, old-fashioned horse manure for centuries without undue consequences, except for stinky neighborhoods when everyone tills it under in the fall." Ice cubes clinked in her glass as she drank.

John felt a twinge of annoyance. "But if I *bother* with the government paperwork, I can sell my produce to buyers of certified organics and earn better profits. Otherwise, folks won't know how the vegetables have been raised. We will need cash for taxes and medical bills, and to buy what we can't grow ourselves." He quickly devoured the rest of his sandwich.

"In that case, it's worth filling out the forms, as long as the bishop approves the idea."

"*Ach*, the bishop." John glanced around the room to make sure no eavesdroppers lurked nearby. "Come outside with me for a spell." He wrapped his second sandwich in a napkin.

Amy frowned. "But I promised Nora—"

"Please, Amy," he interrupted. "This is important."

She tugged her soiled apron over her head and walked out onto the porch. "A touch of fall is in the air, no? At home, things would still be hot and humid."

He took her elbow to lead her down the steps. "This is our home now. Don't you like it here?"

She peered up at him, perplexed. "I do, very much so. It's just force of habit to refer to Pennsylvania as home."

"That's the rest of what I wanted to tell you. The folks at MOFGA gave me a list of properties for sale throughout the county with the number of tillable acres, availability of water, condition of the house—if there is one—and number of outbuildings. Some farms are too far away for us to attend Sunday services, but plenty are close enough to remain part of the district." He took her hand. "The women seem to like you, and we'll be able to stay close to Thomas and Sally."

"Are there prices on these listings?"

"*Jah*, for each one, but you know sellers expect buyers to haggle them down a bit."

"And we can afford these properties?" Her eyes reflected the sun like blue sapphires.

"Some. We won't bother to look at those we can't."

"Then I suppose it wouldn't hurt to check out a few." She smiled up him.

It was the first smile he'd seen that day. The sight spread warmth to the marrow of his bones. "I can't wait. The sooner we buy a place, the sooner we can move from here and start our life together." John peered around the yard. Sally's laundry flapped in the breeze at odd angles because several clothespins had come loose. Hornets buzzed around wormy, fermenting apples because no one had canned them or raked them into the compost heap. A rain barrel lay on its side, forgotten, no longer collecting precious rainwater from the downspout. When he turned back, he saw that she was studying him with a serious expression on her face.

"You don't sound grateful for your family's kindness. That's not like you, John."

The retort hurt, as though one of the drunken hornets had stung him. "Beg your pardon. I do appreciate Sally and Thomas opening up their home to us, but I'm tired of staying in Elam's former room while you're upstairs."

Her face turned cherry red. "But we're not wed yet, or have you forgotten that? And our new bishop doesn't seem in any fired-up hurry to marry us."

Blushing, he slipped his sweating hands under his suspenders. "I haven't forgotten. I can think about little else, but my *bruder* says the 'when' isn't up to him. Last Sunday after preaching, the bishop evaded my questions while asking plenty of his own. He asked me about the fire that killed your parents and about your family back in Lancaster. He wouldn't give me a firm date or even an exact month we could marry. That's why I want to buy land. Once he sees that I'm…that *we're* serious about staying in Harmony, maybe he'll schedule our counseling classes to get this ordeal going."

Amy's chin lifted as she crossed her arms defiantly. "Our wedding is an *ordeal* to you?"

"*Nein.* The ordeal is the long wait." He released a sigh. "I'm not expressing myself well. Why don't you grab your sweater and take a ride with me? I know of a property for sale not far away. The house is vacant, so we can—" He broke off abruptly as he noticed her expression and tapping toe. "What's wrong?"

"You're so excited about this farm that I can't get a word in sideways. I tried to tell you before that I promised Nora I'd ride to town with her. There are some things she needs, and I don't want her going alone."

"Can't this wait for another day?"

"No, she said she needs them today."

John pulled on his suspenders and took a breath. "Of course. I'll hitch up the buggy. I don't suppose anybody will snatch up the property overnight. We can go tomorrow, or at least in the near future."

She nodded on her way up the path. "Soon we'll go. *Danki* for bringing around the buggy." Amy disappeared into the house before he could say another word.

"Don't stay too long. Sally will need help with sup—" But the screen door had already banged shut behind her. John stood with his hands in his pockets, feeling like a dog that just had his bone taken away.

❧

Nora jumped back from the window so Amy wouldn't know she'd been spying. What had John wanted to talk about that had been so important? Surely, the advantages of one type of garden vegetable over another could have waited for later. She could understand wanting to look at farms for sale—every man longed for his own place—but why all the excitement about organic produce? In her opinion, a cherry tomato would always be just a cherry tomato.

"Can we still go?" she asked the moment Amy walked into the house.

"*Jah*, we can. Get your purse. I want to tidy my hair and change my *kapp*. Find your black bonnet too." Amy slanted her a wry expression.

"Okay, but don't expect me to watch for traffic at crossroads wearing that thing. I have to turn my neck so far around, it's a wonder my head doesn't come loose."

Amy rolled her eyes on the way upstairs. "Just be grateful we can go to town again." When she returned wearing a black cloak and her wide-brimmed bonnet, she looked like a widow in deep mourning.

"You will sweat to death in that," said Nora, throwing a lightweight shawl around her shoulders. "It's still summer."

"By the calendar maybe, but I felt a chill in the air." Amy grabbed her purse off the counter and a bottle of water.

Outside, they found the horse and buggy ready at the hitching post, but John was nowhere in sight.

"Where did he go to in such a hurry? No big send-off for his beloved?" asked Nora, climbing up.

Amy settled in beside her, purposefully bumping Nora's hip with her own. "What's gotten into you lately? That was a mean thing to say." She shook the reins and the horse strained against the traces.

"Sorry, I'm out of sorts. Little Jeremiah hasn't stopped crying all day. I'll never get my last dress finished because I can't concentrate with the noise."

"The baby is teething. You could offer to help Sally with him. It might be good to get your mind off yourself for a change."

Nora took no offense. She *had* been mopey and preoccupied lately. "I picked him up and carried him around, but no matter what I tried he wouldn't stop crying. I even sang a song to him."

"Goodness, that would make anybody cry their eyes out." Amy tried to maintain a straight face, but when she glanced at Nora they both broke into laughter.

"I'll keep that in mind tomorrow." Nora leaned back on the seat and slipped on her sunglasses. She wouldn't chance a migraine on their rare afternoon together.

"What did you need so urgently? I thought we stocked up on our last trip to town."

Nora turned her head to watch the passing scenery. "Nothing I couldn't do without, but I needed a break from Thomas's farm." Noting her sister's expression, she grabbed Amy's sleeve. "Wait and listen before you scold me. I just feel so lonely. At home there was always someone to talk to, plus we had lots of *different* projects going on. Life was never dull."

"You think life here is dull?" Amy's voice held no censure, only curiosity and concern.

"Dull as a fifty-year-old knife that's never been sharpened." Nora chuckled with amusement.

"I find it peaceful and serene. Plain lives should contain contentment, *jah*, but not excitement. What did you expect?"

"More people around, I suppose. John is always doing chores. Thomas is either in the fields or poring over his Bible to prepare for Sunday. And running the household and tending her children overwhelms Sally."

"That's not fair. Both of her boys are very young."

"I'm not criticizing her. It's just there are no neighbors here. Nobody drops over for a midweek visit or to borrow a cup of sugar. Folks can spend days without seeing anybody other than their families and, if they are lucky, the mailman. In Lancaster, people were constantly coming and going through *mamm's* back door."

For a few moments their thoughts wandered to a crowded kitchen, voices raised in song and laughter, the comforting smells of baking bread and simmering soup…and to their parents.

"Are you missing home?" asked Amy softly.

"No. I just needed a trip to the market." Nora shook off her sadness like a wet dog in the rain. "Let's get this new horse up to lightning speed. I want to see if there are more donuts left."

"Your wish is my command." Amy slapped the reins and the gelding tossed his silky head, pleased to trot on the flat empty road. They reached the co-op general store twice as fast as they did on their last outing. Both women marched in wearing broad grins and discovered they were the only customers—another testament to the miniscule population of Harmony.

Amy headed down the aisle of spices and seasonings, but Nora immediately felt the sensation of being watched. She turned around and met the gaze of the young clerk, the same man who had rung up their candy purchases before. That trip seemed like ages ago.

"May I help you find something?" he asked, offering a pleasant nod.

Nora marched to the counter, wishing she could pull off her black *kapp*. "What do you have on sale?"

The question left him momentarily dumbfounded. She could practically see the wheels turning behind his bright-blue eyes. "Do you mean marked down? Like about-to-expire cheese or bruised produce?" His eyes sparkled playfully.

"*Jah*, I suppose, but do you have things on sale that aren't damaged?" She offered him her prettiest smile.

"*Nein*. Why would I reduce the price of merchandise if there's nothing wrong with it?" He appeared to chew on the inside of his cheek.

"To sell more items, of course. Women love things on sale."

"Our store only carries what people really need. And when you find something you need, you're willing to pay a fair price for it. I won't undercut our meager profits to make a quick sale, not even for a pretty face."

Nora felt warmth welling up inside her that had nothing to do with the building's lack of air-conditioning. "Who has a pretty face?" she asked.

"You do, Miss King. I noticed it yesterday." He spritzed cleaner on the counter and wiped it up with a cloth.

"How do you know my name?" She arched one eyebrow.

He stopped cleaning and leaned an elbow on the sparkling glass. "Because Minister Detweiler introduced you, your sister, and his brother to the congregation at Sunday school and at the preaching service. *I* happened to be paying attention."

She relaxed and exhaled. "Oh, that's right, I forgot. I didn't see you in church, but I remember you from our last time in your store."

"My *daed*'s store," he corrected. "Maybe you didn't see me because you'd fallen asleep." He winked and then looked around to make sure the gesture hadn't been observed.

Nora leaned forward against the counter. "Was it that obvious? I fought to stay awake, but with this heat my eyes kept closing during the sermons."

He gave the spotless glass one final swipe with his rag. "The heat? I just remarked to my sister that it had sure cooled off recently. Whose sermon did you find particularly sleep-inducing—the bishop's or one of the ministers'?" He paused and then feigned an expression of horror. "Certainly not Thomas's! It would be tough to live in his household if you fell asleep whenever he spoke."

She pursed her lips and considered a response. "Did you plan how to tease me? You seem well prepared."

He straightened up. "I did, actually. There's not much else to do on Mondays, and I knew you would come in at some point."

Nora decided it was time to change the subject. "Where are the donuts? They are the main reason I'm here."

"*Ach*, it's the wrong day. You'll have to come back on Wednesday." He winked his other blue eye.

She narrowed her gaze. "Do you have a name, or shall I call you Impudent Rascal?"

The clerk crossed his arms, drawing Nora's attention to biceps that strained the fabric of his shirt. "My name is Lewis. And I am pleased to see you…awake." He stretched his hand across the counter.

Nora shook his hand as she noticed Amy approaching with an armful of dried herbs and pasta. "Nice to meet you, Lewis. I'll watch for you on Sundays to make sure *your* eyelids stay fully open."

Amy looked at them both curiously as she set down her purchases. "Don't you have anything at all to buy?" she asked.

"I haven't seen anything I like yet. Today's not donut day."

Amy sighed. "I understand your desire for a change from the farm, but I did tell John you *absolutely* had to come to town. Don't you think it will look odd if you come back empty-handed?"

Nora glanced at Lewis. He seemed to enjoy their conversation immensely. "You have a point. Lewis, why not ring up Amy's merchandise and I'll be right back." Moments later she returned with four different varieties of bulk candy.

"Sweets?" asked Amy, putting one hand on her hip. Then she accepted her package and change with a polite *danki*.

"That's right, candy." Nora pushed the bags across the counter. "Lewis explained that this co-op sells *only* essential items. Therefore, a person can assume candy is one of life's necessities. I've felt that way for years."

Lewis took the candy to ring up. "I will give you a ten percent discount, Miss King. Never let it be said our store doesn't run sales." He smiled warmly as he handed her the sack.

Amy glanced back over her shoulder as they headed for the door. Nora kept her focus forward.

"I do believe that man likes you," Amy whispered as they climbed into the buggy.

Nora smoothed her dress. "Of course he does. Why do you sound surprised? I'm a pleasant enough person."

"Pleasant?" Amy shook her head from side to side and clucked her tongue to the horse. "Giddyup there."

"Well, some of the time I am." Nora dug into a bag for a lemon drop.

As the buggy pulled onto a traffic-free road, Amy turned to face her. "Let's just say you know *how* to be pleasant." At that they shared a sisterly belly laugh.

For the first half of the trip home, they remained lost in their own thoughts. Then Amy asked, "Do you like him?"

"Who?" Nora put on sunglasses against the practically blinding sun.

"You know very well who I mean. Lewis."

"He's nice enough, despite not believing in markdowns."

"And rather handsome, no?" Amy persisted. "Especially that smile."

"I'd say he's too tall and thin with rather enormous hands. How does he pick up dimes from the counter?"

Amy released an exhalation of exasperation. "He is *not* too thin, and most big men have big hands. It would look ridiculous if they didn't. And you shouldn't worry about picking up dimes. Concern yourself with finding someone to marry."

"Don't be ridiculous, Amy. I'm only twenty. That's too young to marry."

"Maybe in Lancaster, but not in Maine."

Nora popped another piece of candy into her mouth. "To tell you the truth, I can't figure out why *you're* in such a hurry."

"*Mamm* and *daed* are gone. I needed to establish a new home for myself…and for you, if you'll have it. I took control of my life when I decided to move here. That is the only way a woman can feel safe." The horse danced to the side of the road as Amy's grip loosened on the reins.

Nora pulled off her scratchy bonnet. "If control of your life is what you want, then why get married at all? It seems to me a woman surrenders her say-so to a husband on her wedding day."

She had raised her voice to underscore her opinion. Now the words seem to hang in the crisp late summer air as Amy stared at the road, pouting for the rest of the way.

❧

Three days later, Amy still felt troubled over Nora's comments. John represented love, affection, and stability—a home in which to raise children, a place to grow old with a good man. And John was a good man. But if he took charge of her life—unilaterally making decisions that affected her future—she might not feel as secure as she hoped.

Bad things happen when a woman lets down her guard.

Weak people are no better than rudderless boats bobbing in rough seas.

She'd been that woman in Lancaster, even though she was the oldest daughter...and look what happened to her parents. Suddenly she gazed down at the beans she'd been snapping for supper. At some point she'd stopped saving the beans and began saving the woody stems. "Good grief," she muttered, picking stems from the colander.

Sally glanced her way as she carried her pot of stew to the stove. "Looks like something has you tied up in knots, and it's probably not the beans." She joined her at the sink to sort vegetables from the scraps.

Amy shrugged. "There is much on my mind. It'll be hard to convince the bishop we're ready to wed when he's only here a few days each month."

"He arrives by Wednesday on preaching weeks and stays with his married daughter. That's probably when he'll counsel you and John."

Amy nodded, ashamed she couldn't confess her true anxiety. "Perhaps, if John finds us a farm, the bishop will speed things up." She snapped another bean and threw the stems into the colander.

"All in good time." Sally nudged her aside. "I'll finish these. Why don't you walk down to the road? No one has fetched the mail yet."

"I go too?" asked Aden in *Deutsch*.

"*Jah*, you go too. We could both use some fresh air." Amy dried her hands on a towel and took the toddler's hand. Tension left her back and shoulders the moment she stepped from the stuffy kitchen. Aden's short legs made for slow going, but aunt and nephew were in no hurry to reach the road.

Hollyhocks bobbed their heads in the gentle breeze, surrounding the Detweiler mailbox like sentinels—the only mailbox for as far as the eye could see. Amy dug inside to retrieve the stack of flyers and junk mail, which she shuffled through as she and Aden walked back up the drive. Third from the top, she spotted a Mount Joy postmark and her grandmother's small, precise handwriting.

Amy swung the little boy to her hip and hurried up to the house as fast as she could without running. "Nora!" she called, cutting across the front yard. "We have a letter from home."

By the time she and Aden reached the steps, Nora appeared in the doorway. "Who from? Rachel or Beth?" she asked.

They both expected a letter from one of their sisters or perhaps even from Aunt Irene. All three liked to write frequently. "Neither. It's from *grossmammi*." Amy set down the child on the porch. "Go find your *mamm*." She opened the door and patted his head when he scampered past. She waited until she heard Sally greet him in the kitchen.

"Read it aloud," demanded Nora. She sat down on one of the rockers.

Amy lowered herself onto the other one and with trembling fingers pulled the sheet from the envelope. A letter from their grandmother was rare because her stiff hands made holding a pen difficult. Inhaling a deep breath, she began to read.

> *My dear Amy and Nora,*
>
> *I hope this letter finds you well. We are thriving, but your schwestern miss you terribly. They inquire several times a day what Irene or I think you might be doing at that exact moment. Finally, I told Beth that Amy probably took up lobster fishing, while Nora no doubt stands knee-deep in a cranberry bog.*

"Everyone thinks of cranberries when they speak of Maine," Nora interrupted, "but all we've seen so far have been blueberries and more blueberries."

"We've hardly seen much of the state. Maybe cranberries grow elsewhere. Let me continue." Amy set her rocker into motion and continued reading.

> *What grace the Lord has shown you—running across a quilt made by Prudence, and to find out she had once lived in your community. Grossdawdi would prefer I not speak of her, nor even think of her, but I can't help myself. Your Aunt Prudence lived a sorrowful life through no fault of her own. First, she discovered she was barren. Then her husband fell under the curse of alcohol. He was mean when drunk, and toward the end he was drunk most of the time. Nothing anyone said or did made any difference to him. He refused to seek help, and refused to treat his wife any way other than with hostility. His evil ways drove Prudence to sin.*
>
> *No one was sorry when Leon left Lancaster not long after his fraa left him and filed for divorce. He moved to Holmes County, Ohio, but he stayed mostly to himself. I heard from*

a niece that he died a year or two ago. It was left to her to see him properly buried because she was the only kin in the area. Leon kept drinking until the end, stating he suffered from a broken heart. The death certificate stated acute liver failure due to chronic alcoholism. I believe that cause is the more accurate of the two. May God have mercy on his soul.

Prudence was your mamm's favorite sister, I daresay—the closest in age and in temperament. Her life here had been unbearable torment. I hope she finds peace, and that the Lord will find in His heart to forgive her transgressions.

Danki for telling me that she is well—at least, the last time anyone has heard. I hope you both find your places in the world, even if it must be far from those who love you.

Mammi

The last sentence of the letter had barely been audible because emotion choked off Amy's ability to speak. Tears coursed down her face, dripping unheeded onto her apron.

"Uncle Leon is dead?" asked Nora in a tiny voice.

"Apparently he is. I wish I could say I'm sorry, but I can't. I feel no sympathy for a man who tormented such a gentle woman."

They both just rocked quietly for a few minutes, listening to Sally's wind chimes tinkling in the breeze.

"All right," said Amy, wiping her face with her apron. "Let's say a short prayer for Leon and a longer one for Aunt Prudence." Both women folded their hands in their laps and bowed their heads. But the silent prayer for her uncle did not come easily. Leon was responsible for Prudence's banning. Now she would live out the rest of her life without her family and, more importantly, separated from God's love. Amy seldom thought about the concept of eternal damnation, but she contemplated it now as a shiver of dread ran up her spine.

Please, Lord, don't let that be the fate of my dear aunt.

SEVEN

Could my tears forever flow

Thomas pulled up the collar of his chore coat. It was barely September, but the breeze held a bite as the first autumn leaves swirled around his boot heels. He carried two pails of fresh goats' milk to the house, careful not to let the contents slosh over the sides. Ahead, he spotted a kerosene lamp through the kitchen window, indicating Sally had finished feeding Jeremiah and would be fixing a hot breakfast. A waft of warm air greeted him when he opened the back door. Aden sat in his high chair, and Sally was spooning cinnamon oatmeal into his little mouth. If she fed him as opposed to allowing him to eat by himself, more food landed in his stomach rather than on the floor.

Suddenly an acrid, scorched smell assailed his nose. "What's burning?" he asked, sweeping off his hat.

For a moment Sally froze. Then she dropped the spoon and ran to the stove. "My biscuits!" Grabbing a pot holder, she extracted a charred pan from the oven. A curl of smoke rose to the ceiling from the contents. "They're ruined." She set the tray on the counter and stared at it angrily, as though the biscuits held culpability.

Thomas leaned over to assess the damage. "I'm afraid they are. They have blackened and dried out beyond redemption."

"Maybe if I scrape the bottoms and slather on plenty of butter—"

"No, let's just have toast instead." Using the pot holder, he dumped the pan into the compost bucket.

Sally returned to the table, where Aden had begun feeding himself. "We need to buy a pig. It will eat anything I ruin."

"Most people say that about goats, so I think we'll hold off on more livestock. Where do you want the milk?"

She glanced up from wiping Aden's face. "Next to the stove. I'll bring it to a boil and then chill it in glass bottles I sterilized."

"Where are the Kings?" He poured himself coffee up to the rim.

"Amy's sweeping floors upstairs, and I believe Nora is still sleeping. The girls talked long into the night about that letter. I could hear them until I finally dozed off around midnight."

Thomas carried his mug to the table to await his scrambled eggs. "A letter? Did they hear from Prudence Hilty? The sooner they know their aunt is safe, the sooner they will be able to concentrate on important matters—such as conforming to district *Ordnung*."

"*Nein*. It was a letter from their *grossmammi*." Sally met his gaze over Aden's head. "Prudence's husband is dead. His drinking finally killed him."

"May the Lord have mercy," he murmured, bowing his head. After a minute of prayer, he took a long swallow of coffee.

"At least now the man can never remarry and subject another unsuspecting *fraa* to his malice." Sally wiped the boy's chin with his bib.

Thomas had just opened his mouth to chastise his normally nonjudgmental wife when he heard footsteps on the stairs.

Amy entered, nearly hidden behind a huge bundle of linens. "I stripped the beds. Let me start a load of laundry before I help with breakfast." Her face looked especially pale this morning. Her freckles had faded since her arrival. She disappeared down the cellar steps but reappeared within minutes. "What can I help with?" she asked, pouring coffee and refilling Thomas's mug.

"Make toast, please, while I start the eggs." Sally lifted Aden from his chair and set him on the floor. "We'll forget about the biscuits we planned earlier."

"After we eat," said Thomas, focusing on Amy, "I'd like to start marriage counseling with you."

It apparently would be a day filled with inopportune moments, because John walked into the kitchen and overheard his comment.

"Oh, *gut*!" he said, shrugging off his coat. "I'm glad to get this ball rolling. Did the bishop give permission for you to assume the duty?" Without waiting for Thomas's response, John continued. "I have time before I muck out horse stalls." He reached for a mug from the dish drainer, grinning in the direction of his fiancée. Amy concentrated on lining up bread slices in rows.

Thomas cleared this throat. "Just Amy to start with. I'll speak to you another day."

John set his mug on the table with a thud. "*Just Amy*? How can you counsel a couple for marriage unless they are together?" His forehead wrinkled as his brows stitched together.

Amy's rack of toast hovered in the air for a moment before she slid it into the oven.

"I'd like to talk to you separately before the bishop begins more formal classes. Does that bother you, *bruder*?"

John shook his head. "No. I'm surprised, that's all. Aren't you, Amy?"

Every adult in the room stared at her, but several seconds spun out before she realized she'd been addressed. "I've never planned to be married before, so I don't know what to expect. And I am the eldest daughter." She carried jam, butter, and homemade cheese to the table.

"Don't be afraid of Thomas," said Sally, pouring egg mixture into a sizzling skillet. "He is a lamb beneath his tough skin."

Thomas tried to hide his smile. "That's not true. I'm stern and unyielding, especially when I counsel family members."

"I'm not frightened in the least," Amy replied as she sat down with the plate of toast. In fact, she seemed downright carefree as she bowed her head in prayer.

Once they finished eating, John hovered close to the door with hat in hand. "Should I wait in the living room for my turn?" He spun the brim between his nimble fingers. "No sense getting dirty in the barn if you'll call me in soon."

Thomas refilled his and Amy's coffee mugs. "No, I'll counsel you another day. You can see to your chores, John." He offered him a patient smile.

Wordlessly, his brother put on his hat and left.

Sally lifted up Aden. "Time to try potty-training again," she announced. "So far, we've made little progress."

"I'll clean the kitchen." Amy stacked breakfast plates as Sally carried their son to the bathroom.

"Leave the dishes for now and sit," Thomas ordered.

Amy complied, blanching to a shade of porcelain white.

"You realize lying is a sin, don't you?" he asked as soon as Sally closed the door behind her.

"Of course I do. 'You must not testify falsely'—the ninth Commandment."

"*Jah*, but not telling the entire truth can also be considered lying when a person asks you a question."

She sat very still, clutching the mug tightly.

"It's important that you are completely honest with me."

"I will be, Brother Detweiler. What would you like to ask me?" Her face remained composed, her luminous blue eyes betraying no emotion.

"Is marriage to my brother what you want right now? Think

carefully before you answer. There's no shame in changing your mind."

She took a sip of coffee. "*Jah*, I wish to marry John. I made up my mind about that a long time ago."

"I understand, but much has happened since then. Your parents' sudden and tragic deaths might cloud your judgment, forcing you to take steps you're not ready for. Don't let John rush you into anything. He's always been in a hurry—to ride a horse when he couldn't yet reach the stirrups, to drive a team alone in the fields, to start shaving when he barely had a single whisker. And he can be mulish about getting his way." Thomas clamped his mouth shut. He hadn't intended to disparage his own flesh and blood.

But Amy laughed off the warning. "He can be persuasive, but he hasn't talked me into this. I know he loves me very much, and his love makes me feel secure."

"And you love him?" he asked, though it was an odd question coming from an Amish minister.

"*Jah*, I do," Amy said with an air of perfect poise.

Thomas waited in vain for further elaboration. "Then you still wish to marry in the fall?"

Finally, her mask began to crack. "There is one matter I wish to see through before the wedding. I need assurance that my aunt is fine, and I want to tell her about Uncle Leon's death. John doesn't approve because Prudence is shunned." She folded her hands on the table as though she'd reached a decision. "I don't wish to disobey him or begin marriage being disagreeable."

Thomas ran a hand through his hair. "I see, but understand this: There is nothing you can do for Prudence. The situation cannot be helped."

"But we don't know if she—"

"We *do* know she married Will Summerton as soon as they left Harmony in October of the year past. She is no longer Prudence Hilty."

Amy's eyes seemed to grow larger. "Have you heard from her? I received no reply to my letter."

"*Nein*, I have not. But the bishop checked into this to put the matter to rest. She is married and living on a farm with Will, without contact to an Amish community and without God. She is banned, Amy. Forever." Thomas swallowed the last cold dregs, along with a mouthful of coffee grounds. "Perhaps she will write to let you know she's in good health, but then you must forget your aunt."

Amy winced as though in pain. "The Lord forgave Mary Magdalene. She became one of His devoted followers."

"Mary Magdalene sought forgiveness for her sins and was washed clean. Prudence Summerton hasn't asked to be forgiven. Her behavior has been selfish and willful." Thomas waited, fully expecting the argument to continue.

But Amy clamped her jaw shut. After a few moments she said softly, "I will wait for a while to see if she writes. Then I will proudly become John's bride."

"So be it," he said, exhaling a weary sigh. Thomas patted her hand and rose to his feet, unclear why he felt unsatisfied with the first session.

He would wait before talking to John to let his own questions and insecurities settle, if for no other reason.

❧

Crack! Like a well-oiled machine, John bent down for the pieces of split wood, added them to the growing stack, and placed another chunk on the chopping block. *Crack!* Two more pieces of firewood would keep his brother's family warm that winter— and perhaps the King sisters and himself too, considering how things were proceeding. Thus far, chores kept Amy too busy to accompany him to look at farms for sale. And he hated to make so important a purchase without her input. Of course, at the rate his brother and the bishop were dragging their feet, getting hitched before the first snow seemed unlikely.

Crack! He'd seen one property with a fairly livable home large enough for a growing family, but the majority of land was wooded and had already been signed over to a wilderness preservation organization in a hundred-year lease. Another farm had plenty of tillable acres, but the house need to be bulldozed, not salvaged. He would hate to force mice, raccoons, bats, and snakes to relocate from their habitats. *Crack!* And why had Thomas put him off for the last few days? Since his counseling session with Amy, his brother had avoided him. "All in good time" was his answer for every question other than "Are there any more pickles?"

Crack! Despite cooler temperatures, sweat ran down John's neck and forehead as he hefted another chunk up to the block. He planned to chop wood until his pile stretched to the road or he worked off his frustration, whichever came first.

Another hard to handle aspect of living in Harmony was the separation from Amy. In Lancaster they had been trusted to spend time alone without fear they would behave shamefully. They had gone to a restaurant once a month and swapped tales from childhood, laughing over each other's exploits. He'd taken her on moonlit buggy rides, where they would plan their future without Sally's frequent eavesdropping or Thomas's hawkeyed supervision. If they tarried too long saying good night on the porch, his brother invariably wandered out to offer bug spray or some other thinly disguised interruption. How he missed her companionship, her friendship, and her attention. If he dared to take her hand walking from the barn, she would pull away as though touching a toad. And stealing a kiss as he had under the grape arbor? He didn't dare. How he missed her soft lips, the scent of strawberries from her shampoo, and her tender touch on his arm.

How he longed for her! *Crack!* Another length of firewood split into equal halves.

The sound of squeaky door hinges mercifully distracted him from his depression. Nora struggled to drag his buggy from its parking spot under the barn overhang. He blinked to make sure he wasn't seeing things. *Nora is trying to hitch up the buggy?* Even more shocking than her labor was her attire—the same pale-green dress she brought from Pennsylvania, along with a white prayer *kapp* on her head. Her full-brimmed, black bonnet was nowhere in sight. John set down his ax and wiped his face with his handkerchief. *This is Amy's sister*, he told himself as he approached. *Treat her kindly and don't lose your temper.*

"Can I help you with that?" he asked, reaching her side.

"Ah, John. You're a sight for sore eyes. I can't believe how heavy this is." She dropped the wooden slats that attached to the horse's harness.

"You've never hitched up a buggy before?"

"Never. *Daed* always helped me...or Amy or Rachel. They are fonder of horses than I am." She flashed a smile.

Nora was an attractive enough woman. The reason she had no serious beaus must be her strong opinions and lack of responsibility. No man wanted a wife who hid from distasteful chores and expected others to take up the slack. "Why don't I get the buggy ready while you go change your dress?" John kept his voice mild and nonconfrontational.

She lifted her chin. "Why on earth would I do that? I just ironed this one."

John stepped around her to the buggy. "Where exactly are you going?"

"To the general store in town." She crossed her arms in a woman's typical defensive stance. "I thought I'd go alone to get what I need because everyone else is swamped with chores."

He contemplated several different irritations—such as the

ridiculous number of times a Plain woman *needed* to go to town and the fact that some of those *chores* should be hers. But he chose his battle carefully. "Were you planning to ask before taking the buggy?"

Despite his best effort, anger lifted his voice a notch.

Nora paused, squinting at him as though confused. "I was under the impression the horse and buggy belonged to you *and* Amy. I don't have to ask her for permission."

John felt flummoxed, as though he'd been somehow outmaneuvered. "No, I don't suppose Amy would turn down your request. I doubt she ever denied you a single thing." He had lost patience with his future sister-in-law.

Unexpectedly, she giggled at his sarcasm. "She has told me no once or twice, but I'll admit it's not often. So, *may* I use your half of the horse and buggy? I won't go any farther than Harmony, and I'll give the horse food and water when I return. But you'll have to rub him down," she added sheepishly. "I promise not to pick up hitchhikers, and I'll be back before supper." Once more, Nora offered a glorious smile.

"You may, as long as you put on a dark dress and a full bonnet." John pulled up a long weed to chew.

Her expression changed in a heartbeat. "I look like a frumpy old woman in my new dresses. Sally's patterns must be for feed sacks, and the material is hot and scratchy."

"You're the one who picked out the fabric, Nora. I won't have you flouncing around town like a youth on *rumschpringe*. That is not permitted here." He crossed his arms too, but he immediately regretted his choice of words.

Nora's back stiffened. "They don't have much selection in dress fabrics here, John." She intoned as though speaking to a naughty child. "And I don't *flounce*. I have never *flounced* in my life!"

"While we are living in my *bruder's* home—"

"Goodness gracious! What are you two arguing about?" Amy

materialized suddenly at Nora's side. "Sally heard you inside the house through a closed window." She glared at one and then the other.

"I have no doubt that she did." John hadn't meant to bark at Amy, but her appearance had caught him off guard. He closed his eyes to regain composure. "Nora wishes to go to town. I said that was fine as long as she changes her dress."

"You are not *my* fiancé," snapped Nora. "I don't have to ask your permission to live my life."

Amy turned to face Nora, her mouth dropping open wide enough to catch crickets. "What's come over you, sister? And why are you wearing light green? I thought we buried that dress in the bottom of the bureau."

Nora blushed to a shade of plum. "I hate my new dresses."

"But you're the one who made them." Amy glanced between her sister and John, confused.

"The fabric is stiff and uncomfortable. Besides, I hate that ridiculous bonnet. I don't see the point of not being able to see."

"The head covering is a sign of modesty in public. Prayer *kapp*s are only for indoors. We have already discussed this," said Amy, her own patience waning.

"Why does John control my comings and goings regarding the buggy? I thought it belonged equally to you." Nora focused her cat-green eyes on Amy with a hypnotist's skill. "And he accused me of flouncing around. That word doesn't sound very nice. I'm sure I don't flounce." Nora opted for a more modulated tone.

"No, you don't flounce, and the buggy does belong equally to me." Amy turned toward her fiancé in a slow, measured movement. "Nora is my younger sister, John, not yours. And she is a grown woman, capable of making decisions." Two or three seconds spun out as they stared at each other. "But I do agree her dress is inappropriate, especially considering the temperature today." With the same slow motion, she turned back to Nora. "If you wear your full navy cloak over the dress along with the bonnet atop your prayer *kapp*, you can be on your way. You may remove the outer bonnet once you get inside the store but not the cloak." Amy smiled and laced her fingers together, as though pleased with the compromise.

Nora hurried toward the house for the outerwear.

And John? He stood holding up the buggy without the slightest idea as to how Nora managed to get her way…again.

⌘

Monday brought great relief to Amy, despite the additional workload of laundry day. Yesterday she attended Sunday school, helped Sally serve lunch to the men first, and then enjoyed a companion meal with the other women before the hymn singing. She'd already made a couple of friends in the district—one, an engaged woman like herself, and the other, a newlywed. And she seemed to have attained approval even from the elderly matrons.

Not so in the case of her *schwester*.

Nora drew inside her bonnet like a turtle into its shell during most of Thomas's Bible lesson. Amy had found the trials of the Israelites' exile in Egypt fascinating. But Nora's head bobbed several times as she apparently dozed. She made no attempt to strike up conversations at lunch or as the crowd milled about after the hymn service. Nora pushed food around her plate like a picky child, staring into space, and in general didn't behave like a newcomer seeking friendship. But at least she'd worn her black dress, white apron, and her high-top, lace-up oxfords without argument. Perhaps the reason for her lack of interest was the absence of Lewis during the service. Amy overheard his *mamm* tell another woman that he had come down with the flu.

Amy stretched up on tiptoes to pin another shirt to the clothesline. Overhead, geese honked as they headed south in their annual migration. Insects buzzed in the nearby shrubs, making a final attempt to gather nectar. She heard the comforting sound of John chopping wood. *The Detweilers will stay warm this winter,* she thought, reaching for another shirt.

Nora had enjoyed her trip to town alone once the drama in the yard was concluded. Lewis had given her a personal tour of the co-op, pointing out every product and service they offered. He'd almost flirted with her, according to Nora, but his *mamm* always hovered close by—dusting, sweeping, or stocking shelves. Last night Nora refused her sandwich at suppertime and had gone to bed early, complaining of a headache. Today she was listless and mopey as she helped Amy with the wash.

"Here are more trousers and our dresses," said Nora, setting down the wicker basket. Amy tucked in a stray lock of hair as they heard the sound of a truck shifting gears. "Mail's here," she announced. "Why don't you hang that load while I walk to the road?"

Nora murmured an acknowledgment as Amy strolled down the hill through the tall grass. She hummed her favorite hymn on her way to the rural box, where she found inside something more to be joyous about—a letter from *grossmammi.*

"Nora! We got another letter from Lancaster," she shouted, ripping open the envelope. She extracted a single sheet along with a formal-looking, notary-stamped paper. She glanced at the letter first, feeling familiar pangs of homesickness, and then she studied the other document. "Certificate of Death," she read aloud. *Why would* grossmammi *send me papers about Leon Hilty?* As she skimmed the information, realization of her grandmother's motivation slowly dawned. And when it did she picked up her skirt with one hand and ran like a child. "Nora, look at this!"

Nora dropped a damp garment back into the basket. "What's the commotion? Did you get stung by a bee?"

Amy didn't slow down until she reached the clothesline. "*Grossmammi* sent Uncle Leon's death certificate. One of her cousins from Ohio had mailed it to her, and *mammi* threw it in a drawer.

Neither woman knew what to do with it because Aunt Prudence was gone." Amy handed both papers to her sister.

Nora read their grandmother's letter first and then glanced over the document. "I don't understand why you're so excited. We already knew Uncle Leon had died."

"Look at the date." Breathlessly, Amy tapped a finger on the line. "Leon Hilty died in July of last year."

Nora blinked her eyes, holding up a hand to shield them from the sun. "And?"

"Don't you remember what the bishop told Thomas? Prudence and Will Summerton didn't marry until October. Leon was already dead by then, so she's not an adultress. According to Scripture, a woman may not remarry while her first husband *lives*." Amy exhaled, exhilarated.

Nora patted her shoulder. "That's wonderful news. I'm sure *mammi* was happy to hear it."

"I have to write to Prudence again and send her this death notice. No, wait. I should make a photocopy first in case she has moved again. Because she hasn't written back, we're not sure of her whereabouts. Let's not lose the only copy we have."

Nora picked up one of Sally's dresses. "Where do you suppose you'll do that?"

Amy folded the papers and tucked them back in the envelope. "The library in Harmony," she said after a moment. "I'm sure they will have a copy machine." Slipping the envelope into her apron pocket, she began walking toward the house.

"Where are you going now?" called Nora. "We have more clothes to hang."

"You finish up. The fresh air will do you good." Amy concentrated solely on not tripping in rabbit holes.

From the porch, Amy spotted John at the woodpile. "Can you take a break?" she called. "I have news to share with you and Thomas."

John signaled he had heard and buried the ax blade in the chopping block. Less than a minute later, he strolled in with glowing cheeks.

"Sally, Thomas?" Amy called from the bottom of the steps. "Can I speak with you, please?"

"What is it?" John closed the short distance between them. "Are you sick?" He held the back of his hand to her forehead despite Thomas's warning about no touching.

"I'm fine." Amy brushed away his fingers and pulled the envelope from her pocket. "I received another letter from home," she said as Thomas and Sally entered the room. "*Grossmammi* mailed me Uncle Leon's death certificate." She gazed from one person to next.

Sally shrugged her shoulders and hitched Jeremiah higher on her hip. "But you already knew he died."

Thomas fixed her with his cool blue gaze. "Go on," he prodded.

Amy repeated what she'd told Nora, barely able to contain her exuberance. When she finished, the three reactions couldn't have varied more.

"That's nice," said Sally with an uncertain smile.

John said nothing, looking mildly irritated, as though the news was unworthy of chore interruption.

Only Thomas's response indicated that he understood the significance. He whistled between his teeth as though summoning a dog and stroked his beard several times. "July, you say? If her husband died in July, Prudence committed no abomination. She remarried after he was dead."

"It's not important." John's voice returned at last. "Prudence already turned her back on the Amish community. She made her choice."

Amy felt mule-kicked. She shook her head to dispel the idea all was lost.

Thomas lifted both calloused palms. "He's right, Amy. Prudence can be forgiven for divorcing Leon if she confesses on her knees to God, but she might not be interested in that. This news might not make any difference to her or Will Summerton." He bent to pick up Aden, who was clutching Sally's skirt tightly in both fists.

Amy jammed the two pieces of paper back into the envelope as she collected her thoughts. She had one chance to speak her mind, so she didn't want to whine or stammer. After all, wasn't she always telling Nora to act like an adult and not a child?

"That's true," she agreed. "But because my family in Lancaster considered it important enough to send me, I will forward it to Prudence at her last known address." She turned her focus to Sally, avoiding John. "After I finish the next load of laundry, I'll write a note to enclose with the death certificate. If you can spare me this afternoon, I'd like to go to town yet today. Nora and I will fix dinner tomorrow, giving you a night off."

Sally's eyes sparkled. "Of course you can go, Amy. I cooked by my lonesome before you came. I'm sure I can still manage. But I won't turn down your offer."

John snorted. "Why go to town? Write your letter and then put it in the mailbox with the flag up. The postman will find it tomorrow morning."

Amy smiled patiently at him. "I'd like to photocopy the document at the library first, John. That way I'll still have a copy in case the letter goes astray."

"It's a waste of time, dear heart." John shook his head but softened his voice. "I'm sure the date of Leon's death will be of no interest to her. It's water under the bridge."

"You're probably right, but that is what I intend to do just the same." Amy tucked the envelope into her pocket and marched out the door, leaving behind three astonished faces.

This is the right thing to do. Prudence should know that she could come back if she chooses. And I won't rest until this paper is in her hand.

On her way back to the clothesline, Amy realized that not

EIGHT

All for sin could not atone
Thou must save, and Thou alone

Amy awoke to pots and pans clattering in the kitchen below, the wails of both little boys, and the shuddering snores of her sister. "That girl could sleep through anything," she muttered, slipping out of bed. She wrapped herself in a heavy bathrobe and padded downstairs. She found Sally at the counter, disjointing a chicken on her cutting board. Several more birds awaited their turn lined up on paper towels. Jeremiah sat on a folded quilt on the floor, squalling, while Aden sobbed in his high chair. "*Guder mariye*," she greeted.

Sally glanced over her shoulder. "Good morning to you. Sorry if we woke you. I'm not my normal efficient self today." She half smiled before returning to the chickens. Her face was damp with perspiration, her *kapp* was askew, and flour dusted her dress and apron.

"It was time to get up anyway. What can I help you with?" Amy put on a clean apron and lifted Jeremiah from the floor. The baby immediately quieted.

"*Ach*, there's no help for me. Once again I'll give the district women something to snicker about behind my back."

Amy carried the boy to the counter, bouncing him on her hip. "What's wrong? Why would the women laugh at you?"

Sally bowed her head, frozen, as sudden tears coursed down her cheeks. "*Mir leid*," she apologized. "I shouldn't have said that. It's not their fault I can't handle the duties of a preacher's wife." She walked to where Aden wailed and lifted him into her arms.

Silence filled the room, soothing jangled nerves. Sally carried her son to the window and bowed her head. While she prayed, Aden tried to catch a moth trapped against the glass in his tiny hand.

Amy prayed too, that the balm of silence would remain. After Sally lifted her head, Amy asked, "What has stressed you?"

Sally faced her somewhat composed. "Thomas mentioned this morning that the men are harvesting corn for the Erb family. Cal Erb broke his arm and needs help. Thomas and John left before sunrise to start at first light."

Amy shifted the baby to her other hip, waiting for the rest of the story. Menfolk helping each other with the harvest sounded like business as usual, not a reason for meltdown.

"He gave no advance notice, yet he expects me to serve a hearty meal to the workers at midday. Mrs. Erb just delivered a *boppli* last week and isn't back to normal yet. When he was leaving, Thomas said, 'Fried chicken would be nice.' It certainly would if I had six hands." Sally tried to smile, but her tears returned instead.

"What are the other ladies taking to the Erbs?" asked Amy.

Sally stared as though mystified by the question.

"I don't know. It's up to me to provide the main course and vegetables, while the other minister's wife brings pies and fresh bread. Dora is a better baker than I am."

"And the other women contribute nothing? That's not how we did things in Lancaster."

"We're a small district. At least, we used to be. Even so, most women bring something to a frolic."

"Don't you end up with too much food?" Amy smiled at Jeremiah, who was tugging on one of her *kapp* strings.

"*Jah*, often that's true. We leave leftovers behind for the family so nothing goes to waste. But I never know what's coming. We might end up with fried chicken, Dora's pies, and five bowls of baked beans." Despite her distress, one corner of her mouth turned up.

Amy considered this. "You said the district is growing, with more families each year, so you need to organize this better. Perhaps you and the hosting family could cook the main dish, while the other pastor's wife continues to make pies. But why not assign the women a type of food, such as a potato dish or a green vegetable or a fruit tray? Someone else could bake bread, and another lady could bring a platter of cheese. How does that sound?"

"It might work if I let them choose." Sally pursed her lips while setting her toddler down. "Maybe I could make a list and have them sign up for what they wanted. I wouldn't want to *tell* Agnes Miller what to bring."

"Good idea," encouraged Amy. "And every six months everyone can switch to a different assignment so life doesn't get boring."

Sally's gaze landed on the plucked chickens waiting to be cut up and fried. "*Danki* for the suggestion, but it doesn't help much today." She took Jeremiah from Amy as he began to fuss again.

"That's what Nora and I are here for. Why don't you go nurse your little one, while Aden and I go upstairs to rouse my sister? We'll throw cold water on her if necessary. Nora can feed Aden his breakfast and then watch both *kinner* while you and I cook up a storm."

Sally's relief was almost palpable. "*Danki*, Amy. You are a life preserver today."

"I'm happy to help." She took Aden by the hand. "What are your favorite side dishes to prepare?" she asked from the doorway.

Sally took no time to answer. "I have a delicious recipe for maple syrup sweet potato casserole. And I love making braised purple cabbage whenever I have leftover pork roast to add. It's one of Thomas's favorites. There's some in the freezer now."

"When I come down with Nora, I will bread and fry the chicken while you prepare your favorite side dishes. It's time the district samples some Sally Detweiler at her finest."

Sally headed into the living room with Jeremiah, beaming from ear to ear. As Amy climbed the stairs with Aden, she whispered a prayer of gratitude. *Thank You, Lord, for the return of serenity to this house.*

Several hours later, Amy, Sally, and Nora loaded roasters of food into the buggy and headed to the Erb farm. They arrived just as men were leading the draft horses to the hay wagon and water trough for the midday break. Combines and wagons half filled with corn waited in the fields, temporarily abandoned. Another dozen men walked toward the hand pump to wash.

"Look, Clara and Agnes are already here," said Sally as she parked the buggy. She pointed at several picnic tables in the shade. Her voice held a note of trepidation.

"Don't worry. You have your list ready to go." Amy patted her arm affectionately.

"Let me see it," said Nora, climbing from the backseat. "I was busy bathing the boys and missed the fun." She held Jeremiah in the crook of one arm, while Aden clung to her skirt instead of his *mamm*'s. He'd found a new friend in Nora, who sang to him comically off-key.

Sally extracted a long yellow sheet from her purse. "I listed every woman in the district on the left and put the side dishes they could pick from on the right." She held the paper under Nora's nose. "The women will write their names in two different columns, one for now and another for after March first."

Nora read aloud the categories. "Potatoes, vegetable casseroles, three types of cold salads, breads, cheeses, and desserts. Looks like you thought of everything." She hefted Aden to her other hip.

"It was your sister's brilliant idea." Sally tucked the list back into her purse.

"But the idea to have them choose twice was yours," corrected Amy.

"Food is food. I don't understand what the fuss is about." Nora's interest had already waned.

As Amy unhitched the buggy, a teenaged boy loped toward them to take the Morgan to the water trough. "*Danki,*" she called, lifting the first roasting pan from the back.

"Here goes nothing." Sally stacked two more atop one another and headed to the tables.

"I'm hungry already," chimed in Nora. Because she had both boys, she avoided carrying heavy pans. "I didn't have time to eat breakfast this morning. These two kept me busy."

Nora looked positively radiant, however, not faint from hunger. *Caring for* kinner *apparently agrees with her,* thought Amy. Maybe something finally interested her sister around the farm.

As the three approached the tables, greetings rang out from the other women. Younger women hurried forward to accept the heavy pans.

"We've been here for more than an hour," said Clara, the eldest of the district widows. "We've already washed down the tables and fixed lemonade."

"*Danki,*" said Sally, flashing a smile in her direction. "The men will appreciate tables in the shade." She went to work lining up pans in serving order and moving the sliced pies to the end of the table.

Amy stood back with her hands clasped behind her. This was Sally's time to take charge and shine. She bustled around the buffet like a professional caterer, making sure each dish had the proper serving utensil.

"Aden has fallen asleep," announced Nora. "I'll spread a quilt under a tree for him and read my book there." Off she strolled with both boys without a second thought about helping with lunch.

"What did you make?" asked Clara, lifting a corner of the first pan of chicken. "Smells *gut*."

"Fried chicken, maple syrup sweet potatoes, braised purple cabbage, and cinnamon-spiced baked apples." Sally brushed her palms together while she spoke.

The eyebrows of every woman within earshot lifted simultaneously. "Oh, my, that sounds delicious," said one.

"You've been very energetic. Sure beats cold sandwiches and pickles," said another.

"Maple syrup sweet potatoes?" asked Clara. "I haven't had those in years. Lately, my spuds have been too stringy for anything but pig feed." She lifted a corner of each cover until she found the correct pan. Just as she was about to sample the contents with a plastic spoon, Sally stopped her with a hand on her arm.

"You must be patient, Clara. You know it's our custom for hardworking men to eat first."

Clara straightened her back and squared her shoulders. "No hidden surprises today? No additional animal protein?" she asked in a whisper.

Thankfully, no one overheard the comment but Amy. "Not today, I'm afraid," said Sally. "That's only for special occasions."

Clara burst into uproarious laughter. "Good idea to keep folks guessing." She tucked the spoon in her apron and gazed at the men washing hands and faces at the pump. "I'll fetch them more towels, but you'd better save me some of those taters. My mouth is already watering." She bustled off as Sally breathed a sigh of relief.

Amy watched sheer joy bloom on the face of the young minister's wife—and maybe a touch of pride. Clara, and everyone else, loved both of Sally's special recipes. There wasn't a morsel left in either pan for the slop bucket.

When the men returned to harvesting corn and the women settled in the shade, Sally relaxed against a tree trunk. After a while, Amy nudged her with an elbow. "What about the list? Now seems like a good time."

"*Nein*," she whispered. "I'll save that for another day."

Despite the missed opportunity, Amy understood Sally's reluctance. Sometimes a woman needed to pick the perfect moment to rock the boat.

❧

Sally sipped her morning coffee a content woman. Jeremiah slept soundly in the portable crib from his last feeding, and Aden was eating breakfast on his own, with the majority of oatmeal actually reaching his mouth. She used the few quiet minutes to bask in her success. The women had raved about her side dishes and even asked for the recipes. Many would deem this a small feat, but not Sally. The look on Clara's face upon tasting the potatoes made up for all the slights and jabs she'd suffered since coming to Harmony. "Thank You, Lord," she said. "Please help me to serve my district adequately." She reached out to wipe her son's chin. "And give me courage to approach them with the cooking assignments."

"Who are you talking to, *fraa*?" Thomas had entered the kitchen during her prayer.

"Dah!" exclaimed Aden with glee. The cereal on his spoon flew off and hit the floor with a *splat.*

"Hullo, son." Thomas bent to kiss the top of Aden's tousled head.

Sally sprang up for a wet rag. "I was talking to God. I thought if I spoke aloud, He would be sure to hear." She wiped up the mess and threw the rag into the bucket of soapy water. She planned to wash the kitchen floor after breakfast.

"He hears us. Whether it's a bold shout from a mountaintop or a child's tiny plea—our prayers are heard. What's troubling you?"

"Nothing, for a change." She reiterated yesterday's preparations for the frolic, Amy's suggestion regarding the list, and the popularity of her recipes.

"You doubted yourself?" Thomas sounded surprised. "We all have our gifts, Sally. You're a fine homemaker. Besides, Plain women don't usually aspire to be gourmet cooks. Hearty food so bodies are replenished—that's all that's required."

"Without oven-baked insects?" She shuddered with the memory.

The web of lines around his eyes deepened from his broad smile. "They might be popular in another culture, but not in ours."

His tenderness filled her with joy. "You're not upset about me spreading around the cooking duties?"

"Of course not. Because we've grown more numerous, it's a good idea to share the workload. You'll have plenty of chances for the women to sign up. We see them every Sunday."

Sally refilled their mugs and added milk to Aden's plastic cup. "Amy and Nora helped me so much yesterday. I'm grateful to them."

"Speaking of whom, where are they?" He peered around as though just noticing they were alone.

"Nora is upstairs with a migraine, and Amy is picking cabbages in the garden. We'll make sweet pickled cabbage and can sauerkraut this afternoon."

When Thomas lifted his coffee mug to drink, Aden mimicked the motion with his cup. "John went to check out a house. He looked for Amy before leaving but couldn't find her." He locked gazes with his wife across the table. "Do you suppose she sometimes hides from him?"

Sally felt herself blush as she walked to the window overlooking the garden. After reassuring herself that Amy still toiled among the rows, she turned back to him. "I don't think she hides, but I doubt she's as eager as he is to find a farm to buy."

"Second thoughts regarding marriage?"

"I can't speak as to her heart, but do you really think he's the right one for her?" Sally glanced nervously at the stairwell, not wishing to be overheard by Nora either.

"It's not my opinion that matters. I see no reason why they shouldn't marry based on what they have told me." He walked to the cupboard for a bowl.

Sally hurried to stir the oats and get the pitcher of milk. "*Mir leid, ehemann,*" she apologized. "A man who's been up since four thirty must be hungry by now." She sliced fresh bread and placed it on the table along with jam and butter.

Thomas carried his brimming bowl to the table. He sprinkled the surface liberally with cinnamon, poured on milk, and began to eat. "Do you know something I don't? I would appreciate some insight."

Sally sat down next to Aden, who waved his spoon in the air. "She's said nothing contrary about him. It's just woman's intuition. Did you see his expression when Amy left to go to the library and post office? I've seen milder temperaments on bulls in spring during mating season."

Thomas lifted a brow and bobbed his head toward Aden.

"He's still too young to understand," Sally assured him with a blush. She sensed a small measure of the confidence she had prayed for. Time to pursue the topic that had been long on her mind. "John looked as though he might suffer a stroke after Amy left. He paced the barnyard and then chopped so much firewood we'll be set for subzero weather through May."

Thomas appeared unruffled by her observation. "It's good for a man to blow off steam with hard labor. We are all victims of human nature, *fraa,* but Scripture encourages us to rid ourselves of anger. That's what he was doing."

"But why was he mad about Amy going to town?" Sally cast another wary glance at the steps.

"You don't understand a man's mind. John worries when she takes the buggy alone. She's not familiar with the area or with handling this particular horse. And the impetuousness of her decision unnerved him. My *bruder* has never been spur-of-the-moment. He's a planner, a consider-all-the-options kind of guy. There's not a spontaneous bone in his body."

"You know him better than I." She filled a bowl of her own with oatmeal.

Thomas leaned back in his chair. "When we were boys, he used to plan exactly what he would do on the first nonpreaching Sunday of warm weather while we were still buried under a foot of snow. He studies seed catalogs in January, even though he'll invariably plant the seeds he saved from the previous year."

She reflected on this. To her, the information only underscored her point. "Does this behavior even remotely sound like Amy?"

"No, but opposites attract, Sally. Look at us." He winked one magnificent blue eye at her.

She frowned, even though she agreed with him on some level. Personalities often differed with long-married, happy couples. But something about Amy and John's engagement didn't set right with her. His impatience to marry sent up—what did the *Englischers* call it?—red flags. "I really like Amy," she said finally. "Not that I don't like Nora, but I seemed to have…bonded with her sister."

"That's *gut.* If she stays and marries John, you'll have a friend besides a sister-in-law."

"*If* she stays and marries?" Sally pounced on that like a cat. "Your word choice indicates you have doubts too, Thomas. Your *bruder* needs a more docile, pliable *fraa* than Amy King."

He stood and lifted Aden from the chair. The boy had eaten all he intended to and was now just making a mess. He carried him to the sink, removed his soiled bib, and washed his hands and face. "I have no doubt that the correct path will be made clear for both Amy and John. In the meantime, it's important that others don't unduly interfere." He lowered his chin and fixed her with a cool, steady stare. He set Aden down on the floor, clean and dry again.

"Me, interfere? Surely you jest." Sally used another favorite English expression, even though Thomas's meaning was crystal clear.

Thomas peered out the back window and then dropped the curtain back in place. "She's on her way in, so our conversation about *your* true nature must wait for another day. And she's carrying a heaping basket of cabbages. You two will have your work cut out for you this afternoon."

"Perhaps women need to burn off steam too." Sally cleared the table of their breakfast dishes. "Oh, I almost forgot. Your other *bruder* came home last night, very late. I heard him on the stairs to the cellar. He made quite a racket, actually, as though he kept stumbling."

"It must be too rainy up north to cut lumber. They give the men a few days off until things dry out. Otherwise, heavy trucks could get mired in the muck." He shrugged on his coat, looking ten years older than five minutes ago. "Have you talked with him yet?"

"Only to say good morning. He took a shower, made two sandwiches, and headed toward the fields. He muttered something about checking fence lines."

Thomas nodded as though deep in thought. "No mention as to how long he might stay this time?"

"*Nein*. I've told you all I know." Sally felt a shiver of something dreadful. When Thomas swept open the door, he nearly ran headlong into a streaky-faced Amy.

"Whew," she said, sliding past him. "All picked—the cabbage, squash, zucchinis, and brussels sprouts—every last one of them." She hung her cloak on a peg and headed to the sink to wash.

Sally poured her a mug of coffee. "Thomas said you have a full bushel of cabbage for us to chop and can."

"*A full bushel?*" she asked. "There are five bushels lined up on the porch. He must have only seen me haul up the last one. I hope you slept well last night, because we'll need our energy today."

Sally sighed and then remembered something her *mamm* loved to say: The Lord never gives us more than we can handle. *Five bushels to can? We'll be inventing recipes for cabbage pie and cabbage bread before all those jars are gone.*

❧

"Get up, John, before the morning gets away from us."

With a start, John bolted upright and fumbled for his glasses on the nightstand. In the dark room he sensed rather than saw Thomas looming above him.

"Were you planning on sleeping till noon?"

"I guess not." John threw back the covers. "What time is it?"

"Half past four. Have you forgotten? We're spreading manure today." Thomas backed away, allowing his brother space to get out of bed. "Just like the old days. You can sleep through thunder and lightning, gunshots, and even the snores of our little brother."

John went to his dresser, where a basin and pitcher of cold water awaited. The floor chilled his bare feet. "*Danki* for waking me. I was having a bad dream."

"What about? Did you arrive late to lunch and the man in front grabbed the last piece of chocolate cake?" Thomas raised the window shade, letting it go with a snap. Whereas John could sleep through just about any ruckus, Thomas loved creating them.

"No, Amy and I were on a country dirt road at the height of summer. She kept running away from me, and I couldn't catch her no matter how hard I tried." John gazed into the small mirror before splashing cold water on his face. "She had an expression of pure terror on her face each time she looked back at me. I knew we were approaching the edge of a steep cliff and wasn't able to warn her. Just like spooked cattle, we were doomed to tumble over to our deaths." He shook his head to dislodge the unsettling nightmare. As he buried his face in a soft towel, he felt a hand on his shoulder.

"Get hold of yourself. There are no deep abysses in the area, no dirt roads, and Amy is downstairs with Sally and Nora, preparing to leave."

"Leave? To go where?" John tossed the towel on the bureau.

"Where's your memory today? I mentioned at supper last night that we would spread manure this morning. It's supposed to be sunny for a few days to give it a chance to dry before we till it under."

John reached for his work trousers from the chair. "Why are we fertilizing already? It's still September. We never did this until late October back home."

"Fall comes earlier here in Maine. I'll see you downstairs."

"Wait. Where are the women going?"

"Sally never sticks around while I fertilize. The smell turns her stomach. The women are meeting at Martha's house. Her neighborhood plans to spread next week, so then they will probably congregate here. They will quilt all day long, breaking only for meals and tending to little ones. But I bet they will do as much talking as sewing." Thomas headed toward the door.

"Amy will be gone the entire day?" John tugged a clean shirt over his head.

"Don't worry. Sally will fix a plate of sandwiches for our lunch. And she's making a pot of chili for our supper."

"It's not my belly I'm concerned with. Amy still hasn't seen the two farms for sale that I like."

"All in good time. Patience is a virtue we need to cultivate." Thomas closed the door behind him, not waiting for his brother's response.

All in good time, muttered John, tugging on socks. *At this rate, I'll hobble into church with a cane on my wedding day.*

In the kitchen, chaos reigned as Sally and Amy bustled around making breakfast, lunch, and dinner for them. Aden attempted to eat scrambled eggs on his own, while Jeremiah howled in his portable crib in the corner, demanding attention. However, when John entered the kitchen, the real eye-opener slouched in a kitchen chair. Elam Detweiler—tall and thin but muscular, with dark hair and eyes—was as different in appearance and temperament from his brothers as a man could be. His traditional Amish bangs had grown out, and he had a scruffy three-day beard, forbidden among unmarried men. Before him sat a plate of eggs and toast, barely touched, as he brooded over a travel mug of coffee.

"Good morning, brother," said Elam in English. "Glad to see you could join us. I'd hate to have all the fun of spreading manure without you."

"*Guder mariye.*" John returned the greeting in *Deutsch*. "Some of us work hard every day and are bone tired when we fall into bed." He sat down at the other end of the table.

"Good morning, John," greeted Amy. "I bet you're hungry." She served his plate of breakfast with a pretty smile.

"I am, *danki.*" Their fingers brushed when she set down his food, and the touch electrified him, erasing the last of his morning grogginess. After bowing his head to pray, he directed his question to her. "Did you sleep well?"

"*Jah*, just like a *boppli*," said Amy over her shoulder. She scooped up eggs for the women.

"Babies don't sleep very well in this house," said Elam. "Jeremiah's cries kept me up half the night." He leaned back in his chair and stretched out his long legs.

"I can't see how that's possible, Elam Detweiler." Sally turned from the counter where she was fixing sandwiches. "Your bed is in the cellar, and Jeremiah was in his crib upstairs with us."

Elam laughed and hooked a thumb toward the crib. "You must be immune to the noise, because I'd recognize my nephew's voice anywhere."

John concentrated on his plate of food, tamping down a retort. He had no right to interfere in Thomas's household, however much he wanted to.

When Sally refilled coffee mugs, she served Elam last. "The boy has been fed and his diaper is dry. Sometimes babies just cry. That's life." She flashed him a scowl before she resumed making sandwiches.

"Perhaps someday your future *fraa* will give birth to the first non-crying baby," said Amy between bites of eggs. She stayed by the stove to eat while she stirred the pot of chili. "Then he'll be written about in a medical journal somewhere, and the Elam Detweiler family will be famous."

John took a bite of toast, but it had suddenly turned dry and hard to swallow. For some odd reason, he didn't like his bride-to-be engaging his younger brother in conversation.

Elam smiled at Amy over his cold food. "I don't intend ever to marry, Miss King, but I appreciate your confidence that my son would be extraordinary."

"Never say never. The right woman could turn even your immovable head."

Elam's raucous laughter drowned out the baby's crying. "Someday you will be a lucky man, John, but this gal will keep you on your toes." Elam pushed away the plate and rose to his feet. "Are we about ready to start spreading autumn joy?" His gaze shifted between his brothers.

John wiped up his eggs with a bread crust and then carried the plate to the sink. "I'd like to say goodbye to Amy. I'll meet you outside."

"Isn't young love sweet?" Elam strode out of the house with an arrogant swagger, leaving his full plate on the table. Two pairs of eyes followed him to the door. One pair belonged to Thomas, whose expression remained dour, while the other belonged to Nora King. She'd watched him from across the kitchen with utter fascination.

John swallowed the bitter taste in his mouth. "Have a good day quilting," he murmured to Amy, in the un-private company of others.

When he joined his brothers, Thomas assigned John and Elam to work as a team to spread the liquefied composted manure across the harvested fields. Elam chose to ride in the seat driving the team of draft horses. John would ride on the backseat, assuring that the supply to the spreader remained constant. Other than a few annoying flies, work went well that morning. But after lunch the Belgians became mired in a low, swampy section of field. Without hesitation, Elam applied the whip to the horses' backs.

John swiveled around. "Stop that! Thomas never whips his team, and neither do I."

Elam sneered. "How exactly can I get them out of this quagmire?"

"If you'd been paying attention, you could have avoided the low spot," snapped John.

"It's too late to worry 'bout that now." Elam used the whip again on the straining horses.

"If you strike them one more time, I'll take that whip to your hide," John shouted. There was nothing ambiguous about his intentions. He jumped down into the muck, walked around the equipment, and positioned himself between the Belgians. He patted their sweating flanks to calm them. After a minute he took hold of their halters and led them onto higher ground.

As Elam drove the equipment past him, John climbed back into his seat. "That's how you free a team without using the whip," he called with satisfaction.

"*Jah*, but look at yourself, big brother. You're caked up to your knees in muck. You better not stand upwind of Amy when she gets home. You stink." Elam slapped the reins and the team resumed fertilizing the row.

John gritted his teeth, knowing he had to work all day with Elam. And also because he did, indeed, smell bad. Because they wouldn't enter the house until they were finished, he would have to smell that way until nightfall.

John took his shower first at day's end. While Elam heated their chili and built fires in the kitchen and living room woodstoves, Thomas rubbed down the horses and put them to pasture for the night. Then the three men ate their meal without speaking. Afterward, John walked down the leaf-strewn driveway to fetch the mail. He needed something to take his mind off the fact the women still weren't home. Darkness had fallen more than an hour ago. But in the stack he found more distraction than he bargained for—a letter addressed to Amy from a town he'd never heard of. "Chestnut, Maine," he read on the envelope. Only one person could have written this—Amy's aunt.

He glanced around and then tucked the letter inside his jacket. Later, after the women returned and everyone had eaten and gone to bed, John pulled the letter from his pocket. With no small measure of shame, he slit open the envelope and extracted the single sheet. His supposition regarding the writer had been correct—Prudence Summerton. By the yellow glow of a kerosene lamp, he read the words meant for another pair of eyes.

My dear Amy,

*Your letter filled me with both joy and sorrow—joy to hear
from my beloved niece after all these years, and sorrow to
learn that my sister and her husband have perished. My
heart aches for you and your schwestern. I welcome you to
our fine state and hope you'll find a good life here, but I
must refuse your invitation to visit Harmony. I am banned,
Amy. My choices have closed that door forever. But be
assured that I am well and happier than I have ever been
in my life.*

*May the Lord bless you and your young man in
your upcoming marriage.*

Aunt Prudence

An uncharitable, judgmental thought came to John's mind:
*You are living a godless existence with a man you had no business mar-
rying.* In a weak, impulsive moment, he did something he would
live to regret. He stuffed the letter back into the envelope, opened
the door of the woodstove, and tossed it inside. With grim satisfaction he watched the words from a willful woman to his beloved
Amy reduce to soot and ash.

But, oddly, he felt no satisfaction after removing the threat of a
bad influence from their lives.

NINE

Nothing in my hand I bring

"Pee-ew!" Nora exclaimed, shutting the living room window with a resounding clatter. "I thought they finished spreading that goop yesterday. Why does it still smell so bad?"

Sally glanced up from the tiny sweater she was knitting for Jeremiah. "Where did you say you came from—Lancaster County or New York City?" She enjoyed a hearty laugh with Amy. "The men haven't plowed it under yet. Besides, they are fertilizing more acres on the east side today, farther away from the house."

Nora shut the rest of the windows just as noisily.

"You'll be opening them back up when it grows too stuffy to breathe in here." Amy glared over her half-moon glasses. She had recently started wearing them for small, close stitches. "At least the breeze comes from the west."

"I'd rather sweat to death than smell any more horse dung." Nora crossed her arms to match her mood.

"Go back to work and stop being vulgar." Amy raised her voice for only the second time since stepping foot in Maine.

Nora obliged, but she stuck her tongue out at her sister before returning to the ironing board.

Sally looked from one to the other, considering how best to cool off the room's occupants. "What happened? Yesterday we worked together like a well-oiled machine. Today you two are snapping at each other."

"We were motivated to get chores done so we could spend the day quilting at Martha's." Amy examined her row of stitches. "I enjoyed getting to know the women better. They are all very interesting in different ways. Didn't you think so, Nora?"

Nora paused while her iron reheated atop the stove. "I suppose so. At least the air smelled better at Martha's. But that fish salad at lunch contained an herb or seasoning I didn't like. I can understand egg or ham or even tuna salad, but codfish salad? Very odd. And her cherry cobbler had the sourest cherries and the driest crust. She must have run out of sugar."

Amy dropped her sewing. "Nora King, you are quite mean-spirited today! I wouldn't blame Sally if she buys you a one-way ticket back to Pennsylvania."

Duly chastised, Nora hung her head. "I was only expressing an opinion."

"Which you are entitled to," said Sally, chuckling. "I'll save my money because I thought the same thing about Martha's cobbler. One bite and my eyes squinted shut from the tartness."

Nora's head snapped up. "That's what happened to me."

Amy looked from one to the other. "Well, I must admit my lips puckered a bit too. Maybe she's watching her weight."

"She could have passed around the sugar bowl for those not counting calories." Nora carried her iron back to the board.

"In all seriousness, Sally, your district holds no great advantage over you in baking or cooking, so I don't know why you were so nervous about your food at the harvest frolic."

Sally unwound a long measure of yarn and pondered Amy's

observance. She opted for the truth. "I got off to a rocky start with the women. And it had nothing to do with food or recipes." She knitted half a row as the clock provided the only sound in the room. After a while, she sensed the two pairs of eyes on her.

"Go on. Now you've got us curious," encouraged Nora.

"But only if you're comfortable talking about it," added Amy, the soul of discretion.

"When Thomas and I came to this district, we didn't move here alone. A few others also relocated from Missouri to make a fresh start in Maine. One young woman couldn't stay mum about my past in Paradise, and soon everyone found out. The older women thought Thomas shouldn't have married a woman with...such a colorful history." Sally glanced at Amy, who watched her with saucer-round eyes. "Remember, this is a *very* conservative community without *rumschpringe* for young people."

"But it's a new district. None of those women grew up here." Amy placed her pillowcase back into the sewing basket.

"True. Everyone came from elsewhere. But many Old Order districts are more conservative than those in Pennsylvania or Ohio...or Paradise, Missouri. Because Thomas married me, some thought he shouldn't be nominated for minister. But few men are as knowledgeable about Scripture as he is, so that line of thinking was quickly squashed. Even so, the older matrons didn't find me suitable to lead the wives."

"Who was this big blabbermouth?" Nora sounded ready to retaliate.

Sally shook her head. "I'll not say her name. That's water long over the dam. I'm sure she regrets gossiping."

"What exactly did you do in Missouri?" Nora whispered the words with unconcealed delight.

Amy sighed. "Pay no attention to her. She forgets her manners at times."

"Nothing truly terrible, before your imagination runs away with you." Sally winked at Nora. "But I did cut my hair up to my shoulders and trimmed a fringe of bangs above my eyes." She touched her eyebrows with her fingertips. "I always considered my forehead too high and thought the bangs would soften my features."

"What did your mother say?" asked Amy as curiosity got the better of her too.

"*Mamm* shook her head and muttered that the bangs were crooked. Because I was sixteen and hadn't joined the church yet, she wasn't too worried. But my *daed* didn't speak to me until my hair grew out. He said no man would marry a woman with scarecrow hair!" Sally laughed at the memory.

"Was that it? Just a bad haircut?" Nora set her iron back on the woodstove to reheat.

"Oh, no, that was just the beginning of my *rumschpringe*. I rode in cars with English girlfriends. They picked me up and took me to the ice-cream shop in Paradise at least twice a week. Then I took a job at that ice-cream stand. *Daed* worried I would fall for an *Englischer* because many young men hung out there on warm summer nights. They polished up their shiny cars just to drive downtown for a banana split, and then they sat atop picnic tables watching other cars drive by like a parade." Sally clucked dismissively. "It was really stupid to waste gas like that, the more I think about it."

Nora perched on the edge of the sofa with rapt attention, her ironing forgotten. "You worked in an ice-cream shop? Plenty of Amish girls take jobs for a spell. I had planned to back in Lancaster...until God changed everything." A pinched expression clouded her pretty face.

"*Jah*, well, perhaps if it had been only the job and haircut, my past would have been easier to live down."

Nora almost fell off the sofa. "Go on."

Sally felt uneasy about Nora's enchantment with her behavior, but it was too late to stop now. After listening to make sure her *kinner* still napped, she continued. "Some of the Amish youth held get-togethers that summer—hayrides and cookouts with s'mores and roasted corn. I can still see the giant bonfires with flames shooting high into the night sky."

Suddenly, she realized the thoughtlessness of her words. "Forgive me, Amy, Nora, for talking about fire so carelessly."

Amy shrugged her shoulders. "No, Sally. Don't feel that you have to walk on eggshells around us. Candles light our way, while wood-burning stoves keep us warm on chilly nights. Fire will always be part of life for us. Go on with your story."

Sally knitted a few more stitches in the sweater. "Amish and English alike attended these parties. One night someone brought a large…boom box, I think they are called, and turned the music up loud. My friends and I walked around the barn to where it was quieter. Soon the noise disturbed a neighbor's sleep, and the man called the authorities. The sheriff arrived with several deputies to break up the party. My sister and I went home, but *daed* found out we had been there. An article in the newspaper said beer had been taken away from several underage *Englischers*." She paused to count the stitches in a row. "I saw no one drinking, but, nevertheless, the woman who moved here told everyone I attended drinking parties in Missouri."

A wide-eyed Amy looked sympathetic. "What happened next that summer?" She glanced nervously at Nora.

"Nothing, really. I met Thomas Detweiler in the autumn. He had moved from Pennsylvania looking for cheaper farmland. We began courting, and I never went to another party. He was a bit older than me, so my *daed* insisted that we wait. We married when I turned eighteen, and then we moved here a year later. We've been in Harmony for three years now."

"You're only twenty-two—the same as me?" Amy sounded more shocked by that than anything else.

"I'm nearly twenty-three." Sally cocked her head, listening as Jeremiah began to stir.

"You already have two fine sons and an established home. I've accomplished nothing yet."

"You and John will soon set up your first house. No one's journey through life is the same, except for the path we follow to the Lord."

"Goodness, that was quite a story," said Nora, returning to her pile of shirts.

Amy picked up her sewing again. "Thank you for sharing that with us."

But Sally wasn't happy about her disclosure to the sisters, especially not after she noticed the toe of a man's boot by the doorjamb. Someone had been eavesdropping—a vice she often was guilty of—and she had a good idea who that person was.

❧

John hadn't meant to listen in on the women's conversation. He and his brothers had finished up fertilizing the fields earlier than expected, and with his free time he thought Amy might like to take a drive with him. With the heat and humidity gone, this might be a good day to look at properties for sale. Maybe they could catch lunch together. They might even be able to slip away without Nora tagging along to chaperone. But Amy hadn't been sewing alone in the front room. Sally entertained the King sisters with tales of her wild youth in Paradise.

Did the woman have nary a brain in her head?

Surely she saw the folly of inspiring the already willful Nora with new ideas. That girl needed tamping down, not stirring up, if she planned to remain in Harmony. And, frankly, he didn't like Amy hearing about Sally's past recklessness either.

Cutting her hair? Riding in cars with Englischers? Taking a job at a local teenage hangout? And attending a party where beer had been smuggled in?

No wonder the district's matrons doubted her suitability as a minister's wife. But, truthfully, that unnamed tattletale needed a reprimand by the bishop. The Bible was quite clear about gossiping, and that particular story should have been left behind in Missouri.

John had crept silently down the hallway, through the kitchen, and out the door, hoping he hadn't been noticed. He needed time to think about what he'd heard. Had he made a mistake coming here? If they had remained in Pennsylvania, they would be married in November with all the other engaged couples. Now Amy had learned of a shameful aunt, who had been shunned by her community, and had listened to wild tales from her soon-to-be sister-in-law. John kicked a stone down the driveway as a chill ran up his spine. What kind of woman had Thomas married? What had attracted a devout, quiet man to a young girl with chopped-off scarecrow hair and no more sense than a goat? Although everyone should be forgiven their past sins, Thomas still should have chosen more wisely if he aspired to preach the Word of God. You might be able to put a hat and a bow tie on a mule, but it still wouldn't do much more than pull a plow.

John shook off his uncharitable opinions about Sally. She was his brother's wife and therefore not his problem. But her negative effect on his sweet Amy was his concern, so instead of stewing about the situation, he headed toward the workshop. Thomas usually worked on tables and chairs once farm chores were finished, and today was no exception. Stepping into the pine-scented shop, John spotted Thomas bent over his lathe, working on spindles for chair backs. He wore plastic safety goggles and a long rubber apron, but sawdust and wood shavings clung to just about every inch of him. John cleared his throat. "Mind if I have a word with you?" he asked.

Thomas continued to labor, deep in concentration and oblivious to his surroundings.

John cleared his throat and repeated the request louder this time.

Thomas jumped, peered up, and then switched off the battery-powered lathe. "I didn't hear you come in, John. Has something happened in the house?" A look of panic masked his placid features.

"No, the women are sewing, knitting, and ironing, and all is well, but I wanted to have a private word with you."

Thomas stepped away from the equipment, brushing off his clothes. He pointed at two finished kitchen chairs by the window. "I could use a break."

Once they sat, John scratched his chin, suddenly unsure how to approach a delicate subject. When no insight came to mind, he simply forged ahead. "I overheard Sally talking to Amy and Nora in the living room. I know I listened longer than I should have, but I became curious." He met his older brother's gaze and then looked away, embarrassed by his admission.

"Go on. What did you hear? Some gossip Sally shouldn't have repeated?"

"No, nothing like that." John crossed and then uncrossed his legs, unable to find comfort on the straight-backed chair. "She was explaining about her *rumschpringe* back in Missouri." He glanced at Thomas, who seemed completely devoid of emotion. "She told them how she'd cut off her hair, took a job in town, and rode with *Englischers* in cars—"

Thomas held up a hand. "I'm well aware of my wife's past before she joined the church and married me. You need not spell out every detail with such enthusiasm. I see no point to your eavesdropping, and even less reason to bring this to me."

John felt a flush crawl up his neck, turning his face uncomfortably warm. "You're right. I shouldn't have listened, but I'm worried about Amy and especially about Nora. She seems so flighty and impressionable, not to mention easily confused. I prefer they not be influenced in a negative fashion."

Thomas bristled like a cornered porcupine. "You consider my *fraa* a negative influence?" His normally calm demeanor vanished again, this time in irritation.

"*Nein.* I'm expressing myself poorly. Sally has my utmost respect, but I would prefer that she not share details of her running-around days, at least not until Nora has made the decision to join the church."

"I don't choose the topics for my wife's conversations. Besides, you're worried about something without basis in reality. As I'm sure Sally explained that Missouri's ways are not Maine's. There is no running-around here, so you don't have to worry about Nora or Amy following in my wife's wayward footsteps."

John clutched his suspenders for something to occupy his hands. "You're right, Thomas. I have no cause to either criticize Sally or fear her influence on Amy. *Mir leid.*" He dropped his chin and stared at the sawdust-strewn floor.

Thomas waved his hand absently through the air. "It's forgotten. We have more important things to worry about than sewing circle chatter." His tone turned ominous.

"What do you mean?" John splayed his hands across his knees.

"It's Elam. He's home for a while."

"I've noticed that, but at least he doesn't eat much." John forced a laugh.

Thomas closed his eyes, and then he rubbed them with his fingertips. "He was fired from the English logging crew. He wouldn't elaborate with details, but I believe he caused dissension among the men. Elam turns into a hothead when provoked. That much hasn't changed about our little *bruder.*" Thomas opened his red-rimmed eyes to focus on John. "I'm afraid this isn't good. The no-*rumschpringe* rule doesn't just apply to young women like Nora, but to our brother as well. The problem is that Elam pays no attention to it. When he's between jobs, he comes and goes from his cellar bedroom as he pleases, he doesn't partake in family meals or evening devotions, and he refuses to attend Sunday school or preaching services."

"Maybe he figures the bishop would take exception to his scruffy beard, long hair, and slovenly appearance. And the fact he hasn't joined the church wouldn't set well." John removed his hat and slicked a hand through his hair. "It seems like he's on the fence—he doesn't wish to commit to Amish ways, but he doesn't want to leave and turn English, either."

Thomas blew out his breath. "That's what I would conclude. I know he wears jeans and plaid flannel shirts when he's on the crew. I've seen his wash hanging on the basement clothesline. He wouldn't dare put them in Sally's laundry basket because she's apt to throw them in the burn barrel." Thomas rubbed the base of his neck while rotating his head side to side. "And I've seen him smoke cigarettes while driving the team through the fields."

"At least he wears Amish clothes while home and pulls his weight with chores around the farm," said John, unsure why he was defending his brother.

"I have given him leeway, hoping he would come around. But the older he gets, the more he test the limits…and my patience. I don't wish to send him away from home. We're the only family he has, except for a few cousins in Missouri. But it might come down to that." Thomas locked eyes with John.

"And if it does, I will support you and help if I can."

"*Danki*. That's good to hear. And I'll mention to Sally to stop chatting about her short-haired days." Thomas rose to his feet and returned to the lathe, but he didn't look even remotely relieved.

❧

"Will you stop poking me?" hissed Nora.

"Then stop sleeping in church," Amy hissed right back.

"I can't help it. I keep dozing off."

"If you pay attention to what the bishop is saying, that won't happen." Other worshippers began to notice the girls' distraction, so Amy pulled away.

Nora nodded and straightened her back against the bench. She'd tried listening, but the bishop's quiet voice affected her like a warm glass of milk. Neither Thomas nor the other minister delivered his sermon in such a monotone. She'd tried biting the inside of her cheek, tapping her foot, and counting flies on the painted ceiling, all to no avail. The only thing that kept her upright on the bench was sitting across from her—Lewis from the general store. Every now and then their gazes met across the aisle, and Nora felt a shiver of exhilaration. She had once asked Amy how a woman knew when a man liked her. Amy had answered cryptically that "a woman just knows."

The explanation made no sense at the time, but it certainly did today. Nora *knew* Lewis liked her. Her last two visits to the co-op confirmed what she'd suspected on her first trip to town. And since then he tried to get her to stay as long as possible.

Have you seen our new assortment of lamp oils that just arrived, Nora?

How about a sample of this honey, walnut, and oat trail mix, Nora? It tastes good and is supposed to give people more energy.

I ordered every variety of bulk candy they make, knowing you have a sweet tooth, Nora.

Lewis loved saying her name. And she loved hearing him say it. She might be growing on his *mamm* too, because the woman stopped frowning whenever Nora came into the store. Today his mother actually half smiled when they passed each other in the outer hall. Half a smile was better than no smile at all.

Maybe Lewis would sit with her during lunch, or maybe they

could take a walk to the grove of oak trees by the river. The bright red and orange leaves were so pretty this time of year. "Ouch," Nora yelped as Amy's elbow connected with her rib cage. Heads turned again.

Amy shoved the *Ausbund*, the Amish hymnal, under her nose. "Stop daydreaming and sing," she whispered.

Nora abandoned thoughts of Lewis to raise her voice in praise. But when the interminable service ended, she couldn't wait to get into the sunshine.

But the thorn-in-her-side had followed her. "I'd like a private word with you," said Amy.

"It's time for lunch," Nora protested. "Shouldn't we help Sally set out the food?"

Amy dragged her like a faceless doll clutched by a toddler. "What? You're suddenly interested in women's work instead of playing with *kinner*?" Sarcasm dripped off Amy's words.

Nora rolled her eyes. "You and Sally usually want me to watch the boys. I'd wish you would make up your mind. And stop pulling me!" She yanked her arm back. They had reached the stand of oaks, but it hadn't been her sister that Nora had hoped to see there.

With nostrils flaring, Amy glared at Nora. Amy took full advantage of her four-inch height difference. "Everyone noticed you falling asleep in church. I was embarrassed for your sake."

Nora arched up on tiptoes. "Tell the congregation those migraine pills make me sleepy."

"I won't make up stories. You need to listen to the sermon and stop letting your mind wander. We're here to worship the Lord. What would God think if He saw you napping in His house?"

Nora leaned against the rough tree trunk, tired of her sister bossing her around. Ever since their *mamm* died, Amy acted as though she had stepped into *mamm*'s shoes. "I think God stopped paying attention to the King family long ago."

Amy's eyes nearly bugged from her head like a grasshopper's. She checked over her shoulder, scandalized. "Why would you say such a thing?"

"Because it's true. Where was God when lightning struck our house? And what are the chances of lightning not only hitting the house, but burning it down?" Like a cornered wild animal, Nora lashed out. "Most people would smell the smoke and get out in time, but not our parents. They had no warning and died asleep in their bed." Tears streamed unchecked as the dam of emotion finally broke.

Blood drained from Amy's face as she staggered back. "We are not to question God's will—"

Nora pushed off the tree and ran along the line of trees, away from the meetinghouse and all of the district members. She kept running until she reached the riverbank, where a fast-moving creek tumbled over rocks and ledges. Breathless, she lowered herself to a log, buried her face in her hands, and sobbed. She cried for her dead parents and for herself, stuck in an ultraconservative district in a land of chilly September days and nights that turned downright cold. If she were home, it would be the height of Indian summer, with bonfires, hayrides, or cookouts every Saturday. Singings would be filled with plenty of young folk...because there were so many more people!

Nora had no friends here other than Lewis...not that it was anybody's fault but hers. Feeling like a square peg surrounded by round holes, she'd made no attempt to socialize. Right now, while she hid from the world, district members were enjoying turkey sandwiches with mugs of hot chocolate. Nora squeezed her eyes shut and tried to pray, but she couldn't think of a single thing to say. Certainly not words of gratitude for bringing her to this alien land. Fresh tears clouded her vision, but she fought them back as she sat on her log, waiting.

She waited for inspiration on how to return to the noon meal with dignity.

She waited for insight that God still had a plan for her life.

And she waited for Lewis, who maybe had seen her leave and followed. He would sit down on the log, slip an arm around her shoulders, and tell her everything would be all right. Then they would walk back to the meetinghouse, where he'd saved her a sandwich and cup of cocoa. After the others filed back in for the afternoon hymn session, he would take her home because she felt the beginnings of a headache. They would marvel at autumn foliage at its best while his buggy rolled down the lane toward the Detweiler farm.

But Lewis didn't show up to rescue her. And nothing she envisioned could have taken place anyway. Not here. Not in Harmony.

Damp and stiff, Nora finally struggled to her feet and trudged back to the picnic tables. It was good Lewis hadn't followed her, she realized. At the speed he was capturing her heart, she would end up married and living in his cabin behind the store before Amy and John. Nora couldn't imagine spending her life here, not with so many interesting places in the world to see. Why couldn't John have picked Missouri, where Sally came from, or maybe Indiana or Ohio or New York? She needed to forget about handsome Lewis with his sea-blue eyes, strong hands, and unlimited devotion.

Her future wasn't here. It couldn't be.

At the meetinghouse, the congregation had already gone inside to sing, but Amy sat waiting at a picnic table. John stood behind her with his hand on her shoulder in an old-fashioned pose. Amy smiled as Nora approached. "I'm so relieved to see you," she said. "I've been worried. Forgive me for pinching, poking, and quarreling."

John stood like a stone statue, his face empty of expression.

"I'm sorry too," Nora murmured. "I lost my temper. Just because I'm mad at God, I shouldn't take it out on you."

John cringed from her statement, but Amy remained calm. "God never stops loving us, even when we're angry with Him," she said, rising to her feet. "Are you hungry? I made you a sandwich." She pulled a wax paper packet from her purse.

"*Danki.* I'll eat it on my way home." Nora tucked the sandwich in her bag. "I feel a headache coming on."

"In that case I'm leaving too so you're not alone." Amy turned toward John. "Why don't you go inside without us? I'll see you back at Thomas's."

"Would you like me to drive you?" he asked, spinning his hat brim between his fingers.

"No. I think the exercise and fresh air will do us good." Amy buttoned her cloak and reached for Nora's hand.

John nodded but remained in place, still fiddling with his hat as they headed toward the road.

"Those migraine pills really do make me sleepy," said Nora, once they were out of earshot.

"I believe you, and I'm sorry I kept jabbing your ribs." Amy let go of her hand and put a comforting arm around her shoulders.

"Don't worry about it. I need a jab every now and then." Nora unwrapped the turkey sandwich and took a bite. It had both mustard and mayo, just how she liked it. No one knew her...or loved her...like her *schwester.*

That night, long after the Detweilers had all gone to bed, Nora moved her chair over to the window. Amy snored softly in her sleep, but oddly the sound comforted instead of annoyed her. Nora gazed down on a silent barnyard illuminated by the thin light of a crescent moon as though keeping vigil. She shook her head each time thoughts of Lewis crept into her head. After a while her vision blurred as shapes seemed to form and disintegrate in the shadows.

Suddenly, the outline of a man leading a horse stepped into the area in front of the barn. Nora blinked several times to make sure fatigue wasn't playing tricks on her. But when she looked again, Elam Detweiler lifted one foot into a stirrup and swung his other leg over his black stallion. Hatless and wearing a red-and-black plaid jacket, he kicked the horse's flanks and rode off into the darkness.

Where on earth is he going at this hour? Intrigue replaced the last residue of Nora's melancholy. At least solving a mystery might relieve the relentless boredom of living in Harmony.

TEN

Simply to the cross I cling

John thought he heard the mournful sound of crying while feeding the goats. But when he listened and heard nothing, he assumed it was the wind whistling through missing chinks in the barn silo. It was still very early, so he saw nothing in the inky darkness. After he scrubbed out and refilled water troughs with the hose, he heard the cries again, distinct and undeniable, emanating from the eastern pasture behind the barn. He went in search of Thomas and found him on a stool bathing a cow's underbelly with soapy water.

"You must come and bring the lantern. I believe a heifer's been injured. Maybe she fell into a hole and broke her leg." John's tone conveyed alarm.

His brother, however, continued to wash the cow's udder, unruffled by the news. "*Jah*, I heard the bellowing and investigated earlier. A heifer wandered into the high pasture to give birth. She's

155

in labor and things don't seem to be going well for her." Thomas glanced up with compassionate eyes, yet he resumed his ministrations from the stool.

"Are you just going to sit there? Why don't we help her? The calf is probably breech and she can't deliver. *Daed* used to turn the calf so it would be headed in the right direction. I've watched him do this."

"It's still pitch-dark. Cows usually drop calves with no help but from the Lord above. This isn't good, John. It's too late in the year for her to be birthing. The youngun' probably wouldn't make it through winter anyway." With the udder clean, Thomas began milking with slow methodical pulls.

"So, because she didn't use better family planning, we're going to let her die up there? In pain?" He added the last two words in case Thomas didn't quite grasp the situation.

Thomas nodded. "She's been in labor all night while we slept. Believe me, I don't like it any more than you do, but few vets make house calls and none will come this early, especially if their patient is up in the hills. She's probably too far gone and won't let anyone close to her now. You don't want to get kicked in the head by a frantic heifer. Her uterus may have torn and she's slowly bleeding to death. That's why she separated herself from the herd—to die in peace."

John slapped his hat against his pant leg, sending up a puff of dust. "It doesn't sound very peaceful to me!"

Thomas offered a sad, patient smile. "All right. Go get what we'll need while I finish up here. I'll meet you either by the house or up in the hills."

John hurried out of the barn to find someone else in case his brother didn't come in time. The perfect person to help sat in the kitchen, sipping her first cup of coffee. "*Guder mariye*," said Amy. "Finished with your chores already? We haven't started breakfast yet. Sally's still feeding Jeremi—"

"No, we're not done, but could you help me in the high pasture? A cow giving birth is in trouble. I need someone to hold the light while I assist."

"Of course I'll come." Amy set down her mug and hurried to the porch for her tall boots. While she pulled them on and grabbed an old chore coat, John hunted for what they would need. Within a few minutes they had two lanterns, rubber gloves, a plastic tarp, and two buckets of hot water. Then they started toward the far end of the Detweiler property, each holding a lantern high to light their way. Not fifty yards from the house, Thomas caught up with them.

"*Danki, bruder.* Three sets of hands are better than two."

"Let's hope they will be enough," said Thomas.

"I don't hear anything," said Amy, as the first yellow streaks of dawn appeared in the east.

"I don't either, and that's a bad sign." John closed the gate behind them and turned his gaze skyward to pray for the cow in labor. He asked for a successful delivery, for the restored health of the mother, and for a strong, vigorous baby that could survive a Maine winter. He prayed for creatures who couldn't pray for themselves. Thomas was right. Nature often cleaned house, allowing weaker members to perish during droughts or to fall victim to wild predators. Even hungry coyotes have a right to eat in God's kingdom. But he hoped that *this* particular cow and calf would not perish.

When they finally found her, she was not only still alive but no longer bellowing in pain. She was on her side with a heaving belly slick with sweat, complaining only when a contraction advanced the baby along.

John spread the tarp over the wet ground as Amy gently patted the animal's soft head and Thomas stroked her flanks. After slipping on long gloves, John set about assessing her condition. He spotted the top of a tiny head, surrounded by four little hooves, poised to make a grand entrance. "We've no time to waste," he said, dropping down next to her tail. "Stand behind me, Amy, in case I slide and need some leverage." Thomas moved into Amy's former place, holding on to the cow's head. With Amy in position and Thomas helping to restrain the heifer, John bent his knees to brace himself against the ground and grasped the calf's protruding legs. With each contraction, John pulled, the cow mooed, and a brand-new life inched into the world.

Amy held one of the lanterns over his head, while the other sat on a rock to his left. She murmured, "Oh, my," not less than half a dozen times during the delivery. "I've never witnessed this before. *Daed* always asked for my cousins next door and then sent us girls into the house."

"At least her uterus hasn't torn," declared Thomas.

"It won't be long now." John sounded giddy with excitement, like any proud papa. With no small effort, along with a great push from the heifer, John pulled the calf free on the next contraction. It plopped unceremoniously onto the tarp.

"Is it dead?" asked Amy, bending down to assess. "It's not breathing."

"Patience, dear one. Fetch me one of those long feathery weeds."

"What?"

"Please, Amy. Bring me a weed and you'll see."

Amy carried a lantern to search the fence line and returned with an expression of accomplishment. "Here you go."

"Watch this."

Amy shone the light on the baby Holstein as John inserted the weed's feathery end into the calf's nose. He twirled it inside the nostril until he achieved the desired result.

Ah-choo! With a single sneeze, the calf expelled mucus from his nasal passages and took its first breath of autumn air.

"Praise the Lord," exclaimed Amy.

"Praise Him indeed," agreed Thomas. "I'm amazed." He slapped John on the back.

Within an hour, both bovine mother and child were on their

feet. She drank deeply from a bucket of cool water while the calf preferred fresh milk to quench its thirst. Weary yet exhilarated, Thomas, Amy, and John started down the long slope toward the house.

"I'm starving," John said, dragging the tarp behind them.

"Me too, but first I want a long hot shower." Amy swung her empty bucket like a milkmaid.

"I need to finish a few chores yet, so don't use all the hot water, you two." Thomas headed off toward the barn. "Good work, John, and thanks."

Once they were beyond Thomas's censuring eyes, John slipped an arm around Amy's waist.

"You were wonderful. You saved her, and I was so proud!" Impulsively Amy leaned over and kissed him. Not a peck on the cheek but a full, on-the-mouth kiss—short, but infinitely sweet.

The sky opened above John's head while angels trumpeted the astounding turn of events. Or…maybe the sun simply broke through the clouds and migrating ducks created a ruckus. Either way, he was one happy man as they walked through the pasture brushing shoulders. Inside the house, Amy headed straight for her shower. John pulled off his boots, cleaned their rubber slickers on the porch, and waited his turn to wash off the scent of cow.

When everyone was seated around the table with toast and eggs, Thomas cleared his throat to draw their attention. "You did good, little *bruder.* For your reward, I'll muck out the horse stalls today. And that cow and calf are yours when you and Amy buy a farm. You now have the beginnings of a herd." He scraped more eggs onto his plate.

"*Danki*, Thomas. That heifer and I have bonded. I can assure you she'll never end up on anyone's dinner plate." John poured himself another cup of coffee.

"I'll see you outside later. Oh, and no one got yesterday's mail, so I brought it up." Thomas nodded toward the counter.

John stared at the neat stack of mail folded inside the weekly newspaper. An ominous premonition robbed his joy as though someone had pulled a plug. He lingered in the kitchen until everyone left the room and then thumbed through the letters and bills. Sure enough, at the bottom of the stack was a letter for Amy from the same Maine town. Without thinking, he tore open the envelope and began to read.

> *My dearest Amy,*
>
> *I am grateful for your thoughtfulness. Seeing the letter in my mamm's own handwriting warmed my heart, but I'm not sure why you sent the death certificate of Leon Hilty. His life or death is of no concern to me, although I hope the Lord will have mercy on his soul. My life is here in Chestnut with Will, where I am thankful for a fine home and good health. I will continue to pray for you each night. Please remember, our door will always be open should you ever decide to visit.*
>
> *With loving regards,*
> *Aunt Prudence*

John's hand cramped from his tight grip on the paper. *Visit the home of a banned ex-Amish woman? Then the bishop might never agree to marry us!*

On the other hand, he knew that not telling Amy about the letter was the same as lying. Plus, he had heard that destroying mail was against English law.

On and on his intellect warred with his emotions. If he showed her this letter, she would certainly find out about the previous one. And he would prefer going to federal prison than facing the woman he loved in shame.

With a shaking hand and a sick feeling in his gut, he opened the door to the woodstove and tossed the letter inside. Prudence's words burst into flames and quickly disintegrated. A few minutes later, Amy returned to the kitchen with her hair dry from the living room fire. She flashed him a smile as she slipped on her *kapp*. John had never felt so unworthy of her love.

ॐ

For the first time since those first grim days following the house fire, Amy couldn't fall asleep at night. She tossed and turned, punched the pillow, and kicked off the covers. After twenty minutes of fitful dozing, she would awaken freezing cold and bundle up under the quilt. Then the whole process would repeat itself. She would climb from the tangled sheets, move her chair to the window, and pray until dawn. Each morning she asked for guidance and direction, yet her earnest prayers failed to bring her peace.

Finally, one late September morning, she realized what she had to do. "Wake up, Nora. We have a full day ahead of us." Amy shook her sister gently at first and then with determination. Nora tried to bury her head, but Amy yanked back the covers. "I need to go to town today. How would you like to come with me?"

"You're waking me this early for a trip to Harmony? I think I'll pass and see you at supper." Nora stuck her head beneath her pillow.

With one quick motion, the pillow flew across the room. "I thought you liked going to town. We can stop at the co-op." Amy purred like a contented cat in someone's lap.

Nora struggled to sit up, clutching the edge of the quilt. "Have you lost your senses, Amy? I'm cold. Let me sleep."

Amy released her grip but not her determination. "Please come with me today. There's something I must do that's important, and I don't want to go alone. Anyway, I thought you enjoyed spending time with Lewis when the store's not busy. It could be a way to chat to your heart's content."

Nora stopped struggling and climbed out of bed. "That's not

a very good idea." She shuffled barefoot to the wall pegs and then wrapped herself in her warm robe.

Amy retrieved the pillow from the floor and pressed it to her chest. "Don't you like Lewis anymore? What happened?"

Nora leaned back on the door. "I still like him. He's the sweetest man I've ever met." She whispered her admission as though afraid someone might overhear.

"Then what's wrong?" Amy knew instinctively she wouldn't like the answer.

"If I let this go any further, I'll end up here in Harmony for the rest of my life."

"Would that be so bad?" Amy plumped the pillow into place and drew up the sheet and quilt.

"*Jah*, it would." Nora crossed the floor to take Amy's hand. "Stop making the bed and look at me." Amy complied with the request. "As much as I love you, I can't see my future here—not now, and probably not ever."

For a moment Amy didn't know what to say. In her heart, she knew every woman must make certain decisions on her own. Then she forced a smile. "Okay, I'll stop needling you. Shall I arrange your trip back to Lancaster while I'm in town today? I need to consult schedules too, and they can arrange transportation to the bus station."

Nora looked startled. "Lancaster? No, I'm not going back there. And why are you interested in bus schedules?" She plopped down ungracefully on the just made bed.

"I'd planned to explain along the way." Because she'd discovered Sally's fondness for eavesdropping, Amy lowered her voice. "But I might as well tell you now." She sat next to her sister and whispered, "I've decided to visit Aunt Prudence."

"How can you do that? She hasn't even answered your letters."

"Maybe she's had no time to write. I'll take a bus to her town. If there's no bus route, I'll hire a driver to take me. They will know at the co-op how to arrange a trip that far." Amy formulated her plan as she talked, growing more confident by the minute.

Nora straightened her slumped posture. "Are you serious? Do you know how expensive this could get?"

"I don't care. I have money from my share of the farm sale. John shouldn't need my entire legacy to buy land."

"He certainly shouldn't. Besides it's your money. What did he say about the idea?"

"It's *our* money since we're engaged, but I certainly have a say as to how some of it should be spent. Regarding my visit, he doesn't know about it. I wanted to fine-tune the details before telling him. Otherwise, he'll worry without cause."

Nora scrambled to her feet, all thoughts of sleep forgotten. "I think it's a wise choice to get your ducks in a row first. Will you travel by yourself?"

"How would you like to come with me?"

Nora pondered that for less than three seconds. "No, I don't think so. Buses make me sick to my stomach and trigger migraines. How exactly will you find Aunt Prudence?"

"I'll start with her last known address. If she's not there, maybe a neighbor will know where she's gone. I'm not a child. I'm sure I can track her down."

"And if she moved to Kansas?"

"I don't know where Kansas is, but I'm sure buses and trains go there too."

"What if John says no when you tell him?" Nora appeared to be holding her breath.

"I'm sure he won't, not after I explain how important this is. And it's not really up for discussion anyway."

Nora grinned and swept open their bedroom door. "Go down and help Sally with breakfast. I'll be there as fast as I can. I've changed my mind about driving to Harmony. Whether I run into Lewis or not, this is one adventure I don't want to miss."

Within two hours and a minor amount of discussion about a trip into town, the two sisters were driving down the road at a good pace. Around them, farmers were preparing their fields for winter, even though October was still a few days away. Colorful leaves crunched under the buggy wheels while the trees glowed brightly from reflected sun. Both women had wrapped themselves in wool cloaks for the ride.

"This morning you mentioned you didn't want to return to Lancaster," said Amy, breaking the silence. "Have you given any thought as to where you would like to go?"

"If you report back that Chestnut is a beautiful town, maybe I'll move there."

"Be serious. You would know even fewer people there, and I know you're lonely here in Harmony."

Nora stared off at the distant hills that were less green than a week ago. "True, but I can't go back to Mount Joy."

"Why can't you?" asked Amy, sensing that whatever had been lurking beneath the surface was finally about to be revealed.

"This past spring I made a mistake—one I've deeply regretted ever since. I met a boy at singings from one district over. He took me home a couple times. I thought he truly loved me, so…I let things go too far." Nora shrank down inside her cloak, becoming barely visible.

"And you discovered he didn't love you?"

"No. He started taking someone else home from singings after I…surrendered to him."

The enormity of her sister's admission hit Amy like a brick. "You gave him what should have been saved for your future husband?" she gasped.

"I did." Nora's answer was flat and unemotional, as though she referred to someone else.

"Oh, no." Amy's response summed up all that could be said.

"I know. I'm sorry for what I did, but now you understand why

I haven't joined the church. And why I can't go back home. What if he's told people about my disgrace?"

"The disgrace also belongs to him. You didn't engage in sin alone."

"No, but it's always worse for the woman."

Amy couldn't argue with that conclusion, despite the unfairness. She focused on the road, hoping for some insight as how to handle this. Unfortunately, none occurred to her by the time they reached the general store parking lot. "I don't know how to advise you, Nora. During my upcoming trip I'll pray for guidance—for the right path for you and for me." Amy clutched her sister's hand tightly. "We'll find a way through this together."

⁂

"Perhaps you two should continue this conversation in private." Thomas's announcement shocked everyone at the dinner table, Amy most of all. Thomas never let them spend time alone. Now he was sending them outside together?

The news about her trip to find Aunt Prudence had not gone over well.

John stood abruptly, almost knocking over his chair. "*Jah*, let's take a walk."

Amy exchanged a look with Nora and headed to the pegs for her outerwear.

After opening the door for her, he followed her down the steps. "So that is where you and your sister went spur-of-the-moment this morning. All the way to the bus station?"

She tightened the cloak around her shoulders against the wind. "No, only to the co-op. They arranged transportation for me. We found out that a bus goes upstate to Bangor every Tuesday. From there it's only a twenty-minute taxi ride to Chestnut." They stopped walking at the goat enclosure.

"On a whim you're tracking down a shunned district member who might not even live in Chestnut by yourself?"

"Yes. Nora doesn't wish to travel with me, so I bought only one bus ticket."

"Nora wouldn't be much help anyway if you ran into trouble." John shifted his weight from one foot to the other.

Amy huffed out her breath. "Be that as it may, I'm going to find her. She's not just a *garden variety* shunned district member, John. She's my beloved aunt. I have little other family here in Maine."

He stepped closer and softened his voice. "I am your family now, Amy, and Thomas and Sally and the boys. What do you hope to accomplish if you do find her? She's not coming back to Harmony, and we're not moving up north. Let her remain a pleasant memory from your childhood."

For a moment, Amy watched a nanny goat chewing grass with her comical, green-stained teeth. Then she turned to face him. "No," she replied, without elaboration.

"What do you mean by no? What if I forbid you?" He removed his glasses to rub the bridge of his nose.

"You wouldn't forbid me, John Detweiler, because that would be a stupid thing to do. And you are not a stupid man. I want to make sure Prudence understands *when* Leon died so if she ever wants to return to Harmony, she knows she could start over."

He stared at her, stunned. "Do you no longer love me, Amy? Have you changed your mind about marrying me? If so, tell me now so I will stop pestering you like a pet dog." He unbuttoned the top button of his shirt to loosen his collar. "Is that why you've refused to look at properties for sale with me?"

"No, John, I've not fallen out of love with you. And I do want to look at farms with you, but it seems Sally always needs me to help with housework. I hate leaving her to manage with only Nora. I promise to visit possible properties as soon as I return from Chestnut…or from wherever Prudence happens to be. Please don't worry about me—I am a grown woman." Amy began to shake violently. "Right now, I'm cold, so I'm going inside. I will leave on Tuesday, but I'll be back as soon as possible." Amy turned on her heel and marched to the house. She knew if she remained he would continue to argue or attempt to reason with her. And, frankly, she'd had enough *reasonable* behavior to last a lifetime.

৯৩

"Please don't spy on them, *fraa*," said Thomas from the doorway. "You cannot hear what John and Amy are saying, and you shouldn't speculate."

Sally dropped the kitchen curtain back in place, only mildly flustered she'd been discovered. "I'm concerned for Amy's sake. You know how fond I've grown of her." She picked up a plate to wash.

Thomas carried his Bible to the table, deciding he would prepare for Sunday school here instead of in the living room. He was curious too, but it was John's actions that had him worried. "If there's something Amy wishes you to know, I'm sure she'll tell you tomorrow. How about fixing me a cup of tea with honey? If you join me, you won't look nearly so obvious." He patted the chair beside him.

"A wonderful idea!" Sally filled the kettle with water and then set out two mugs and the honey pot.

Before the water came to a boil, Amy pushed open the door. She looked pale, her teeth chattered, and her fingers were bright red. "If you don't need me anymore tonight, Sally, I think I'll read in my room." She dabbed her nose with a tissue.

"The dishes are almost done. How about I bring you a cup of tea later?" asked Sally.

"Please don't trouble yourself. I'll probably go to bed early." Amy disappeared up the stairs without another word.

Sally perched her hands on her hips. "Your brother upset her and that's not right."

Thomas closed his Bible without jotting down a single verse of Scripture. "Let me handle this. It's part of my job as minister."

"Do you need the wooden spoon?" she asked. "Your *mamm* said it worked on you and your *bruders*."

"No, and please leave the curtain closed. We don't want you getting chilled from pressing your face to the glass." Thomas shrugged into his coat. "I'll be back before you can even miss me."

Sally snorted as she grabbed the next bowl to wash. "Your tea will be on the table. I'll add an extra teaspoon of honey. It'll sweeten you up." She flashed a grin over her shoulder.

It would be the last smile Thomas would see that night.

He found John in the barn, brushing burrs from his horse's mane. A sole kerosene lamp burned from a hook on the post. Although his strokes were slow and methodical, the set of his jaw revealed a sour mood. "I'd like a word with you," said Thomas.

John glanced up and then resumed grooming the Morgan. "What would you like to talk about?"

"I didn't like how you raised your voice at the supper table tonight. You know better than that."

"*Mir leid.* It won't happen again." The brothers locked gazes before John turned back to the horse. "Amy's harebrained idea to go traipsing upstate pulled the rug out from under me."

"It shouldn't have." Thomas leaned against the stall wall.

"What do you mean?" John sounded suspicious.

"She's been obsessed with Prudence Summerton since the day she bought that quilt in town. After her *grossmammi*'s letters, finding her aunt seems like a logical progression."

"Not to me, it doesn't." John brushed with renewed vigor.

"That's because you don't like Prudence. And perhaps you're judging her for her past actions. That's not your place."

"It's hard not to, Thomas. She behaved selfishly without regard for anyone but herself. And I fear Amy might follow in her foot-steps. She knows my feelings and yet plans to travel to Chestnut anyway."

"You cannot and should not bully her."

"I don't want to bully anybody, but maybe if *you* told her not to go she would listen. You are her minister, and Prudence is shunned."

Thomas couldn't deny that John's request contained some logic, but he still couldn't comply. "Perhaps she would listen, but I won't tell her what to do—not as her pastor and not as her future brother-in-law. I want Amy to accept our *Ordnung* and our ways of her own choosing. I won't order her around just to make you happy."

"No, of course not. You won't lift a finger to help me, yet you let Elam come and go as he pleases with your blessings."

The accusation stung. "Not with my blessing, I assure you. The matter of Elam will be resolved in due time." Thomas heard the brittle edge to his tone, so he took several deep breaths. "And it wouldn't be helping you if I ordered Amy to cancel the trip. I fear it would only drive her further away. You must let her make her own choices or she'll not be happy as your wife."

John pressed the brush against the gelding's shiny coat. "A wife should mind her husband."

"But she will never become your wife until you grow up. You're not ready for marriage and neither is she. A marriage is a partner-ship based on love and respect, not an authoritative dictatorship. You must first surrender your own will to God if you want Amy to surrender hers."

John's eyes flashed with anger and then unexpectedly filled with tears. "*Daed* was always in charge of the Detweiler household. What other example do I have? *Mamm* seemed content in her role as his wife and our mother. I want my home to be as happy."

Thomas's heart rose into his throat hearing his brother's pain. "We have no idea how *mamm* and *daed* were during their courting days. I can only advise you regarding here and now." He reached for John's shoulder.

"*Danki*. I'll think on what you have said." John shook away his tears and his brother's touch and continued to brush.

Thomas could do nothing more than return to the house, praying those thoughts would lead John in the right direction.

ELEVEN

Naked, come to Thee for dress
Helpless, look to Thee for grace

B e sure to watch for moose," had been Nora's instructions.
        "Don't set your purse down in the bus station and walk
away from it," had been Sally's sage advice.

"Those batteries in your new cell phone will only hold a charge
for so long, so you'd better come back as soon as possible," had
been John's last-minute warning.

"Turn to the Lord for strength and guidance during the trip."
Amy had appreciated Thomas's words best of all. Who else did
she need as long as she had God? But in the taxi from Bangor to
the last known address of Prudence Summerton, Amy lost most
of her confidence. The town of Chestnut was little more than a
crossroads, with one blinking traffic light; a small grocery store;
one bank; a combination town hall, post office, and library in
one building; and a gas station that also sold Subway sandwiches.
Apparently, they also served ice cream in warm weather, but that

window had been shuttered. Picnic tables used to enjoy summertime snacks were stacked on their sides in preparation for winter.

Amy saw no evidence of anyone Amish living in the area—no
hitching posts or water troughs. Electric wires ran to every farm or
modest ranch house she passed. She began to doubt the wisdom of
her rash decision. What had seemed a bold and independent idea
in Sally's warm house now felt foolish and reckless in the backseat
of a car careening down narrow country roads at breakneck speed.
If she hadn't been both tired and hungry, maybe she could have
enjoyed the grandest adventure of her life.

The day had started at dawn when John drove her to the bus
stop in Harmony. He cautioned her about every possible danger,
from an early snowstorm to a bout of food poisoning. He'd purchased a prepaid cell phone at the hardware store and taught her
how to use it, even though she fully understood the device thanks
to English neighbors in Lancaster. The bus ride from Harmony to
Bangor took several jarring, stomach-churning hours. Then she
had to find a cab to take her to her aunt's address. She planned on
using the new phone to arrange a ride back to Bangor.

She should have had more than a hot dog to eat.

She wished she'd brought some kind of hostess gift.

And she should have figured out what to say to an aunt she'd
not seen in a decade.

"Here we are, miss," said the driver, turning into a rutted lane.

"Please don't leave right away. I'm not sure if the Summertons
still live here, and I don't wish to be stranded." Amy leaned forward to peer out the windshield.

"It said 'W. Summerton' on the mailbox." The driver smiled
into the rearview mirror. "Besides, I don't see any power lines to
the house. You might have found the right place." He stopped the
vehicle with a spray of gravel.

Amy squirmed on the seat. "I don't think my relatives are still
Amish, so that doesn't mean anything. You could take my bag from

the trunk, but please don't leave. I'll pay you what I owe you now, but I may need you to take me back to Bangor." Her voice cracked and sputtered out, exposing her insecurity.

He opened the back door for her. "I understand. Try to relax. Things will probably turn out okay." He flashed a grin as she stepped out. In front of her stood a white two-story house, very simple without shutters or porches, but late-blooming mums flanked both sides of the walkway.

Amy counted out the fare while the driver retrieved her bag, and then she climbed stone slabs to the front door. No one answered her first knock or her second or her fifth. She glanced over her shoulder. "No one seems to be home," she called, trudging down the steps.

"Try over there." The driver, who had been leaning against the taxi with crossed arms, pointed his finger toward the side of the house.

In the distance Amy spotted someone working in the garden. The stooped-over woman was shrouded in a heavy cloak and bonnet. *Could it possibly be?* A fist-sized lump rose up in Amy's throat as she took several mincing steps toward her. She hesitated and looked back again with childlike shyness.

"Go on," he encouraged. "I'll wait right here till you tell me otherwise."

"Turn to the Lord for your strength." Remembering Thomas's words, Amy forced her stiff legs toward the cabbage and squash patch. "Hello?" she said meekly while still fifteen feet away. "Prudence Summerton?"

The woman arched her neck to peer at Amy. Then she slowly straightened her back and dropped long-stemmed beets into a basket. "Amy? Amy King?" she asked. Breaking into a grin from one ear to the other, she opened her arms wide. "Goodness, I can't believe you've come all this way."

Amy dropped her purse in the tall grass as she ran. "You recognized me after all these years? I can't believe I haven't changed."

"Who else could it be?" Prudence dragged her across a garden row.

"Dear me, Aunt, I'm trampling your pumpkin runners." Amy allowed herself to be enfolded as her heart swelled to near bursting.

"Don't worry about them. I have tons of squash but few nieces who come to visit." Prudence held Amy against her wool cloak for a moment and then drew her back to arms' length. "My, you have indeed changed. You were in school the last time I saw you and as skinny as a reed. I don't think I would have known you if you hadn't written." She lifted Amy's chin with one finger to study her face.

"You got my letters? How many?" Amy tugged off her outer bonnet as her scalp started to perspire.

"Two. And I wrote back the next day both times." Prudence slipped an arm around Amy's waist. "Let's get you something to drink. Are you hungry? Wait until my Will gets back. He's cutting up deadfall in the hills for firewood."

Amy scooped up her purse as they walked by and then remembered the taxi. "I'll be right back." She took off running for the driveway. "It's her!" she shouted to him. "I found my family!"

"That big hug told me as much." His grin was almost as wide as her aunt's. He climbed back into the car. "Enjoy your visit. Call me when you're ready to return to the bus station."

"*Danki*—I mean, thank you." Amy waved her hand.

Prudence waited on the threshold, holding open the front door. "I can't believe you traveled alone. Your *mamm* would be proud. We would have met you in Bangor had we known you were coming."

Amy followed her inside, down a hallway, and into a large airy kitchen at the back of the house. Everything was tidy but austere. Judging by her aunt's appearance and the sparse furnishings, the Summertons were still Plain. "When I received no replies to my letters, I took a chance on finding you. I didn't want you to tell me not to come."

Prudence pointed at a chair. "I can't imagine why my letters never reached Harmony, but I wouldn't try to keep you away. Tell me about your trip."

Over two cups of coffee, a bowl of vegetable soup, and a tuna sandwich, Amy described the bus ride and her life at the Detweilers, minimizing but not avoiding John's reluctance for her to come.

"John is wisely being cautious. He wishes nothing to impede your acceptance in your new district. I'm banned, Amy. Nothing will ever change that."

"But that's why I had to see you. If you got my letters, then you saw the death certificate of your first husband. You didn't marry Mr. Summerton until *after* Uncle Leon had died. You're no adultress." Amy had spoken the harsh word without thinking. "I beg your pardon. I don't mean to be offensive."

Prudence set a pot of steeping tea on the table. "You didn't offend me, child. No one can call me anything I haven't called myself." Her face paled from the unpleasant memory.

"Well, I'm here to set things right."

She patted Amy's hand. "Everything *is* all right, so your work is done. Now you can relax and enjoy yourself."

At that moment a tall bear of a man entered through the back door. He hung up his hat and raked a calloused hand through thinning grey hair. "Who is this, *fraa*?" He studied Amy curiously.

"My sister Edna's oldest girl has come to see how I'm faring."

"That's what I supposed." He nodded at Amy while taking the seat across the table. "Supper 'bout ready?"

Prudence laughed hard enough to set her *kapp* ribbons swinging. "Supper? I just reheated soup for Amy and fixed her a sandwich. I've been nibbling along with her."

Will Summerton leaned back in his chair. "A bowl of soup and sandwich sounds fine to me, providing you have some pie left. You can fuss over dinner tomorrow."

When he smiled fondly at his wife, Amy relaxed. She'd been right to come. Time hadn't changed her aunt. With one glance, anybody could tell the woman was happy here. "I'm pleased to meet you...*oncle* Will."

Later that evening, after Will had gone to bed, Amy asked Prudence the question that had been bothering her. They sat in the front room, quietly rocking next to the woodstove after catching up on the news of each other's lives.

"Why did you divorce Uncle Leon? Amish couples don't ever get divorced."

"I wondered when you would get around to asking that."

Amy felt heat climb up her neck into her face. "If you'd rather not—"

"Don't be silly," she interrupted. "You deserve the truth after what you undertook to get here." *Clack, clack, clack.* The wooden runners of her chair rolled over the polished floor. "I divorced Leon because he often drank. And when he got drunk, he used to beat me—sometimes with his belt, sometimes with his fists. He'd say he was sorry the next day once he sobered up, but it never changed anything. It started up again the next time he bought a bottle. Folks would pretend they didn't see the bruises, or they would make excuses for him."

Clack, clack, clack.

"Why not just live apart? Our *Ordnung* permits that in certain cases." Amy spoke with the barest whisper.

"Because he would find out where I was staying and make me come home. Under alcohol's influence, Leon was evil. One day I decided I'd had enough. I didn't care if they shunned me. I went to the police for a restraining order. They got me a legal aid lawyer, and she found me a place to stay—in Harmony. Then I met Will. That's the story in a nutshell."

Clack, clack, clack.

Amy stopped rocking. "But you continue to be Plain. How can that be?"

Prudence's face filled with compassion. "You're still so young.

My brethren might have turned me away, but I never turned from my faith."

"Are there other Amish around Chestnut?"

"*Nein*. We have no district. Will and I hold nightly devotions, and on Sundays he reads aloud from Scripture. We sing the hymns we can remember too, although our bad voices don't make much of a joyful noise."

Amy reached for her aunt's hand. "Then you two should return to Harmony. All can be forgiven if you repent on your knees. You can become part of a district again...and part of my family. Nora isn't very happy in Maine. She might go back to Lancaster or move elsewhere. I'd love to have you close by." She clamped her jaw shut before she said too much, such as *John might not let me visit again after we're wed since you're banned.*

Prudence squeezed her hand tightly. "As much as I would love to take your *mamm*'s place in your life, Amy, we are content here." Tears filled her soft brown eyes.

"But the Bible instructs us to live in community with other Christians, not apart from each other like hermits." Amy's desperation rose in her voice.

Her aunt reflected on this before replying. "I cannot come back and take the kneeling vow because I would have to repent for marrying Will. And if the truth be told, I'm not sorry. If I had to do it all over, I would do the same."

At that, Amy couldn't think of a single thing more to say.

❧

Cold drops of water trickled down Thomas's neck. He repositioned his felt hat and tugged up his collar to no avail. The way the wind whipped the rain around, he would find no protection from the sudden storm. The sooner he finished fixing the break in the fence, the sooner he could dry out in his warm kitchen. After one last twist with the pliers, tightening the top wire, he restored a barrier between his Holsteins and the rest of Waldo County—at least until his bull decided again to judge for himself whether the grass was greener elsewhere.

On his way back to the house, movement caught Thomas's attention from the corner of his eye. He turned his face into a blast of cold rain and spotted Sally's laundry still on the clothesline. Shirts, pants, and towels flapped in the wind, certainly wetter now than after Sally had cranked them through the wringer. Thomas looked down at the flagstone path just in time to avoid calamity. Aden's blue plastic wheelbarrow, purchased last summer at a garage sale, had been left on the walkway. His son used the toy to haul stones in between the rows in Sally's garden, providing hours of helpful distraction for mother and child alike. Now discarded and filled with muddy water, it almost sent Thomas stumbling.

He stomped his boots on the porch, shed his soggy coat while still outdoors, and stepped into a scene of chaos. A pot of something green and sticky bubbled and spattered on the stove. Jeremiah wailed from his cradle. Aden sat at the kitchen table, playing in rather than eating his oatmeal. And Sally? His *fraa* was up to her elbows in flour, baking powder, and solid shortening.

Thomas toed off his boots to leave on the rubber mat. He strode to the stove, waiting to converse until after pouring a strong, hot cup of coffee fortified with two spoonfuls of sugar. Then he cleared his throat. "It's quite a downpour outside, and you forgot about your laundry on the line. Will you have to start from scratch?" He watched her over the mug's rim.

"I don't know," she replied, not glancing up from kneading dough.

"I nearly broke my neck on Aden's wheelbarrow. Why did he not put it in the shed or at least tuck it under the porch?"

"Dunno." Her single word expressed no reaction whatsoever. But with the mention of the child's name, Sally looked at her son and said in rapid-fire *Deutsch* the equivalent of "Stop playing with it and eat!" Then she slapped the dough ball down on her floured baking board, sending up a white cloud into the air.

Thomas took a long, slow sip of coffee. With Amy King gone for two days, his household had deteriorated into worse shape than before the sisters' arrival. And his normally cheerful wife had turned snappish and sullen, a condition he was rapidly tiring of.

"Where is Nora on this fine autumn morning?" He leaned back on the counter and focused his attention on her.

"I don't know, *ehemann*. Would you mind asking me a question I *can* answer?" Her eyes flashed with anger when their gazes met, and then she stared down at the piecrust.

In that instant he'd seen the quiver of her lips and knew she was on the verge of tears. "All right, I will," he said mildly. "But first I'll get you some help for setting this kitchen to rights." Thomas walked to the foot of the stairs and called in a voice that could be heard in the attic, "Nora, come down here, please!" He waited only a moment for the sound of stirring overhead. Then the young woman appeared on the landing and slowly descended. Her blood-shot eyes were deeply shadowed by dark smudges—a sure sign she was suffering from a migraine.

"I'm sorry if you feel poorly," he said gently, "but Sally needs help."

"Of course, Thomas," she murmured. "The pills I took should take effect soon." Nora stepped into the room, took a quick perusal, and hurried to Aden's high chair. The boy giggled and raised his arms over his head. "You must not be hungry anymore or you wouldn't make such a mess." In a blink of an eye she lifted him from the chair, grabbed up Jeremiah, and disappeared into the bathroom, presumably to give both boys baths.

Silence never sounded so sweet to Thomas's ears.

Sally remained bent over her pie dough, no longer rolling it out but merely staring at the mound.

"Sit down a minute with me. Pour yourself some coffee."

She complied but didn't look at him until seated with her beverage. "What's your next question?" she added. "I'll do my best to figure out a response. I must admit I have grown too dependent on Amy these past weeks. That won't do. Soon she and John will wed and move into their own place." One corner of her mouth lifted.

Thomas wrapped his fingers around the mug, ignoring the handle. "Are you happy here in Harmony with me?"

Her half smile vanished, replaced by fear and uncertainty. "What kind of question is that?"

"It's simple enough, Sally. Are…you…happy?"

"Of course I'm happy. I love you, Thomas, even if I don't ever say it. Plain folk don't go around saying 'I love you' as often as 'Hello' or 'Goodbye' or 'Have a nice day' like *Englischers*." She laughed uneasily.

"*Jah*, I know you love me, but I was thinking maybe you don't want us to remain in Harmony. You were overheard going on and on about your former life in Paradise to Nora and Amy."

"Was that you listening?"

"No, it was John."

Sally relaxed visibly as she swallowed some coffee. "I didn't mean anything about my reminiscences. Nora seemed in need of a pep-up story, so I provided one. But I don't have a hankering to live anywhere else than right here." She rose and returned to rolling piecrusts, assuming her response would satisfy him.

It didn't. "If you are happy here and wish to stay, then you need to act like it. Look at this kitchen." He gestured around the chaos with a wave of his hand. "Once again you've assumed all the tasks for the lunch after Sunday school instead of lining up helpers. I notice you're even making pies."

Sally blushed a shade of scarlet. "Dora is sick with a bug. I told her I would bake."

Thomas set down his mug. "That's all the more reason to implement Amy's suggestion. Why haven't you done that yet? I thought the women were going to sign a list of who would cook what."

She dug her hands into her apron pockets. "I've been afraid. What if they don't like my categories?"

"Then they can make up new ones. I see you take the suggestions of Amy and Nora readily enough, either with a *jah* or *nein*, without getting nervous about the conversation. And those Lancaster women seem to have a better way of doing everything," he added wryly.

She stopped rolling. "That's because I really like Amy and Nora, and I can tell they like me too. So it's different." She placed a palm on the table for support.

"You've let them get close and allowed them to like you. Other folks you practically hold off with a clothes pole."

Sally opened her mouth to object but changed her mind. She chewed on a fingernail instead. "Let me think about this a moment."

"You should think about it a long while, and if you come up with the right solution, this might be the last Saturday you find yourself in such a state." He gestured around the room again. "Reach out and make friends, Sally. Once this district gets to know you, they can't help but like you."

Sally abandoned her baking and came to him. She squeezed onto his lap, wrapped her arms around his neck, and hugged him the way Aden loved to do. "*Danki*, Thomas."

He patted her back and whispered in her ear. "If you give your heart freely, it won't matter who's the best butcher, baker, or candlestick maker. And even an ill-placed fly cannot ruin an otherwise perfect day."

❧

Nora peered out the living room window into a dismal down-pour. It had been raining all day, and cold gusts blew in anytime a person opened a door. Jeremiah slept soundly in his cradle after his last feeding, while Aden played on the rug with wooden blocks. On a happier note, her headache had abated and the Detweiler storm cloud in the kitchen appeared to have blown over. Sally hummed as she fixed ham-and-cheese sandwiches to accompany the split pea soup for tomorrow's lunch. Nora had volunteered her help after bathing the boys, but Sally insisted the ironing needed more immediate attention. So she'd been ironing near the window for almost two hours, after she'd rewashed the load of laundry and rehung it on the covered porch lines.

At least it was toasty warm in here. Thomas kept both the kitchen and living room fires burning hot so warm air would reach their bedrooms for comfortable sleeping. He doted on Sally, that was for sure. If her *daed* had entered a house that looked the way Sally's had today, he would have thundered, "Does something ail you, *fraa*? If not, I suggest you turn this pigpen back into a respect-able room." And her *mamm* would have replied, "Now that I've chased my muck-makers outdoors, Samuel, I'll have this room normal before you can wash the dust off." And *mamm*'s disasters couldn't hold a candle to Sally's.

Thomas had remained calm, never raising his voice or ruffling a single feather. Nora hoped John would treat Amy just as indul-gently, or at least as respectfully as her *daed* had treated *mamm*. The image of her parents sitting together during evening prayers flick-ered across her mind, bringing a wave of painful emotion. *Do not cry. Your headache will come back.*

Nora folded the final shirt, placed it on John's pile, and mas-saged the muscles of her lower back. John had barely said five words to her since Amy left to track down Aunt Prudence. Actu-ally, she agreed with him that the idea was harebrained, but if Amy felt so strongly, no one should interfere. Far be it from her to talk a sister out of a far-fetched notion, because lately her own actions hadn't been too rational.

Sally bustled into the room, interrupting Nora's daydreaming. She gawked at the clothes neatly stacked into piles. "You're done already? My, you've been busy." She grinned widely, revealing a gold cap on a back tooth.

"Idle hands make easy work for the devil," said Nora.

Sally flinched. "Our bishop says we should never invoke the evil one's name. It's not a good idea."

"I'll do my best to remember that." *Along with everything else on the long list of Harmony rules,* she added mentally. "What can I help you with?"

"Nothing. We are in fine shape for supper and for the after–Sunday school meal. I'll ride herd on these two if you'd like to take a nap."

Nora shrugged as she spotted a tall basket of umbrellas and carved walking sticks. "*Nein, danki.* I think I'll bundle up and stretch my legs. Fresh air will do me good."

"There's a plastic rain poncho hanging on the back porch. Unfortunately, it's bright blue. The outlet had sold out of black."

The sudden pop-pop-pop of gunfire drew Nora to the window. "That sounds close by. Who's shooting behind the house?"

Sally cocked her head to listen. "Oh, that's just Elam. Don't worry about him. He'll be able to tell the difference between you and a squirrel. He's hunting for his supper."

Nora pictured the cute, furry creatures with bushy tails and shuddered. "Why on earth would he choose to eat a rodent instead of sitting down to table with us?"

Sally reached in and lifted Jeremiah from his bed. "Who knows? I stopped trying to figure out that man long ago. Elam digs up his own potatoes, onions, carrots, and turnips from the garden and cooks a huge pot of squirrel stew on the old stove in the basement. He'll eat from that for days and then go hunting for a rabbit or a possum."

Nora wrinkled her nose, just as a bunny would. She grabbed an umbrella from the basket and followed Sally down the hall and into the kitchen. "I'll be careful to give him a wide berth."

"You do that," Sally said as she headed into the bathroom with her son.

But once Nora was outside, the sight of Elam standing tall and straight in the harvested field drew her like a magnet. His long hair danced across his shoulders in the wind, while his skin looked ruddy and tanned from many hatless hours on the logging crew. Meandering in his direction, she kept the umbrella well positioned.

Elam wore an *Englischer*'s gray flannel shirt tucked into black plain trousers with suspenders, work boots, and no coat. Rain dripped from his black felt hat, yet he didn't seem to notice. A double-barreled shotgun lay across his forearm.

"Aren't you freezing?" she called, not wishing to startle him.

He turned with a smile, but he didn't seem surprised to see her. "You're a brave woman to approach a man with a loaded gun. And no, I'm not the least bit cold. You'd better waltz back to Pennsylvania, Miss King, if you're cold in this kind of weather. You're in for a rude awakening in another month or two."

She advanced until she was just a few feet away. "I'm quite comfortable with my wool cloak, a rain slicker, and this." She shook the umbrella, sending water droplets in all directions. "And I'm confident your eyes can tell me apart from a squirrel."

Elam faced her squarely then. His slow gaze started at her toes and traveled up to meet her eyes. "I would have my hands full getting you into my cook pot." He winked one dark eye.

An odd sensation spiked up her spine, but she ignored it. "Why on earth would you eat rodent stew when you can sit down to Sally's chicken-and-dumplings? Plus, we're having creamed succotash and sweet pickles, and cherry cobbler for dessert." Nora shifted her weight to the opposite hip.

Delight replaced his former neutral expression. "My, that

sounds downright delicious!" Elam yanked off his hat and slapped it against his leg. More water flew everywhere. His hair hung in thick waves around his head, growing damper by the moment.

It took all her effort not to stare at his handsome, rugged features. "And eating with your family will allow some hapless squirrel to return to *his* family tonight." Nora couldn't hold back a smile.

"I haven't seen a critter in more than an hour, so don't worry about possible orphan squirrels." He laughed with a careless, near-giddy sound. "And if the right person were to ask me, I'd come willingly to the Detweiler table."

It took slow-as-molasses Nora nearly half a minute to comprehend his meaning. "Being that I'm a guest, it hardly feels right, but...would you please come to supper tonight, Elam? I believe there's room for you, and we'll certainly have enough food." She smiled sweetly even as her knees knocked beneath her skirt.

He slicked a hand through his wet hair and repositioned his hat. "I'll get myself presentable right now so I don't get under ornery Sally's skin by being late." He cracked open the barrel and removed both shotgun shells. He hollered toward the silent, distant hills, "You, squirrels, can relax now and come out to play." Then he walked toward the house, leaving Nora staring at his back for a long while.

That night Elam appeared at the table in proper Amish attire, except for his lack of a haircut. He bowed his head in silent prayer when everyone else did. If Thomas, John, or Sally were surprised by his appearance, they hid it well. Sally's only question was, "All the furry animals evade your eagle eye today, *bruder*?"

"*Jah*, they bested me, I must say." Elam reached for the bowl of dumplings.

"What is the north country like, Elam?" asked Nora, followed by, "How many moose have you seen? Have you caught sight of those funny-looking striped cows that I saw in a postcard at the co-op? What are the *Englischers* you work with like? Do they cuss, chew wads of tobacco, and then spit in the dirt? Who does the cooking while you're logging? Does the crew ever eat deer meat?"

Nora peppered Elam with questions throughout the meal. In each case he answered politely without much embellishment. Each of his responses triggered another spate of inquiries from her. In her mind, life sounded so free, so unrestricted up north.

"Calm yourself, sister," said John during dessert. "You don't even like snow, and soon the northern counties will be buried by several feet of it."

Nora turned to face her brother-in-law-to-be. She'd almost forgotten other people sat at the table other than Elam Detweiler. But John's flushed face and Thomas's pale appearance brought her back to reality. Neither man was smiling. In fact, she'd seen Jeremiah, hungry and with a wet diaper, looking happier.

"True enough," she replied. "I'm just curious about other places in Maine besides Harmony." From the corner of her eye, Nora caught a glimpse of Elam. That particular Detweiler brother was downright elated.

TWELVE

Foul, I to the fountain fly
Wash me, Savior, or I die

Nora stood by her bedroom window, unable to sleep. Men sure had a habit of making a big deal out of nothing. John and Thomas had both overreacted to her questioning Elam about upstate Maine. She wasn't about to move to moose country to take up backpacking in the wilderness or apply for work on a logging crew. She simply wanted to find out if the rest of Maine was as dull as this part. Maybe if she had somebody who cared about her, like Amy or Sally, things might be different. But single women had few opportunities here, and after the mistakes she'd made last spring, single might be all she would ever be.

Beyond the pane of glass lay a dark and silent world. A full moon rose in the east, illuminating the fields and meadows. Nora pushed upon the window a few inches to listen but received only a chillier room for her efforts. In Lancaster, night sounds used to comfort her whenever sleep wouldn't come. Barking dogs, slamming car doors when the neighbor returned from a night shift, faraway train whistles, and the constant hum of truck traffic on Interstate 30. Here in Maine, she heard *nothing*—even dogs, crickets, and hoot owls went to bed early and slept soundly. Couldn't John have picked a happy medium between constant-tourist hubbub and quiet as a tomb?

Nora closed the window, and as she turned away a flicker of light caught her attention. She focused on the back pasture until she spotted it again—a tiny red dot where there were no outbuildings or road. Without blinking, Nora watched the soft glow approach. Then a man stepped into a ring of moonlight just beyond the house. Clad in dark clothing with his hat brim pulled low, he approached the outside entrance to the cellar. Nora was certain it was Elam. He dragged on a cigarette and then tossed it into the weeds by the steps.

He was smoking—a habit frowned upon even in more liberal Lancaster. She couldn't imagine what the Harmony bishop or Thomas or John would say about that. Sally certainly had few nice things to say about the youngest Detweiler brother. Usually she rolled her eyes or made a clucking noise with her tongue whenever someone mentioned his name.

Nora had read that smoking caused everything from bad breath to lung cancer, yet watching Elam somehow imbued the nasty habit with an odd appeal. He was like no other man she knew, here or back home. Men either left the Amish faith or conformed to the district's ways once they left *rumschpringe* behind. But Elam seemed to be Amish by his own set of rules—a freethinker in a culture that didn't encourage independence. A black sheep. Shivering in the cold room, she slipped under her quilt to contemplate the puzzling man.

Why did he sleep in the cellar instead of his own room? Why had he come to supper when he usually avoided his family? And where had he been in the middle of the night, on foot, while everyone else slept like the dogs, crickets, and owls? Without her sister to rein her in, Nora decided to search out Elam in his private, subterranean world the first chance she got.

&

The next day Nora's investigation proved easier than expected. Thomas announced at breakfast that he and Sally would visit the other minister to discuss district business. "Would you like me to watch Jeremiah and Aden for you?" she asked over her plate of scrambled eggs.

Sally shook her head. "*Danki,* but no. We'll be gone most of the day, so I'll need to feed the baby. And Aden loves to play with their son. Being with someone his own age will do him good. Maybe he'll stop seeing food as playthings."

"Would you like to come with us?" asked Thomas. "Otherwise, you'll be alone on the farm. John left to visit more properties for sale."

"*Nein, danki.* I have a book I've been meaning to read."

"Could you put the chickens in the oven around three o'clock? I've already stuffed them with celery-and-sage dressing."

Nora nodded. "I'd be happy to," she said, grateful that Sally had already prepared them for roasting. "I'll cook some vegetables and maybe boil some cranberries for a relish."

After the Detweilers had loaded up and left, Nora headed into the bathroom for a hot shower and a fresh dress. She chose one of her Lancaster favorites because no one remained to criticize the unsuitable shade of color. Half an hour later, she was tiptoeing toward the outdoor entrance to the cellar. The door lay wide open, probably to catch some of the last sunny weather after a string of rainy days. Nora crept down the stone steps like a thief after a king's gold. Her stealthy approach fooled no one, however.

"Who goes there—friend or foe?" a deep male voice boomed from the unseen recesses.

"Friend, I think," she called, steadying herself against the damp walls. "It's Nora King. I'd like a word with you."

Elam's face appeared in the opening at the bottom. "Oh, Nora *King*, as opposed to one of the dozen other Noras around here." He smirked, showing off two deeply-set dimples.

"Smarty-pants." She marched down the steps as indignation bolstered her confidence. "Can't you just say 'Hello' or 'How are you?' like most decent folk?"

"As you probably suspected, I'm not a decent sort of person, but as you're my first visitor down here, I'll say anything you like." Elam bowed low. "Hello, Nora. How are you?" He straightened up and looked her in the eye. "Are you breathing easier with my brother gone for the day?"

"I breathe fine every day, *danki*. Thomas doesn't bother me," Nora said as she turned slowly to assess his living quarters. He had a metal bed with a ragged patchwork quilt, an oak dresser with missing knobs, a stack of towels by a plastic stationary tub, a kerosene lamp hanging from an overhead beam, and a second lamp at his bedside. His table had been fashioned out of apple crates. An array of magazines was spread across the coverlet, with two or three open to glossy photos. She walked toward them curiously.

"What have you got here?" She reached the bed before remembering some English men liked to look at pictures of half-dressed women when their *mamms* or wives weren't around. But she needn't have worried. Every one of the pictures was of a vehicle of some sort—car, truck, or motorcycle. Some sported flashy stripes or orange flames, shiny chrome, or huge knobby tires to raise the vehicle feet off the ground. Every imaginable paint color was represented in the photographs.

"You found out my secret. I'm afraid I have developed a

fondness for more horsepower than my Standardbred can deliver."
He plopped down on his bed and pawed through the magazines.

Nora picked up one that showcased a two-seater convertible
with a name she couldn't pronounce. "How much would this little thing cost?" She shoved the cover under his nose.

He didn't need to read the fine print. "About seventy-five thousand." He leaned back on his elbows, completely relaxed.

"Seventy-five thousand dollars?" she squawked. "According to
John, you could practically buy a farm around here for that."

"True enough, but that sports car would be way more fun."

She thumbed through another issue. "How much for this van?"
She held up another photo.

"Less than half that much, somewhere around thirty grand."

"That makes no sense. The little car will only fit two people,
while the van will seat at least eight comfortably." She clutched the
magazine to her chest.

Elam didn't laugh or make fun of her. Instead, he spoke in
a patient voice. "It's hard to explain. You are paying for a high-
performance engine and an expensive interior with leather seats
and fancy instrumentation. But most of all you're buying the pres-
tige that's associated with the automaker's name. This German
company will make very few of the sports car, so that makes it
especially pricey."

Nora nodded to indicate she understood when, in fact, she
didn't at all. "I think I would rather buy the van with plenty of
room." She tried not to stare at the man lying across the bed on
his elbows. She focused on his hairbrush on the apple crate. It was
loaded with long strands of shiny dark hair. They looked as though
they would be silky to touch.

"Maybe if you rode in the convertible just once, you would
change your mind." Elam rose and began stacking the magazines
into a pile.

Her heart thudded against her chest wall as she watched him. "Where did you get all of those?"

"From the nice librarian in Harmony. Every six months they throw out the old issues, and she saves them for me."

"Doesn't she find it strange? You being Amish and all?"

"If she does think that she hides it well."

When he stopped tidying up, they were uncomfortably close. Nora felt a sensation wavering between excitement and fear in her belly. "I saw you smoking last night from my window," she blurted out.

"Now you know two of my deep, dark secrets, and I know none of yours."

"I don't have any secrets," she said, sounding disappointed.

"Everyone has secrets, whether they are Amish, English, or Eskimo. Can I trust you with mine?" He cocked his head to one side.

"I don't know. I guess so." She backed up until she bumped into the washtub.

He stretched his arms over his head and touched the beams. "Why are we in a damp old basement on such a fine day? Let's take a walk, Nora King, down to the river. After all, Thomas isn't here to say we can't."

"Why not?" she asked, pulling her bonnet from her pocket. Without giving it a single thought, she ran up the steps into the bright sunshine.

As they strolled through harvested cornfields toward the woods, Nora saw Thomas's farm from a new perspective. Maybe it was because sunshine warmed her back or because hawks soaring above lifted her spirits too. But most likely it was because Elam asked questions, encouraging Nora to talk about herself.

Once they left sight of the Detweiler house, he seemed to relax even more. "I heard a rumor you're courting Lewis. Is it true?"

They had been casually comparing Lancaster to Harmony, so the offhand question took her by surprise. "No, it's not true. At least, not anymore," she stammered. "Lewis is very nice, but courting him means staying here for the rest of my life. And I'm not sure I want that."

Elam grabbed at an overhead branch, sending down a cascade of red leaves on their heads. "So you're not content having lived in only two states? Where do you wish to go next?" His words contained no sarcasm whatsoever.

"I don't know...maybe Ohio or Missouri—or Germany, to the town where they made that little red car. I wonder if Germans have ever seen Amish people."

"Probably not, so everyone will learn something new." Elam took her arm as the lane sloped downhill to the river. A strong current carried dead leaves and branches onto the next logjam. Close to the water's edge, he stopped and drew a cigarette from the pack in his jacket pocket. He lit it, inhaled, and released a puff of smoke with a satisfied sigh.

"What do those things taste like?" She had to peer up at him because he was at least half a foot taller.

"Like smoke. Not very good."

"Could I try one?"

He considered her. "I don't think so. You won't like it, Nora. Besides, it's a nasty habit I really wish I never started."

"Please? You don't want me to confuse you with Thomas, do you?" She arched her neck and balled her hands into fists.

His eyebrows lifted. "No, I surely don't." He shook out one from the pack. "Suit yourself, but don't come complaining to me later."

"I won't." She studied both ends of the cigarette.

"Put the filter end in your mouth and light the tobacco."

He flicked his green lighter and Nora leaned forward close

8194MARY ELLIS

enough to smell something spicy. *His aftershave? His hair tonic? Is that why his hair is so shiny?* She tried to identify the scent while drawing air through the cigarette into her lungs. Suddenly, the noxious smoke caused her to gag and cough.

"What did I tell you?" Elam folded her arms over his broad chest. "I said you wouldn't like it." He tried to pull the offender from her lips.

But Nora quickly turned her back on him. "I took too big a puff. Let me try a smaller one." Nora took several short puffs and tried to hold the smoke inside, to no avail. She coughed and sputtered same as before.

"Give me that thing before it makes you sick." He reached around to take it away from her.

But the damage had been done. Without warning, the leaf-strewn riverbank tilted before her eyes. Her belly churned as though she'd eaten something spoiled. Nora took a few steps toward the thick holly and mountain laurel bushes that grew nearby. Yet privacy during her personal humiliation wasn't to be. Eggs, orange juice, and two cups of coffee surged up her burning throat.

Without a shred of dignity or decorum, Nora vomited into the weeds and mud at the water's edge. And she had to listen to Elam's hoots of laughter all the way back to Sally's house.

༄

John set down his ax to catch his breath. He gazed at the enormously long pile of stacked, split firewood with little satisfaction. He needed to stop distracting himself with physical labor and figure out what to do before it was too late.

Thomas's admonishment in the barn had been an eye-opener for him. It wasn't Sally's stories of her Missouri adventures turning Amy's head. And the problem wasn't Amy's sister. Either

Nora would adjust to Harmony's rules or the bishop would send her back to Pennsylvania. The problem was himself. Every time Thomas turned around, he and Amy were arguing about something. The bishop would never agree to marry them if they couldn't get along. Although he would have preferred Amy not to have visited her aunt, what was done was done. He hoped the bishop wouldn't make an issue of the trip during their marital counseling...if he ever scheduled their sessions. Prudence Summerton was banned and wouldn't be moving back to town. The only threat she presented was the one he created from his insecurity.

For the third time that hour, John withdrew his cell phone from his pocket and checked for new messages and the battery strength. He'd ridden his horse to the gas station in Harmony just to charge up the battery, fearful he would miss Amy's call. But he hadn't. She called yesterday to say she was coming home this evening. She provided few details regarding the visit, only that she'd found her aunt at her last known address.

It was time to put this ordeal behind them. He aimed to welcome the woman he loved home the best way he knew how. Burying his ax into the chopping block, John marched to the house to shower and start preparations. He would enlist Sally's help and maybe Nora's too. Tonight Amy would wonder why she'd traveled north in the first place, once he started acting like the man she'd fallen in love with.

Three hours later, when she climbed from the bus, John could barely restrain himself. How he yearned to lift her up into a bear hug. She looked so small and helpless bundled in the heavy cloak with her oversized bonnet. But because some of other passengers were Amish ladies, he didn't dare. Instead, he stretched out his hand to shake. "Welcome home, Amy. How was the ride? Are you hungry? Dinner is ready for us back at the house." He rattled on like Aden after a nap.

Amy handed him her bag with her left hand and shook with her right. "I'm fine, John, and eager to be home. *Jah*, I'm hungry, but I hope Sally hasn't held dinner for me. The rest of the family will be starved by the time we get back." They walked toward the buggy shoulder to shoulder in the brilliant autumn sunshine.

"*Nein*. I told everyone to eat because I planned a surprise for your homecoming." He helped her step up to the seat.

"What are you up to, John Detweiler? This doesn't sound like you."

"If I told you, it wouldn't be a surprise, would it? Just be patient and all things will be revealed. Tell me about your aunt...and Will Summerton." He clucked to the horse to get the buggy moving.

"She's well and still lives at the address provided by the bishop. She was working in her garden when I arrived. She knew who I was because she'd received both my letters."

John focused his gaze on the road ahead, keeping the buggy as far to the right as possible.

Amy tugged off her outer bonnet once they left the co-op parking lot. "She received Leon Hilty's death notice but hadn't realized the significance. Yet when I explained that her marriage occurred after her first husband's death, it didn't make an ounce of difference to her."

"Is that right?" he asked, feigning interest. The sooner they finished talking about Prudence, the sooner they could discuss important topics, such as the farms he'd seen.

"She said it didn't matter. She would have to repent for marrying Will to be restored to the Harmony community. And she's not sorry—not one little bit."

"You can't tell other people how to live their lives, Amy. You can only hope they make the right choices."

"I know that, but it's not fair. She left Uncle Leon in the first place because he beat her. He used to get drunk and then strike her—many times, not just once or twice."

John hated to hear about abuse. Women should be treated with respect and kindness, considering that God made them the weaker of the sexes. He felt a stab of guilty remorse about burning Prudence's letters. It had seemed like the right thing to do at the time, like patching the hole in the roof before it started to rain. "I'm sorry to hear that, Amy, but even though she had good reason to divorce, we can't go around changing the *Ordnung* to suit individual circumstances."

"I know, but I find this incredibly sad." She leaned her head on his shoulder.

The gesture sent his blood pumping through his veins twice as fast. "Perhaps she'll change her mind someday," he murmured.

"They still live Amish. They wear Plain clothing, don't use electricity, and keep the old traditions. They have nightly devotions with the German Bible and try to hold preaching every other Sunday, even though they have no district."

"They didn't turn English when they were banned?"

"No. They still kept their faith."

He nodded and then tried to steer conversation away from the Summertons. He succeeded in getting Amy to talk about the bus ride. Just when he started to describe the farms he recently visited, she pivoted on the seat to face him.

"Oh, I almost forgot to tell you. My aunt said she wrote two different letters and mailed them right after she received mine. Isn't that odd? They never arrived."

Shame roiled up his throat into his mouth. He endured the bad taste for the rest of the drive, yet he said nothing. How could he confess now when they desperately needed to mend broken fences?

In the Detweiler yard, Thomas met their buggy with a warm smile. "Welcome home, Amy. You two go in to supper. I'll tend the horse and put away the buggy."

"*Danki, bruder.*" John grabbed her bag and helped Amy down.

They entered an empty kitchen from the side door. Only one small candle burned on the table.

"Everything has already been put away. Maybe Sally thought we would eat in town. I'll see what I can heat up without much fuss." She washed her hands at the sink.

"No, you won't." John splashed cool water on his hands and face, recovering some of his confidence. "A surprise awaits you on the back porch."

"What on earth?" Amy ran down the hallway and threw open the back door. "Oh, my," she whispered.

John had covered the picnic table with a white cloth. Three kerosene lamps burned from one end to the other, besides two more hanging from porch rafters. Two places were set with plates covered with foil, glasses of milk, and slices of cherry pie. A huge bouquet of flowers graced the center of the table. He had picked every garden mum and wildflower he found growing along the fence. A small box of chocolates waited next to where she would sit.

"How beautiful! Did you do all this for me?" She hooked her arm through his.

He blushed up to his hairline. "Sally cooked the food, but I got everything ready. Do you mind eating outside? If you get cold, we can carry the meal into the house. I just thought we could be alone without interruptions from people going to the bathroom." He glanced away, embarrassed.

She giggled and reached up to kiss his cheek. "This is very sweet of you. I would love an autumn picnic." She sat down and opened the heart-shaped box. "Chocolates with caramel centers—these are the best."

"I bought them the same day as your new cell phone when you weren't looking."

She unwrapped one and popped it in her mouth. "*Danki*, John. We haven't had a private dinner since leaving Lancaster."

"Thomas wasn't keen on the idea but he agreed, providing that the kitchen curtain remains open and we have plenty of lamplight." He pointed at the window behind her.

"I think we can live with those terms."

"For your dining pleasure, we have fried chicken, sweet corn, coleslaw, and cherry pie," he announced, pulling off the foil covers.

"You remembered all my favorites." She smiled so sweetly his palms began to sweat.

"I thought of nothing other than you the whole time you were gone." He sipped from his glass to hide his shyness. Then they both bowed their heads for a moment of silent prayer.

"My aunt asked me if I was happy here. I told her I'd found the man I wished to marry and he was busy looking for our new home." Amy picked up a chicken breast and took a bite. "The only thing that could make my life better would be if Aunt Prudence moved closer."

And John began eating too, reassured his life was finally on track.

THIRTEEN

While I draw this fleeting breath

Y ou mean the whole district will be there?" asked Nora.

Amy counted to five before replying. Losing her temper with her sister wouldn't help the situation. "*Jah*. If you had been paying attention during my first two explanations, you would know. Singings aren't only for young people in Harmony. The entire district shows up and joins in if they so choose. And the Stolls are hosting a pig roast along with the singing."

"Will Elam attend?" she asked.

"I have no idea, but I know Thomas, Sally, and their boys will be there besides John and me, so you'll know plenty of people. You'd better hurry, though. We're leaving in a few minutes."

Nora walked across their bedroom to stand before the row of pegs on the wall. She studied her assortment of everyday garments as though unfamiliar with them. "Can I wear one of my Lancaster dresses?"

"You most certainly cannot." Amy began tapping her toe with impatience. "We have discussed this before, Nora."

"But these dresses look so shabby. May I wear my Sunday dress?"

"To eat barbequed roast pork and corn on the cob? No one will be in their Sunday best. Please stop dawdling. I'm going downstairs to carry the pies I baked to the buggy and help Sally with the boys." Amy moved toward the stairs before the temptation to shake Nora's shoulders got the better of her. She hoped the girl's sudden interest in Elam would end up being a passing curiosity. John mentioned that Nora had monopolized the dinner conversation with questions for Elam while she'd been up in Chestnut. Apparently, Thomas didn't care much for Nora's newfound concern for Maine's northernmost counties. Leave it to John's little *bruder* to select a night she was gone to finally dine with his family.

From the kitchen window, she spotted John leading their horse and buggy toward the house. Sally and Thomas were packing food, diaper bags, and their little boys into their own buggy. Amy hurried to wrap three pies snuggly with aluminum foil before loading them into a hamper. As she finished, John's head appeared in the doorway.

"About ready, dear heart?" he asked. True to form, a blush stained his freshly shaven cheeks from using an endearment.

"*Jah*, Nora and I will be out in two shakes of a goat's tail." She offered her cheeriest smile. He had no way of knowing how much she'd loved their private dinner on the porch. Despite rather chilly temperatures, the sweet gesture had warmed her heart.

"We're taking two buggies so we won't be so crowded. Maybe Nora can ride with Thomas and Sally on the way home. I'll see what Thomas says." He winked, blushed even deeper than before, and then disappeared down the steps.

That man is turning into a romantic after all. Amy wiped down the countertops and swept breakfast crumbs into her dust pan, during which Nora still hadn't arrived downstairs. With a quick huff of exasperation, Amy called at the landing. "I'm taking my pies out, *schwester*, and then we're leaving. I suggest you come *now* if you wish to ride the three miles to the cookout." She turned on her heel, grabbed the hamper, and marched out the door.

After climbing up next to John, she said, "Let's be off. But slowly, if you don't mind."

John nodded with comprehension and released the brake. The wheels began to roll from the horse's prancing.

"Wait! I'm here." They heard Nora before her head appeared at the side window. John pulled on the reins almost imperceptibly. "Please stop so I can climb up," she pleaded, jogging alongside.

Amy offered her a hand along with a scolding. "You truly must learn self-discipline."

"I'll work on that starting tomorrow." Nora tugged her cloak closed and settled herself on the seat.

Amy remembered the second part of Nora's favorite expression—the part Nora added after their parents were no longer in earshot: "But everyone knows tomorrow never comes." Amy decided not to share this tidbit with John as they enjoyed the warm fall sunshine and gorgeous display of foliage along the way.

But all was not silent in the buggy. John described some of the properties he recently visited. Apparently, real estate agents used expressions like "spacious," "well-maintained," or "contains excellent agricultural potential" when the exact opposite condition was the case. Amy laughed at a lean-to henhouse described as an outbuilding. Their lighthearted conversation screeched to an abrupt halt, however, when Nora's long cloak fell open to reveal a rose-hued dress. John pointed an accusatory finger at the garment. "Nora! I thought you understood that those colors aren't permitted here."

Amy's earlier annoyance with her sister ratcheted up a notch. "I asked you to wear an everyday dress."

Nora tugged the cloak closed. "Nothing was clean and pressed, and this is the most subtle one of the batch. We'll be outdoors all day. I'll keep my cloak on and closed. No one will notice, I promise."

John shook the reins to keep up with Thomas's buggy and didn't speak to Nora for the rest of the trip.

Amy could tell he was clenching down on his back teeth by the set of his jaw. "See that they don't," she said. "And the next time this happens, you'll climb out and walk back home."

Nora folded her hands in her lap and pouted silently. Amy hated acting like their *mamm*, but she didn't see much alternative.

Once they were at the Stolls', she and Nora sat on the women's side for the singing, while John squeezed onto the bench opposite them. Sally and Thomas visited with district members who didn't wish to participate. With some relief, Amy noticed Lewis on the men's side. The handsome young man tried to get Nora's attention between songs, to no avail. If only she would agree to court him, perhaps her transition wouldn't be two steps forward followed by one step back. By the fourth song, Amy forgot the family melodrama and lost herself in hymns of praise. If only she could abandon herself this freely to God each day, all day, maybe her own life would smooth out. But once the last melody lifted toward heaven, Amy started wondering where Nora had gone.

"Ready for a glass of apple cider?" asked John, offering his elbow and a bright smile. "They put out snacks to stave off starvation until the pork is done." He nodded toward a bounteously laden table.

"I don't know where Nora hurried off to."

"She's a grown woman, not a toddler. Let's get something to eat and drink."

Amy followed him to fix a plate of vegetables and dip, along with cheese and crackers. John located two about-to-marry couples, who eagerly shared their marriage counseling experiences while they nibbled. He hung on to every word they uttered to glean valuable advice. But Amy couldn't keep her mind on the conversation no matter how hard she tried. Unsettledness stirred beneath the cheese and crackers in her belly. "Excuse me a minute, John.

I wish to find my sister and refill my glass." She smiled politely at her new friends.

"I'll fetch us more cider while you reassure yourself Nora hasn't fallen down a well." He laughed easily, as did the other four.

"*Danki*. I'll be back soon." Amy strode toward those clustered around the snack table but recognized no familiar face. She looked outdoors, where some young people were gathered around the roasting pit. No Nora. Next, Amy scanned the front porch, where a knot of women stood in a circle gossiping. Her sister wasn't among those interested in local news. She checked the bathroom, the kitchen, and then rechecked the buffet line. Panic began to intrude on her otherwise enjoyable afternoon. Finally, on a harried walk around the barn, she spotted the objectionable rose-colored dress near the pasture fence. Her sister had wandered far from the crowd after the singing concluded.

Amy thought Nora was alone until she spotted Elam Detweiler sitting on the fence in front of her. The two were chatting and laughing as though old friends. Amy blinked several times. Elam hadn't been at the singing, yet there he was perched on the top rail. *How did he know we were coming here? And where is Nora's cloak?* Her sister socialized in the brisk autumn air in a lightweight dress with a black apron as though it were a balmy July day. Amy took a few steps toward the pair and then hesitated. Thus far no one had noticed the rare appearance of Elam Detweiler or Nora's inappropriate outfit. Any scene she caused would certainly draw unwelcome attention.

"Amy? Come back inside," called John from the doorway. "Sarah and William are talking about the farm they purchased on Waterville Road."

She smiled, deliberating only a half minute longer. He was right. Nora was a grown woman, and Amy wasn't her mother. If the girl earned a chastisement from the bishop for wandering off unchaperoned, then so be it. Amy tucked a stray lock under her *kapp* and returned to John's side. She enjoyed getting to know the two engaged couples who were about their same age. Before long, Nora crept back into the barn with her full-length cloak covering her dress. She filled a glass of cider and walked to where Sally chatted with other young mothers.

Several English families wandered the Stolls' mown backyard as more continued to arrive, bringing side dishes or plates of cookies to share with their neighbors. The Stoll family seemed to be well-liked in the community among both the Amish and English. Younger children organized a game of dodgeball using a striped beach ball, while older youths played volleyball over the clothesline strung between house and barn. Men carried the roast pig to the paper-covered table for carving as Beth Stoll organized the buffet table into salads, hot dishes, platters of pork, and desserts at the far end. Nora chose Aden for her dinner companion, and she held Jeremiah while Sally ate supper.

When the sun dipped below the Dixmont hills, Amy and John joined those at the bonfire nibbling cookies, sipping cider, and counting stars that appeared one by one. Soon the sky was filled with a million diamond-bright points of light.

"More stars are here than back in Pennsylvania," whispered John into her ear. They had found a quiet bench to sit on, close to others yet separate enough for private conversation.

Amy felt a rare sense of intimacy with the man she loved. "Another reason to like Maine," she said, winking fondly.

"I'm hoping you like it here enough to start looking at farms. I narrowed them down to two or three I'd like you to see." John placed his hands on his knees and appeared to hold his breath.

"I think I can tear myself away on Monday." She leaned toward him—close enough to smell his spicy shaving soap, but she pulled away with the arrival of Thomas and Sally.

"I believe Aden is finally worn out." Thomas carried his sleepy-eyed son on his shoulder. The boy clung to his father with a fistful of shirt. Sally cradled a sleeping Jeremiah wrapped in a quilt in the crook of her arm.

"We're headed home. Three of us are tired, but I believe Sally could talk with the women until the rooster crows tomorrow."

"I keep thinking of more things to say," said Sally, beaming at Amy.

"Where's Nora?" asked Thomas, scanning the fireside crowd. "Is she riding home with us or staying longer with you?"

Amy arched her back like a startled barn cat. She hadn't seen Nora since they had eaten roast pork with all the trimmings. In fact, she hadn't even *thought* of her sister during the last hour. She jumped to her feet. "I'd better go look for her."

John rose to his full height lazily. "Relax. She's probably taking a stroll with Lewis and his *schwestern*. You know he carries a torch for her."

"I don't think so. Lewis is over there talking to Abe Stoll." Thomas pointed a finger toward the woodpile. "It looks like Nora will be riding with you two." He settled his son more comfortably on his shoulder and put his other arm around Sally. "See you at home. Don't tarry too long."

John waited until they left before he muttered under his breath, "Confound your sister. Now she'll chatter the entire ride back."

"I'll go find her." Amy hurried toward the pasture—the last-seen lurking spot—but she didn't have to search for long. A flush-faced Nora stepped from the darkness near the phone shed. Her cloak hung open, and the hem of her dress was wet and muddy. "It's time to leave," announced Amy, not hiding her irritation.

"I figured as much." Nora sauntered past her in the direction of the buggies.

While John hitched up the horse and Amy retrieved her pie carriers from the buffet table, Nora rocked on her heels, looking oddly disoriented before she climbed into the backseat. *Maybe she'll fall asleep*, thought Amy, settling herself next to John.

Conversation during the ride home centered mainly on the succulent pork and variety of side dishes until John mentioned the unexpected presence of his brother. "Did you notice that Elam showed up?" he asked Amy. "He skulked in the shadows like a possum, trying to fix a plate of food without having to socialize with folks." John laughed with little humor.

"I don't know about that," said Nora. She leaned forward in between them to interject. "I spoke to your *bruder*, and he was downright conversational with me."

Nora's having to voice a contrary opinion led to her undoing.

John's head recoiled with shock and disgust. "Have you been drinking? I smell beer on your breath."

Nora blinked like an owl and retreated from close proximity. "How would you know what beer smells like?"

"I know. Never mind how, but I know, and I smell it distinctly on you."

Amy turned around and stared at her sister. "Is it true? Were you drinking? I saw you off with Elam by the fence after the singing. And you were gone a long while after we ate supper."

Nora shrunk against the bench back, partially hidden in darkness. She neither confirmed nor denied the allegation, but in the ensuing moments her silence spoke volumes. What had been an unseasonably warm fall evening turned chillier by the minute. For the remainder of the drive no one spoke. Amy's mind whirred with possible outcomes to Nora's misdeeds—and none of them were good.

When John stopped the buggy by the stone walkway, he unhitched the gelding with a stony expression. Nora climbed out and approached with downcast eyes. "John, I just wanted to say—"

"Save it," he interrupted. "I don't want to hear another word from you. Just go to your room and stay there."

Nora ran to the house and disappeared inside without a backward glance. Amy had never heard him speak like that before. It was as though his heart was filled with hatred. She lifted her containers from the back and trudged up the path. Halfway to the side door she paused and glanced back. "Perhaps it would be best if you waited until morning to discuss this with Thomas so that cooler heads might prevail."

John stepped into the moonlight, holding the horse's bridle. "No, Amy. If Thomas is still awake, I'll tell him tonight. You have coddled and babied your sister long enough. It's time she grew up and took responsibility for her actions." He turned and stomped off toward the barn without bothering to offer a civil *"gut nacht."*

ॐ

Thomas stretched out his calf muscles under the warm quilt, wiggled his toes, and worked the kinks from his spine one vertebra at a time. Despite being the one at the gathering who wanted to talk until dawn, Sally had fallen asleep as soon as her head hit the pillow. Thomas thought it had been a successful social—Amish and English coming together to celebrate a good harvest and talk of their plans for next spring. The logic many had presented for obtaining organic certification convinced him to submit the necessary paperwork over the winter. God was good. He had blessed Harmony with fine weather this day so they could enjoy one last outdoor event. Thomas was about to surrender to sleep himself when a tap at his bedroom door jarred him alert.

"Thomas, are you still awake? I'd like a word with you."

He bolted upright at the sound of his brother's voice, and then he jumped out of bed before a second knock awoke Sally. Opening the door quietly, he peered into John's deeply lined eyes. "What is it? Can't it wait until morning?" He stepped into the hallway and closed the door behind him.

"*Nein*, it won't." John spoke in a harsh, exaggerated whisper. "I smelled beer on Nora's breath on the drive home. She had been drinking at the Stolls' cookout, and the only person Amy saw her with was our brother." He crossed his arms, tucking his hands beneath his braces.

"Elam? Are you sure?" Thomas tried to clear the cobwebs from his tired brain.

"Who else in the district would do such a thing? I saw him there with my own eyes, slinking in the shadows like a fox near the hen-house. He wanted to get supper without interacting with folks." John met his gaze and held it, expecting him to say or do something as the eldest Detweiler and a minister of the district.

Something I probably should have done a long time ago. "Give me a moment." Thomas crept back into the room to retrieve his robe and slippers. Then he marched down to the first floor as determination and ire rose with each step. John followed close on his heels.

How many casual conversations had he had with Elam? How many times had he gently corrected infractions of the rules without anger or judgment? He had bent over backward to tolerate Elam's continued fence-sitting while others would have been given an ultimatum—join us and abide by the *Ordnung* or leave to make a life elsewhere. He provided a home for his wayward *bruder* without asking for a dime from his paycheck toward food or shelter. At long last, Thomas's blood began to boil.

In the kitchen he grabbed a flashlight from atop the refrigerator and handed John the battery lantern from the peg. "Let's check his quarters before he returns from the party," he said, heading down the cellar stairs. He had every right to discover what went on inside his house—a house paid for with his life savings and restored by the sweat of his brow. Thomas hung the lantern from an overhead hook, and the two brothers began rummaging around the austere room.

It didn't take long to find snack food, several packs of soda pop, an assortment of car magazines, a battery-powered radio, and a charger for a cell phone. But where Elam would plug in the thing was a mystery to them. John also discovered a pint of whiskey under the mattress and a carton of filtered cigarettes on the ledge above the washtub. He tossed those two items on the bed with the outdated library publications.

"Under my nose, in my own home," moaned Thomas. "This is how he repays my patience and continued indulgence." The words tasted bitter on his tongue, like grapes left too long on the vine. He swallowed hard as they heard approaching footsteps from the outside entrance.

Elam appeared in the doorway, hatless and disheveled, as if he'd run all the way back from the Stoll farm. "Looking for something specific?" he sneered. "Or are you just invading my privacy for no particular reason?"

Thomas closed the short distance between them. "You aren't entitled to privacy in my home—not anymore, not after tonight." He pointed at the whiskey bottle and carton of cigarettes. "You get liquored up and smoke in my house while my *fraa* and *kinner* sleep?" He didn't hide his revulsion.

Elam's brown eyes darkened to almost black. "I've never smoked in the house or enjoyed an evening nip indoors. I give in to my weaknesses away from your precious abode."

Thomas felt no relief whatsoever. "Tonight you shared your weakness with Nora King. Is it not so?" He couldn't control the anger in his voice.

"I didn't offer it to her. She came upon me eating supper in my buggy and saw a six-pack of beer under the seat." He shrugged with defiance. "She took a can of her own accord."

"I suspect she drank more than one." John spat rather than spoke the words. "I smelled it strong on her breath."

"Like I said, it wasn't my idea she partake in the first place." Elam moved from the doorway to the bed to assess his magazines.

Thomas narrowed his focus. "It's time you looked for another logging job. And in the meantime, you will not bring forbidden alcohol or tobacco into my home again."

Elam glared first at John and then at Thomas, thinning his mouth into a hard line. Yet he remained silent.

After several uncomfortable moments, Thomas demanded, "Do you understand?"

The two brothers engaged in a stare-down before Elam glanced away. "I understand," he mumbled.

Thomas and John stomped up the steps to their beds, yet both would suffer restless sleep despite their fatigue.

ॐ

Nora finally found a Sunday school lesson that didn't put her to sleep during the first five minutes. Thomas had spoken about the parable of the mustard seed. It was the smallest of all seeds, but it became the largest of all garden plants, providing long branches for birds to make their nests. She loved how Jesus taught in parables but explained what He meant to the disciples so there would be no confusion.

Now, if only they would replace these hard, uncomfortable benches in the meetinghouse. Why couldn't this district meet in people's homes or outbuildings the way every other Amish community in America did? She'd read that Plain folk lived in twenty-eight different states, including Colorado, Texas, and Florida. Couldn't John have picked some place warm to move to instead of this wilderness?

"Are you going to slice those loaves of bread? Or do you expect people to tear off a chunk to make their sandwich?" asked Sally, studying her with interest.

The sarcasm jarred Nora back to her present circumstances—helping to set out the noon meal. Sally arranged meats and cheeses on a platter while Amy scooped pickled eggs and beets into bowls wearing an equally hawkish expression. Amy had watched her every move since they returned from the pig roast, as though if she turned her back for a second, Nora might pull out a bottle of beer.

Nora giggled with the mental picture of guzzling a Budweiser in plain sight. Now the other women might fear her mad, besides a reckless drunkard. But if she admitted the truth, she didn't much care for the taste of beer. She would rather drink a Pepsi or cherry soda. It was Elam Detweiler who caused her to do crazy things— not by suggestion but by example. She'd never met anyone who lived by his own rules, not caring what others said or thought about him.

"Do you think your brother-in-law will show up for lunch like he did at the pig roast?" asked Nora of Sally. She sliced the whole wheat loaves uniformly and arranged the slices artfully on the tray.

"Who, John?" asked Sally. "He's standing over there by the cider barrel with Thomas." Sally bustled around directing the ladies where to put their contributions, glowing with the success of her food lists.

Why she hadn't thought of it sooner was a mystery to Nora. "No, not John. I mean Elam." Nora dropped the carving knife into the tub of soapy water.

Amy looked as though she might faint dead away, but Sally closed the distance between them in a heartbeat. She stood practically nose to nose and hissed under her breath, "You're in enough trouble, young lady. I strongly recommend you forget about Elam. A walk down that road will only lead to certain ruin."

Nora opened her mouth to remind Sally of Scriptures such as: "Do not judge others, and you will not be judged." And "Let the one who has never sinned throw the first stone." But men suddenly formed a sandwich line, thwarting the opportunity. By the time everyone had been served, Nora had lost her appetite. She grabbed an apple and sat alone on the meetinghouse steps. No one joined her to chitchat or offer a sample of their secret recipe brownies or walnut tarts. No one liked her. She was as much an outcast in Harmony as Elam. But at least Elam would find another job to take him away from the ceaseless boredom.

Nora bit into her apple as movement caught her eye. Lewis from the store waved and pointed at the empty spot next to him on the bench. He was eating lunch with several of his sisters. They motioned for her to join them. How the sight of him stung. He was so kind and gentle, so attentive to her. Yet one glance at his dull, drab sisters indicated exactly what lay down that road...to paraphrase Sally Detweiler. Nora grinned, held up her apple, and gestured it was all she desired. Then she left to find her sister in case Lewis decided to become persistent.

She found Amy and John with four people she didn't know. "Join us," said Amy. "Where's the rest of your lunch? Do you want half my sandwich?" She scooted over to make room.

Nora shook her head. "No, I'm not hungry. If it's okay with you, I'll start for home."

"Walking?" Amy looked suspicious.

"*Jah*, I'm just going home to rest. Please don't worry so much." Nora headed toward the road. For the remainder of the day, she stayed in her room napping and praying to be released from her Harmony incarceration. She ventured downstairs only long enough to eat a tuna fish sandwich and a hard-boiled egg. No one had called her to supper. In the living room Amy sewed by the fire while the Detweilers read. Their sons played with toys on the braided carpet. Dejected and filled with self-pity, Nora climbed into her bed fully dressed and fell asleep. When she awoke a few hours later, Amy was sleeping in the other bed while a bright-yellow moon beckoned her to the window. Nora sat on the straight-backed chair daydreaming of home until something in the yard drew her nose to the glass.

Elam hauled the open pony cart from the shed into the barnyard. From her vantage point she watched him hitch the sleek, black stallion he'd been grooming the first day they met. Where was he going in the middle of the night? It took her less than a moment to decide to find out.

Creeping silently downstairs, Nora grabbed her cloak from the peg and closed the door behind her. A mouse couldn't have made less noise.

Elam looked up as she approached, but his expression remained bland. "Aren't you already in enough hot water because of me, Miss King?"

"You haven't done anything. I only have myself to blame, if I were to blame someone…which I don't choose to do." She stepped closer.

"That's a lot of words when a simple *jah* or *nein* would have sufficed." He finished attaching the bit to the bridle and then faced her. "What exactly do you want out here tonight? Couldn't sleep, so you wondered what the family black sheep was up to?"

She didn't flinch or look away. "I wanted to know where you were going at midnight on the Sabbath."

He ran a hand down the horse's mane to calm his eagerness. "It's not the Sabbath anymore. If the Harmony bishop or his ministers cared to consult Scripture, the Sabbath ended at sundown. So folks should be allowed to sow by moonlight or take a late night buggy ride if they choose. At this time of day the roads are empty of Amish buggies or English cars—nothing to worry about." Elam climbed into the pony cart as the stallion pranced. Apparently, he wasn't the only one eager to feel the wind in his hair. Elam studied her face long enough for her to grow uncomfortable from the perusal. Then he stretched out his hand. "Want to join me on the fastest ride of your life?"

Without hesitation, without consideration for the consequences, Nora looked him in the eye and replied, "You bet I would."

FOURTEEN

When mine eyes shall close in death

R eady to go?" asked John. "I'm free until suppertime. In fact, if we miss supper and are forced to grab a bite in town, so be it." He beamed with way more energy than usual for a Monday.

Amy didn't feel half so peppy, even though her chores had been less tiring than his. "I'm not sure this is a good day to go after all." She hung up the damp dish towel to dry.

John wasn't remotely deterred. "This is a perfect day to go. Thomas will be gone all day on district business, and Sally went next door with her little ones. We are free as birds." He wiggled his eyebrows.

"I'm a bird with a clipped wing." Amy sighed while glancing toward the stairs. "Nora still hasn't come down yet. She just moaned and buried her head beneath the quilt when I tried waking her this morning."

"And why would that affect our looking at farms for sale?" He leaned against the kitchen counter.

"I don't know if she has one of her migraines or is simply being lazy." Amy wiped down the kitchen table for the second time.

John pursed his lips while pondering this. "Either way, we're not talking about Aden or Jeremiah. We're discussing Nora, who is capable of taking care of herself while we're gone."

Amy tossed her rag into the sink. "I know, but I'm afraid if we leave that she might get into trouble." Her voice dropped to a whisper. "I'd planned to ask her to come with us today."

John's eyes nearly bugged from his face. "Why would we take her along? I don't need her negative comments when this will be *our* farm."

"But look at the stunts she pulled at the pig roast when I let her out of sight."

This time he rolled his eyes. "You can't watch her every minute of the day to prevent bad things from happening, Amy. You are not her keeper."

"I know that, but maybe we should keep tabs until Elam returns to his logging crew."

"He was fired. Who knows if he'll find another job away from home? Besides, the real estate agent is meeting us at the first property. Everything is set up for today." He opened his hands, almost in supplication.

"Then let me get my outer bonnet," she agreed. But inside Amy felt anything but agreeable. Nora needed to stay out of trouble or Thomas might send her back to Pennsylvania. And who would look out for her there? Their grandparents were too old to understand a young woman testing her wings before settling down. Nora might make irrevocable mistakes without Amy's guidance. She might not be able to control Elam, but she could prevent Nora from ruining her reputation with him.

A few minutes later Amy had her bonnet and purse, but Nora still hadn't come downstairs. So she had no choice but to paste on a smile and leave the Detweiler farm with her husband-to-be. She couldn't expect John to wait forever for the perfect opportunity.

When they arrived at the first farm, the English Realtor was pacing the length of the porch. "There you are," she called in a melodic voice. "I should have picked you up instead of meeting you here. We would have saved time. Hi, I'm Jane Chadd." She pumped their hands in turn, wearing the whitest smile Amy had even seen. Then the woman marched up to the front door and threw it open with a flourish.

"Now, don't be shocked," said Mrs. Chadd. "No one has lived here in ten years. Once those holes in the roof are patched and the broken window glass has been replaced, you can start on the interior one room at a time."

Amy followed John inside a building that should have been torn down, not put up for sale.

"Mind your step," the Realtor cautioned. "The last tenants left behind some unfortunate souvenirs."

"Oh, good grief!" Amy quickly pulled up her apron to cover her mouth and nose.

"Now, Amy," murmured John. "It doesn't smell anymore. Those were left last winter. Raccoons prefer living outdoors until the snow starts to fly." He stepped over the dung and followed the Realtor on a whirlwind tour of the dilapidated hovel.

"Is there plenty of good fertile land that comes with the house? Is that why we're looking at this property?" Amy whispered conspiratorially to him so as not to offend the agent. Broken windowpanes, sagging floorboards, and missing stair treads indicated a house beyond repair in her estimation.

"*Nein*. More than half the acres are wooded, while the tillable land has lain fallow for years." John leaned on a saggy post that threatened to give way.

Apparently, Amy's facial expression indicated she needed no further elaboration.

"Are we ready to see the next place, folks?" asked the bubbly Realtor. "Why don't we leave your buggy here and take my car to save time? I'll bring you back when we're finished."

Amy couldn't exit the shack fast enough. It hadn't contained one redeemable feature. Climbing into the backseat of the sedan, she let John ride up front with the Realtor.

"I believe you'll like the second property better, Miss King." Mrs. Chadd spoke to Amy's reflection in the rearview mirror. "It hasn't been vacant for nearly as long."

It would be impossible not to. "That's refreshing to hear." Amy kneaded her knuckles in her lap and stared at the passing scenery.

John turned around to face her, practically strangling in the seat belt. "We are touring in the reverse order of my preference. I saved the best property for last."

If the first one was any indication, perhaps we should skip ahead to the end, she thought, but she asked, "You visited these earlier while I was gone?"

"*Jah*, several times. Plus a few others I already eliminated."

"I don't see why you didn't eliminate the raccoon hotel." Amy's tone sounded more sarcastic than she'd intended.

"I included that one because it was close to my brother's house, knowing how fond you've grown of Sally."

"Well, that would be an advantage." She smiled politely as a twinge of motion sickness began. Backseats wreaked havoc on her stomach.

The second farm was indeed in better condition, but the one-story house had small, cramped rooms. Amy longed for large, airy second-floor bedrooms. She marched through the house as though running a marathon—in through the front door and out the back in record time. "On to the next property, Mrs. Chadd," she announced.

"Absolutely, Miss King. I aim to find the perfect home for you two." The Realtor's smile never faltered the entire afternoon, as though smiling was part of her job description.

The third stop yielded no house whatsoever. Eighty acres of till-able farmland on a high plateau suitable for a homesite were up for sale. Another forty acres of backwoods could be optioned, along with stream access for an additional sum.

"What do you think of a three-story, four-bedroom frame house set maybe fifty yards from the road?" John used his hands to form a picture frame in the direction where he would position their house.

"Sounds like an awfully long driveway in the winter. Plus, we have no architect or builder, and where would we live during the construction? We shouldn't rely on your brother's generosity indefinitely."

"If I had my way, we would be married already," he whispered into her ear. "Thomas is the one dragging his feet regarding our wedding date."

"How much are the owners asking?" she asked Mrs. Chadd. Amy gasped upon hearing her reply. "But that's more than the first property. And it had a house."

"Not one you would live in." John's veneer of patience began to crack.

"True, but that price sounds high for bare land." Amy tightened her cloak against the wind.

"Didn't your fiancé mention you moved here from Lancaster County?" Mrs. Chadd's demeanor also faltered a notch. "The price per acre here must be much cheaper than back home."

"I suppose so, but I wasn't in the market to purchase anything in Pennsylvania." Amy rocked on her heels, chewed on her lip, and tried not to look at either of them.

"Not to worry, *liewi*. I've saved the best for last." He offered her his arm. "We have plenty of daylight left—"

"I'm starving," she interrupted. "Could we stop for lunch? I didn't pack us a hamper."

John's lips thinned as he frowned. "I suppose so, but I want you to have enough time to see the final property."

"I know just the place," chirped Mrs. Chadd. "We can grab a quick sandwich and cup of coffee and still get out to Thorndike.

Have you tried the deli by the railroad crossing? They make the best homemade soups and salads."

On the woman prattled while Amy and John climbed back into the car. It was a good thing Mrs. Chadd was talkative because Amy needed a chance to think. Four different properties in one day seemed too much to evaluate.

But she found herself in better spirits after lunch, revitalized by food and caffeine. Her interest piqued with the Realtor's description: seventy acres—equally divided between pasture and corn-fields—and only one year fallow. The former owner had farmed organic, so the soil contained no pesticide residue. And the property was being sold to settle an estate.

"The elderly couple died ten months ago, within weeks of each other," said the agent, heading out of town toward Thorndike.

"How sad," Amy murmured. She rolled down the window for fresh air.

"That often happens when people have been married as long as the Morrells had."

"And you said when we looked at this property before that nei-ther of their children wishes to take over the farm?" John said, turning toward the agent.

"That's right. Both kids are lawyers in Boston. They just want the property sold to finalize the estate."

"That's the truly sad part." John shook his head from side to side. "Giving up their family's heritage."

"The eldest son would love to sell the place to a farming fam-ily rather than see it cut up into development lots." Mrs. Chadd grinned at Amy over her shoulder.

Amy shrugged, but she felt her excitement build as they drove up the Morrell driveway. Perched on the highest point, the house commanded a view of almost the entire property. It faced south, so the front windows would catch the afternoon sunlight in the win-ter. A stand of pines directly behind the house would block frigid winds from the north. It had a dark-green metal roof, white siding, and black shutters. A windmill spun lazily in the breeze on an adjacent hill. Shrubbery and flower beds looked as though they had been tended this past summer. "Oh, my. Is that the kitchen garden?" she asked, pressing her face to the glass. A white picket fence enclosed a quarter-acre plot. Hollyhocks and sunflowers stood sentinel along the fence line.

"Pretty, isn't it?" Mrs. Chadd parked the car near the back porch. "The landscaping service tilled everything under last spring to await the next live-in gardener, except for those flowers. They were too lovely to chop down."

Amy jumped out when John opened her door. "There are two barns?" She gazed up at two huge, gambrel-roofed outbuildings.

John beamed as though the property already belonged to him. "Yes, one for livestock and one for grain storage with a small office and a workshop. The office and workshop have a concrete floor and electricity, but the wiring can easily be removed. Even inside the house, wires run through conduit, not hidden inside walls. The electricity had been added after the house was built."

The agent scanned the computer printout. "The house is well constructed too. There are no shoddy materials in this old beauty." She opened the front door, allowing a few leaves to blow onto a faded area rug. "Remember, no one has lived here for more than a year. But with fresh paint and a little elbow grease, this could be a showplace again."

"We're not interested in showplaces, Mrs. Chadd," corrected John. "Only a sturdy Amish home in which we can raise a family."

She grinned, taking no offense. "Then we'll forget about custom drapes. Go through the Morrell homestead on your own. Take your time. I'll wait for you right there." She pointed at an antique bentwood rocker, the sole item of furniture in the room. "Whoever cleaned out the parents' possessions decided to leave this piece behind."

Amy stood behind the chair to assess the view from the front room window. Rolling hills and valleys stretched as far as the eye could see. She hurried through the first two floors and up to the attic, and then she wandered through the whole house slowly a second time. John kept pace with her but wisely remained silent, allowing her to form her own opinion. In short, she loved it. It had a huge country kitchen with an L-shaped dining area, a large front room, a small nursery or den, and one bathroom on the first floor. Four additional bedrooms and another bath sprawled across the second floor. The third-floor attic had two dormer windows from which she was certain you could see the ocean on a clear day. The basement offered an outside entrance and plenty of cold storage space for vegetables.

No broken windows, no gaping holes in the roof, and no tenant family of raccoons. "This is a very large house," she said to John. Amy clasped his hand as they stood in an attic dormer, transfixed by the panoramic view.

"It is, but the Morrells never turned it particularly fancy with floor tiles, wall-to-wall carpeting, or carved staircase bannisters."

"Would Thomas or the bishop think it too much house for a young couple just starting out?" She couldn't hide her mounting excitement. It was the nicest house on the prettiest piece of land she'd ever seen.

"I think they'll agree it's a tremendous value for the money."

"This wouldn't be too many acres for you to handle alone? It will be years before our sons are old enough to give you a hand...if God graces us with sons, that is," she added with a blush.

"No problem. I suddenly feel as though I possess the energy of five men." He squeezed her hand.

"Then let's ask Mrs. Chadd what we need to do to put down a deposit or down payment or whatever." Amy began digging in her purse for her checkbook.

"I just *knew* you would like it as much as me!" He enfolded her in a hug. "I've already given her a thousand dollars earnest money to put a hold on the place. I didn't want someone snapping it up while you were out of town in Chestnut." He released his embrace unexpectedly. "Let's go back downstairs. I told her the full down payment wouldn't be a problem because you have already deposited your inheritance at a Harmony bank. Come, my love. Let's not keep Mrs. Chadd waiting." John disappeared down the attic steps to the second floor.

Amy was left feeling as though that faded, threadbare rug had just been pulled from beneath her feet. *He put down a deposit before I even saw the place? What if I hadn't liked it? Would that have even made a difference?*

ॐ

If John lived to be a hundred years old, he still wouldn't understand women. Amy had said she loved the house. He reassured her it would neither be too big for them, nor too many acres to farm. Yet for some reason her back had stiffened as though someone slipped a two-by-eight under her dress.

She said to Mrs. Chadd, "Give me a couple of days to think about this" at least three times in response to the woman's questions, including, "What did you think of the separate tub and shower in the upstairs bathroom?"

Mrs. Chadd kept glancing at him to say or do something, but he couldn't engage Amy in a serious discussion in front of an outsider. Finally, after the Realtor dropped them off at their buggy, he tried to open up a conversation. "Would you care to enlighten me as to what's wrong?" He spoke softly so as not to intimidate her. "I thought you liked the Morrell farm."

Amy pulled the wool blanket over her knees. "I truly did like the house, but I panicked when you said you already gave her a deposit. Things are moving too fast." She drew the cover up to her chin, even though she wore a heavy cloak.

"I understand, but I feared someone else would snap it up. It hasn't been on the market for long. And their asking price was more than fair." He pulled gently on the reins to slow the pace. The horse was eager to get home to his hay and a bucket of oats, but John wanted some time to talk. "I was unsure how long you would linger in Chestnut."

She leaned her head back and closed her eyes. "If someone else bought the farm instead of us, then it would have been God's will."

John bit his tongue to keep his temper. "Sometimes God expects us to step up and show some initiative. He never promised to hand life on a silver platter to His believers."

She snorted. "At that dear price, I'd hardly say we're being handed anything."

He flinched from her sarcasm. "Is that what this is about? You're afraid we'll overpay? Amy, because you've never shopped for real estate, you have no idea what land costs." He patted her knee. "I assure you I've looked at plenty of farms, both here and back in Lancaster. This one is a good deal. That's why I don't think it'll remain long on the market."

Amy cocked her head to one side. "The earnest money you paid Mrs. Chadd—how much time does it give us before someone else can place an offer?" Clouds drifted across the sun, bringing an immediate chill to the air. He would have preferred any other question. She didn't need additional excuses to drag her feet. John floundered for the best response.

"How long do we have, John?" she repeated.

"A bit less than three weeks. We had a month total."

She sighed with obvious relief. "*Gut.* I won't feel pressured to decide in a day or two. It's a big decision. Most folks will only buy a big house like this once in their lifetime. I might wish to look at one or two more properties for comparison." Amy buried her hands beneath the wool.

He couldn't argue with her logic. But if she hadn't put off viewing farms for sale, he wouldn't have taken so rash a move in her absence. "We're permitted thirty days but not required to take that long. So why don't we play it by ear?" He forced his most benign expression.

"All right. That will give us time to see bankers about a mortgage in case we decide to go ahead and buy before our wedding."

His smile vanished. "Mortgage? What are you talking about? With your share from the sale of your parents' farm, along with the money I've saved, we won't need a mortgage."

Amy threw off the covering. It fell into a heap by her feet. "If we pay for the farm in full, I won't have anything left to my name." Her face scrunched into such unpleasantness that no one would misunderstand her opinion of that idea.

John began breathing hard through his nostrils. "Amy, you know Plain folk don't borrow money unless absolutely necessary. It is unavoidable back in Lancaster because of real estate prices, but that's not the case here. We have enough cash to pay for the farm in full and not have to pay a single dime in interest." He appealed to her practical nature while guiding the buggy up Thomas's driveway.

She shook her head back and forth like a stubborn mule. "Again, I must ask for more time. You're throwing too much at me at once. You picked out our home by yourself while I was out of town. And now you have already decided how I'll spend my entire inheritance from my late parents. Have I no say in matters?"

"*Jah*, of course. That's why we drove out there today. If you didn't like the Morrell homestead, Mrs. Chadd would have refunded our deposit. She assured me of that." He sounded weak because he felt as though a stubborn mule had just gut-kicked him.

"Well, that's good to know." Amy jumped down as soon as the buggy stopped, not waiting for him to come to her side.

John hopped down to grab the bridle of the hungry, prancing horse. "I acted with your best interest in mind. I thought this house would make you happy. I apologize if I overstepped my bounds as your fiancé."

Her features softened considerably. "And it probably *will* make me happy someday, but not today. I'm tired and cranky and need to figure out if we should give every cent we have to this fancy-dressed *Englischer*. How much common sense does the woman have to wear high heels to show people a farm?" Her crankiness grew ever more apparent.

He considered explaining that their money would be given to the Morrell heirs, not to the overdressed Mrs. Chadd, but he wisely held his tongue. Unsure as to how to proceed, he tipped his hat ridiculously, like some elderly *grossdawdi*. "Good afternoon, then. I'll tend to the horse and see you in the house later." He turned on his boot heel and led the gelding to his oats and a rubdown inside the barn. An errant, shameful idea crept from the recesses of his mind. *It wouldn't be all the money we have if you hadn't sold your farm to your cousins for a song.*

❧

Thomas knew something must have happened while John and Amy toured properties for sale, but he didn't have the heart or the energy to inquire what it was. He and Sally were tired after visiting with the other minister, but a consultation with the other ministerial brethren had been long overdue. Tomorrow, he would call on the bishop at the home of his married daughter. Their church leader usually arrived in Harmony the Wednesday before a preaching Sunday to prepare the main sermon and conduct district business. Minor disputes were brought to him for an *Ordnung* decision or some sort of compromise between members. It was time Thomas discussed the problem of Elam. He needed to tell the bishop about his brother's latest fall from grace.

While Thomas pondered tomorrow's meeting, everyone else at the supper table apparently had their own crosses to bear. Amy pushed the food around her plate untouched, gazing anywhere but at her intended spouse. John hunched over his supper eating as though he was a condemned man at his final meal. Even Sally seemed distracted and distant. The only one with any enthusiasm or appetite was Nora King, for a change. Despite the fact that she hadn't crawled out of bed by the time they had left this morning, Nora smiled dreamily and ate her chicken-and-rice with unusual zeal. There was no figuring out these King sisters. Were the two who remained behind with their grandparents equally as enigmatic? That must have been some household.

After evening chores, Thomas opened his Bible to the book of Revelation. If a person read some of the most depressing and hard to comprehend Scripture, everyday conundrums seem small potatoes in comparison. When he finally drifted off to sleep that night, his dreams were filled with fiery lakes and plagues of locusts and earthquakes that tore huge rifts through Waldo County and the rest of Maine. Elam appeared in the nightmare, passing out pint bottles of whiskey to the youth of Harmony, aided by a wild-eyed Nora King. When Thomas shook himself the next morning, he had no more anxiety about seeing the bishop. Difficulties with a willful brother fell into perspective after battling swarms of insects devouring crops and bottomless chasms between farms.

Blessedly, the world appeared unchanged during his ride.

"*Guder mariye*," greeted Andrew, sweeping open the door. "How did you know my daughter was baking pumpkin pies today? They are your favorite, *jah*? Come in, come in. Let's have coffee." The white-haired clergyman limped into the kitchen.

"Is your rheumatism worse today?" asked Thomas, pulling out two chairs.

"*Jah*, always so when the weather turns cold and damp. Maybe I'll visit the homeopathic doc in town for one of his cures. Those compounds usually work wonders till your body adjusts to them. Then they are not so effective." Andrew massaged his kneecaps with a grimace, while his *fraa* placed two large slices of pie, the coffeepot, and two mugs before them. His wife, meek and retiring, never spoke unless directly addressed.

"*Danki*," said Thomas. "But I'm not here for a social visit. I've come to discuss my *bruder* Elam."

"Still sitting on the fence, is he?" The elder man pulled his long white beard sagely.

"I'm afraid it's more serious than a man who cannot commit. He showed up unexpectedly at the Stoll pig roast, though I doubt the hosts even knew he was there. He ate by himself and clung to the shadows, mostly."

"Seems like a long way to go for a free meal." Andrew gave his beard another pull.

"True enough, but one of my houseguests, Nora King, came upon him eating supper in his buggy. He gave her...or allowed her to take...a couple of his beers. He brought a six-pack to the party. Later I searched his basement room and found both cigarettes and whiskey."

Andrew recoiled from the words. "Send him back to his English logging crew! Those sort of pastimes might be acceptable among them, but not here. Tell him he can't return to your home until he is willing to accept your rules." The bishop cut into his pie with a fork.

"That's part of the problem. Elam was fired from his job—for fighting, I think. He has no crew to return to and no other place to stay other than my cellar." Thomas took a big swallow of coffee without sipping it first and scalded his throat with the hot liquid.

"That is, indeed, a problem." The bishop focused on his food while mulling the matter over. When he finished his pie, he riveted

Thomas with his gaze. "You have been too lenient with him because he's a family member. And now he's caused another, Nora King, to stray from the path. Speak to him man-to-man. Insist that he give serious thought to his future instead of bouncing from one experience to the next. Ask him to also consider his eternal future—the hereafter. His soul is at stake. Invite him to join our district and commit to the faith of his parents and their parents. But make sure your meaning is crystal clear. The time has come for him to decide. Set a date, Thomas."

"How much more time should I give him?" Thomas finally cut into his dessert, heartened by a corner turned.

"Why not till Christmas? That will give him seven weeks to give up his English habits. Or he must leave your home and not return until ready to be baptized and join the church."

Thomas nodded and then voiced his confirmation. "I will speak to him soon and honor our decision come December."

FIFTEEN

When I soar to worlds unknown

Are you sure you don't want me to come with you?" asked Amy. "Maybe there will be more work to do than you figure."

Sally smiled over the lid of their largest picnic basket. "No, you're a big help by keeping the home fires burning. I'm not sure when I'll get back, so if you will serve dinner at our regular time, I would be obliged." She loaded the stuffed chicken, pan of roast pork, and sweet potato casserole into the hamper.

Amy wiped her hands on her apron. "Nora and I will make sure none of the menfolk starve to death while you're gone." Then her pretty face furrowed with concern. "How did you find out that Agnes Miller was ailing?"

"When Thomas visited the bishop yesterday, his daughter mentioned that Agnes was suffering from a flare-up of gout. That can be very painful."

"Aren't you afraid to visit her alone?" asked Nora. "That woman has always been critical of you, Sally. Never a kind word comes from her mouth." Nora turned back to her sink full of dirty dishes.

"Oh, I don't know about that. When I brought out my sign-up sheet, she was the first to pick a category." Sally squeezed half a loaf of bread next to the casserole in the basket.

Nora laughed with a caustic, unpleasant sound. "*Jah*, but she also made a wisecrack about not having to contend with turkey sandwiches week after week."

"Is any room left in the hamper?" Amy went to the pie safe, angling her sister a glare along the way. "Please take the Millers this extra Dutch apple pie. I'll cut the other into smaller slices so that one will be enough for us tonight." She quickly wrapped her contribution with foil.

"Good idea," agreed Nora over her shoulder. "Bribe your way onto her good side with sweets."

Sally shook off Nora's skepticism. "You girls, really, with your worries. I'm going to give Agnes a hand with housework and take them supper for a few days. Her *ehemann* is too old and in too poor of health to help when Agnes feels sick."

"Well, I hope she won't criticize you. After all, you're on a mission of mercy. Because the Millers have no children, they must rely on district members for help." Amy set her pie on top of the other food. "Let that be a lesson to those planning never to marry and bear *kinner.*" With great animation, Amy turned toward her sister.

"I'll carry Jeremiah to the buggy," volunteered Nora, turning off the water. She stuck her tongue out at Amy on her way to pick up the baby.

"And I'll carry the hamper." Amy lifted the handles and headed out the door.

"Come along, Aden." Sally reached for his hand and the diaper tote. "It looks like we're ready."

Outdoors, Sally saw no sign of Thomas, John, or Elam. Waving goodbye to the two women, she felt relieved to spend the day away from the farm. John had remained out of sorts since the house-hunting excursion with his bride-to-be. Amy explained only that they needed to work through a few minor details. If minor details could cause so much tension, Sally predicted a rocky road for their first couple of years together.

Thomas confided that today would be his long overdue showdown with his brother. Last night, as they huddled under their heaviest quilt, he told her about his conversation with the bishop, along with a blow-by-blow account of what happened during and after the cookout.

"It's about time," she mused aloud now as she guided the horse along the road.

"For what, *mamm*?" asked Aden, peering up from under his dark eyelashes.

"For you to snuggle under the blanket." Sally pulled it up to his neck. Usually, once the boy was toasty warm, he would fall asleep against her side. Today was no exception, so Sally spent the forty-five-minute drive to the Millers' mulling over how to help Amy and John. The man did love Amy despite his stubborn streak. And she seemed devoted to him. But if they kept arguing, Thomas would never bless the marriage. Sally wasted no time thinking about her younger brother-in-law. The sooner that thorn-in-her-side returned to his English friends, the better. She thought there was little chance Elam would hop down on the Amish side of the fence.

Sally spent so much time contemplating the rocky romance of her houseguests that she forgot to fret about the upcoming visit. She was negotiating the ruts and potholes of Agnes's driveway before she knew it. Unfortunately, peeling paint on the house, sagging porch steps, and overgrown flower beds indicated that the Millers hadn't felt well in a while. Thomas had suggested that the district help with major chores, but his offer had been soundly refused. The elderly couple didn't seem to recognize that their property was falling into disrepair.

After tying her horse to the post, Sally inhaled a deep breath and marched up the path with her sons in tow. "*Guder mariye*," she greeted the moment her knock was answered.

Agnes Miller stood in the doorway wearing a spattered, wrinkled apron and a prayer *kapp* that hadn't been starched or ironed.

"Sally Detweiler, what are you doing here?" Her gaze scanned the baby carrier and Aden with little joy. "I hope you hadn't planned to ask me to babysit for a few hours. I'm really not up to it." Agnes sounded fatigued beyond description.

"Goodness, no. I just brought them along for the ride when I decided to come visit today." Carrying Jeremiah, Sally pulled Aden by the hand into the room, fearing an invitation to enter might not be extended. Her peripheral vision took in more clutter and disorganization than normal for a Plain home, even by her own modest standards.

The older woman wrung her hands. "I wasn't expecting company." She looked around her kitchen with apparent unease. "I hope you won't gossip that Agnes Miller allowed her house to go to seed." She forced a laugh and moved to block Sally's view of a sink filled with dirty dishes. "My gout has flared up something awful."

Sally placed the baby carrier on a chair and bent down to Aden. "You sit next to your brother and do not move." Her tone of voice meant business. "Of course not," she said to Agnes. "The fact that you're under the weather is why I'm here." She held up a hand when the other woman began to protest. "Hear me out, Agnes. You did me a great service after a preaching service not long ago. You came to my rescue, so I'm here to return the favor. And I won't take no for an answer."

Confusion pinched the woman's face. "How do you mean?"

"You were first to volunteer to bring potato salad for the after-service meal. Once you stepped forward as a district elder, the other women followed your lead."

"I'm no elder, unless we're only talking age." But her features softened while her posture relaxed. "And why shouldn't I have? It was a good idea. We should have started doing that a while ago. No sense in one woman bearing all the work and expense while the rest of us sit around."

"I appreciated your support because the women respect your judgment."

Agnes nodded modestly and then gestured toward a kitchen chair. "Care to sit a spell and tell me how you aim to return the favor? I have coffee that's still warm."

Sally grinned. "Coffee sounds *gut*, but I need to get something from my buggy and unhitch my horse into your paddock." She hooked a thumb at her sons. "I promise you'll only be stuck watching them for five, maybe ten minutes at the most."

"That long I can handle." Agnes opened her cupboard for mugs.

Once Sally returned with the food, she noticed the woman had donned a fresh apron.

"What have you brought?" Suspicion returned to Agnes's voice.

"Well, because you haven't been feeling well, I made a few meals to tide you and Joseph over. I expect you'll do the same for me one day when I'm ailing."

Agnes peered into the picnic basket. "Is your pork roast with braised purple cabbage in here? And maple syrup sweet potatoes?"

"They are." Sally lifted out the pie. "Amy King insisted I bring this pie she baked, even though everyone knows *your* Dutch apple pies are the best around."

Agnes lifted a corner of the foil and sniffed. "That may be, but I've had plenty of practice. And there's no reason to hurt the young woman's feelings." She carried the pie to her windowsill as though it were still cooling from the oven.

When light from the window illuminated her face, Sally saw just how much Agnes was suffering. "Why don't you sit down? I heard from Thomas about your gout and know it's really painful."

"It's my own fault. That doctor in Waterville gave me a list of foods I shouldn't eat, but most of my favorites are on it. Don't eat meat or broth? All Joseph ever wants is either meat and potatoes or a big kettle of soup. How can you make soup without broth?" She limped toward the table and lowered herself slowly into a chair.

"That can be a challenge. But that doc didn't say anything about purple cabbage or sweet potatoes, did he?"

A smile brightened the color of Agnes's cheeks. "*She* did not."

Sally perched a hand on her hip. "Now, you sit and tell me the district news. I'm going to wash those dishes, scrub the kitchen floor, and maybe run a few loads of laundry. I'll bet the cellar steps are nearly impossible these days."

"I can't manage them or the ones up to our bedroom. I started sleeping on the living room couch. Joseph refuses to spend the night apart, so he sleeps in the recliner." She lowered her voice to a whisper. "The wash is frightfully overflowing the hamper."

"Then I will start on that first. I'll ask Thomas and John to stop by to move the washing machine from the basement to the back porch. That should make things easier. And I have a foldaway bed no one is using. Why don't you borrow it just until this flare-up passes? That'll give Joseph the couch—better for his back, *jah*?"

Agnes stared down at her liver-spotted hands. "*Jah*, truly so. *Danki*, Sally. You're a godsend to me today, especially because I'm not the most deserving woman in the district for your kindness." She didn't lift her gaze from her hands.

"Nonsense. I'm still figuring out everything a minister's wife is supposed to do. So don't be surprised if I come to you for a little advice now and then."

When Agnes looked up, Sally saw tears in her eyes. "I'd be happy and honored to help."

Sally pulled crayons and a farm animal coloring book from her tote bag for Aden. "Don't forget, while I'm downstairs with the laundry, you're stuck babysitting my *kinner* up here." She winked impishly.

Agnes hooted with laughter. "I had a notion you would rope

me into that, Sally Detweiler! But I suppose I can manage these
rascals for a little while." She smoothed back a lock of Jeremiah's
hair as a tear ran down her face.

Sally left to search for the overflowing laundry hamper before
she started crying too.

                                    ❧

Amy waved until Sally's buggy reached the bend in the road.
Nora was already halfway back to the house. "You shouldn't have
reminded Sally about Agnes's comment on the turkey sandwiches."
She ran to catch up.

"Why not?" asked Nora, waiting for her on the steps. "A person
should be prepared to enter the lion's den."

"And what would you know about that?" Amy held open the
door.

"I attend services here in Harmony, don't I?" Nora walked into
the warm, cozy kitchen. "What shall we mice do while the cat is
away?" She winked one shiny green eye. "Maybe call the hired
van to take us shopping in Waterville? We can bring home pizza
for supper."

Amy stared at the girl. "Have you lost your mind? I assured
Sally we would tend to chores in her absence—not run off the
moment she turned her back. We have lunch and dinner to make.
And I thought we would wash walls to start fall cleaning."

"I'm not sure who we're cooking for. I've haven't seen hide nor
hair of Thomas or Elam. And John seems to be avoiding you lately."

"He has chores, same as us. You finish up in here while I scrub
the bathtub." Amy walked away from her sister before she lost her
temper. The woman had landed too close to the truth—John *did*
seem to avoid her. But, after all, hadn't she requested some thinking time? Perhaps he was only giving her the space she wanted.

Their self-imposed separation ended at lunchtime. The side door banged against the wall as John paused long enough to toe off his mud-caked boots. Then he bounded into the room like a stallion jumping a fence. "Where are you, Amy?" he called.

"I'm right here!" She stepped from the walk-in pantry into the kitchen, flashing him a smile.

"Sorry about shouting. I didn't see you." He hung up his chore coat and hat. "I talked to Thomas in the barn. The bishop agreed at last to let us join the marriage counseling classes. Thomas will provide any information we might have missed during the first class." He grasped the chair back but didn't sit down. "Isn't that *wundabaar?*"

Amy felt a surge of affection for his excitement. Few men approached mandatory marital sessions with such enthusiasm. "It is. I'm glad he finally realized we're not running back to Pennsylvania on the next train from Portland." She pulled bags of cold cuts, cheese, and condiments from the fridge for their lunch.

"A few new rules won't scare us off. Not since we've come to the land of milk and honey."

"And where would that be?" Nora materialized in the doorway. "Surely you don't mean here. The thermometer says it's only twenty-five degrees outside. The bees are all dead and milk would freeze solid."

John swallowed hard. "I am speaking of Harmony, sister. When someone is ready to buy a new home, he or she appreciates properties still affordable by the common man."

Nora set the loaf of bread on the table and turned toward Amy. "It's too late to marry this season. November is half over."

"Couples in this district can marry anytime—December, January, February. There's no wedding season here," said Amy. "At least we can join the group that will marry before Christmas."

Nora shrugged her thin shoulders. "They have no season because the district is so small. Who would come to these weddings that you don't already see each and every Sunday?" She slumped into a chair.

"Probably so," agreed John, building himself a huge sandwich.

Nora placed a modest portion of ham on her multigrain bread. "I wonder who'll be here for Thanksgiving dinner. Will it just be the six of us....and maybe Elam?"

Amy heard the note of delight at the mention of Elam's name but said nothing. But she set jars of pickles and beets down with a thud.

"It will be the same people who eat here every Thursday evening." Thomas had entered through the back door silently and walked to his seat at the table. "The English holiday has no place in a Plain household." He bowed his head in silent prayer as did the others.

When they finished, Nora stared at him. "What's wrong with Thanksgiving? It's simply a time to give thanks for the bounty of the Lord."

"We need a special day on the calendar to do that?" Thomas aimed his piercing blue eyes at Nora. "We should express our gratitude daily, without fail."

Nora picked up her sandwich but met his gaze. "I agree, but I don't understand the harm in this particular English celebration. It's just family and friends coming together to share a big meal."

A muscle jumped in Thomas's jaw. "I've been to Thanksgiving dinners on occasion. Folks usually stuff themselves until painfully uncomfortable and then they fall asleep in their chairs. That's nothing but an exercise in gluttony."

For several seconds no one spoke. Then Amy said quietly, "I do like the holiday, but you're right about overeating. I've been guilty of that myself in the past."

"So, no Thanksgiving in Harmony?" Nora pressed the issue while nibbling her sandwich.

"*Nein.*" Thomas scooped pickled beets onto his plate.

"What about Christmas?"

He stared at her. "Surely back in Lancaster you didn't decorate a Christmas tree, hang stockings by the fire, and place a wooden Santa with sleigh and reindeer across the roof?" His tone was soft but deadly serious.

Amy exchanged an uncomfortable look with John. He held his giant, gluttonous sandwich in midair.

"Nooooo." Nora dragged out the word. "But we baked pretty Christmas cookies to share, sang carols at church and singings, exchanged inexpensive gifts, and had another *big* turkey dinner." Amy's gutsy sister didn't back down.

Thomas didn't reply to that, but his brows coming together above his nose and a mottled red complexion adequately expressed his opinion. He started to eat with urgency, as though suddenly remembering somewhere he needed to go.

"Well," interjected Amy. "The meaning of Christmas is remembering the arrival of the Savior. I'm sure we can read the three accounts of His birth in the Gospels on Christmas Eve."

Thomas nodded at Amy. "*Jah*, of course, you can. That's how we usually mark the holy day."

John cleared his throat and changed the subject. "I told Amy that the bishop will allow us to take the marriage classes."

Thomas fixed his blue eyes on Amy. "*Jah*, the bishop said you can join them. Is that your desire, Amy, to wed over the coming winter months?"

"It is. We would be married by now if we hadn't moved here."

"But you did make the move. I hope you have found our district satisfactory to make a home in."

"I have." She set down her glass, squirming a little under his assessment.

"In that case you need to be at his daughter's house at three o'clock." Thomas rose to his feet, pushing back his plate. "*Danki* for lunch."

"*Today?*" squawked Amy.

"*Jah* and every other week for four sessions, always on the Thursday before a preaching Sunday."

John was already shrugging into his coat. "I must check livestock in the pasture and clean stalls. Be ready to leave by two, Amy. An hour should be ample time to get there. His daughter doesn't live too far away." He smiled gloriously, donned his hat, and left by the side door, as did Thomas.

"Does this mean we don't have to start fall cleaning today? I hate washing walls." Nora pulled apart her sandwich to eat only the meat, cheese, and tomato slice. She tossed the homemade bread into the compost bucket.

A ripple of irritation nearly made Amy's eyes cross. "Nora King, if you're not the laziest person in this state, I don't know who is! We've enjoyed Sally's hospitality for *months*, yet you barely lift a finger to help her out. You should be ashamed of yourself. *Mamm* would be ashamed of you."

Nora's eyes quickly filled with tears. She dropped the remnants of her lunch onto her plate. "I was only joking. I assumed we would at least start on one room."

Amy carried a stack of plates to the sink. "Well, today you're not very funny. And we'll do more than just start a room. While I do the dishes, you move the furniture away from the walls in the living room." She turned her back on her sibling, who left without uttering another word.

By the time Amy had cleaned the kitchen, her temper had cooled. She found Nora in the front room washing windows with vinegar and newspapers. The rug had been rolled up and the furniture sat in the center of the room. Yet despite her restored calm, she couldn't bring herself to apologize to Nora. That girl had pushed the limits of polite behavior for too long.

Unfortunately, because they toiled in silence, Amy couldn't stop work until the room was finished. Once they moved the last chair back in place, Amy hurried to the bathroom for a long, refreshing shower. The hot water cascading down her sore muscles brought soothing relief. Her respite, however, proved short lived. A knock on the bathroom door broke her pleasant daydream of sunny weather back home.

"Are you about done in there? We need to leave within the next few minutes to arrive on time."

Sheer panic paralyzed Amy under the stream of water. Why on earth had she let her hair get wet? But the warm water had felt so good on her prickly scalp. "I lost track of time. *Mir leid*, but I promise to hurry."

"Amy, it's our initial meeting. What kind of an impression will we make if we're late?"

"I wanted to clean at least one room before Sally returned." She shut off the water, grabbed a towel, and stepped from the tub, chillier than the room's temperature would warrant.

"Do you mean to say you're still dripping wet?" His tone was half growl, half mutter.

"The more we talk about the situation, the longer it will take me to get ready. Please, John, wait for me outside. I won't be long."

Amy King kept her word. Never before had she dressed, towel-dried her hair, and braided it into a coil so fast. She grabbed her purse, bonnet, and cloak from the peg without taking the time to search for her sister. Supper would be Nora's sole responsibility. Amy ran out the door to their buggy. Yet her intended *ehemann* brooded all the way to the home of the bishop's daughter. Even though he trotted the Morgan as fast as he dared, they were still ten minutes late.

Once they were inside, Mary took their coats. "Did you get caught in a downpour?" she asked, studying Amy curiously. "I don't believe it rained here."

"What? No, it wasn't raining along the way." She gingerly touched her damp prayer *kapp*.

"Excuse us, Mary. We don't want to keep folks waiting longer than we already have." John took Amy's arm and guided her down the hall and into the living room. Conversation ceased as all eyes turned in their direction. A moment later fond greetings of welcome sang out.

Amy tried to explain their delay, but Bishop Andrew shook his head. "All's well. Come sit close to the fire. You look cold."

The group's friendliness, along with the bishop's patience, soon put Amy at ease. She noticed that even John stretched out his long legs and unclenched his hands after a while. They listened intently while the expectations of *fraas* and *ehemanns* were clearly defined. Then Andrew explained in detail the customs and procedures for the wedding day. Afterward, each couple shared their plans for starting married life. In most cases the young couple would live with one set of parents until able to build a home on the family farm.

"I understand you bought a farm on Waterville Road." The bishop directed his statement toward William and Sarah, their new friends from the pig roast.

"Yes, but the place needs lots of work before it can be called a home," said William. "We plan to live with Sarah's parents until the spring. John and Amy won't have to wait, though. They bought a really nice house on Thorndike Road—biggest house in the neighborhood."

All eyes fastened on them. John seemed to puff up larger, but Amy shrank into her chair, not comfortable with William's boasting. Pride was never encouraged in any Amish community.

"Large, *jah*," she said. "But that house needs plenty of work too. It hasn't been lived in for a while, and the elderly owners weren't able to do much upkeep when they were still there. If that's even the one we purchase…we're having a bit of disagreement about it."

"How so?" asked Andrew, looking directly at John.

John deflated inside his shirt and vest. "I want to pool our money and pay cash, avoiding a mortgage altogether."

"But that would deplete our funds," interjected Amy, "leaving nothing for repairs or necessary furnishings or unexpected doctor bills." She spoke louder than she'd intended. The hardwood floor, without the softening effect of an area rug, didn't help.

The bishop gazed at John and then at Amy. "I understand your concern, but it is the Amish way to avoid borrowing money whenever possible. God will provide for your needs, including furniture. And you'll have the entire district's help with major repairs or medical expenses." He possessed the calm, gentle voice of a wise old man.

"I'll give it some thought. But in our case, we don't need to rush into anything." Amy folded her hands and leaned back in her chair.

She didn't look at her fiancé, because she truly didn't wish to see his expression.

෨

"It's pitch-dark already," murmured Amy, stating the obvious.

John hitched his horse to the buggy as a sharp wind blew through his thin coat. It was time to start wearing his heaviest wool. "I imagine it's about half past six." He kept his tone as pleasant as possible.

"It sure makes a difference when we take the clocks off of daylight savings time." She settled herself on the seat and wrapped the blanket around her legs.

"Some districts don't change to fast time, but Harmony isn't one of them."

"I would like daylight savings time all year round."

John had no comment to this, so he merely grunted. With a cluck of his tongue, the buggy began to roll down the driveway toward home. Trained Amish horses could find their way back on the darkest nights, even if the driver fell sound asleep.

After a minute Amy turned to face him. "You're awfully quiet, John. Is something bothering you? Why not just come out and speak your mind."

He inhaled a deep breath and released it. "Okay, then, I'll do that. If you disagree with me, I wish you would wait until we're alone to voice your opinion instead of doing so in front of our friends and certainly not in front of the bishop. He might not choose to marry a couple who quarrels over minor details."

Amy wrinkled her nose. "I see your point to a certain extent. But if I let the matter go, it would be like lying because I haven't made up my mind about paying the full amount in cash. And I would hardly describe my inheritance—my entire life savings—as a *minor* detail."

John considered the "what's yours is mine" aspect of most marriages but decided to hold his tongue. Maybe he would feel differently if he had inherited more than a hundred thousand dollars. So he selected a benign response. "All right, but when you come to a decision could you let me know?" He tugged some of the lap robe over his legs.

"You shall be the first I tell." She angled a wry grin. "I wish I'd eaten more cookies with my cup of hot chocolate. I am starving."

"Me too. I wonder what Sally and Nora fixed for supper. I sure hope they saved us some." He let the horse pick up speed on the straightaway.

"Oh, no!" she exclaimed. "Sally's away today helping a sick district member. She'll be gone until late. Supper was left up to Nora and me, but then we were called to the couples meeting." She gripped the edge of the seat for support. "I didn't tell Nora what to do."

John patted her arm. "Relax. Nora is twenty years old, not nine. I'm sure she saw us leave and figured out that making dinner was her job. Goodness, Amy. Sometimes you treat her like an English houseguest, not a grown Amish woman."

She smiled weakly. "You're absolutely right. We'll eat whatever she's made even if it's soup and day-old bread."

"I'm so hungry I'll probably fight you for the last stale crust, but all will be well."

But all was not well. When John drove the buggy inside the Detweiler barn, he found his brother tending livestock by lantern light. "Good evening," he greeted and unharnessed the horse as quickly as he could. "I hope you saved us something to eat. We only got a few women-type cookies with cherries stuck in the center. That stanchion of hay is starting to look good."

Thomas fixed him with his blue-eyed stare. "You'll find cold cuts and cheese in the refrigerator in their usual location."

John led the Morgan to his stall and began brushing with serious intent. "What do you mean by sandwich fixings? Is that what you ate?" He spoke over the stall wall.

"It was." Thomas strolled to where John worked. "A sandwich and a cup of reheated coffee. A pie had been cut into slivers, but I left my share for someone else. It didn't seem enough to dirty a plate."

John's empty gut rumbled. "I know Sally has been away, but wasn't Nora home all day?"

"She was, but she got caught up in fall cleaning and forgot to make supper." Thomas held his brother's gaze for a moment before returning to his own chores.

John carefully drew the brush through the mane and tried to tamp down his anger. He didn't succeed. When he finished the rubdown and fed and watered his horse, he headed to the house as though on a mission. The kitchen was empty, but he heard water running in the bathroom. "Amy?" he called at the door.

"I'm frozen solid, John," she called back. "I'm drawing a tub. Give me a little time and I'll reheat something from dinner."

John marched into the living room. He knew dinner had not been prepared and put away. He found Nora by the woodstove reading a library book with her feet on a stool. A crocheted shawl was draped around her shoulders.

"Is it too much for you to take up the slack when Sally and Amy are both gone?"

Nora blinked her catlike eyes. "I did. I scrubbed the house all day until maybe an hour ago. My hands are red and cracked from the cleaning solution." She set her book on the floor to give him full attention.

"That's all well and good, but you need to assume responsibilities when they are left in your hands. Have you never heard of multitasking? As fond of *Englischers* as you are, surely you've heard of the concept. While cleaning, you could have stewed some beef or baked a chicken."

Nora narrowed her focus into a glare. "Amy left without saying a word. I thought she planned to return in time for supper. I would have been happy to take care of it if she'd mentioned—"

"You shouldn't need to be told or left a reminder on a Post-it," interrupted John. "You are an adult, Nora. If you wish to be pampered like a child, then I suggest you move back to *grossmammi*'s. Which is exactly where I will send you if you don't straighten out!"

Her mouth fell open with shock and humiliation. Nora King was utterly speechless for the first time in her life.

John clamped down on his molars, shocked by his vehemence. The stress of the counseling session and near starvation had taken their toll.

"That is not your decision to make, John Detweiler." Amy stepped from the doorway into the room. "Nora is *my* younger sister, so she is my responsibility, not yours." There was no mistaking the strength of her conviction. "We are not man and wife yet... and at this rate, maybe we never will be." Her voice trembled with exasperation. Stress and fatigue had taken its toll on her too.

He spoke without thinking. "You sound just like her, Amy, which makes you far too willful to be my wife."

John strode quickly from his brother's house and ran down the lane toward the road. He kept walking until his rage dwindled to impotent frustration. When he turned toward home, shame, fear, and regret filled his heart. As he sat down to eat bologna-and-cheese in a dark, cold kitchen, he found that his sandwich offered little sustenance.

It stuck in his craw alongside his mean-spirited words.

SIXTEEN

See Thee on Thy judgment throne

Awave of relief like a summer shower washed over Thomas as Sally's buggy pulled up the driveway. Although he hadn't expected her home much before then, he worried whenever she was on the road after dark. And tonight both of his sons had been with her. "Whoa," he said to the horse, catching the bridle on his second attempt.

"He's eager to get to his oats in the barn." Sally pulled on the reins. "But not quite as eager as I am to relax with a cup of tea." She handed down a drowsy Aden.

"How did it go at the Millers?" Thomas held on to the horse with one hand while he clutched his son to his chest with the other.

"*Gut.* Better than I hoped in my fondest dreams." Despite her fatigue, Sally's face glowed with the joy of accomplishment. "At first Agnes didn't want me to see how....*verhuddelt* things had become around the house."

"Mixed-up, you say?" he asked. "That's hard to imagine, but

maybe that's why she had to swallow her pride. She's used to keeping a tidy home."

"Her gout is bad, Thomas, and her husband is too frail to help much. The district should hold a work frolic there before winter comes. The Millers need their home made handicapped accessible, including moving the washing machine from the basement to the ground floor." She climbed down, carrying Jeremiah asleep in the crook of her elbow.

"It will be done as soon as possible." Thomas set Aden on his feet because the boy awoke without the lulling movement of the buggy.

Sally stepped closer to him instead of toward the house. "Oh, Thomas, Agnes made me feel so welcome and appreciated. She praised my cooking as though I'm one of those famous Boston chefs. And she thanked me several times for cleaning and doing her laundry. I have made a true friend in the district." Her eyes sparkled with delight.

"If you have won the heart of Agnes Miller, everyone else will be easy as pie." He placed a tender kiss on her forehead. "Shall I help you put the boys to bed?"

"*Nein*, I can manage while you tend the horse. The sooner you put him away the sooner we can get to bed. I'll brew us cups of chamomile tea to help us sleep." She started up the path and then stopped. "How was supper? Was my *cuisine* put to shame by my Pennsylvania gourmet sisters?" She winked with amusement.

Thomas removed the bit from the horse's mouth. "Let's just say I'm not going to bed hungry, but we won't bring up the subject of tonight's dinner in the foreseeable future."

She shifted the *boppli* to her other arm. "Oh, dear, what happened? You must tell me."

"Nothing to worry about. I'll tell you once we're warm under the quilt. Go inside before you get chilled. I'll join you soon." Thomas watched as Sally lifted Aden to her hip, despite her weariness and his rapidly increasing weight. A wave of emotion seized his heart and lodged in his throat. Danki, *Lord, for bringing Sally into my life and for bringing my family safely home.*

But Thomas found more than a cup of tea waiting in the kitchen once he finished his chores. John sat staring at the wall with a half-eaten sandwich and a cold cup of coffee.

"Aren't you worried about that stuff keeping you awake?" Thomas shrugged off his coat and hat.

"No. If I can't sleep tonight it'll have nothing to do with caffeine." He took another gulp and grimaced.

"Did you have words with Elam?"

John shook his head.

"With Sally?"

His brother's head snapped up. "Of course not. Sally made tea and took hers upstairs to drink while she readied the *kinner* for bed." He pointed toward the stove, where another mug steeped. "She said you shouldn't tarry."

Thomas carried his tea to the table, relaxing his tight shoulders. "Tell me what's wrong if this can't wait until morning."

John glanced up with the eyes of a cornered animal. "When I returned from the counseling session, I lost my temper with Nora for not cooking. I told her when the other women are away, she must stand in their place." He rattled off his two sentences as though the words tasted bitter from the second chewing.

Thomas reflected before speaking. "If you had simply asked for more assistance without allowing your temper to enter the discussion, it would have been a reasonable request." He sipped his cooling tea.

John downed the contents of his mug with another frown. "*Jah,* I came to that conclusion while eating this dry bologna-and-cheese."

"Would you like some mustard or mayonnaise?" Thomas consulted his pocket watch, ready to put the interminable day behind him.

"Nothing will help my parched mouth." John pushed away his plate. "I lost my patience with her."

"That much I gathered."

"She is so dreamy and unfocused, content to stroll through life as though it were a summer garden." He gritted out the words through clenched teeth.

"She does have more maturing to do before all is said and done."

"That's an understatement. I don't like the way she takes advantage of Sally and Amy, letting them do the lion's share of the work."

"I haven't observed that to be the case, John, but if it is, I believe my wife and your wife-to-be won't put up with it for long."

John crossed his arms, shaking his head. "There's more. I'd better tell you everything." He sucked in air as though preparing for a deep-sea dive. "I told Nora that if she doesn't straighten out, I will send her back to Pennsylvania. Amy overheard me and said I had no right to deliver such an ultimatum."

Thomas allowed a few moments to pass. "Amy is right. You don't."

John's face clouded with confusion and resentment. "But I brought the women here from Lancaster. I feel they are my responsibility."

"They are not." Thomas rose to his feet. "At least, they're not under your authority. You shouldn't have threatened her in such a fashion. You need to deal with Nora with patience and kindness or not at all." He rinsed out his empty mug.

John struggled up and carried his dishes to the sink. He glanced around to make sure they wouldn't be overheard. "Frankly, I'm confused. Didn't the bishop tell you to give Elam just such an ultimatum? He must conform to our ways or leave by Christmas." He peered up with earnestness.

Thomas knew he was treading along a slippery slope, so he chose his words carefully. "Indeed he did, but the situations aren't the same. As his brother and minister, I have been patient and tolerant for years. I've overlooked his refusal to follow the *Ord-nung*, hoping he'll join the church family and commit his life to God. But it never happened. Now that he's led another to stray— to sin with drunkenness—I must draw a line in the sand. Such is not the case with Nora. She's been here only a few months and is still learning our ways. She's younger than Elam, and the recent deaths of her parents have no doubt affected her judgment. We need a far gentler hand with her than with our wayward *bruder*."

John ran a hand through his tangled hair. "What should I do?"

"Reach out with love as the Savior taught us. Maybe Nora will adjust and conform, or maybe she'll return to Pennsylvania. But either way, your anger is just as onerous a sin as her willfulness."

John gazed out the window. Darkness offered nothing to look at as he mulled things over. "It's true she hasn't been here that long."

"And, I must add, if and when Nora's behavior needs correction, it should come from me as her pastor, not from you."

John's brows lowered to the bridge of his nose while a muscle jumped in his neck. "Nora will become part of my immediate family, not yours. Won't her actions reflect on Amy?"

Thomas placed a hand on John's shoulder. "Go to bed. Tomorrow life might not seem so grim. Fatigue always magnifies our anxieties." Thomas walked wearily to the stairs and climbed them with the gait of a seventy-year-old man.

❧

Nora drew the quilt over her head and pretended to be asleep when Amy came into their room after her bath. She didn't know what had been said between John and her sister because after John left Nora had fled to their room like a scared rabbit. Feeling as though she'd been slapped, she undressed quickly and hid under the covers. Never before in her life had she been spoken to in such a way—not by *mamm* or even *daed*. *Daed* had waited for a cooler head before correcting his children's bad behavior.

Mamm *and* daed...*why did you have to go and die? Now the family has been split apart and our lives surely ruined.*

At least hers was ruined here in Waldo County, Maine, where she was nothing but a thorn in everyone's side. How could she face John tomorrow at breakfast, or at supper, or any other time after causing trouble with Amy? She should have stayed home with Rachel and Beth and not come to the land of tall pines and long winters.

The next morning she stayed in bed while Amy dressed, pinned up her hair under a fresh *kapp*, and went downstairs. Nora watched by the window until John and Thomas headed to the barn before she ventured below to the kitchen. She preferred to encounter no males until she had a chance to talk with her sister. Amy and Sally were eating creamed wheat with smoked sausages when she entered the warm room.

"How are you feeling?" asked Amy, immediately rising to pour her sister some coffee. "I hope your migraine hasn't returned." She set the cup next to Nora's place at the table.

"No, I feel okay. Just a little hungry. I'll fix lunch today by myself since I didn't help with breakfast." Nora sipped her coffee, believing the beverage had never tasted so good.

Sally placed a mounded bowl of hot cereal in front of Nora that had been liberally sprinkled with cinnamon and sugar. "We'll worry about lunch when it gets here. You just eat and don't give another thought to my cranky brother-in-law." Sally patted Nora's back fondly.

Amy scooted her chair closer. "No one will send you anywhere you don't wish to go, Nora. Sally is right. John was cranky due to hunger and because of something I said at the marriage meeting." Amy patted her arm.

Nora felt like a pampered lapdog instead of a sister from all the petting. "Dinner *should* have occurred to me. You told me we were in charge, and I saw you leave with John. But I got caught up in housework and let time slip away."

"It happens to all of us," said Sally from her position next to Aden. She kept watch to make sure food reached his stomach and not the floor.

"I don't do my share." Nora ate one bite, followed by a second, and then she began to gobble up her breakfast. After yesterday's spat with John, she'd skipped dinner altogether.

"You often don't feel well. Besides, it's not John's place to correct you." Amy reached again for the coffeepot on the stove.

"And Thomas told him exactly that when he came inside last night. You were already upstairs."

Nora looked from one to the other and smiled. "*Danki*. You are both very sweet to stick up for me."

"What are sisters for?" Amy filled the sink with sudsy water to do dishes.

Although Nora appreciated their kindness, it also filled her with shame. *I am causing nothing but problems in Amy's life. Defending me last night may have driven an irreparable wedge between her and John. Why should she be forced to choose between us?*

Nora performed her chores that day as though in a fog. Even Aden's and Jeremiah's amusing antics couldn't dislodge the sorrow that had settled around her heart. She was no longer a traveler from another state—a houseguest recovering from the painful loss of her parents. She was a pariah who had overstayed her welcome...like Elam. Not for the first time, she felt a kinship with the youngest Detweiler brother.

That night, while Amy slept, Nora took up her vigil at the bedroom window. She watched the moonlit backyard for any sign of movement while wearing her socks and tennis shoes. Deep within her heart she knew her footwear wasn't for protection from chilly floorboards. For hours Nora stared into the darkness, waiting, hoping, fantasizing.

Her patience finally found its reward.

Elam appeared on the lawn beneath her window. He paused to light a cigarette, pull up the collar of his coat, and tug his hat down over his ears. During his brief hesitation, Nora flew from their bedroom like a bat and crept down the steps. She lifted her outer bonnet and full-length cloak from the peg and closed the back door behind her, careful not to make a sound.

She decided to follow him simply to see where he went.

At any time he could have turned around and spotted her because the harvested fields provided few hiding places. But he didn't turn. Elam strode through rows where corn had recently stood, hopped a fence, and then crossed the pasture where goats and cows happily comingled. Only darkness hid Nora's stealthy trail as she climbed the fence with far less grace.

Exhilaration kept her from noticing the cold gusts that cut through her wool cloak. Sheer determination kept her moving when one mile dragged into two.

Finally Elam jogged down a slope, ducked between fence rails, and jumped a ditch. He landed on a dirt-and-gravel lane that led into the wooded hills. As Nora watched from the high ground, he lit another cigarette. But before he'd smoked barely half, a vehicle approached from the main road. The driver slowed and flashed his headlights, illuminating Elam's broad shoulders and straight profile. Elam stepped forward, waving his hat as the car came to a stop.

Nora observed from her vantage point behind a bush, transfixed by the mystery of a late night rendezvous. Elam climbed not into the passenger side of the car, but the driver's side. He turned the vehicle around with only two jockeying maneuvers as though he'd been driving for years. The taillights soon disappeared into the night as the car exited at a far faster speed than its arrival.

Nora trekked back to the house unaware of hidden puddles soaking her shoes and dampening the hem of her dress. Her head whirred with questions. *Where was he going? How did he learn to drive like that? Who moved over on the seat and gave him the wheel?* She felt neither the November wind whipping down from frozen Canada, nor the droplets of rain starting to fall. Catching Elam in his clandestine activity had distracted her from the foul weather. Even crossing unfamiliar, alien land in total darkness didn't frighten her.

Nora slipped in the back door and crept through the kitchen like a mouse. The possibility that someone—Thomas, John, Amy, or Sally—might be waiting for her, expecting an explanation, had never occurred to her. What could she have said? *Oh, I saw Elam leave like a thief in the night, so I decided to sneak out after him.* She couldn't face another scene like yesterday's and didn't want to make more trouble for her sister.

But no one lurked, ready to pounce, in the kitchen. The house's occupants slumbered peacefully as Nora dripped on the floor mat, considering what to do next. A sane woman would have hung up her wet garments and returned to bed, satisfied with the late night adventure.

Apparently, Nora King didn't fit that description.

Leaning on the countertop on both elbows, she waited at the kitchen window for the secretive man to return. Sometimes she dozed, only to be awakened by her head bobbing to her chest. Other times her tired eyes spotted imaginary phantoms drifting across the frost-kissed fields. But when Elam finally approached the outside entrance to his cellar bedroom, Nora was neither asleep nor daydreaming. She sprang out the door, went around the corner of the house, and landed directly in his path.

"Holy cow, Nora, you almost gave me a heart attack!" Elam clutched his chest with both hands. "What are you doing out here? It's the middle of the night."

"I know what time it is. What are *you* doing?" Nora purred soft as a cat with her hands clasped behind her back.

He stared at her, mystified. Then the corners of his mouth lifted into a smile. "You were spying on me." His expression of confusion changed to pleasure.

"True. After all, what else is there to do around the farm for entertainment?"

"You're the only woman I know who wouldn't lie about spying on a man." He glanced up at the second-floor windows.

"I see no reason to lie about anything." Nora lifted and dropped her shoulders. "I saw you get into that *Englischer's* car."

Judging by his face, this information shocked him. "You followed me that far?" Elam pulled her down a few steps so they wouldn't be seen or overheard. "You'd better keep mum about that unless you want me run out of town on a rail."

"I'll keep quiet if you tell me where you went," she whispered with newfound boldness.

"Nowhere, really. We just cruise around. My friend taught me to drive and lets me practice with his car. I memorized the English booklet of rules and regulations from cover to cover. We don't go far—only to the shopping center lot so I can practice maneuvering around cones. I already have my temporary permit and I'll take the test next week." Elam's black eyes danced in his head.

Nora didn't understand about "temporary permit" or "cones," but that hardly mattered. Elam was taking the English driver's test. She'd known only one Amish man ever to do that. "Whatever for?" she asked, peering up at him. "All you have is a buggy and a fast horse."

"Don't be a little goose. I don't plan to stay in Harmony forever, especially if another logging job doesn't open up soon. And I can't very well walk or take a buggy where I'm going." He lifted her chin with the gentlest of touches. "Now go on inside. You're starting to shiver. And you don't want to get caught with a no-good man like me."

Before she could argue, he grabbed her hand and pulled her up the steps to the lawn. "Good night, Nora. Sweet dreams," he whispered. After a courtly tip of his hat, he disappeared back down into his subterranean cave.

Nora stood in the dark with a racing heart and skin tingling where he had touched it. Elam didn't need to remind her to keep quiet. Wild mustangs couldn't have dragged the secret from her.

❧

Amy sat at the kitchen table with her second cup of coffee, trying to understand how her life had tangled into such a snarl. Every mental avenue she traveled down appeared to be a dead end. In her state of turmoil, she wasn't aware that Sally had entered the room until she spoke.

"What are you doing up? It's not yet five a.m. Even the rooster hasn't crowed."

"I couldn't sleep. I'm trying to figure out how to patch up things with John. Just because he lost his head doesn't mean I should have lost mine. You know what they say about two wrongs."

Sally reached for her favorite mug and the coffeepot. "First, you need to decide what you want, Amy King."

"What do you mean?"

"Why did you come here? Spell it out for me. I have plenty of time. Both boys are still asleep."

Amy considered the question carefully. "I came to make a new life for myself with John."

"And Maine is where you wish that new life to be?" Sally squinted as though in bright sunlight.

"Definitely. I've fallen in love with Harmony."

"And John is the man you want to marry?" Sally added two heaping spoonfuls of sugar to her mug and stirred her coffee slowly.

"*Jah*. I can't imagine my life without John in it."

"Then why do you keep fighting him at every turn?" The teaspoon clattered onto the table.

Amy flinched—annoyed, then frightened, and then saddened by the question. After an uncomfortable minute she answered, "I don't know why. I suppose I'm afraid to surrender to him and give up my independence. I need to maintain control, especially for Nora's sake."

Sally tilted her head, looking genuinely perplexed. "What do you suppose would happen to Nora if you let down your guard?"

"I'm afraid to think about it. I know she doesn't want to return to Lancaster," she whispered, ashamed she might be betraying a confidence. "I must make things work for her here."

"You're capable of doing that?" Sally stared without blinking. "You can make another person's life run smoothly?"

Amy fussed with her paper napkin. "I must try, Sally. I'm her only confidant since our parents died. Although, John is right about one thing—my pampering and overprotecting will only cripple her. I might have done that already. This morning when I shook her so we could talk, she snapped at me. She said she needed to sleep and that I should leave her alone." Amy gulped her coffee black, needing all the fortification she could get.

"No one would describe her as a morning person." Sally's giggle dissipated some of the tension.

"Nora pays lip service to helping around the house more, but then she sleeps in until ten o'clock." Amy leaned her head back and shut her eyes. "But we've gotten off track. I need to fix things with John, not map out my sister's future."

Sally finished her drink before speaking. "Okay, you wish to make a life here with John. What else is important to you?"

"I love having family around me. That's why I want Nora to stay in Maine and the house we purchase to be near you and Thomas and your boys…" She heard the childish tone in her voice and stopped herself.

"Go on," prodded Sally. "It's just you and me and God. Get this off your chest. There's nothing you can't admit to me, not with my checkered past."

Amy wiped her eyes, moist with unshed tears. "That's one reason I wanted to reconnect with Aunt Prudence. She was so much like my mother back in Lancaster. *Mamm* is gone, but I still could have Aunt Prudence if she would only move to Harmony. In some odd way I need her in my life, and she turned her back on me. I wonder if she really did write two letters or if she just said that to cover her tracks. Why wouldn't I have received them?" Her voice trembled, betraying her insecurity.

Tick, tock, tick, tock—the clock on the wall marked the passage of time. Amy heard stirring overhead. Thomas must be getting up, rising from his knees after morning prayers. She scrambled to her feet. "I had better start the bacon. The men will want a hot meal when they finish chores."

"Sit!" ordered Sally. "We're not done yet. Breakfast can wait."

Amy plopped down. She'd never heard such vehemence from the woman before. "What is it?"

For several moments Sally stared at the ceiling as though it might reveal the answers. "She did mail the letters, Amy. Prudence Summerton wrote back to you just like she said."

"How do you know that? What happened to them, then?"

Sally's face contorted as if she were chewing on a sour lemon. "I know, that's all. Can't you just take my word for it?"

Amy shook her head back and forth. "*Nein*, I can't. You're the one who started this bare-your-soul conversation, so you cannot stop midstream. Tell me what you're hiding."

Sally sighed, sad but resigned. "I know the postman delivered letters here shortly after you wrote to Aunt Prudence. John found them. Who else could they have been from with a Chestnut postmark?"

"If that's true, where are they?" Icy fingers clawed along her backbone, despite her proximity to the woodstove.

"He threw them into the fire. I saw him do it. Later I poked through the ashes after he left the room. The Summertons' return address was still visible on the envelope."

Amy heard movement behind her as she tried to process Sally's news. She turned to see John Detweiler in the doorway as her belly took a tumble. He stood mute and motionless as though struck by a paralytic fit.

"Is it so, John? Did you burn my aunt's letters?"

"*Jah*, I did."

With those three words, everything changed in Amy's life. Everything she had trusted and loved and believed in changed in an instant.

SEVENTEEN

Rock of Ages, cleft for me

If the kitchen floorboards had suddenly heaved apart, opening a deep chasm to the center of the earth, John would have jumped in without hesitation. Certain death would have been preferable to the shocked and miserable expression on Amy's face. He'd awakened that morning with the clear understanding that Thomas was right. Nora's business wasn't any of his. He'd overstepped his role as Amy's fiancé, causing her additional frustration. Dealing with a willful sister must be hard enough without him adding unnecessary pressure.

As he washed and dressed for the day, he planned how he would apologize first to Amy and then to Nora. If they had any future together, he must rein in his need to control situations and have the final word in every discussion. Wasn't marriage a partnership between a man and woman—a meeting of minds as wells as bodies to form a new whole, greater than either half alone? The male wasn't the "big" half, like a pie haphazardly split between siblings.

He heard Amy's voice in the kitchen as soon as he'd left his room. He prayed to know what to say—to have the right words that would undo his badly misguided behavior. He hadn't minded hearing Sally's voice too. After all, how could Amy refuse a sincere apology delivered before a loving witness who only had their best interests at heart? But he hadn't been prepared to hear his grievous sins—sins that shame had forced to the recess of memory—brought forth to convict him on the spot.

"He threw them into the fire. I saw him do it... The Summertons' return address was still visible on the envelope."

The floor, however, didn't rend like an earthquake fault line. John was left facing the only woman he had ever loved.

"Is it so, John? Did you burn my aunt's letters?"

And he had no choice but to admit the terrible truth. Amy turned deathly pale as she ran for the door, grabbing her cloak as an afterthought. "Amy, please wait," he begged. "Let's talk about this. I can explain."

With her hand on the doorknob, she glared at him. Her eyes turned as cold as a high-country stream in spring. "How could you *do* such a thing? You knew how much Aunt Prudence meant to me!" Then she was gone with a resounding slam of the door.

John looked at Sally, who sat motionless at the table, mortified by what she had done.

"I kept your secret for as long as possible," she whispered. "But I couldn't allow her to believe—"

"Stop," he pleaded. "You owe me no explanation. I'm the one who did wrong, not you." He slumped into the chair recently occupied by Amy. "Because of my bullish inflexibility, I have ruined my life."

Sally flinched from his assessment, her forehead creasing with worry. "Maybe not. Everyone makes mistakes, John. If you explained to her why you acted so, perhaps she'll take pity on you." Her grip on her coffee mug tightened.

"And say what? I had no rational excuse for my actions, only the desire to remove what I considered a bad influence from her life. That sounds nothing but mean." He fought back self-indulgent tears. All his troubles, all his misery was his own fault.

"That might be true, but Amy has a generous heart. Maybe she'll forgive you." Sally hesitated and then reached out to pat his arm. "Worth a try, no?"

He nodded. "Worth everything in this world to me. If I die a lonely old man, at least I'll know I tried to make amends." He jumped up, grabbed his coat, and ran from the house. At the end of the driveway he scanned the road in both directions, calling Amy's name. Then he swiftly searched the barn, workshop, and henhouse. Finally, he spotted a solitary female figure walking through the pasture. In the thin light of dawn, she moved like a specter as fog swirled and eddied around her legs. Her head was bent low as she watched the ground for hidden obstacles.

John ran pell-mell after her, heedless when a gust of wind blew his hat from his head. "Amy, wait up," he called once he'd cut the distance between them by half.

Hearing her name, she picked up her skirt and ran. A split rail fence stopped her like a high stone wall. Just as she was ducking her head to climb through the rails, John reached her side.

"Please give me a minute of your time, even though I don't deserve it." He touched her arm.

She recoiled. Hurt, anger, and betrayal filled her glare. "Say your piece, John Detweiler, but be quick about it. And keep your hands to yourself."

He stepped back a pace. "Regardless of what you decide to do, I want to say how truly sorry I am."

"Sorry about what? That you got caught? I'll bet so. If not for Sally, I never would have known of your deception." She crossed her arms, erecting a hostile barrier between them.

How could he answer that? He had no idea if he would have

someday confessed his guilt. "I knew the moment I burned Prudence's letters it was wrong, that I was making a mistake—"

"Then why did you do it not once, but *twice*?"

"I was afraid of losing you." He uttered the words so softly he didn't know if she'd heard. "I feared that an independent woman like Prudence would advise you not to marry. At least, not marry me, a man without means to properly provide for a wife. With your share of the inheritance you could support yourself anywhere until a more suitable candidate came along. I'm sure your aunt wished she had never married Leon Hilty in haste." John stared at wild morning glories, still clinging desperately to life despite several hard frosts.

"*Candidate*?" Amy spat out the word like tainted food. "You weren't a name on an *Englischer*'s election ballot. You were the man I'd fallen in love with. I didn't search for Aunt Prudence for relationship advice. I sought her for the comfort of family around me." Her eyes grew moist and shiny. "You have Thomas and Sally—and even Elam, for that matter. As fond of them as I am, I still yearned for loved ones from home. Prudence was no threat to you. I certainly wouldn't want to emulate her sorrowful life."

"I realize that now and can only beg your forgiveness, Amy. I will regret what I've done till my dying day." He raised his head but the moment their eyes met, he knew his answer. There would be no mercy for his shameful behavior.

There would be no future for them.

She lifted her chin, creating a sharp, angular profile as she turned toward the fence. A black crow had perched on the top rail not far from where they stood. Superstitious people thought those birds carried spirits to the afterlife or were the harbingers of bad news. John thought this time those *Englischers* might be right.

"I may be able to forgive you, John," she said, "but that's as far as it goes. I have no faith that you won't do such things down the road. And I won't marry a man I cannot trust."

Her words rang a death knell for his future. The crow issued an irritated *caw, caw,* took flight, and disappeared into the mist and fog. "You don't love me anymore?" he asked. With shaking fingers, he caressed her cheek with his thumb. The bold act wasn't born from hope, only from the desire to touch her sweet face one last time.

Amy brushed away his hand as though a mosquito on a warm summer day. "I won't marry you, and love has nothing to do with it." With that she walked away from him, down the slope, and out of his life.

John didn't try to stop her or change her mind. He knew it was hopeless.

"Pride has ruined the lives of many good men." The words of his long-dead father rang in his ears as though spoken yesterday. John had heard the warning many times but had never understood its meaning. After a horrible buggy accident took his parents away, he'd never been able to ask for an explanation.

Now he understood. Although he would be hard-pressed to call himself "a good man."

ॐ

Nora had a bad feeling when she awoke that morning, coming on the heels of one bad dream after another. *Ah-choo!* The sneeze brought her upright along with a full recollection of the previous night's events. *Ah-choo!* She reached for a tissue from her nightstand. She shouldn't have snapped at Amy when she tried to wake her earlier. The woman wanted to talk—a normal reaction after taking her side during the argument with John. How could Amy have known she had followed Elam Detweiler through rain, cold, and muddy fields on his late night escapade?

But it was worth catching a cold for it. She'd discovered Elam's secret and formed a special bond with him.

Nora washed her face, pinned up her hair, and donned the

plainest, drabbest dress she owned. She would need to wear sack-cloth and ashes around John to make up for coming between him and his beloved Amy. Though it hadn't been her intention, that had been the final result.

Halfway down the stairs she heard Aden let out a wail. Nora hurried back to his room and found him still prisoner in his crib with both rails up. Many times the boy climbed over the side, but today he stood there crying. "I'll set you free." Nora lifted him up and out, setting his bare feet on the floor.

"Norrah," he said, hugging her around the knees. Then he pad-ded out of the bedroom in search of his mother.

"Hold up there, young man," she called in *Deutsch*, to no avail. Nora grabbed socks from his bureau drawer and followed after him. On her way to the kitchen, she heard Jeremiah crying in the living room portable crib. That sound meant a hungry *boppli*. She was no help there. Nora expected to run into Sally scurrying to her child. Instead, she found her staring out the window with her face pressed to the glass.

"*Guder mariye*," greeted Nora, heading straight to the coffeepot. "I believe Jeremiah wishes for his breakfast."

Sally glanced over her shoulder. "What? Oh, *jah*, of course." But she took one more look at the backyard before leaving the window.

Her strange behavior sent a frisson of anxiety up Nora's spine. Sally never was reluctant to tend her *kinner*. "What's wrong? What has happened?"

In the doorway, Sally wrung her hands like an elderly woman. "Amy ran out of here furious with John. Then he took off after her. From what I can tell, they won't be kissing and making up, as the *Englischers* say." Sally shivered as though outdoors without a coat.

Nora felt her hunger pangs vanish. "Is this my doing? Is this because I forgot to cook supper? I thought Amy decided to smooth things over with him."

Jeremiah's wails grew more insistent. Sally looked torn between two pressing needs. "She came downstairs this morning aiming to do exactly that. But then…" Sally's voice trailed off as she hurried from the room to her baby.

Nora set down her mug to follow her. She waited until Sally had Jeremiah nursing comfortably in the rocking chair and Aden playing with blocks at her feet. As Nora knelt to put on his little socks, she demanded, "What happened? Tell me the whole story."

Sally closed her eyes and rocked. "I told Amy that I'd witnessed John burning Prudence's letters in the stove when he thought no one was around. Amy was furious. I think she'll break up with him now. The marriage will be canceled, and it's my fault."

"John burned Aunt Prudence's letters?" Nora pressed her knuckles to her lips. "If she does break their engagement, it will be John's doing, not yours." Nora realized she took no pleasure from the possibility.

"I must stop eavesdropping and spying on people. No good can come from that." Sally's vehemence echoed off the polished wood floors.

"This has been a week for bad behavior," mused Nora. She wandered from the room to give Sally privacy and took up her post at the kitchen window. As expected, Nora spotted the unhappy couple by the fence. Amy stood with her arms tightly crossed. That posture never boded well for the other person.

Backing away from the window, Nora reached for her cloak from a peg. She slipped out the side door and headed in the opposite direction from Amy and John, preferring to avoid either of them for the next several hours. Unfortunately, only selfish thoughts crept into her mind: *If Amy and John part ways, Amy will return to Lancaster. And that means I must return with her.* That was something she'd pledged never to do. For the past few weeks, she had worried about Thomas or John sending her back to *grossmammi*'s because her adjustment had been less than sufficient.

Never in a million years had the idea of both King sisters board-ing the train with their tails between their legs crossed her mind.

She had to think of something. There had to be a way—*Ah-choo!* An explosive sneeze caught her unaware and sent birds flee-ing from overhead branches.

"God bless you," called a voice. "Are you all right? A sneeze like that could burst a blood vessel." Smirking, Elam stuck his head out from around the outdoor stall wall.

"I truly hope He does, because I can use all the blessings I can get today." Nora walked to where her sole friend groomed his sleek stallion. "You know this nasty cold is your fault." She dabbed her nose with a tissue.

His smirk broadened into a wide ear to ear grin. "Don't dump this on me, my lovely Miss King. I didn't tell you to tail me in the dead of night in the cold rain—without your galoshes, no less." He added an aged, scratchy inflection to his last words. "Spies have only themselves to blame when plans go awry." Elam patted the horse's flank affectionately.

My lovely Miss King? Nora peered up into his dark eyes. "I sup-pose you're right, but suffering a cold is preferable to dying of bore-dom on the Detweiler farm."

His raucous laughter caused the horse to prance against the cross-ties. "Don't get too close, Nora," he warned. "There's no tell-ing what this feisty boy will do." Wiping his hands on a rag, Elam stepped out of the stall. "Did chronic boredom send you search-ing for me two days in a row?" He shook his long hair from his eyes.

"Not exactly. John and Amy are fighting. I thought it best to stay out of their way, especially as I'm partially to blame for their disagreement."

"I'm sorry to hear that. Your sister seems very nice. My brother will never do better than her for a wife." Elam leaned a shoulder against the barn wall.

"But Amy and John are only part of the reason I came outside."

Nora inhaled a breath of clean, cold air. "I was curious about something you said last night."

"About my getting a driver's license?"

"No, I understand why a man would want to learn to drive. I'm interested why you're leaving."

"For the same reason you followed me last night. Harmony is a tad too quiet for my taste. Besides, Thomas hasn't given me much choice." Elam pulled a half-smoked cigarette from his pocket to relight.

"What do you mean?" She inclined her head toward him.

Elam struck a match on the rough-sawn wood. "I have until Christmas to make up my mind—either join the Amish church or mosey on my way. I don't think it'll take me long to decide." He exhaled the smoke in a series of tiny rings. "There are no jobs around, not until the spring anyway. I don't relish another winter spent in Sally's basement twiddling my thumbs. It's time for me to move on. And I plan to pick someplace warmer."

Nora tried not to reveal her excitement from his announcement. "*Jah*, that cellar must get depressing in cold weather. Tell me, Elam, where will you go?"

"I've tweaked your interest, no?" His dimples deepened as he smiled. "I'm going to Missouri where some relatives live—a couple of aunts and a whole bunch of cousins. It's an Old Order community like this one, but, according to Sally, a lot less conservative than here."

"Sally told you about her *rumschpringe* days in Missouri?" Nora couldn't hide her surprise. "I thought she wasn't very fond of you."

"*Jah*, she actually liked me when I first moved in with them a couple of years ago. Now she's bound and determined to become the perfect preacher's wife, so I've become nothing but bad news." He shrugged with nonchalance.

Nora scratched her chin. "She has been trying hard to live down her past."

"And I'm eager to *start* living my future." A gust of wind buffeted them from the south, and a hard rain began to fall. Elam turned his focus toward the sky. "You'd better head for the house, even if the squabble between Amy and John isn't over. We're in for a storm. This might turn to snow. After all, we are in Maine." He winked an expressive brown eye.

Butterflies took flight in Nora's belly from his flirtation. "One more question before I go," she said. "What's the name of that town in Missouri where Sally is from? She mentioned it once, but I don't recall."

Elam resumed grooming his horse with long, gentle strokes. "In Missouri, even the names of towns sound appealing. I'm headed for Paradise, sweet Nora. One of these days, you'll wake up and I will be gone." This voice had taken a dreamy, faraway sound.

"Just for the record, I'm not that sweet." Nora flashed her prettiest smile before stepping from the barn's protection into the rain. But she neither ran, nor even walked fast toward the house, despite the downpour. She was too busy plotting how to win the heart of Elam Detweiler before it was too late.

❧

Amy left her conversation with John with a singular purpose in mind—to get as far away from him as one house, in one small town, would permit. What a conniving, controlling, duplicitous man he was! She would not shed a single tear over her broken engagement. As her *mamm* used to say, any woman who married a schemer must have rocks in her head.

What would mamm *say about this sudden turn of events? Good riddance to bad medicine? Better now than later?*

Yet by the time Amy reached the porch she found herself checking to see if the despicable letter-burner had trailed after her. She had half a notion to call the postmaster general and have John arrested. Destroying mail that didn't belong to you was a federal offense, punishable by a fine or time in prison. Perhaps solitary confinement with a steady diet of bread and water would do him some good.

But John hadn't followed her. He remained at the pasture fence with his back bent and his forehead resting against a post. She hoped he would remain there until dark, sparing her the ordeal of seeing his face. She entered Sally's kitchen, toed off her muddy shoes, and hung up her cloak. Her cup was exactly where she'd left it on the table. Refilling it with coffee, Amy carried it to the front room. Thomas had stoked the woodstove, making the room toasty warm.

While her iron heated atop the stove, Amy planned her day. She would iron every garment in the laundry basket and then sew until bedtime. But the embroidered pillowcases and sheets seemed pointless now that she was no longer a bride-to-be. Perhaps reading would offer more diversion, although she could skip the bishop's assignment of First Corinthians. Instructions to husbands and wives no longer had bearing on her life. She needed to figure out her future. *If the wedding is off, how can I continue living with Thomas and Sally?* Amy pressed the first shirt zealously. *Should I catch the bus to Bangor and then another to Portland where I can board the train?* The dull ache between her eyes soon spread across her whole head.

"Amy?" asked a soft voice. "May I join you, or would you rather be alone?"

She glanced up to find a bedraggled Nora standing in the doorway.

"*Jah*, come in. Why are you wet? Never mind. You were obviously out walking. Go stand by the fire until you dry." Amy turned her attention back to the shirt.

Nora crept into the room and took a position by the woodstove. "Sally said you and John had a horrible spat."

Amy didn't look up from her ironing. "That is true." She volunteered nothing more than three flat words.

"She told me he burned Aunt Prudence's letters."

Amy bit the inside of her cheek. "If it's just the same, *schwester*, I'd rather not rehash the details right now. I'm trying to control my anger, not fan the flames."

"That would be wise." Nora held her hands above the stove. "You need to consider your options here."

Amy set down the iron to reheat. "And what options would those be? I...we...have no choice but to return to Lancaster. I can't very well stay if the wedding is off, especially as Harmony is a small town. I would run into a Detweiler every time I turned around." She hissed the words under her breath, not wishing to be overheard.

Nora sneezed repeatedly into her tissues. "Oh, dear, this is even worse than I imagined."

Amy glowered at her. "What are you talking about? You're the one who didn't want me rushing into marriage. I thought you would be pleased that I broke my engagement."

"Not at all. I don't want you making rash decisions, and that appears to be what you're still doing."

Amy was in no mood for an enigmatic sister. "This was no garden-variety disagreement. John's actions uncovered a major character flaw. It's better that I found out now rather than later on." She walked to the front window, where rain pelted the glass, underscoring the prevalent mood in the room.

"A character flaw?" Nora blew her nose. "I'm sure you're overreacting. You're about to make an important decision—one you shouldn't make without serious consideration and plenty of prayer."

Amy's patience began to fray. "You're a fine one to advise—"

"Hear me out," interrupted Nora. "I know I'm dispensing medicine I don't usually take, but that doesn't make it less worthwhile. You don't really want to move back to Pennsylvania and neither do

I. But I will if that's your decision," she added hastily. "Why not give this a little time to see if you feel differently? Let's say a week."

"A week? You want me to live here and try to avoid John for seven days? Don't you think that might be uncomfortable?"

"It might be, but if you explain this is a seven-day cooling-off period, he'll probably cut you a wide swath."

Amy shook her head mulishly, but she had lost the desire to continue arguing. Her confrontational side was plum worn out for one day. "I suppose I can wait that long."

Nora's expression turned victorious. "One week. Then we'll pack up and head to the bus depot. You'll have the rest of your life to hate his guts."

Amy had always loathed that expression. "I could never hate John, no matter what final choice I make."

"All the more reason not to go off half-cocked."

"Where are all these English phrases coming from?" asked Amy, grateful for a change in subject.

"I ran into Elam on my walk in the rain. You know he's more English than Amish these days." Nora flashed a toothy smile. "You finish the ironing while I scrub the bathroom and kitchen floor. I have much to atone for, and I heard hard work goes a long way... especially in Maine." In the blink of an eye, she was gone.

Amy put her sister's odd comments out of mind. She had more to contemplate than any sane woman could handle at the moment.

EIGHTEEN

Let me hide myself in Thee

Dampness seeped through the leather soles of Thomas's work boots. Time to buy a new pair on his next trip to the Harmony co-op. Last night's surprise blizzard brought more harm than cold feet and sloppy pastures. An ancient, dying sycamore had split down the middle as wet snow clung to the heavily laden branches. Half the tree fell into the cornfield, leaving a deep furrow between the rows, while the other half brought down a section of pasture fence. Fortunately, his cows had chosen the barn to spend the night in due to the storm and hadn't yet discovered their path to freedom. Shielding his eyes as the sun rose higher than the eastern treetops, Thomas spotted the approach of his brother.

John's head was bent low. He was either watching for pockets of icy water hidden under the fresh snow, or miserable from an unhappy encounter with Amy that had already spoiled his morning. When he reached the stump, his pinched face told the story. Thomas felt a jab of compassion for the man, who often emulated a confused moose blundering into town.

"What happened?" asked John. "Did the storm knock down a tree?"

Considering the presence of an ax, chainsaw, and bail of wire, along with snippers and the flatbed wagon, the question seemed superfluous. Thomas answered him with courtesy anyway. "*Jah*, but by noon most of the snow will be gone. It's supposed to be sunny today. We'll have time to get the wood moved down to the house."

Without a word, John started the chainsaw and began cutting the fallen tree into stove-sized pieces as Thomas returned to fence repair. The two men worked at least thirty minutes before his brother, perspiring and red faced, set down his tools.

Thomas picked up the signal that his brother was ready to talk. "More trouble with Nora?" he asked.

"No, I can't shift the blame this time. Amy broke our engagement this morning for something she'd found out about me." He sat down on the stump used as a chopping block with a grim expression.

"She canceled her plans to buy the house and marry you?" Thomas dropped the wire cutters into the toolbox and devoted his full attention to his brother.

"She can never marry a man she cannot trust."

"Maybe you should start at the beginning and tell me the whole story."

John recounted the events factually, with little emotion, but as soon as he was finished he began to cry. Thomas hadn't heard his brother cry in many years. The sound broke his heart, yet at the same time it stirred a sense of hope. A man never changes until forced to, until he's brought to his knees. John had fallen from the straight and narrow path. This could be his first step back. Thomas let his brother weep until he had exhausted his sorrow and self-loathing. Finally John wiped his face with his handkerchief, blew his nose, and straightened his back.

Thomas closed his eyes to recollect a passage of Scripture. "In

James chapter five, verse sixteen, we find good advice. 'Confess your sins to each other and pray for each other so that you may be healed.' You have confessed your sins to the Lord and to Amy, so now your healing can begin."

"Perhaps God will forgive me, but Amy never will. She won't forget my pride and arrogance and judgmental behavior. I condemned her aunt and her sister as though my hands were clean. I maneuvered to keep Amy and her aunt apart, fearing I would lose control. And in so doing I destroyed our life together." John locked eyes with Thomas. "You're my minister and my brother and my only friend. Please help me change my ways. I don't want to live another day in my skin."

Thomas had never heard his brother so vulnerable and penitent. "Pray daily—no, hourly—for deliverance. Let the Holy Spirit fill your heart, give you strength, and guide you. Your future will be revealed in due time, but for now put Amy out of your mind. You're allowing her to monopolize your every thought. Dwelling on your missteps, no matter how onerous, won't help the situation." He placed a hand on John's shoulder. "In the meantime, you're not finished making amends. You need to confess what you've done to Prudence and apologize to Nora. Those two acts will go a long way in your healing."

John rose to his feet. "You're right. I will do this and pray it will be enough."

"A contrite heart will be sufficient to the Lord, but Amy must arrive at her own conclusions. Many things said during heated arguments are later regretted. Give her space and time. If your hearts are true, there are few obstacles that cannot be overcome. But if you do part ways, this union was never meant to be."

"*Danki, bruder.*"

"*Gern gschehne,*" murmured Thomas. "Before you go to bed, turn in your Bible to the third chapter of First John, verses nineteen and twenty. Start there for help." He reached out his hand to John. They shook heartily and returned to their tasks. Within a couple of hours the fence had been repaired, the tree cut into manageable lengths, and the branches cleaned up. John loaded the firewood onto the flatbed wagon to be split another day. The dead sycamore would provide warm nights next winter. The hard physical labor distracted John from his woes, which is exactly what Thomas had in mind.

Later that night, when John retreated to his room, weary from a day of backbreaking work, he discovered two things that would help him sleep a bit easier. Amy had written a note and slipped it under his door. With shaking fingers he unfolded the single sheet and began to read:

> *Dear John,*
>
> *Although my mind-set remains the same, Nora has advised me to wait a week before leaving Harmony and Thomas's gracious home. I regret losing my temper, but since I did, waiting is probably a good idea. I hope you will respect my privacy and give me time to plan a course of action. Don't try to coerce me or influence my decision.*
>
> *In Christ's love,*
> *Amelia King*

Amelia—all these years he'd never known her formal given name. Now the word tumbled around his head like a beautiful melody, constricting his heart with unbearable melancholy. *Amelia, what have I done?* Dropping into the rocking chair, handmade long ago by his *grossdawdi*, John turned to the passage in First John that Thomas had suggested and read aloud words to change his life.

> This is how we know that we belong to the truth and how we set our hearts at rest in his presence: If our hearts condemn us, we know that God is greater than our hearts, and he knows everything.

Nora didn't think she'd ever spent a more uncomfortable three days. They had to endure the Sabbath's Sunday school class, and then a rather somber noon meal at the meetinghouse, followed by an afternoon of quiet reading and meditation devoid of any sociability. Everyone walked on eggshells so as not to strain already frayed nerves. Monday and Tuesday hadn't been much of an improvement. At least laundry, baking, cleaning, cooking, and child care occupied female hours, while John and Thomas managed to stay busy despite fallow fields. Even the Detweiler goats had stopped producing milk during the dullest season of the year. Thomas had to own the tidiest barn in Waldo County, Maine, considering how many hours the men spent out there. Thomas occasionally left on district business or to run errands, but John had to be worn ragged trying to stay out of Amy's way.

Poor John. Nora pitied the man she had so recently held in low regard. His emotional state was painful to witness, yet he sought no consolation from anyone. He arrived promptly for meals, bowed his head to pray and then ate as though ravenous wolves nipped at his pant legs. Amy kept busy slicing bread or vegetables, or suddenly remembering a condiment they needed from the cellar. She didn't sit down to her own meal until John dabbed up the last drop of gravy with a bread crust and left the table. She also appeared lost in a world of isolation but refused to discuss the matter since the morning Sally had disclosed John's misdeeds.

Nora stared out the living room window at snow falling fast and flaky. Soon the brown fields would be covered with an insulating mantle that would remain until spring. According to Thomas, Maine seldom enjoyed a January thaw—a midwinter reprieve to lift low spirits—the way they had in Lancaster County. *Where will I be come spring?* The sound of footsteps soon jarred her from her daydream.

"May I speak with you, Nora?"

She turned to find Amy's former betrothed nearly nose to nose.

"Of course, but I have no news for you. Amy has said nothing to me about her plans."

John forced a smile. "I've not come to talk about your sister. I want to apologize for my behavior the night of our marriage class. I had no business judging you or threatening you or even speaking in that fashion. I hope you can forgive me." He clutched his felt hat brim between chapped, reddened fingers and appeared to have lost ten pounds during the last few days.

"You weren't wrong in your assessment of me." Nora offered an overdue olive branch. "I've spent years trying to avoid chores. My *mamm* said she needed to tether me to a project if any progress was to be made."

His blue eyes softened. "Whatever your work ethic, I acted cruelly, and for that I am sorry." He reached out his hand.

Nora clasped it and shook. "The matter is behind us and we won't talk about it again." She pumped his hand like a well handle.

John shifted his weight nervously, seeming uncertain what to do with his hand once she released it. "*Danki*, Nora. I'll leave you to your storm-watching. The weather is supposed to get worse. I'm glad we have enough food and firewood to last us a while." He nodded and strode out the door, maybe standing taller than when he arrived.

Nora trailed him as far as the kitchen. With her mouth and throat parched dry, a cup of tea sounded good. Filling the teakettle at the tap, she noticed Elam exit his basement quarters and head for the barn. Suddenly, he halted on the path and glanced back, as though aware he was being watched. Water overflowed the kettle, cascading down her wrist and soaking her sleeve as Nora stared at the man who monopolized her every dream and waking thought.

Elam lifted his hat brim and mouthed the words, "Meet me in the henhouse."

Nora shut off the water but otherwise froze in place, unable to acknowledge she understood the exaggerated five-word sentence.

Elam repeated the attempted communication and waited with

an expectant glint in his eye. Standing in the falling snow, with large flakes clinging to his hat and jacket, he took on the visage of a winter storybook character.

She peeked over her shoulder before nodding affirmatively to his request. *What am I doing? This isn't exactly atoning for past mistakes while keeping a low profile.*

Elam smiled and then sprinted off. Without exception, it was the craftiest, slyest grin Nora had ever seen. The comic snowman vanished, replaced by a handsome temptation a woman would be wise to resist.

Yet, resist him Nora could not. She set the kettle on the stove and then ducked into the bathroom to rinse with mouthwash and add a touch of blusher—a keepsake from her *rumschpringe* days in Pennsylvania. For a fleeting moment, Nora contemplated changing from her hideously drab dress but nixed the idea. *No sense in keeping him waiting,* she thought, forgetting about her notion of sackcloth and ashes. She listened at the door, and when she was certain no one had come into the kitchen, she left the bathroom. With her heart thudding in her chest, she grabbed her cloak and slipped outside.

Snow dampened her face as she closed the door, a chilly reminder that she had forgotten her heavy bonnet. But the sight of Elam's boot tracks heading to the henhouse sent ripples of delight across her skin.

Get hold of yourself. He probably just wants to borrow twenty bucks to buy gasoline. That sobering thought reined in her imagination before she embarrassed herself. Pausing outside the little outbuilding, she steeled her nerves and ducked her head through the low doorway.

"Nora, so glad you could make it." Elam leaned against a stack of feed bags—a picture of casual disregard.

She opened her mouth to reply, but the smell of closely confined chickens assaulted her nose. She began to cough and gag.

Her reaction was met with snickers. "I thought you had lived on a farm back in Pennsylvania, not a high-rise loft in the city."

She pulled a handkerchief from her pocket. "I did, but I refused to enter the henhouse in winter. I only gathered eggs at our outdoor coop, which we moved around the yard on wheels to keep things fresh. I could collect eggs without entering the enclosure, while the chickens roamed free." She stifled another wretched cough.

"Such clever girls, you King sisters. Care for a feed sack or an upturned bucket for a chair? I apologize for the amenities, but this is the only spot where we won't be interrupted. Sally gathers eggs in the morning, always at first light, like a windup toy. You can count on her routines." Elam fastened his coal-black eyes on her and didn't look away.

Nora concentrated on breathing through her mouth. "What, no cigarette dangling from your lips?"

He laid a hand across his heart. "I would never endanger the lives of my poultry friends with a stray spark. Lately, they are the only friends I seem to have."

She clenched her hands into fists deep in her pockets and whispered, "You have me."

One of his dimples deepened and then the other. "I was hoping you would say that." Elam waited as though for some dramatic effect. "Because I have a favor to ask you."

Nora stifled another sneeze and forced her expression to stay neutral. "Sure, how can I help?"

He held up both hands. "Wait, you'd better hear me out before you agree. This favor involves sneaking around, freezing your tailbone off, possibly foregoing a good night's sleep, and driving my buggy at night. I take it you're still unfamiliar with Waldo County roads, but could you control my Standardbred? I can't waste time with one of Thomas's old nags."

She inhaled a steadying breath, finally ignoring the odor of chicken manure. "I know how to handle a buggy horse. And I proved the other night that rain, snow, and frigid temperatures don't deter me. Miss some sleep? I've slept so much since coming here that skipping a few hours will probably do me good." Nora fluttered her eyelashes.

Elam reached down to pet a hen that pecked corn near his boot heel. "Wow, you are ready for some adventure and intrigue before settling in for a long winter's nap."

Nora shook off the image of deathly quiet Harmony, buried under several feet of snow for months. "What do you have in mind?"

He sauntered to the building's sole window and rubbed a patch in the frost. "I listened to the weather report on my radio. This snow will dwindle to flurries by six o'clock and then stop altogether, but tomorrow we're supposed to get a nor'easter down from Canada bringing along a major blizzard. We might be snowed in for days. The state highway workers will clear main routes first, so it could be a week before these back roads are dug out, depending how bad things get." He tucked a lock of hair behind his ear. "I need to go tonight before I lose my chance."

Nora waited as tiny hairs stood on end at the back of her neck. She ignored them. "I hope you don't expect me to guess the destination," she said after a moment.

He laughed with abandon. Several startled hens ran for cover in their nesting boxes. "Waterville, my lovely Miss King. In case you haven't studied a map of Maine, it's a city past Thorndike, which is five miles or so beyond Harmony." He lowered his tone to a whisper, even though chickens weren't known to spread local gossip. "I bought a car from a guy on the outskirts of town. I had a mechanic check it out for me. Everything's been tuned up and ready to go—decent tires, plenty of antifreeze in the radiator, and the radio and heater are in good working condition." Elam's eyes nearly danced out of his head. "It might not be one of those cream puffs in a magazine, but it'll get me where I'm headed." He slicked his hair back with a callused hand.

"Congratulations on the purchase," she murmured politely.

"Thanks. I'll pay him the balance of cash tonight. He'll sign the title over, and I'll take possession of the car." Elam leaned against the post. "The seller promised to fill the gas tank to the brim."

"Where do I come in?" she asked.

"Use your head, Nora. The *Englischer* won't take my horse and buggy in trade. I need some way to get them home while I drive my new car." He rubbed a stubbly jawline. "Unless, of course, you would prefer to drive the Chevy." He lifted her chin with one finger.

Though his touch electrified her, she batted away his hand. "No, thanks. Fast cars upset my stomach. I'll drive the buggy. What do you plan to do with this car? Show Thomas after breakfast tomorrow and then take him for a spin?" She matched his sarcasm with her own.

He snorted. "My friend said I could store it in his barn for a while. They don't use the building anymore because his *daed* gave up farming. I'll cut across back land to get home—the same general path you took the other night."

Nora needed to exit the crowded henhouse, not because of chicken odor—she'd grown accustomed to that—but because of his proximity. But Elam caught her sleeve before she reached the door. "We probably won't be home until almost dawn, and there's a chance you might get caught. I want you to understand what I'm asking you to do."

She spent no time pondering her decision. "What time do we leave for Waterville?"

"That's up to you. Whenever you can slip away from Amy and leave the house unseen, I will be ready. Just tap lightly on the cellar door. The buggy will be hitched with warm blankets inside."

She nodded, dry mouthed and a bundle of raw nerves.

He took hold of her face a second time. "Thank you, Nora. I'll owe you a favor—a big favor." Then, without warning, he leaned over and kissed her on the lips.

Nora savored the kiss, and then she fled the coop as though the chickens had all decided to attack at once. She didn't stop running until she was inside the kitchen, belatedly brewing her cup of tea. But the taste and sensation of his kiss would remain fixed in her memory for an eternity after that.

$\approx$

Amy dressed by the window and gazed across fields glistening with reflected sunlight. The diamond brightness hurt her eyes. The storm six days ago lasted forty-eight hours, dumping several feet of trouble on the residents of central Maine. Her cloistered period of contemplation grew only more claustrophobic as the women remained housebound. Finally, Thomas, John, and Elam shoveled paths to the barns and sheds, and then to the street so they might receive mail and view an occasional passing car or buggy.

Propping up the hand mirror, she studied her wretched face for a long moment. Amy King was absolutely miserable. This past week had been unbearable. Not that John had pestered her or in any way pressured her. On the contrary, he'd behaved as a perfect gentleman, similar to visiting a distant cousin she barely knew. He finished chores, ate his meals, and read his English Bible more than all previous Bible sessions combined. When John told Thomas that his High German was inadequate to study effectively, Thomas provided an English translation.

And neither Sally nor Nora caused her distress. Both had allowed her plenty of privacy. Amy simply couldn't create a plan for the rest of her life. Although her anger with John had waned, her feelings of betrayal and mistrust had not. There was no way she could marry him this winter. And yet the prospect of leaving Harmony with a suitcase of memories scared her to the bone.

Her prayers had gone unanswered. Her nightly devotions hadn't led to any great epiphanies regarding the future.

With a sigh she tucked the hand mirror in a drawer, pinned up her hair, and donned a *kapp*. Trudging down the stairs, Amy heard a knock at the side door. When she reached the bottom, she heard the soft rap escalate into vigorous pounding. "Nora? Sally?" she called. "Someone's at the door."

Amy stuck her head into the living room. Sally sat in the rocker nursing her son, while Nora was reading a library book. Neither appeared concerned about whoever waited on the porch. "Did the storm knock out your sense of hearing?"

Sally arched an eyebrow. "We decided *you* should answer the door."

Nora only shrugged and refocused on her book.

Because the other females apparently suffered from some storm-induced malaise, Amy hurried to the kitchen before the person splintered the wood. Yanking open the door, she gazed into the face of Prudence Summerton, bundled head to toe in heavy wool with knee-high farm boots. "Aunt Prudence!"

"Is this the kind of hospitality the Detweiler and King household offers?" Prudence sounded piqued, but her brown eyes twinkled with affection. "You would allow a middle-aged woman to freeze to death while you sip tea by the fire?"

"Come in and warm up." Amy threw her arms around her. "Are you hungry? How about some hot chocolate?" She started to drag the woman across the threshold.

"Wait, wait." Prudence extracted herself from her niece's embrace. "I need to pay the cab before his meter bankrupts me. I wasn't sure if I had the right farm or not. Snowbanks obscure most of the address posts." She gingerly walked down the salted steps and shoveled walkway.

"I'll fix you something hot to drink," called Amy. She watched to make sure her aunt didn't fall and then hurried to heat coffee

and cinnamon rolls left over from the men's breakfast. By the time
Prudence returned, Amy had the fire stoked and a warm meal for
them both.

"Oh good, coffee," Prudence said. "Cocoa is for afternoons, in
my book. And that had better not be decaf, dear niece." She hung
up her outerwear and tugged off her boots. Unburdened, she shed
fifteen pounds.

"*Nein.* It's good and strong too." Amy stared at her aunt as she
drank half a cup before sitting down. "How did you manage to
arrive so early?" It was the first of many questions.

"I spent the night in Harmony at a motel. I didn't want to look
for this place at night with the roads only partially plowed." Prudence finished her drink and refilled the mug from the pot.

"How did you find us?" Amy pushed the plate of rolls across
the table.

"I had your address, remember? It's a cab driver's job to know
the roads in his area."

*Why would you pick such a day to change your mind about visit-
ing?* Amy conveyed the question without opening her mouth.

"You're wondering why I'm here." Prudence bit into a cinnamon roll.

"Only why you would pick December and not during warmer
weather. But I'm very pleased to see you no matter what the season."

Prudence licked white icing from her fingertips. "The way I
heard it, time was of the essence. If I didn't come and talk sense
into you—and fast—you would soon be back in Lancaster."

Amy stared, wide-eyed. "You heard I broke my engagement?
From who?"

"From whom," Aunt Prudence corrected. "The letter was signed
only 'interested bystanders.' But I suspect it was from the same
people eavesdropping in the hallway." She took a large bite of her
treat.

Amy sprang to her feet and caught the interlopers before they could escape. She dragged Sally and Nora into the kitchen. "What have you two done? You made our aunt travel in this weather when she chose not to visit Harmony on a warm summer day?" Amy directed the admonishment at her sister.

Nora slipped from Amy's grip. "You said you needed Aunt Prudence's advice, and you sure weren't listening to anybody else."

"Settle down, both of you. No one forced me to do anything. Now, let's get better acquainted. Nora, I remember you from Mount Joy, and you must be Sally." Prudence held out both hands to the women. For thirty minutes, they chatted and drank copious amounts of coffee. Amy kept glancing from one woman to another, oddly miffed but not sure why.

Then Sally scrambled up and announced, "Come, Nora. Help me in the henhouse. We'll give these two some time to talk alone." Sally smiled at Amy.

Nora looked dubious, but she bundled up and followed Sally out the door.

"What's this I hear about your breaking your engagement?" asked Prudence the moment they were gone.

Amy could only nod her head in agreement.

"You had a spat and you threw in the towel? Is that what my sister raised you to be—a quitter?" Prudence clucked her tongue.

"Perhaps when you hear the whole story you'll understand, especially because it involves you." With that, Amy launched into an account of recent events. However, she noticed the retelling generated little anger in her listener.

Her aunt sipped coffee without interrupting. When Amy was finished, she said, "He messed up badly, no doubt about it. And because *you* have never messed up, you can't forgive him. I understand." She nodded her head sadly.

"No, I've made mistakes in my life too—ones I will regret forever." Amy stared at the tabletop, terrified to purge her soul of past sins.

The clock ticked, the wood shifted in the stove, drops of water hit the bottom of the sink at regular intervals as they sat together, waiting. Unable to keep quiet any longer, Amy whispered, "I bought smoke detectors at the Mount Joy hardware store back in Lancaster. My *daed* refused to install them. He said they weren't permitted by the *Ordnung* and insisted that God would protect us." She lifted her gaze to meet her aunt's. "I should have put them up anyway. I could have hidden them in places he wouldn't have noticed. If I had done that—taken the initiative like an adult— then maybe my parents would still be alive."

Prudence's eyes filled with tears. "My dear child, their deaths were part of God's plan. Nothing you could have done would have changed the outcome. English smoke detectors aren't more powerful than God when He calls someone home. Now you and your sisters must carry on."

"But don't you see? I've made my own mistakes. Forgiving John isn't the point. I've already forgiven him. But this whole marriage thing—a husband always getting the final word—what if he makes the wrong decision? Like depleting our bank account to avoid a mortgage. Is that wise? I don't know."

Prudence shrugged her shoulders. "I don't know either, but you could ask a bank how much money you'd pay in interest during the loan. Maybe then you would have a better idea."

"Is that how it must be? A woman must surrender her will to her husband and lose control of her life?"

Prudence studied the ceiling as though choosing her words carefully. "A Christian woman must surrender her will to God. He promises never to forsake you and will mark a clear path. Don't try to figure out your entire life at twenty-two. You must trust, Amy. It's the hardest and yet the easiest thing to do."

Amy's face grew hot with pent-up emotion, and when she couldn't contain them any longer, she let her tears fall. She cried for several minutes, cleansing her soul of guilt and regret. "I do still

NINETEEN

I will put you in a cleft in the rock
and cover you with my hand.

EXODUS 33:22

From the open door to the barn loft, John and Thomas had seen the taxicab arrive. They had been restacking hay bales and feed sacks, sweeping the floor, and checking for rodents' nests. They had just about exhausted their list of possible chores when the vehicle crawled up the driveway.

A middle-aged woman, indistinguishable in a heavy layer of clothes, climbed from the backseat and peered around with interest. She said something to the driver through the open car window before picking her way carefully toward the porch. With the sun simultaneously melting snow as the cold ground refroze the liquid, ice had formed in cleared areas.

"Who do you suppose she is?" asked Thomas, leaning on his broom handle. "She's not anyone from the district."

John rubbed the back of his neck to loosen tight muscles. "Don't know," he answered, but deep inside he had a feeling he knew exactly who had arrived. "She might be Amy's Aunt Prudence," he added after a bit.

"You think so? All the way from Chestnut after that blizzard we had?" Thomas pulled on his beard as the newcomer knocked on the door. "We'll find out soon enough. Let's finish this loft and feed the goats. Then a cup of coffee sounds about right."

By the time they climbed down the ladder to the first floor, Sally and Nora entered the barn. Sally carried a wicker basket brimming with fresh brown eggs. Nora's breath condensed into puffs of white vapor.

"Have our hens done their part to keep us well fed, dear *fraa*?" asked Thomas of Sally.

"We have more than enough for omelets tomorrow and to bake a cake this afternoon." Sally held up the basket for their perusal.

"What brings you ladies out here?" asked Thomas. "An inspection, perhaps? To make sure we've been working hard enough?"

Sally emitted a charmingly undignified snort. "The condition of the barn is your domain, *ehemann*. We're here to give Amy some privacy with her aunt." She turned to face John before continuing. "Prudence Summerton is here. Nora and I wrote and asked her to come, but we weren't sure if she would."

John balanced his rake against the wall. "*Danki* for writing to her. I considered it myself but no longer had her address and…I felt too ashamed."

Nora stepped forward. "You're *glad* she's here?" She sounded more shocked than skeptical.

"*Jah*, I am," he said. "Amy had wanted to reestablish a relationship with her while in Maine. I feared she would return to Pennsylvania without seeing her one more time." He tugged off his gloves and stuck them into a jacket pocket.

Nora's green eyes softened. "Well, I hope Aunt Prudence can talk some sense into her."

John had no idea what kind of "sense" Nora would prefer, but nevertheless he nodded and dipped his head toward his former sister-in-law-to-be.

"She paid the taxi driver and he left, plus she brought an overnight satchel. So that's a good sign she'll stay a day or two." Sally looked at one man and then the other.

John nodded at her too, feeling like a rooster pecking for grain with his bobbing neck. He left the barn as though he remembered an urgent task, but in fact he couldn't stomach all the furtive, sympathetic glances and innuendos. He didn't want to talk about Prudence's visit with anyone except Amy. And because he couldn't imagine *that* happening, he needed to get away, period.

John walked down the road, careful to watch for oncoming cars. Should one approach, the roadway was too narrow from the banked snow. He would have to leap into a drift to save his life. But no cars ventured down the Detweiler road, leaving John to muse of what might have been if he hadn't been a loathsome man. When he could no longer feel his toes, he turned back, exhausted yet relieved he was too tired to think. As he reached the porch steps, their new guest stepped out the side door. She wore a wool afghan around her shoulders and carried something steaming in her mug.

"Aunt Prudence?" he asked, a bit ridiculously. "Mrs. Summerton?" he corrected.

"I am, but you were right the first time. Call me Aunt Prudence." She offered a broad smile that erased years from her features. "You must be John Detweiler. Pleased to make your acquaintance."

Then you must not know what I've done. The thought shamefully flitted through his mind. "I'm glad to meet you. And I would appreciate a word with you if you don't mind."

"I have all the time in the world, young man. Should we sit there?" She pointed at a forlorn porch swing lightly dusted with snow.

It looked very unappealing in the stiff breeze and dropping

temperatures. "*Nein*. Let's talk indoors where you'll be warmer." John moved to open the door for her.

"No, let's stay out here. This house seems to have busybodies afoot, and I think we would both enjoy some solitude. We'll survive a little cold and snow." Prudence plunked down on the swing without bothering to brush off a patch.

He laughed at her astute observation as his nervousness dwindled. "*Danki*. I appreciate that. You've only been here a few hours, and you've discovered a key characteristic of the Detweilers."

"It's an Amish shortcoming." She pulled down her sleeves to cover her hands.

John leaned against the porch rail, buttoned his coat, and crossed his arms. "Thank you for responding to Sally and Nora's letter and coming here. I'm aware of your earlier reservations about visiting Harmony. Amy enjoyed her trip to Chestnut because she so wanted to reconnect with family. She would have regretted leaving Maine without seeing you again." He locked gazes with the woman's warm brown eyes. They contained only compassion, or perhaps it was simply his wishful thinking. "I will be forever grateful for your comforting Amy today, no matter what the outcome."

Prudence slapped the armrest of the swing. "Stop sounding so grim. Good grief, one would think somebody died the way you're going on and on." She tightened the shawl around her shoulders. "All is not lost. There's still hope for you."

He shook off the notion of hope. "I've more to say, Aunt. I wronged you. You sent letters to your niece and I read them and then burned them. I'm no better than a common criminal, but I'm sorry for what I did." He swallowed hard, not looking away from her.

"Amy told me about your mischief and the reasoning behind your actions." She studied him like an interesting moth trapped in a web. "You might be a criminal, *jah*, but I suspect you're not the least bit common, John Detweiler. You have my forgiveness and my blessing for a long and happy life with my niece. Now, let's go in the house. I want to see if any more cinnamon rolls are hidden in the cupboards. I forgot how much I loved those things."

When John opened the door for the older woman, he found Amy blocking their entrance with her hands on her hips. "Both of you should know better than to talk right under the window. I'm afraid Sally's habit has rubbed off on me." Her face held a long-absent peaceful expression.

"Your *mamm* would swat your backside if she'd caught you, young lady," said Prudence to Amy, stepping around her. "And folks wonder why I choose Chestnut over Harmony." She made a dismissive noise. "I'm going to forgo my snack and take a hot tub soak instead. Cold has settled in my bones. Call me when it's lunchtime." The bathroom door clicked shut behind her.

Amy glanced toward the living room and lowered her voice to a whisper. "I heard your apology, John. That was very brave."

"It needed to be said." He tried to find something to focus on other than her beautiful face. "I'm glad she arrived before you left for home. Above all, I want you to be happy, and if that's in Lancaster with someone else, so be it." Surprisingly, he no longer felt the familiar sadness, only a vague sense of resignation. He forced himself to smile.

Amy pulled him inside and closed the door behind him. "I'm glad to hear you want me happy, because that means I'm staying right here in Waldo County. This is where I want to be, John, with you, as your wife."

He couldn't believe his deceptive, malfunctioning ears. "But—"

"Stop. Not another word. People make mistakes. I've made some of my own and will probably make a few more before I die. But those who love, forgive. That's what we've been taught every Sunday since we were little *kinner*. And I certainly love you."

There they were—the words he'd longed to hear for a long time. And he could do nothing more than just stand there, staring at her.

Tick, tock, tick, tock…the clock marked passing moments in their lives, ones they would never get back. But John realized he would have plenty of other moments—millions, really—with the woman he loved. He pulled her into his arms. "And I love you, Amelia King."

They hugged until she finally squirmed away. "Before we get too mushy, I need to see if Elam's cell phone still has a charge."

"Whatever for?"

"I want to call Mrs. Chadd to say we need to close that real estate deal for the Morrell house."

"You needn't make any rash decisions, Amy. Much has happened today. Enjoy your aunt's visit, and then in a few days—"

"No, John. I've made up my mind. I don't want another family snapping up my dream house while I bake cookies, sip tea, and get caught up on news. I'll have plenty of time for that later. I've dragged my feet long enough, so please walk me down to the cellar to borrow Elam's phone. You know how frightened I am of spiders."

❧

Elam heard two pairs of boots stomping down the inside basement stairs before he saw John and Amy. They sounded like clumsy heifers trying to climb a ladder. He made no attempt to hide what he was doing because his plans to get on with life were underway, the wheels finally in motion. When his brother and Amy walked around the clothespress and crates of canning jars, Elam reclined against the wall. His stack of magazines were scattered across the bed as they had been the day pretty Nora had come calling. However, the beer he held was far more damaging, along with the three empty bottles in the cardboard carton by his feet. Most onerous of all was the burning cigarette in the ashtray on the floor.

Like a matched pair of marionettes, John and Amy looked at

him, the open bottle of beer, and then the burning cigarette, in that order.

Elam bent down to stub it out. "Has the happy couple patched up their differences? If so, I'm glad to hear it." He resumed his casual pose against the wall.

While Amy blinked several times from the smoke, John cleared his throat. "We have, *danki*, but Amy has a favor to ask. She would like to use your phone if it happens to be charged up." He kept staring at the smoldering butt, which gave off a foul, burnt-paper odor.

Elam pushed off the bed and strode to where his heavy work jacket hung from a hook. "No problem. Are you two calling a cab? Maybe running away to get married in Portland and then honeymooning on the coast?" He angled his smile straight at Amy. "Of course, summer would have been preferable for a seaside vacation. Walking the beach on days like today could lead to serious frostbite."

Amy wrinkled her nose. "A taxi? No, I wish to call a real estate agent about a farm for sale here in Harmony."

Elam extracted the phone from an inside pocket, snapped it open, and handed it to her. "Sorry to hear that. You folks would do better to take that trip to Portland and keep going south."

John cleared his throat but held back whatever comment he had with great effort. "I appreciate the loan. We'll return the phone soon." He took hold of Amy's hand.

Elam hooked a thumb toward the entrance directly outside. "Best reception is at the top of those steps."

Amy managed a verbal response. "*Danki*, Elam. I am in your debt."

"Not for much longer you won't be." He grinned at his brother's bride-to-be. *Pretty, but not as pretty as your fireball younger sister.* It was too bad he was going before he and Nora could get better acquainted. That green-eyed, speak-whatever-came-to-mind Nora

King would be his only regret about leaving Maine. He slumped back onto the bed with a car magazine until his brother returned alone with the phone a few minutes later.

John held it out in an outstretched palm. "Thomas asked you not to smoke inside his home," he stated flatly.

"*Jah*, I recall, but I've been very careful to keep ashes only over the concrete. The weather's been too nasty to sit outside to smoke."

A muscle jumped in John's neck. "Children and women sleep on the second floor of this house and could easily become trapped should fire break out in the basement." John spoke very slowly, enunciating each word to make sure his meaning was clear. He stared him in the eye without blinking.

After a moment, Elam glanced away. "I won't do it again, *bruder*. I promise."

John took a couple of steps toward the inside stairs and stopped. "*Danki* again for letting Amy make that call. Why don't you join us for supper tonight? I heard Sally's making fried chicken. Isn't that one of your favorites?" He looked back over his shoulder.

The invitation left Elam momentarily speechless. "*Jah*, it is, or used to be. Let me think about it and consult my social calendar." He laughed humorously.

John left the stale-smelling cellar as fast as his legs could carry him.

ॐ

Thomas savored his mashed potatoes topped with cheese, enjoying the lively table conversation. Amy chatted with John, Sally, and her aunt as though she'd been gone for a long time and needed to catch up. Sally, of course, filled Prudence in on news of Harmony district members she might remember—marriages, deaths, new *kinner* and *kinskinner*—the events which defined their lives.

Prudence had originally seemed nervous around him, as

though she might not be given a warm welcome. A shunned member could be offered shelter, food, and any other necessities, but those meals shouldn't have been at the table with the family. However, Thomas had no intention of following the strict letter of the *Ordnung* on this matter. If he faced censure from the bishop, so be it. Prudence Hilty Summerton had suffered much in her life through no fault of her own. He wouldn't add to her sorrow.

"Some pie, *ehemann*?" asked Sally, breaking his woolgathering.

"*Jah*, please."

"John?" she asked, pie server in hand.

Her brother-in-law continued to gaze from Amy to the current conversationalist and back again. Amy seemed to have put the man into a trance with her feminine powers.

"John, my wife asked you a question." Thomas thumped his brother on the arm.

"*Mir leid*," he apologized, surprised to find Sally at his elbow. "No, I've had enough to eat." He turned back to focus on Amy's description of the house they both loved. The real estate agent hadn't answered their phone call yet, but the message left after the beep had been clear: "We wish to proceed with the purchase of the farm without delay." Amy's face glowed as she described the huge kitchen, the number and size of bedrooms, and the incredible view of the Dixmont hills in the distance.

Prudence oohed and ahhed at appropriate intervals, sharing her niece's enthusiasm. The only quiet person at the dinner table was Nora. The young woman replied if directly addressed yet otherwise picked at her meal listlessly. Sibling rivalry was normal enough, even among the most devout Christians. It couldn't be easy to be a rudderless orphan with few prospects for the future. As Thomas considered another cup of coffee before heading out to evening chores, the cellar door swung open and banged against the wall. Seven pairs of eyes turned toward the commotion as all conversation ceased.

"*Oncle Ee-um*," said Aden, lifting his small fingers in a wave.

"Elam," murmured Nora. "Glad you could join us."

The other five adults stared, slack-jawed at his appearance.

John leaned slightly toward Thomas. "I invited him to supper when Amy and I borrowed his cell phone."

Thomas nodded his acknowledgment. However, it wasn't Elam's arrival that startled him but the younger man's appearance. He had on faded blue jeans and a plaid flannel shirt open at the neck. The sleeves had been rolled to the elbows, revealing his thermal undershirt beneath. He wore a leather belt rather than braces, and what looked to be brand-new, expensive work boots. His freshly washed hair had been slicked back from his face, bangless and utterly too long. His high cheekbones looked more pronounced, as though he'd lost weight. And most irritating to Thomas was the man's three-day-old beard, well beyond normal stubble by day's end.

Beards were only grown by married Amish men, a badge of honor that they had committed their lives to one God and one woman. Elam wasn't a married man, and as far as Thomas knew, he had no prospects along those lines. Thomas cleared his throat as the others remained silent. He seldom felt anger, but he was beginning to feel the first red-hued sensations deep in his gut.

"You come to my supper table dressed like that?"

Elam stood at the stove, loading his plate with four pieces of fried chicken. "As our brother already told you, I got an invitation." He slapped a dollop of mashed potatoes next to the chicken, and then he ladled on a topping of rich brown gravy.

"It is your clothing I object to, not sharing a meal with you, Elam." Thomas wadded up his paper napkin into a tight ball.

"You have served many *Englischers* dressed like this at the meetinghouse and here at home." Elam balanced two buttermilk biscuits atop his mound of food, grabbed a fork from a drawer, and walked to the table. He set down the plate but didn't sit.

"Is that what you consider yourself to be—an *Englischer*?" Thomas sounded more like a growling dog than a man addressing a member of his family. Up until now Elam had left his logging crew clothing below and come upstairs in traditional Amish garb.

Elam glared at him. "Not usually, only today. I understand we have a special guest." He flashed a pearly-white grin at Prudence Summerton.

Amy set down her glass of milk. "Elam, this is my Aunt Prudence, visiting from upstate. Aunt Pru, this is John's younger *bruder*, Elam."

Elam took a huge bite of biscuit and talked around the food. "Pleased to meet ya." He swallowed and then shoved the remainder in his mouth.

"Likewise, I'm sure." The older woman smiled, oddly amused.

"And I hear the lovebirds have patched things up. That's good news. John ain't never gonna find a prettier gal than this one, that's for sure." He waved a chicken leg in Amy's general direction and then bit off a chunk. Crumbs of breading dropped onto the polished wood floor.

Amy turned bright pink, John a shade of deep plum, and Sally faded to ghostly white. Nora giggled, popping a brussels sprout into her mouth.

"So the weddin's back on? Hope I can stick around long enough to go to that. Plenty of good eats at a weddin'. Folks pull out all the stops whenever another good man bites the dust." Elam licked his fingertips before selecting a thigh to eat next. Standing to dine didn't seem to bother him in the least.

"This man, however good or not, is *not* biting the dust." John's words hung frozen in the warm kitchen air. He glared at Elam but made a great effort to release his clenched hands, one finger at a time.

"Just an expression, that's all." Elam winked at John before turning his attention to Aunt Prudence. "So what do you think of

Harmony these days? A few more families, but not much else has
changed. Ever get the idea that somebody closed the door and time
just stopped here?" He lifted the plate up to his chin to shovel in
an enormous amount of mashed potatoes.

Prudence tilted her head to one side. "People don't often fix
things that aren't broken." She dabbed her lips daintily with the
napkin.

"Why don't you sit down before you make a mess on our
freshly washed floor?" Nora added a schoolmarm inflection to
the scolding.

Elam's face flushed to a particularly bright hue. Too bright.
And his black eyes were entirely too shiny. At that moment
Thomas realized something that might have been obvious to a
more astute man: His brother was inebriated. Thomas rose to
his full height and pushed back his chair. He reached the end of
the table in a few long strides. Once they were eye to eye, Elam
continued to eat as though the plate might suddenly be pulled
from his hands. Thomas smelled the sour stink of cigarettes on
his clothing and the faint but distinct odor of beer. "You may not
sit with us," he said. "Take your supper down to your room. I'll
speak to you later."

Elam's color heightened. "I won't eat Sally's tasty vittles down in
a damp old basement." And with that, he strode out the side door,
grabbing another piece of chicken as he passed the stove.

Thomas exchanged glances with his pale, wide-eyed wife. "The
time has come," he whispered, more to himself than anyone else.
To Prudence he nodded and said, "I apologize for my brother's
behavior." Then he threw on his chore coat and followed Elam
out the door.

His youngest brother hadn't gone far. He sat on the porch
swing chewing meat off the bone as though at a summertime picnic. "Ya know? That Sally does make some good fried chicken." He
smacked his lips to emphasize his point.

Thomas advanced until he stood a foot from the swing. "You're drunk." It was a declaration of fact, not a question.

Elam wiped up the last of the gravy with his buttermilk biscuit. "Might have had a nip to take the edge off...meeting new relatives and all." He laid the plate of bones beside him on the swing.

"You have no right to come to my table drunk and stinking of your infernal cigarettes." His breath vaporized into white fog.

Elam lifted his chin and squinted. "I thought I'd like to have one final meal with my family before I leave. I will truly miss your wife's cooking. She's improved considerably since the early days, *jah*?"

Thomas ignored the second compliment to Sally, concentrating on the new information. "Where are you going? Did you find another job?"

"Nope. But I'm moving on, taking a road trip before we get buried in another avalanche. I'm heading south. Thought I would stop in Lancaster to see if anybody remembers me, and then I'll move on through Kentucky and on to Missouri. Maybe stop and see the Ozark Mountains, wherever they are." Elam leaned back on the bench.

"How do you plan to get around? Hop freight trains?"

Elam scowled, not taking what he considered an insult lightly. "I'm no hobo, Thomas. I'm driving. I bought a car. I got my license and saved a few bucks. Making a fresh start where there's more to do than watch icicles drip five months a year."

Thomas shifted his weight. "Is that right? Then I suggest you be on your way." There was nothing warm or hospitable in his tone.

Elam glared from under his black eyelashes. "I'll start packing. It won't take me long." He rose unsteadily to his feet with false bravado, stomped down the steps, and disappeared around the house.

Thomas gazed toward the empty fields feeling a pervasive sense of loss for someone not yet gone. *How did this happen? Was there*

*something I could have done to keep Elam from turning away from
his heritage, his family, and his faith?*

For the life of him, Thomas didn't know.

⁊ᆫ

Two days later the sun rose to its winter zenith, offering a decep-
tively pleasant ambiance to the world despite frigid temperatures.
Nora, Amy, John, Thomas, Sally, and their two sons stood in for-
mation to bid Prudence goodbye. As the taxi driver loaded her
suitcase into the trunk, even Nora felt tears moisten her eyes. Aunt
Prudence was a remarkable woman—kind, patient, and gentle, yet
still feisty and independent. She'd had a difficult life, but the Lord
had blessed her with happiness in her later years.

Nora hoped to be like her one day. But not in the near future.

John hugged Prudence in his shy, backward fashion. Sally
embraced her with spine-snapping vigor for so small a woman.
Amy stood mute and teary-eyed, despite Aunt Prudence's assurance that she and Mr. Summerton would return for the wedding.
Thomas promised to smooth matters with the bishop and district
to make that possible. Nora gave her a hug, and then Amy kissed
their aunt on both cheeks like a tourist before Prudence climbed
into the backseat of the cab. With a toot of the horn, the taxi
crunched down the driveway to the street and on to the bus depot.

"Don't worry. She'll be back." Nora slipped an arm around
Amy's waist, while John hovered on her other side.

"I know," Amy murmured. "I'm just sad about all the wasted
time."

John waited until the others wandered off before buzzing a kiss
across Amy's forehead. "See you at lunch," he said next to her ear.

"Dinner, more likely. Could you hitch up the buggy, please?"
asked Amy. "The roads aren't bad, and I'd like to run some errands
in Harmony."

"It'll be ready before you can layer on your warmest clothes." John practically ran to the barn.

Amy watched him go with a sly expression on her face. Then she said to her sister, "Why don't you bundle up too and come with me? I have some phone calls to make and wish to stop at the bank. I'll treat you to lunch and a cappuccino later."

Nora thought for a moment. "Why don't you just use Elam's phone again? I'm sure he wouldn't mind."

Amy's carefree countenance faded. "Because he's gone, Nora. He left yesterday."

"*Gone?*" Nora moved into face-to-face position. "What are you talking about?"

"Yesterday morning I went downstairs to ask to borrow his phone. I wanted to leave another message on the Realtor's answering machine. Elam was packing his stuff into two ratty old duffel bags. He said the battery was dead on his phone anyway." Amy paused, as though *this* were of primary significance.

"Go on," prodded Nora.

"He told me best wishes for the wedding and that I should tell everybody goodbye after he was gone. He wanted a day's head start so there wouldn't be any embarrassing scenes."

Nora stamped her feet on the frozen ground to improve circulation, fighting the urge to shake the details out of her sister. "You didn't bother to ask where he was going?"

"Of course I did. He said he'd be taking a grand tour in his new car. Can you believe it?" she interjected. "Unbeknownst to everyone, he got his driver's license and purchased an automobile!"

Nora looked away, ashamed of her deception.

Amy didn't notice. "He's stopping in Pennsylvania and Kentucky, and he wants to see the Ozark Mountains of Arkansas for some strange reason. Then he'll settle for a while in Paradise where Sally came from. He said by then he'll be broke and will need to get a job."

A dozen questions rose up Nora's dry throat, but suddenly Amy stomped her own feet. "Goodness, that wind cuts right through this shawl. We'll talk more on the way to town." She bolted toward the porch, leaving her sister thunderstruck.

Nora waited until the kitchen door closed, and then she ran around the house to the outside cellar entrance. Half slipping down the icy steps, she entered the former residence of Elam Detweiler. Inexplicably, her heartbeat quickened as though she would soon face the man impossible to stop thinking about. She focused on the twin bed, neatly made with Sally's patchwork quilt, the rag rug beside it, and the rickety old bureau that leaned to one side. Several drawers were still open, as though he'd packed in a hurry. Nora gazed at the spots where Elam had stored his worldly possessions—the upturned milk crate, the shelf above the stationary tub, the row of pegs along the wall. Empty. Nothing remained of the occupant other than settling dust motes and the faint, stale odor of tobacco.

She felt an overwhelming, near-paralyzing sense of abandonment. How could he leave without as much as a simple goodbye? She stood in the gloom until the damp walls with hidden spiders began to close in on her. Then she ran up the interior stairs, not stopping until she reached the sanctity of her bedroom.

Later, as she drove to town with Amy, wrapped snuggly in a lap robe, her disappointment only increased with each passing mile.

"Are you warm enough?" asked Amy.

"*Jah*, quite. It was nice of John to heat the blankets by the woodstove."

Amy grinned. "Sure was. I can't wait to talk to Mrs. Chadd. I checked the date. We're still within the thirty-day hold for the earnest money deposit. We haven't lost our chance for the house." Her tone equaled that of someone heralding a cure for cancer.

"I'm happy for you. I look forward to seeing it...on a warmer day."

"Oh, you'll be seeing it plenty, *schwester*, while you help me paint the bedrooms." Amy laughed uproariously. "We'll swing by the bank first to set up a transfer of funds. John and I will pay cash for the farm so we'll own the place free and clear, without any encumbrances." Her tone now implied the end to global hunger.

Nora politely waited until Amy's exuberance waned a bit before asking, "Elam just left? He had no message for me? I'd thought we had become friends during the short time I was here—my only friend in Harmony."

"*Mir leid*, sweet sister, I've been self-absorbed. There was a message. He said to tell you that it was nice meeting you and that you should stay adventurous. And not to let Harmony moss grow up your backside." Amy giggled like a schoolgirl with the mental image.

"He said that?"

"*Jah*, he did. Apparently, he appreciated your short friendship too. I know he had few other pals in town." Amy slapped the reins lightly on the horse's back. "I hope he finds what he's looking for. He surely wasn't happy here. That's why he indulged in those bad habits."

Nora struggled not to expose her turbulent emotions. "What do you suppose that is? What does Elam want in life?"

Amy shook her head, hidden inside the oversized bonnet. "I haven't the slightest idea. I can't stop fixating on the meatball sub with a big cappuccino I plan to order for lunch."

Nora sank down into her heavy wool cloak and layers of blankets for the rest of the ride. Yet two particular words that Amy used earlier regarding Aunt Prudence settled in her head and refused to dislodge.

Wasted time.

Nora was no longer thinking about Amy or Aunt Prudence or even Elam.

TWENTY

All by His hand and for His glory

Three months later

God graced the ecstatic bride and nervous groom with abundant sunshine on their wedding day. The sky was a fathomless blue with wisps of white clouds so high it seemed they could barely be in our solar system. No one appeared to mind that temperatures had dropped into single digits, even though it was the beginning of March.

While Nora slept, Amy knelt beside her bed to send up prayers of thanksgiving. She had found the answers she had been seeking. By nightfall she would be Mrs. John Detweiler, and Amy couldn't think of anything that would make her happier.

She bathed and dressed and wound her hair into a tight coil. Tonight, in the privacy of their bedroom, John would see her waist-length hair down for the first time.

And today would be the last day he would shave off his whiskers.

She didn't mind that her new dress wasn't the soft shade of blue it would have been in Pennsylvania. And there would be no reception with tables brimming with gifts and sweet desserts, including a multitiered frosted wedding cake. Their Harmony bishop would cringe at the gluttonous excess of a Lancaster wedding meal. But none of that mattered. Amy could eat stale saltines washed down with well water and still enjoy herself.

When she emerged from the bathroom, Sally had the kitchen in a flurry of activity.

"Well, there you are! I thought you would never finish." Sally pushed up the window and shouted. "John, get in the shower! Time's a'wasting." She slammed it shut to stem the draft of cold air.

Amy assessed the countertops. "Did you even sleep last night?" Several types of pie cooled on metal racks, while one huge roaster of braised purple cabbage with roast pork and another of her maple syrup sweet potatoes waited by the door. "Is anybody else cooking food today?" she asked.

Pleasure mingled with pride on Sally's face. "*Jah*, the ladies are making their new assignments from my list. But I couldn't stop myself. I wanted to make this day special for you." Impulsively, she threw her arms around Amy's waist and squeezed. "The bishop will shake his head and grumble under his breath that there's too much food, but he'll allow the feast for you and John as long as nothing goes to waste."

"*Danki*," murmured Amy, feeling emotion clog her throat for the first of many times that day. "What's in here?" She lifted the lid on a huge stockpot, releasing the fragrance of celery and onions.

"Your sister insisted on making traditional Lancaster wedding soup. Except she had no written recipe and guessed at the ingredients and proportions. Nora admitted she never cooked it before, only watched your *mamm* a few times." Sally's dimples deepened. "We'll hope for the best. I haven't sampled it yet."

John stomped into the back mudroom and shrugged off his outerwear. He called "*Guder mariye*" to Amy with an ear to ear grin before disappearing into the bathroom. There was no rule against the groom seeing the bride before the ceremony as in the English world. He emerged fifteen minutes later with his damp hair neatly combed, dressed in his Sunday black coat, pants, and crisp white shirt.

Amy leaned against the kitchen counter, savoring the details of the Detweiler household. She wanted to remember her wedding day forever. For a few moments she thought about her parents, picturing what her *mamm* would be doing and saying to her. Then she forced those memories away, not wishing to cry. No bride wanted to look blotchy and swollen-eyed. Her sole regret was that her sisters, Rachel and Beth, and her grandparents couldn't make the trip with the unpredictable weather. Late winter still packed plenty of wallop for stalwart New Englanders.

In a few months she and John would take a wedding trip once mild weather returned. Who wanted to walk the rugged Maine coastline in forty-mile-an-hour winds? They would honeymoon in Portland at a bed-and-breakfast near the water. Amy would view the ocean for the first…and perhaps last…time. But it didn't matter. Whatever God had planned was fine with her. Then they would travel by train to Philadelphia, on to Harrisburg, and finally to Lancaster County by bus. A taxi would take them to *grossmammi*'s farm for a month-long vacation. Amy planned to sleep little to enjoy the maximum visit with her sisters, aunts, uncles, cousins, and, of course, her grandparents. Time marches on, bringing new *bopplin* and taking away those whose allotted days on earth are over. Only our faith in the hereafter softens the sting of the relentless cycle.

Just as Sally bustled away to tend her children, Nora appeared in the doorway. "Won't be long now," she murmured.

"Bring it on!" Amy used her sister's favorite English phrase to the girl's utter delight. They both erupted into a fit of giggles like many times before. "Don't forget the crate of surprises," Amy cautioned once she regained her composure.

"Not to worry. It's already on the porch." Nora rocked back and forth on her heels. She looked very young and pretty today, even in her drab olive-green dress.

"Thank you for standing up as my attendant." Amy studied her sister to memorize every detail, even though it would be weeks until she and John moved into their new home.

"Who else would do it? I'm your only sister in Maine." She rolled her eyes and hurried to the stove. "Why don't you see if Sally needs help? I want to be alone when I sample my pot of soup in case it needs last-minute adjustments or a quick dump into the compost pile."

On feet barely touching the floor, Amy did as Nora suggested, feeling more cherished than any woman had a right to.

Later that morning Amy and John listened with heightened awareness to two sermons, plenty of Scripture readings, and tuneless singing by the congregation. When the three-hour service ended, the bishop married them in a simple but reverent exchange of vows before a crowd of joyous faces. Will and Prudence Summerton sat in the back row on their respective sides of the meetinghouse. They would kneel and confess their sins at a later date to be restored to their former Amish community. Perhaps they would someday move back to Harmony or, more likely, they would remain in their quiet world up north. But Amy would never be far from her aunt's support again.

As they were joined together as man and wife, John's face glowed, while Amy couldn't stop holding her breath. Then the newlyweds moved to the front steps to greet their guests. Inside, men moved the benches and set up long tables. Women carried in roasters of food from their buggies for Sally to organize into a buffet. As her special soup reheated atop the wood-burning stove, Nora set out the sisters' pre-wedding handiwork. She placed jelly jars filled with cut celery sticks on each table; their leafy tops lending the appearance of flower bouquets.

Sally flitted among the ladies like a trained tour operator. She directed, organized, and praised everyone's contribution, smiling the entire time. Women young and old turned to her as their leader. Agnes Miller followed Sally around, eager to assist wherever needed. Agnes had not forgotten Sally's intervention and never would. The younger woman gained a new adopted *mamm* for her act of Christian compassion. The change in Sally over the last six months had been astonishing. Amy experienced a rare moment of pride that she'd helped transform her into an exemplary pastor's wife.

Once Sally organized the buffet, she ladled small bowls of Nora's creamy soup for the meal's first course. Amy and Nora delivered the bowls to the tables, determined to transplant a Lancaster tradition to central Maine. They watched one wedding guest hold his soup to his nose and sniff. Another man took a spoonful and lifted his eyebrows. Most, however, began eating and didn't stop until the soup was gone. After Amy and John finished their lunch of chicken, stuffing, mashed potatoes, coleslaw, applesauce, and warm bread, they wandered between tables to thank the guests for their gifts. People lingered over coffee and dessert in no hurry to venture into the cold. Amy presented each woman with a packet of celery seeds for their spring gardens. If the district enjoyed the soup recipe, the new tradition might catch on.

Only two young faces didn't seem to enjoy the jubilant occasion. After doing her share of serving and cleanup, Nora stood along the meetinghouse wall like the proverbial wallflower. A few women attempted conversations with her, but their interactions were brief. Nora, in her drab dress, black *kapp*, and high-top shoes, looked shrunken and forlorn. But whenever Amy looked at her, Nora's face bloomed into a smile.

She so wants me to be happy, thought Amy. *Can't she understand I want the same thing for her?*

The other melancholy wedding attendee was Lewis. He talked softly with his sisters, listened to his brother's enthusiastic plans for spring planting, and helped move benches and tables whenever necessary. But all the while he watched Nora from the corner of his eye with his broken heart glowing like a neon sign along the highway. What a shame Nora had lost interest in the handsome, hardworking shopkeeper's son.

But Amy shook away her disappointment. Her sister was a grown woman, capable and entitled to making her own choices. The overprotectiveness started by their mother and continued by her had done nothing but hobble Nora. To find her place in the world, she needed to stand on her own two feet.

As though Nora knew Amy's musing centered on her, she slipped an arm around Amy's waist. "I believe the celery soup was a crowd-pleaser. The kettle has been scraped dry. There's not a drop left. I think those seeds might just get planted this spring." Nora leaned close to whisper. "Will celery even grow in Maine's rocky soil, or did we just waste our money?"

Amy hugged her tightly. "Thomas said it would do fine and that organic celery is the best. There's always a good market for it in Boston."

"Sounds like you and John have discovered the perfect cash crop for your new farm." Nora tightened the embrace. "Did you enjoy your special day?"

"I did. *Danki* for all your help."

Nora waved her hand dismissively. "Think nothing of it. *Daed* would be pleased that the eldest daughter is finally married off." She hooted with laughter.

For a few minutes, they stood side by side as parents rounded up *kinner* and collected empty food containers. Young married men crowded around John to slap his back and offer last-minute advice to the new husband.

"If you don't mind, I'll start for home," whispered Nora.

Amy's head snapped around. "It's still cold outside. We'll all leave within the hour."

"I know, but the fresh air will do me good. I feel the start of a migraine. Besides, Lewis has already cornered me twice in conversation. He's so nice, but I feel nothing but guilty when I'm around him. Be happy, my dear *schwester*." Nora buzzed a kiss across Amy's cheek and headed for the hallway for her cloak.

As expected, Lewis watched Nora exit like a red-tailed hawk perched on a telephone wire. But Amy turned her attention on John, her new *ehemann,* who was coming toward her. He didn't wrap her into a bear hug or plant a sloppy kiss on his bride's lips— no demonstrations of affection were permitted in an Amish community. But his heart was also pinned to his sleeve, like Lewis's.

Amy felt certain their story, like a fairy-tale romance, would have a happy ending.

❧

Nora gazed over the frozen landscape of late March. Drifts of gray, dirty snow banked up to fence lines, while icy rivulets crisscrossed the acres from melting and refreezing snow. The sun rose higher in the sky each day but offered little warmth.

None of the Waldo County farms had started plowing their fields yet, and certainly nothing had been planted. She wrapped her quilt around her shoulders against the morning chill and watched a world where nothing moved or showed the tiniest proof of life. Her breath on the cold pane created a fog of white. With the tip of her finger she drew the letter *e* on the glass, followed by an *l, a,* and then an *m.* She stared at the letters until they blurred and dissolved into condensation.

"Missing me already?" Amy bustled into Nora's room, interrupting her sister's thoughts.

Nora quickly rubbed the glass with her sleeve and pivoted in her chair. "You're finally moving into your house? There isn't another ceiling for me to paint or maybe more windows to wash?" She arched a brow.

"I am going today. John has two wagons packed with our wedding gifts, the quilts and linens we sewed this winter, and everything I brought with me from Pennsylvania. Thomas gave John tools and implements that had been duplicates, so he won't have much to purchase to begin farming." Amy's cheeks were especially pink today. "He will attend a livestock auction this Saturday to buy a pair of Belgian draft horses along with a mule. He insists we need a mule—I can't imagine why, but they are rather cute critters, don't you agree?" Amy dropped onto her twin bed.

"I do, especially when they wear somebody's old straw hat." Nora wiggled her eyebrows.

"I'll look for a hat on Saturday. There's a flea market near the auction barn." Amy leaned back on her elbows, the picture of newlywed bliss.

"What can I help you with?" asked Nora, feeling a rush of anxiety over what was to come.

"Not a thing. Everything is ready to go."

A lot had happened to the newlyweds' home since the wedding. John and Thomas had de-electrified the house, patched and replastered the walls, and then the whole family had painted every room. They pulled up the moldy carpeting and sanded, stained, and sealed the hardwood floors.

"What was Sally carrying to the wagons in those crates? I saw her at first light from my window."

Amy rolled her eyes. "Goodness, that woman never stops. She talked the district ladies into donating canned fruits and vegetables, homemade noodles, dried herbs and spices, and a side of beef. Then she organized a potluck to start me off so I won't have to cook for a week." Amy stretched out her long legs. "I guess I'll lounge around like an English movie star with everything already done for me."

They laughed at the absurd idea. "Enjoy yourself. Those casseroles and the pampering won't last forever."

Amy sat up straight, sobering to her normal demeanor. "What you can do, Nora King, is explain why you refuse to move to one of our spare bedrooms. You know I have plenty of space and would love to have you close by. Do you still harbor hurt feelings from John's behavior last fall?"

Nora jumped to her feet. "Not at all. We made our peace the day he apologized. I never think about that anymore." She paced to the other end of the room.

"Then why do you choose to stay here with Thomas and Sally? Is it because of their sweet little boys? Someday, God might bless us with *bopplin*, and I'll need your help because *mamm* is gone." Amy had never sounded so earnest.

Nora leaned her back against the rough-sawn pine door as a wave of sorrow washed over her. *Someday, my dear* schwester *will give birth and I will be miles away.* Yet no matter how many times she shuffled and reconsidered the repercussions, she couldn't bring herself to stay in Harmony. "I pray He blesses you with a houseful of children," she said. Nora drew in a quick breath to steady her nerves and blurted out the difficult words. "I'm not moving with you because I'm not staying in Maine."

Amy froze on the bed. "Go on."

"I haven't been content here, Amy. That should come as no surprise, but I waited to see you happily married. After all, I couldn't miss your wedding. Then I remained to help you ready your new home. Now that is done. Today I will help you move and then come back to pack my own possessions." Nora pushed off the door and paced to the window. "I've already bought my bus and train tickets. The schedules and my traveling funds are in my purse."

Amy rose with the stately dignity of a matron. "Where will you go, dear heart? Back to Lancaster? I will soon join you there. Once John plants his seeds in the ground, we'll be off on our wedding trip."

"*Nein*. I don't want to live there, either." Regrettable scenes of the young man she thought she'd loved flooded back, unbidden. She had given herself to him instead of saving herself for marriage. But his affections proved to be short-lived. Nora shook away the painful memory.

"Where will you go?" asked Amy. A note of alarm shaded her words.

"Missouri. I plan to go to Paradise, the town Sally came from."

"Whatever for? You don't know a soul—" The sentence hung in the air as comprehension dawned on the elder King daughter. "Elam Detweiler. You're going to see him?"

Nora looked across the room at the woman she knew better and respected more than any other. "I love Elam. I want to see if I can share my life with him."

"*Love?*" demanded Amy, as though Nora had used the term in context with boa constrictors. "You don't even know him, and yet you wish to travel halfway across the country?"

Nora crossed her arms and leaned against the windowsill. "I do know him. I told you we had become friends during the fall."

Amy's forehead crinkled into worry lines. "So you knew he'd taken the driver's test and bought a car?" She whispered, even though no one was close enough to overhear.

"I did." Nora's response couldn't have been more succinct.

Amy's mouth pulled into a thin, tight line. "You knew he'd planned to leave Maine?"

"*Jah*, but I didn't know exactly when. That's why I was blindsided when he actually made his move. I can't blame him, of course. With this changeable weather, a person has to travel when they can or become trapped by a blizzard for weeks. I'm sure he's not that good a driver yet." Nora snapped her mouth shut, suddenly aware she was rambling.

Nora could practically see the wheels spinning in Amy's head. "This…friendship with Elam. Exactly how close did you two become?" They locked gazes. "You didn't…"

She didn't complete the question. She didn't have to.

"No!" snapped Nora, "It was nothing like that. He really liked me and I liked him. And while getting to know him, I fell in love."

"I beg your pardon, Nora. I didn't mean to imply anything." Amy's relief couldn't be more apparent. "Have you written to him? Did he invite you to visit? Perhaps kin of Sally's can put you up."

Nora exhaled a frustrated sigh as she paced across the room again. "He doesn't know I'm coming. I want it to be a surprise. I'm not like you. I don't need each *i* dotted or *t* crossed before I walk to the street for the mail. I want some adventure in my life!" Nora hadn't meant to sound quite so abrasive.

Amy's reaction startled them both. She laughed and nodded in agreement. "You're right, I do tend to overthink and overplan everything. I prefer my adventures to be on the pages of a book." Amy walked to where Nora stood and took her hand.

Feeling defenseless and vulnerable, Nora said in a low raspy voice, "I love you, Amy, and I will miss you terribly, but I must follow my heart. I want to see if my future lies in Paradise."

"Then go with my fondest wishes, but always remember— trains and buses and even slow-moving Amish buggies travel in both directions. You can come back anytime. There's no shame in changing your mind. After all, it *is* a woman's prerogative." Amy kissed her forehead and then swept from the room like a whirlwind to finish packing the two wagons.

But Nora remained where she was as tears streamed down her face. How she would miss Amy, the sole connection to their former life.

Please, Lord, bless my sister and her husband as they corner the market with organic celery for folks in Boston.

After sending up her heartfelt prayer, she wiped her face and dressed in her oldest clothes. Today was the big moving day. There would be no lurking on the sidelines or dodging work for Nora King.

But before she headed down the steps, she whispered an addendum to her prayer.

Wherever I go, no matter how far from family I am, may I never falter on my path to You.

❧

Sweet-and-Sour Red Cabbage
Old German Recipe
Rosanna Coblentz (Old Order Amish)

½ cup butter, divided into two ¼ cup portions
4 medium apples, peeled and sliced
½ red onion, chopped
1 head red cabbage, finely shredded
1 cup apple juice (red wine optional)
4 whole cloves
⅓ cup brown sugar
2 bay leaves
¼ cup vinegar
Juice of ½ lemon
Sliced or cubed cooked pork roast (optional)

Melt ¼ cup butter in a 4-quart Dutch oven. Add apples and onion and sauté slightly. Add cabbage, apple juice, cloves, sugar, and bay leaves. Simmer, covered, for about 1 hour, and then add the remaining ingredients, making sure the last ¼ cup of butter melts and incorporates completely. Serve immediately. Makes 6 servings.

Note: For a hearty main dish, add sliced or cubed cooked pork roast, as much as desired, and add a half hour to cooking time.

Sweet Potato Casserole

Anna Beachy (Old Order Amish)

6 medium sweet potatoes
Butter for browning
2 T. flour (white or whole wheat)
Salt
1 cup maple syrup

Peel and cut sweet potatoes into 1-inch cubes. Fry in butter (use enough butter to coat potatoes well while cooking) until browned. Then sprinkle flour over the potatoes while still cooking. Stir and add salt to taste.

When the potatoes are lightly browned, place in a baking dish and cover with maple syrup. Bake at 350 degrees until potatoes are soft, about 30 to 40 minutes. Makes 6 servings.

Amish Cream of Celery Wedding Soup

4½ cups chopped celery

1½ teaspoons onion salt

9 T. butter

6 T. all-purpose flour

3 teaspoons salt

1½ teaspoons celery seed

1 teaspoon pepper

3 cups rich chicken broth

7½ cups milk

Celery seed for garnish (optional)

Cook the celery as desired, whether by sautéing or boiling, until it is soft enough to puree with the onion salt in a food processor, blender, or food press. Set aside.

Melt the butter in a large soup pot. Add the flour, salt, celery seed, and pepper, stirring well until mixed. Remove the pan from heat.

Add the chicken broth and milk, stirring with a wire whisk. Gradually blend in the pureed celery. Return the pan to the stove and simmer on low heat until the soup is desired consistency, stirring constantly, approximately 10 minutes. Serve hot with a dash of celery seed. Makes 18 servings.

DISCUSSION QUESTIONS

～

1. Why do you think the Harmony bishop insisted that Amy and John wait before they marry and also before they took marriage counseling classes?

2. Describe the mixed bag of emotions Sally experiences with the arrival of two women from Lancaster. How would you feel if you were in her place?

3. Maine offers exactly what John is looking for, so why does he doubt Nora will be able to adjust to the new community? Why is he so eager to send her back to Pennsylvania?

4. In the fabric shop, Amy discovers a quilt she's certain had been sewn by her Aunt Prudence. How does this open a can of worms for Amy?

5. Why does the English community of Waldo County welcome the Amish with open arms, and how is their agriculture very different than what John left behind in Lancaster?

6. Still water runs deep with Thomas Detweiler. How do his duties as minister often conflict with his roles as husband and brother?

7. Why do the district women hold Sally in such low esteem?

8. Elam Detweiler is the quintessential fence-sitter. Why do you think it would be so hard for an Amish young man to leave his *rumschpringe* days behind?

9. Nora finds someone inside the general store and organic co-op who puts Harmony in a different light. Why would his attraction cause such wardrobe problems for her?

10. Receiving the death certificate from her late uncle gives Amy a mission to accomplish before her marriage. Why is the date so significant and how does this put her at odds with John?

11. Why does John find Sally a poor role model for his bride-to-be and future sister-in-law?

12. Prudence Summerton welcomes a visit from Amy, and yet she has no interest in moving back to Harmony. Why is she content to live apart from an Amish community?

13. Nora's attraction to Elam Detweiler runs deeper than good looks. What does he offer that the handsome Lewis Miller does not?

14. John backs himself into a corner with Amy. How does one sinful act lead to another until he practically destroys the relationship he holds most dear?

15. What from Amy's past in Lancaster prevents her from committing herself to John? And how does Aunt Prudence help free her from guilt?

Don't miss Nora's continuing story in
Book 2 of The New Beginnings Series
by bestselling author Mary Ellis

LOVE COMES TO PARADISE

༻

One

"Are you lost, miss? This is the bus to Columbia."

Nora King almost jumped out of her high-top shoes. She turned to find a kind ebony face inches from her own.

"I don't think I am. Do you mean Columbia, Missouri?" She shifted the heavy duffel bag to her other hand.

The bus driver chuckled, revealing several gold teeth. "It's the only one we've got. You're a long way from South Carolina. Want me to stow that in the underbelly, or do you want it in the overhead?" He pointed at her bag.

The question dumbfounded Nora as people jostled past on both sides. "I'm not sure," she murmured. In fact, there wasn't much she was sure of since leaving Maine. Who would have thought it would be so hard to get to Missouri? It certainly hadn't been such an ordeal to travel from Lancaster County, Pennsylvania, to Harmony, Maine, last year.

The bus driver straightened after stowing several suitcases into a large compartment above the wheels.

"It's a little more than two hours to Columbia from here, St. Louis." He pointed at the ground, in case she truly was lost. "Is there anything you will need from your bag during the drive—snacks, reading material, personal items?"

"*Jah*...I mean, yes." Nora flushed as she lapsed into her *Deutsch* dialect. "Sorry, I'm Amish."

He offered another magnificent smile. "That much I figured out on my own. Because your bag isn't too large and you'll need things, feel free to stow it in the rack above your head. But you'll want to climb on up and find a seat. It's time to go." The driver pointed at the steps and then resumed packing luggage into the compartment.

Nora had no idea why she was acting so uncertain of herself. She'd ridden plenty of buses in her lifetime—just not on any this side of the Mississippi River. She was in the West and in the new home state of Elam Detweiler. That thought left her weak in the knees. Nevertheless, she joined the queue boarding the bus in the St. Louis terminal and started the second-to-last leg of her journey. Soon she was inside the vehicle and looking for a seat.

"Nora? Nora King?" An unfamiliar female voice sang out.

Nora gazed over a sea of English faces, yet none seemed particularly interested in her.

"Back here, Nora." A small hand waved in the air, midway down the aisle.

Nora inched her way back, careful not to bump anyone with her overstuffed bag. Her sister Amy had sewed her several dresses, along with lots of white prayer *kapps*, and then bought her brand-new underwear. Nora should have brought a bigger suitcase. After hefting up her bag and jamming it between two others, she looked into the blue eyes of the person calling her name—a pretty girl around her own age.

"You're A-Amish," she stammered.

"I am. Did you think you would be the only one?" The girl became even prettier when she smiled. "Sit here with me and stop blocking the aisle." She patted the vinyl seat beside her.

Acutely aware people were growing impatient behind her, Nora did as she was told. "*Danki*, I will."

"I'm Violet, and I'm your official welcome-to-Missouri committee. My mother and me, that is." She hooked a thumb toward the rear of the bus. "My *mamm* moved to another seat so you and I could get acquainted during the ride." Violet straightened her apron over her dress with an expression of joy with her idea.

Nora peeked over the seat. Two rows back a middle-aged woman lifted her hand in a wave. She appeared old enough to be the girl's *grossmammi,* not her mother. "*Danki* for saving a seat and for the welcome, but how did you know I would take this bus?"

"Our meeting was arranged by Emily Gingerich, sister of Sally Detweiler, sister-in-law to your sister Amy Detweiler. Hmm, does that make Sally your sister-in-law too? I don't know how that works, but it doesn't really matter because you're here now, and soon we'll be in Columbia. My father arranged for a hired van to take us the rest of the way to Paradise. He'll be waiting at the terminal." Violet finally sputtered out of air.

Nora blinked like an owl, bewildered despite Violet's long-winded explanation. "I see," she said unconvincingly.

"Forgive me for chattering like a magpie. My *daed* says I run off at the mouth to make up for the fact I can't run around." She laughed without restraint.

"I don't mind. Talk all you want. But are running or jogging frowned upon in your local *Ordnung*?" Nora was eager to learn the rules and regulations after her experience in the ultra-conservative district of Harmony, Maine.

"Goodness, no. You can run until you drop over with a side-stitch if you like. But I can't due to bum legs." She patted her dress where her kneecaps would be. "I fell from the barn loft when I was four years old. I'd sneaked up the ladder when my sisters weren't looking, even though my parents had warned me a hundred times to stay away from it."

"Oh, my. You're lucky you weren't killed." Nora noticed with pleasure that Violet's dress was a soft shade of sea-blue. The Harmony district had allowed only dark or dull colors: navy, black, brown, or olive green.

"That's the truth. I don't have to stay in a wheelchair all the time. I can hobble around on crutches, but I tire out quickly."

"At least a wheelchair is more comfortable than those hard, back-less benches during preaching services. And you'll always have a place to sit at social events."

Violet threw her head back and laughed. Her freckles seemed to dance across her nose. "You have a great attitude! You're not uncomfortable with me being handicapped?"

Nora stared at her as the bus pulled out of the depot. "Of course not. What difference does it make whether or not you can run? I can always push your wheelchair fast if you need to get some place in a hurry."

Without warning, Violet threw both arms around Nora and squeezed. "You and I might end up being good friends."

A perfect stranger until ten minutes ago.

An expression of affection from a human being other than her sister Amy.

"That would be nice. I don't have any friends in Missouri. I only had two in Maine, and I didn't have many in Lancaster, either." Nora smoothed out the wrinkles in her mud-brown dress, wishing she'd worn one of the new ones.

Violet's eyes rounded. "You once lived in Lancaster? I've heard stories about how crowded that county has become. Plenty of Old Order folks have resettled here because they couldn't find affordable farmland to buy in Pennsylvania."

Nora's stomach lurched, and it had nothing to do with the bus gaining speed on the freeway entrance ramp. "Please don't tell me that where I'm headed has only a dozen families and a town the size of a postage stamp. There were just a couple hundred Amish people in three communities in the entire state of Maine."

"You're moving to a place you know nothing about?" Violet drew back, clucking her tongue. "There are nine thousand Amish in Missouri in thirty-eight settlements and at least ninety districts. Does *that* brighten your day a bit? The city of Columbia is only an hour away with beautiful parks and nature areas and a super-duper mall." She leaned over conspiratorially. "But don't tell my *daed* that *mamm* I went there twice after doctor's appointments. We didn't buy anything except for a giant pretzel. We just looked around at the stuff *Englisch-ers* spend their hard-earned money on. My father has no use for English malls, but I think they are quite fun."

Grinning, Nora relaxed against the headrest. She liked Violet already. "Harmony would be nice if I were ready to marry and raise a family, like my sister Amy. But for a single woman, not ready to settle down, it was deader than an anthill in January."

"In that case, you'll like Paradise. We have almost forty Amish businesses in town and spread throughout the county. Lots of bakeries; mercantiles; doll shops; and quilt, craft, and antique stores as well as manly businesses, such as lumberyards, feed-and-seed stores, leather tanners, and carriage shops. You'll have no trouble finding a job." Violet dug a package of cheese crackers from her purse and offered some to her companion.

Nora took one to calm her queasy stomach. "You mean your *Ordnung* permits women to work?"

"Of course women are allowed to work. Where did you say you came from—Maine or Mars?"

Nora choked on a bite of cracker. "The two were pretty much the same thing," she said after a sip of water. "Women were forbidden to take jobs outside their homes."

"Usually women here quit work once they marry and the *bopplin* start arriving. But until then, people will scratch their heads or shake a stick if you sit around the house twiddling your thumbs." She leaned over to whisper into Nora's ear. "Don't you love that quaint expression, 'start arriving,' as though babies take the Greyhound to the Columbia depot, call for the hired van, and show up with a fully packed diaper bag?"

Nora snickered. "It does paint a different picture than a mother in hours of painful labor." She pulled another cracker from Violet's pack. "I'm glad Paradise isn't as stodgy as Harmony. There was little to do, especially during the winter, with few social events other than singings. And the church singings were for *everybody*, not just young single people. Plus, there was no *rumschpringe*."

Violet's hand, holding the last cracker, halted midway to her mouth. "You're pulling my pinned-together leg, right? No *rumschpringe*?"

"I assure you, I don't joke about the district I used to live in. They were very conservative and tolerated no running-around time."

"How on earth did folks court, marry, and then add to the rapidly growing Amish population? Or are you saying most Harmonians lived and died lonesome, celibate lives?"

Nora smiled at that. "People still managed to meet and fall in love, in spite of the incredible obstacles placed in their path." She gazed out the opposite window as memories of tall, handsome Lewis Miller flitted through her mind. She could easily have fallen in love with him if not for the monotony of central Maine...and if the irresistible, black-eyed, wild-as-an-eagle Elam Detweiler hadn't changed everything for her. She shook off thoughts of both men and turned back to her companion. "So you know Emily Gingerich—Sally Detweiler's sister? I will be staying with her, at least for a while, but we have never met."

"Of course I know her. Paradise might be larger than Harmony, but we have plenty of social occasions to meet each other. Besides, Emily owns Grain of Life Bakery." Violet lowered her voice. "They are the best bakery in town, but don't tell my *mamm* I said that. One of her *schwestern* owns another of the shops."

"So far you've shared with me one secret to keep from your father and another from your mother, Violet. We just met today. I could be the world's biggest blabbermouth."

"You don't appear to be, and I'm a good judge of character." Violet studied Nora with narrowed eyes, not the least bit nervous. "Tell me, are you up to the challenge, Nora King, to not divulge the confidences you've heard today?"

"You bet I am. It's been a long time since anybody trusted me." Nora sighed, remembering Elam and his secrets.

Violet reached down to rub her leg, generating a metal-against-metal sound. "My leg braces itch like crazy sometimes." She winced, as though her scratching had touched a sore spot. "And now that you're privy to several of my dark secrets, you must confess one of yours."

Nora's head snapped around. "What do you mean? What makes you think I have any?"

"Come on. My legs might not be perfect, but there's nothing wrong with my mind. You just moved halfway across the country to a town that's a complete mystery and are staying with a couple you've never laid eyes on. I smell a secret as strong as cheese left out in the sun." Her stare practically bored holes through Nora. "Don't you trust me?"

Typical of her impetuous personality, it took Nora no time to decide. Something about Violet appealed to her enormously. She wanted nothing to nip their friendship in the bud.

"I fell in love in Harmony with the wrong sort of man," she whispered. "I don't know if he plans to stay Amish, and he doesn't even know I'm coming. But when he left Maine, he said he was heading to Paradise. So I pointed myself in this direction." Nora leaned back in her seat. "Now you know *my* secret."

Violet stared at her, wide-eyed. "That is the most romantic thing I've ever heard in my life. I will take your secret to my grave if need be."

And if her expression of awe could be trusted as an indicator, Nora had just made a new best friend.

❧

"I'm coming," called Emily from the hallway. She pulled off her apron, tossed it on the counter, and swept open the kitchen door. Before her stood a small woman, not more than a girl, really, in a dusty cape and wrinkled brown dress. Her clothes looked too big for her, as though they were cut from a pattern meant for someone else. But she had the prettiest green eyes Emily had ever seen.

"Mrs. Gingerich?" the girl asked, peering up through thick dark eyelashes. "I'm Nora King, Amy Detweiler's sister. I've come from Maine."

"Thank goodness. For a moment I feared you were here to sell me a new set of pots and pans or some of those English cosmetics." Emily grabbed her sleeve and pulled her into the kitchen.

Nora waved at the hired van idling in the driveway as she passed through the doorway.

"No, ma'am. I hope my arrival hasn't come at an inopportune time." She clutched a large duffel bag with both hands, gazing out from inside a huge outer bonnet.

"I was joking, Nora. Please sit and get comfortable. I expected you today and hoped you would enjoy the company of Violet and Rosanna on the ride from St. Louis. Isn't that Violet a hoot? She never fails to make me smile within five minutes of being in the same room with her."

Nora removed her cloak and the hideous bonnet, and then she hung them both on a peg. "She seems nice and is really quite funny. *Danki* for arranging them to meet me. I was a bit discombobulated in St. Louis." She stood behind the chair as though waiting for a certain sign or signal.

"Sit. Take a load off. They travel to Columbia once a month for physical therapy and twice a year for a specialist's reevaluation of her legs. The doctors want to keep them as strong as possible because Violet insists on using crutches whenever possible." Emily filled the kettle and placed it on the stove. "We'll have tea and cookies. Dinner will be in an hour or so."

Nora sat and folded her hands like a schoolgirl awaiting an assignment or admonishment.

"Unless you're starving now," Emily said, "in which case, I'll make you a sandwich."

"No, ma'am, tea will be fine. I can wait until supper." Nora remained very still, as though too frightened to move.

"Please, no more ma'ams. My name is Emily." Without the bonnet, the girl had delicate, small-boned features. Wisps of strawberry blond hair escaped her prayer *kapp* and framed her face. "Are you *sure* you're the Nora King my sister wrote to me about? Or have I admitted an imposter into my house?"

Nora paled significantly. "I am she, although I have no iden-tification. Shall I describe Sally's home or her two sons, Aden and Jeremiah?"

Emily placed some oatmeal cookies on a plate and sat down across from the scared rabbit. "Because I haven't met my nephews yet, nor have I ever been to Sally's home in Maine, I'll take your word for it. And I'll stop teasing until we get to know each other better." She filled two mugs with hot water and tea bags. "Welcome to our home, Nora. My husband and I are happy to have you and hope you'll soon like our humble part of the world."

"Everyone has better senses of humor here." Nora took a cookie from the plate to nibble. "I'm afraid I lost mine when I left Pennsylvania."

Her earnestness tugged on Emily's heartstrings. "Sally told me what happened to your parents in a letter. You have my deepest sym-pathy. A woman is never prepared to lose her *mamm*, even if she's sev-enty years old. At your tender age, the loss is especially painful."

"I try to focus on the future instead of the past. I did too much star-ing out of the window and crying in Harmony. I'm eager to make a new beginning in Paradise."

"Then you've come to the right place. The Amish population of Missouri has tripled in the last twenty years. Folks move here from all over—Ohio, Indiana, and Illinois. We still have plenty of cheap land, and farming is what ninety-nine percent of us do."

Nora gasped. "That's not like Pennsylvania at all. Most folks there have had to learn a trade or start a business."

Emily stirred sugar into her tea. "Well, my *ehemann* is actually part of the one percent. His brothers work their family's land, but Jonas started a lumberyard. It does fairly well, selling to Amish and English, if you'll forgive me for some prideful bragging."

"I will forgive just about anything if I can have another cookie. They are delicious." A dimple formed in Nora's cheek, the first sign her shyness might be ebbing.

Emily pushed the plate across the table. "Eat to your heart's content. You can stand to gain a few pounds, whereas I cannot." She gently slapped one rounded hip. "Didn't my sister feed you while you lived there?"

"Sally certainly tried to, but I get migraines from time to time. They take my appetite away for days."

"Migraines can be triggered by stress. I aim to see you relaxed and not worrying so much."

Nora reached for another cookie and consumed it in three bites. "Was your Old Order district formed by people moving here from Pennsylvania?"

"No, we were settled sixty years ago by a group who came from Iowa."

"Iowa? Where is that?"

Emily smiled. "And to think you traveled all the way from practically the Atlantic Ocean. The Lord be praised! He pities those with a poor knowledge of geography."

"I prayed plenty on the way here. I took the Downeaster train from Portland, Maine, to Boston; the Lake Shore Limited from Boston to Chicago; and then I caught the Texas Eagle to St. Louis. I tried to learn the layout of my country along the way. What are the states near Missouri?" Nora possessed the innocent, curious expression of a child.

"Iowa is to the north, Kansas is to the west, Arkansas is due south, and Illinois lies to the east. A corner of us touches both Kentucky and Tennessee. A long time ago I pronounced our southern neighbor as 'Ar-kansas,' so it rhymed with our western neighbor. Finally, an *Englischer* in my shop corrected me. She whispered the correct pronunciation softly so I wouldn't be embarrassed. But what's to be ashamed of? I had never heard anybody say the word before."

Both of them laughed.

"These Iowa Amish—do you think they are similar to the Maine districts?" asked Nora, taking another cookie.

Emily realized where her guest's queries were headed. "Sally wrote to me about Harmony's no-*rumschpringe* policy. And about the fact that you haven't joined the church yet. I assured her that no one would pressure you to commit to the Amish church until you're ready."

Nora released an audible breath of air, relaxing for the first time since her arrival. "I'm happy to hear that. It wasn't so much that they pressured me to be baptized, but every time I turned around I was breaking another rule. Truly, Harmony was too small to be my cup-of-tea." She drained the contents of her mug and then set it back on the table. "Violet mentioned that your bishop allows social events for young people, regular-type courting, and jobs for unmarried women. That sounds more like what I'm used to after being raised in Lancaster County."

Emily considered her reply before speaking. Should she mention that their district might soon become far less liberal if one of their ministers got his way? She glanced at Nora and quickly decided to hold off on full disclosure. *The woman had just arrived in a strange land where she knew no one...and the bus back to St. Louis doesn't even run tomorrow.*

"We're more liberal than the districts near Seymour, Missouri," she said. "But why don't you wait to learn all the details? Let me show you to your room. You can bring up your bag and start to unpack."

Nora rose gracefully to her feet. "Will I share the room with your daughter? Sally didn't mention whether or not you had *kinner*."

"We haven't been blessed...yet." Emily hoped her greatest sorrow wasn't obvious as she walked toward the doorway.

"*Danki* for opening your home to me, Emily." Nora followed on her heels. "I so wanted to move here after Sally described her childhood and *rumschpringe* while courting Thomas."

"*Jah*, but I wish he hadn't taken my sister so far away. At least she's happy in Maine, so that's what counts." Emily led the way up to the bedrooms and chose her words for the second delicate topic in almost the same number of minutes. "Sally mentioned her brother-in-law's relocation had something to do with *your* coming to Missouri." Emily opened the door to the guest room, which would be Nora's for as long as she wanted it.

She walked straight to the blanket chest and deposited her bag. "Partially, I suppose. Elam and I became friends when I lived in Harmony. But it really was Sally's description of Paradise that fascinated me." Nora smiled with genuine warmth. "The fact her kin still lived here helped me decide because I didn't want to return to Pennsylvania. I hope to run into Elam if he's around. He mentioned taking a grand tour in his new car. He even planned to see the Ozark Mountains, wherever they are."

"He brought a car?" asked Emily, shaking her head. She pulled down the window shade against the night. "The Ozarks are in Arkansas, to the south. A cousin said Elam lives somewhere in the county, but he hasn't shown his face here or at a preaching service yet, I might add." She fluffed both of the pillows. "You'll find him, I suppose, if it's meant to be."

Emily walked to the door. "You have time to unpack and take a nap before dinner. Come down about five o'clock. I wound the clock on your bedside table."

Nora hurried toward her hostess and embraced her shyly. "I am so grateful to you."

"There's nothing wrong with making a fresh start." Emily hugged the thin woman, patting her back.

Who has made her afraid of her own shadow? And what has gone on in my sister's home? Thomas Detweiler seemed like a good man when he married and took away Sally five years ago.

❧

"Giddyup there, Nell. I can walk faster than you're pulling this buggy." Solomon Trask shook the reins above the mare's back, but he did not slap them down. No sense in startling the old girl. She was probably enjoying the warm April sunshine on her flanks, the sweet smell of apple blossoms tickling her nose, and the absence of traffic on the county road—increasingly rare for Saturdays.

The horse dutifully picked up the pace to a *tad* quicker than he could walk.

Solomon tilted his head back, letting the sunshine reach his face beneath his hat brim. How he loved spring! Overhead, songbirds filled the crystalline blue sky with their music, red-tailed hawks soared on wind currents, and waterfowl crossed the Great Plains back to Canada. Life was good. The Lord had richly blessed him with a *fraa* and six fine *kinner*, including four boys who had built their homes nearby. His sons had taken over farm duties so he could minister to the district, keeping the members on the straight-and-narrow path. If he failed in his responsibilities, the Lord might not continue to bless their growing community.

Since the drawing that had made him one of two district ministers for life, he had endeavored to adhere to the Bible. God hadn't provided His holy book as mere suggestions or helpful advice. His Word was law, and only through strict adherence could a man find direction in this life and salvation for the next.

A hollow, uncomfortable rumble in his belly reminded Solomon it had been hours since lunch, and at this pace it would be hours before supper. Should he stop to buy a dozen cookies at the next farm—one of the district's three bakeries? After all, his wife would appreciate an extra pie or two in case she hadn't found time to bake.

It wasn't long before he turned off the main road. Pricking up her ears, Nell trotted up the drive as though oats and a good rubdown waited up ahead.

However, Nell hadn't heard the whinny of another horse but the sound of a car radio. Loud, discordant music blared from a pickup truck parked in the side yard of the Morganstein farm. Solomon climbed from the buggy slowly and then tied the reins to a hitching post. As usual, his back spasmed from sitting too long.

"*Guder nachmittag*," greeted one of the Morganstein sons.

"Good afternoon to you," said the minister. "Could you bring my mare a bucket of water and maybe a little grain?"

The boy nodded and scampered off as Solomon trudged past the truck. He headed toward Levi's leather shop, an outbuilding that had become popular on Fridays and Saturdays with English tourists. Solomon hadn't gone twenty paces when a sight stopped him in his tracks. Two of Levi's sons, both in their late teens, were talking with two English girls of around the same age. Doubtless, the girls belonged to the red truck. One was swigging soda from a bottle, while the other moved her body suggestively to the beat of the infernal music. Solomon's gut twisted into a knot. Both girls wore shorts far above their knees and blouses that didn't come close to covering their stomachs. He approached the foursome with building ire.

Luke Morganstein spotted him and spoke first. "Hullo, Minister Trask. My dad's in his shop and my mother is the house."

Solomon noticed the boy spoke in English, not their dialect of German. He addressed the *Englischers*. "Where are *your* parents?"

The taller of the two girls smiled brightly. "My dad's buying a new jacket. You guys make the best leather stuff in the state. And my mom's over there checking out free-range chickens. She loves the idea of no cages and will buy every last egg available."

Solomon followed the girl's long purple fingernail in the direction it pointed. The sight made his jaw drop agape. A middle-aged woman in a sweatshirt and tight blue jeans focused her camera, snapping pictures of the youngest Morganstein child, a girl of around three years old. The woman was actually posing the child by the henhouse. Bile inched up his throat, souring his mouth.

Sol turned to the teenagers. "Go back to your truck, turn off that loud music, and stay there if you don't have additional clothes to put on."

The pair stared, blinked, and then bolted down the drive. The Morganstein sons vanished into the barn before Solomon could take two steps toward the chicken coop.

"Stop that," he said. He hadn't raised his voice, but the woman froze and then turned like a corned animal.

"Stop what?" she asked, glancing around nervously.

"Do not take pictures of our people. They are graven images and are forbidden."

She blushed to deep crimson. "I'm sorry. I didn't know that. What about the chickens and goats. Can I photograph them?" She sounded utterly sincere.

Solomon sighed. "Yes, animals and buildings are fine. Good day to you."

He picked up the little girl and strode toward the house. Dealing with *Englischers* wasn't his calling—dealing with members of his congregation was. He opened the back door without knocking, a common practice among the Amish, and stepped into an overly warm kitchen.

"*Guder nachmittag*, Sol." greeted Sarah Morganstein. "You look hot. How about a cool drink of water?"

After he had set the child down, she scampered for her mother's skirt.

"*Jah,* that would be *gut*," he said, breathing in and out as he tried to control his temper.

Sarah handed him a glass filled to the brim. "I suppose you heard from the deacon that Levi worked on the Sabbath. He hadn't intended to, and it was only one time, but he had to fill a large order of leather chaps on a tight deadline. Of course, the deacon stopped by that particular Sunday and found Levi in his shop." She tugged on her dangling *kapp* ribbons. "He's mighty sorry and told Jonas he would never do it again."

The glass of water almost slipped from Sol's sweaty fingers as he sorted out the new information, although he had no idea what "chaps" were. "No, I hadn't heard. I wanted to say your sons are cavorting with half-dressed English girls and a woman was taking photographs of your little one." He spoke in a raspy whisper.

Sarah blanched as she drew her daughter to her side. "I didn't know about the pictures. The tourists buy much from Levi and the bakery, helping pay the medical bills from my last surgery. But I'll keep a better eye on little Josie and my boys."

"See that you do." Solomon drained the glass and handed it back to her. "Tell your *ehemann* he broke the Fourth Commandment and must confess on his knees on Sunday." Then he marched from the house to his buggy without buying pies or speaking to Levi.

This wasn't the first time he suspected members were doing things they shouldn't on the Lord's Day. He would take the matter up with the entire congregation—and the sooner the better—before things spiraled out of control.

Books by Mary Ellis

The Miller Family Series
A Widow's Hope
Never Far from Home
The Way to a Man's Heart

The Wayne County Series
Abigail's New Hope
A Marriage for Meghan

The New Beginnings Series
Living in Harmony

Standalones
Sarah's Christmas Miracle
An Amish Family Reunion

❧

Mary loves to hear from her readers.
She has a blog at **www.maryeellis.wordpress.com.**
Please also check out her website and sign up for her
newsletter at **www.maryellis.net.**

To learn more about other Harvest House books
or to read sample chapters, log on to our website:

www.harvesthousepublishers.com

HARVEST HOUSE PUBLISHERS
EUGENE, OREGON